SHIPLORD

EARTH'S LAST GAMBIT

VOLUME 3

FELIX R. SAVAGE

SHIPLORD
EARTH'S LAST GAMBIT, VOLUME 3

Copyright © 2017 by Felix R. Savage

The right to be identified as the author of this work has been asserted by Felix R. Savage. All rights reserved. No part of this book may be reproduced in any form or by any electronic or mechanical means, including information storage and retrieval systems, without written permission from the publisher or author.

First published in the United States of America in 2017 by Knights Hill Publishing.

Cover art by Christian Bentulan
Interior design and layout by Felix R. Savage

ISBN-10: 1-937396-26-6
ISBN-13: 978-1-937396-26-8

SHIPLORD

EARTH'S LAST GAMBIT

VOLUME 3

FELIX R. SAVAGE

CHAPTER 1

Jack Kildare, pilot and acting commander of the *Spirit of Destiny*, clung to the ship's truss tower just north of the bioshield. He stared up at the bloated disk of Jupiter. He was sick of the sight of it, and was actually looking for something else: the *Cloudeater,* the alien shuttle that should be descending at any moment from the looping orbit that had brought it up from Europa's surface.

The *Cloudeater* had made dozens of trips up and down to the *SoD* in the last three months. When the alien colossus known as the *Lightbringer* burned out of orbit, it had left the *SoD* stranded. The *SoD's* magnetoplasmadynamic (MPD) engine ran on water. And the *Lightbringer* had drained it dry.

But now the bioshield tank—the manifold for the SoD's primary water cycle—was full again, as were the external tanks mounted at the back of the ship, near the reactor. Large plastic bags nuzzling the bioshield held still more water. You can't really have too much.

All that H2O—radioactive as hell, but it does the job—had come from Europa. Ice chunks mined on the surface had been slung into low orbit by a mass driver built from hoops of meteoroid iron, and then the chunks had been collected out of orbit by the *Cloudeater*.

And here came the *Cloudeater* now, a bright speck on Jupiter's equator. Jack relaxed a tad as he visually confirmed its trajectory. Descending, the speck resolved into a wide-body Concorde with a bulbous conical tail. A skirt of spiky fins behind its swept-back wings dumped the heat from its fusion reactor.

The alien shuttle's beautiful lines never failed to give Jack a frisson of awe, but that didn't change the fact that the *Cloudeater* was *just* a shuttle. It had limited tankage, crappy delta-V, and no life-support capacity to speak of. All it could do was go up and down.

Now its work was done, and it was coming up for the last time.

"Looking good, Keelraiser," Jack said into the radio of his Z-2 spacesuit.

"I see you," said Keelraiser, the *Cloudeater's* pilot. "Engaging thrusters for final deceleration."

Plasma, ducted from the main drive, boiled from the *Cloudeater's* auxiliary thrusters. Although the shuttle was still a kilometer away, the telemetry display in Jack's helmet registered a brief external temperature spike.

"Relative velocity three meters per second," Keelraiser said.

The *Cloudeater* drifted lower. It blocked out Jupiter. Jack suppressed a flinch as the undercarriage dropped towards his head. For an instant he felt sure Keelraiser was going to mess up. Orbital docking maneuvers were like playing football with an orange in four dimensions, as Jack knew well, having docked the space shuttle with the ISS in low Earth orbit before.

"Little bit to the right," he said.

"Get your eyes tested, Jack," Keelraiser replied.

They had done this dozens of times.

"Relative velocity one meter per second."

"Mind the bioshield!" Jack teased, grinning.

"Oh," Keelraiser said. *"Whoops."*

The Cloudeater completed its descent, without, of

course, hitting anything.

"Yawing a tad," Jack said, not kidding anymore. The *SoD* had no visual yaw or roll indicators for Keelraiser to look at. These two craft had not been designed to dock. They hadn't even been built in the same star system.

"Yes, I know," Keelraiser said. "Hang on."

Minute puffs of exhaust gusted from the auxiliaries, turning the *Cloudeater* around its axis. Now the shuttle was sailing through space in perfect synchronization with the *SoD*, as if glued in the vacuum two meters above the truss tower. Its tail stuck over the bioshield, which protected the *SoD's* crew from gamma rays shooting out of the reactor. But that was OK. The *Cloudeater's* own rad-shielding would protect its passengers.

"Standing off," Keelraiser said. "Stable."

Inside the truss tower, feeling like a monkey clinging to the bars of its cage, Jack turned his head. He couldn't see past the cylindrical bulk of the storage module. "Alexei! Ready?"

"Ready," answered Alexei Ivanov, Jack's crewmate and co-pilot.

"Let's do it."

Jack pulled himself out through one of the diamond-shaped gaps between the struts of the truss tower, taking the arc-welding kit with him.

Alexei flew towards him, under the *Cloudeater's* belly, wrangling three 4-meter angle irons.

Just nickel steel, actually.

Forged on Europa, in the same furnace that made the hoops for the mass driver.

Full of impurities, you bet. Even alien technology

couldn't achieve high-quality steel production in a bunker under the ice of Europa. The nickel and iron comes from a melted-down meteoroid. But it's all we've got, so we'll just have to cross our fingers and hope.

And do a bloody good job with the welds.

Jack rose up towards the alien arabesques of pilot lights on the *Cloudeater's* belly, visually measuring the distance to the lifting lug above the nearer wheel well. Alexei passed him one of the angle irons, and tied the others to the truss to keep them from floating away. They'd run out of everything, even duct tape. They were using rope manufactured by the rriksti on Europa from chopped-up plant stems.

Jack flipped back the cover of the *Cloudeater's* lifting lug and shoved one end of the angle iron into the dent. To his relief, it fit.

"Got it."

"Got it," echoed a new voice in his helmet.

"Got it."

"Got it."

Lithe black shapes materialized out of the void. Brbb and its friends had come out to help. Their elongated bodies writhed like bipedal squids moving backwards. Their hair swirled like tentacles stirred by an ethereal tide. They wore their work lamps on their chests, which made them look a bit inhuman. That was understandable, as they weren't human. They were rriksti, like Keelraiser.

Brbb and company used to be bad guys. Now they were good guys. The *Lightbringer* had left them behind without so much as a see-you-later. They had been living on the *SoD* ever since, lending a hand with everything from hydroponic gardening to ice-melting ...

... and now, welding a shuttle onto the truss.

"Watch out for the spatter," Jack said, setting his teeth. Everything's trickier in freefall. And that definitely includes welding. With no gravity to hold things down, a pool of molten metal is a whimsical and dangerous beast. Nudge it the wrong way, and it might detach from the work piece and go wobbling out to sear through your spacesuit.

One of the rriksti held Jack's legs while Alexei and the other rriksti held the angle iron steady. The electrode holder coughed sparks over the hull. Too many cooks! Everyone was jostling, trying to help. Jack squinted at the dazzling arc, muscles trembling from the effort it took to just stay *still*. Sweat oozed out of his pores and detached from his face to form a suspended rainfall inside his helmet. Thank God the rriksti had built this shuttle on the ground, so it had lifting lugs in the first place. On Imf—which was what the rriksti called their home planet, known to humans as Proxima b—advanced manufacturing in orbit had been banned. Too easy to weaponize. Of course, that hadn't stopped the rriksti from wrecking their planet. *Everything* can be weaponized.

"Having fun out there?" Keelraiser said.

"Unlike you, I only have five fingers on each hand," Jack gasped, "but consider one of them raised in your general direction."

Alexei said, "The real fun will start when we hook up the plumbing." They planned to splice the *Cloudeater's* onboard plumbing into the *SoD's* potable water cycle. "When we built the *SoD* in Earth orbit," Alexei went on, "we had to learn this stuff. I am an elite cosmonaut, OK? Go make Russia proud. That's what they told me. Then they made me learn plumbing. I fucking hate plumbing."

Jack had had the same experience except they'd made him learn welding. He let out a shout of laughter. "Alexei, remember when we calculated our hourly wages? I'd have made more money as a welder in the UK than I did working on the *SoD*."

The rrikstis' hair danced. "We think it is funny that you had to build your own spaceship," Brbb said, speaking for its friends, who had not mastered English.

"Oh yes, I agree, it's downright hilarious," Jack said, shaking his head violently to get the sweat out of his eyes.

"On Imf, families of specialists built spaceships by the dozen. The crews were rock stars. Is this correct?"

"Do you mean they spent most of their time drinking and shagging?"

"Yes, yes." Rriksti laughter. "Until the last war." No more laughter.

They completed the weld, and then welded the other end of the angle iron to the truss. Now the *Cloudeater* was secured to the truss at a single point.

They moved on to another lifting lug on the opposite side of the cargo bay.

"Watch out for the power cord …"

The arc-welding kit ran on a rechargeable power pack the size of a car battery. The rriksti had batteries the size of a smartphone that held kilowatts of charge, even in Europa's sub-glacial cold. But they didn't have a welding kit. They had fled the *Lightbringer* in a hurry ten years ago, taking only what they could cram into the *Cloudeater,* with a priority on edibles. What they'd managed to do since then, with no raw inputs except scavenged meteoroids and plant husks, was nothing short of amazing. It proved that stuff expands to fill the space available, even if you live in a bunker on a Jovian moon. The *Cloudeater* had had to make several trips to bring everything, and everyone, up to the *SoD* .... and even so, loads of stuff was getting left behind. It would freeze on Europa in the derelict bunker, an archaeological puzzle for spacefarers in the distant future.

Jack glanced down in the direction of Europa. They were orbiting over the moon's nightside, and all he could see right now was afterimages of the electrode arc, anyway. That was fine with him. If he never saw that barren, radiation-drenched moon again, it would be too soon.

"Jack!" Giles Boisselot, another survivor of the *SoD's* original crew, spoke from the bridge, where he was monitoring their EVA.

Jack guessed immediately that something was wrong. "What, what is it?"

"Ice chunk," Giles said, in the same sort of calm voice that Jack's father, thirty-five years ago, had used to tell his space-mad son that the *Challenger* had exploded.

Keelraiser broke in. "Yes, I see it. I'm ranging my comms maser on it now."

"How big is it?" Jack demanded.

"Size of a fucking house," Giles said in the same unnaturally calm voice. "It is five klicks away. It is coming this way." Pause. *"Merde."*

CHAPTER 2

"Keelraiser!" Jack yelled. "Can you deflect it?"

"We'll see."

Suddenly, the angle iron Jack was holding jerked in his gloves. He let go. It speared down through a gap in the truss. The one they'd already done sprang loose at the bottom like an unstrung bow.

"Damn. Have to re-do that weld," Jack said, striving for calm. As the Cloudeater settled a few inches to port, everyone on the truss tower dived inside the lattice to safety.

"Sorry," Keelraiser said. "My payload shifted. In other words: everyone got out of their seats and stampeded for the exits."

"Tell them to sit down and fasten their fucking seatbelts!"

"I have," Keelraiser said, its impatient tone hinting at the limits of its authority over the other rriksti.

Jack wrapped one arm around the truss, the other around his precious welding gear, and closed his eyes. It killed him that he wasn't on the bridge of the *SoD*. He had scored a string of successes, in the emergencies of this type that had arisen now and then in the last couple of months, when ice chunks wandered too near the ship. Supposedly the mass driver had flung the ice from Europa into a much lower orbit, but the whole thing was one big seat-of-the-pants hack, and it was actually a miracle that the *SoD* hadn't suffered a collision yet. At 30,000 kph, even a snowball could be a lethal projectile. So you had to make sure they missed.

What Jack did was train the comms laser on the offending snowball and pour on the power. Do that for long enough, and the ice would sublimate in jets of water vapor, which nudged the snowball off its collision course and onto one that passed harmlessly by. Smaller chunks just exploded.

He'd learned this trick from Keelraiser, who had had to pick off a lot of inconvenient snowballs while gathering ice chunks in orbit.

The *Cloudeater* had a comms *maser*, more powerful than the *SoD's* laser. Masers used microwave energy. Tune it to the absorption spectrum of water, and watch the target start steaming like food in a microwave oven.

Would that be enough?

"I didn't actually think there were any left this big," Keelraiser said. "I thought I'd picked them all up."

"Is it going to hit us?" Jack demanded. His own helplessness was driving him bonkers.

Keelraiser let out a creaky chuckle. "We'll know in a moment."

"Ten o'clock high," Giles interrupted. "It is sublimating like crazy! *Ou la la!*"

Jack, Alexei, and the rriksti in the truss tower turned their heads as one, staring in the direction Giles indicated.

A white blur hurtled past. It was blurry because, as Giles had said, it was trailing a tail of water vapor like a comet. "The maser does the fucking job!" Jack whooped.

The work crew broke into a cheer.

"That was a *piece* of it," Keelraiser said calmly. "Here comes the other piece."

For a microsecond, the black slice of space visible beneath the Cloudeater's belly turned white. A sharp vibration jarred through the truss into Jack's gloves. The craggy white mass shrank into the blackness. The size of it stunned Jack. He had excellent spatial perception. He could judge sizes and distances quite well in space, and he knew that if there were air up here, they would've felt the wind of that thing passing like a truck on a killing spree.

"That was not an ice *chunk,*" he said slowly. "That was an ice*berg.*"

"Yes," Keelraiser said. "Any damage down there?"

"A piece of it hit us," Alexei said. "It shattered on the truss. One foot to the left, and I would have ice splinters in my faceplate."

"Jesus," Jack said. "Anyway, Keelraiser, you cut it in *half!* That maser is the business."

Alexei started to laugh. "Giles said *ou la la.* I've never heard him say that before. Giles, I thought the French only say *ou la la* in movies!"

"One day they will make a movie about us," Giles said. "Attack of the Killer Icebergs. Directed by Michael Bay."

Jack laughed with the others. "All the same," he said. "that was too close for comfort. I can't wait to get out of here."

"My passengers seem to feel the same way," Keelraiser said. "They are getting out."

"No! We haven't finished the welds yet …"

By a combination of shouting and disabling the airlocks, Keelraiser contained the *Cloudeater's* traumatized passengers until Jack got the welds done. The angle iron that had popped loose turned out to have bent. It couldn't be used. There went the spare, so now they only had three angle irons. "It'll do for now," Jack said. "Three points is enough to stop it from moving around."

NASA had bullet-pointed checklists for changing lightbulbs. When they set out on this voyage, they'd done everything by the book. Now they were in unregulated territory. The loss of that safety net gave Jack a permanent sense of low-level uneasiness, though it also energized him. He loved finding solutions to problems that shouldn't exist.

The slag around the last weld had hardly cooled when Keelraiser opened the *Cloudeater's* cargo hold. A ramp hinged down. Spacesuited rriksti spilled out, clinging to ropes. Their voices filled the men's helmets in a racket of high-pitched squeals.

"You're hurting our ears," Jack yelled urgently. The rriksti did not use their mouths to talk. They communicated by bio-radio, in a range of 800-2600 KHz, which unfortunately included several frequencies that set up harmonics with the men's suit radios. The rriksti had to remember to tune their voices to avoid the harmonics, and when they were agitated, they often forgot. The noise was nails on a blackboard, a jackhammer digging into your brain—it made Jack want to hit someone. "Stop it!"

The harmonics abated. The rriksti floated past Jack and Alexei, lowering their heads apologetically. They carried bales and bundles. Their hydroponics had come up separately—the *Cloudeater* had made five trips to transport that lot alone. The pathetic flock of refugees broke Jack's heart. He was offering them an escape from Europa, but what did he actually have to offer? About 400 cubic meters per person, a lot of that unusable. NASA's studies recommended 800m3, minimum. On the way out, the crew of the *SoD* had had ten *thousand* m3 each, and even then they'd fought with each other.

The storage module's airlock only took two people at a time. It would be a long while before they all got in.

Jack gave the welding kit to Alexei and drifted the other way, into the *Cloudeater's* unpressurized cargo hold. Dull red light gleamed on the heavy machinery riveted to the floor. They had brought the two 3D fabbers and the 'upcycler,' an indispensable tool for turning rubbish into fabber feedstock. Alien technology for the win.

On top of the upcycler sat a figure wearing a skintight rriksti spacesuit. It was, however, the wrong shape for a rriksti—shorter legs, narrower torso, no hair. In fact it was Skyler Taft, the fourth surviving member of the *SoD's* crew.

"Sky!" Jack flew up and hugged him, clumsy in his Z-2. They hadn't met in months, as Skyler had been down on the surface, helping with the mass driver. Skyler's idea in the first place. There was more to Skyler Taft than met the eye: some of it bad, more of it—Jack had begun to hope—good.

"I'm just staying in here until the crowd thins out," Skyler said, via the transmitter attached to his air supply mouthpiece. That, plus the goggles he wore under his suit, made him look snouted, bug-eyed. "Some rad-shielding is better than none at all."

They had all had terrible experiences with radiation exposure during their time at Europa. By rights they should all be dead. Those memories made Jack uncomfortable. "Great stuff," he said. "I'll be right back."

He unclipped his tether from his belt, leaving it attached to a handle on the upcycler. He pushed off from the floor and flew up to the airlock. It opened at the touch of a button—no wearisome hatches to undog, not in the technological future where the *Cloudeater* came from. The chamber also cycled quicker than on the *SoD*.

He rose into the dimly lit passenger cabin. Discarded garments drifted in the air amidst globules of vomit—evidence of the panic caused by the killer iceberg, or just space-sickness? Another terrible thing about the rriksti's plight was that maybe ten of them were astronauts. The rest were civilians, the rriksti equivalent of senior public servants, who'd signed up with their families 70 years ago for a voyage to Earth that had *not*—to put it mildly—gone as planned. They came from the future, technologically speaking, but for that very reason, they weren't used to the rough-and-tumble of space. They were used to things *just working*. Their exile on Europa had been a nightmare for them. Travelling on the *SoD* was going to be ten times worse.

Jack flew forward through the cabin. His heart beat faster with anxiety. He felt nervous about seeing Keelraiser again. They'd worked together so closely during the ice delivery operation that they almost lived inside each other's heads. But for all these months, Keelraiser had just been a voice on the radio. They hadn't met face to face since April. Now it was August. On Earth, people would be picnicking, going to the beach ... staring up at the summer sky and wondering what was going to break out of it in two years' time.

A narrow, dark corridor led to the cockpit. The door was open and Jack flew straight in. Smaller than the *SoD's* three-man bridge, the *Cloudeater* only had two crew couches in the cockpit. The commander's seat was empty.

Keelraiser sat in the pilot's seat, sweeping its seven-fingered hands across the banks of consoles that projected from the forward wall, powering the shuttle's systems down. Jack's mouth went dry. "Well, we did it," he said cheerily. "Should be smooth sailing from here on out."

"I thought that might be you," Keelraiser said. Its mouth opened, but its grave, musical voice did not come from its lips. Like all rriksti, it spoke with the bio-antennas swirling around its shoulders like snaky hair, in the radio frequencies. Keelraiser's bio-antennas were black. Its face was paler than Jack's, a foot long, flat as a shovel, pointy-chinned, dominated by huge dark eyes. Minimal facial mobility limited the rriksti to a bare few expressions. Mouth-opening could indicate distress, or delight, or the complicated rriksti emotion that Jack understood as amusement. "Do you need help getting out of that thing?"

"No, I think I'll just evolve double-jointed shoulders," Jack said dryly. The rriksti had double-jointed shoulders. Humans did not. However, the Z-2 could only be doffed via the rear entry port, which the wearer couldn't reach on his or her own. Way to go, NASA.

Keelraiser floated over to him and unlatched the port. Jack writhed free of the bulky suit, into steamy heat and a salty smell that pulled at things low in his belly. This was how the rriksti liked it. Christ, they were going to be miserable on the *SoD*. That was one of the things he'd come to talk to Keelraiser about. The other was …

"The killer iceberg," Keelraiser said, proving again that they lived inside each other's heads.

"Yeah. That." Flapping his sweat-soaked t-shirt away from his chest, Jack drifted into the center of the cockpit. The ceiling swept down into a concave forward wall, making a curvilinear arrowhead-shaped space. Electronics filled the tip of the arrowhead, but when Jack hovered in just the right place, behind the pilot's seat, the whole cockpit turned transparent, and he seemed to be floating in space, wearing nothing but a t-shirt and underpants. The illusion induced vertigo, it was so perfect.

However, the *SoD's* rotating hab took up most of the view. It rose in front of the *Cloudeater's* nose like a steel wall with a curved top. The view to starboard was not much better—that is, Jack could see Jupiter, which he was heartily sick of seeing. He glanced to port. No icebergs.

Not that he'd be able to see them coming with his unaided eyes. He looked around for the optical telescope, and saw that Keelraiser was talking to him, its hair undulating. But the turbines aft made a fair bit of noise, and he couldn't catch the faint words coming from his Z-2, which drifted in the air between them like a fat, dark gray corpse. He was so flustered he'd forgotten his headset. He retrieved it from the Z-2's thigh pocket. Rriksti electronics: better than wearable—*crumplable,* and they still work. He uncrumpled the headset and jammed it onto his dirty blond curls. It transposed rriksti bio-radio frequencies into the audible range. The integrated mic did the same thing in reverse.

"I was just saying you haven't got your headset on," Keelraiser said, its hair dancing, picking up red and green glints from the lights on the consoles. The 'hair' was bio-antennas. Iron particles mixed with keratin.

"Very funny. Before that."

"There may be more icebergs where that came from. I've set the optical telescope to scan the whole sky. The computer will alert me if it sees anything. But there's a blind spot in my coverage ..." Keelraiser joined Jack behind the pilot's seat. "... the shape of your rotating hab."

Jack nodded, looking down at the length of the *SoD*. The truss tower beneath the *Cloudeater* enclosed the secondary hab modules. The *SoD* embodied the unspoken human rule that spaceships had to be steel gray. The spacesuited rriksti queueing outside the storage module provided an incongruous splash of color. They were a tall people, between six and eight feet, not counting their manes of bio-antennas. Their spacesuits sported lurid patterns that apparently alluded to Imfi flora.

"It's like stepping back in time," Keelraiser whispered.

"I see what you mean about the telescope coverage," Jack said awkwardly.

"Yes. Can you set your telescope on the bridge to scan the forward regions of the sky?"

Jack sighed. "No. The computer can't traverse the telescope, and we haven't got software that could analyze the feeds from the external cameras to look for snowballs. It's all got to be done manually." He hated to admit how primitive the *SoD's* systems were, in comparison to the *Cloudeater's*. But it was no secret to anyone. "I've had someone on ice chunk lookout duty whenever I'm not on the bridge. Usually Brbb or one of its friends. Giles caught this one. He just happened to be looking in the right direction. The computer had nothing to do with it."

"Maybe we could integrate the computer systems," Keelraiser said, without much hope. The *SoD's* flight computer was state of the art circa 2010—rad-hardened electronics always lagged a few years in terms of performance. The *Cloudeater* had a quantum computer. Yes, a freaking *quantum computer*. Scientists on Earth would wet their pants. You might as well try to integrate a jet engine into a WWI Sopwith.

"Not worth the risk of breaking both things," Jack said. He was not a person to weight fat-tail risks too heavily, as a rule. 'Have a go' was his motto. But since being named mission commander, he had felt compelled to play it safer than he normally would. He was trying to model himself on their previous commander, Kate Menelaou, who'd been murdered by the bad guys on the *Lightbringer*.

Keelraiser's hair stirred and subsided, producing a noise like a sigh. "Well, the lookout idea is good."

"So you think there are more where that one came from," Jack said.

"Yes."

"Right." Jack had reached the same conclusion. "It wasn't one of ours."

CHAPTER 3

"That iceberg had a motor on it," Keelraiser said.

"You're fucking kidding me."

Keelraiser turned a portion of the forward wall into a screen. The *Cloudeater* had captured video as the iceberg hurtled towards them. In slow motion, you could see the plumes of water vapor erupting from the iceberg as Keelraiser traversed the maser across it. Jack spotted shards of metal debris embedded in the ice.

"It's a flying nail bomb," he marvelled.

A crude engine bell also protruded from the ice. Keelraiser explained how it would have guided the iceberg to its near-fatal rendezvous with the *SoD*. Jack was not all that interested in the engine. It was just a little solid-fuelled thing he could have made in an afternoon in a decent machine shop. He was interested in where it came from.

He stared into the vastness of space beyond Jupiter. At the moment, he knew, he was actually looking towards the outer solar system. But in his mind he saw the *Lightbringer,* a five-kilometer whale with a hole in its side. A wounded planet-killer. It had escaped from Europa orbit three months ago, after Jack fired a plutonium round at it, and missed.

"They can't think we're a threat to them," he said, feeling incredulous.

"No," Keelraiser agreed. "It's just …"

"The principle of the thing?"

"Yes."

"I tried to nuke them, so now they're throwing icebergs

at us?" Abruptly, Jack started to laugh. It was a reaction to the stress and fear of the close call they'd had. "Icebergs!" he hooted. He had to wipe his eyes, as tears of mirth built up, but could not fall in zero-gee. "Fucking remote-controlled *icebergs!*"

Keelraiser's hair danced. "Exactly! The good news is that this proves they haven't anything *else* to throw at us." Keelraiser's mouth closed in a somber line. "At least … not at the moment."

Jack gave voice to a fear that had nagged him ever since the *Lightbringer's* departure. "Everything was trashed. But they've got railguns. A HERF mast. Muon cannons. Right? They'll try to mend that stuff along the way. Do you think they can?"

"I would not underestimate the ingenuity of the *Krijistal.*" The *Krijistal* were the rriksti special forces now in command of the *Lightbringer.* "Water and power. That's all you need. The rest is chemistry."

The quote invoked the memory of Eskitul, the *Lightbringer's* Shiplord. Towards the end of their long voyage from Imf, she had changed her mind about invading Earth. That was all very noble, but then she'd changed her mind *again* when the *SoD* showed up. Betraying her faithful followers, she'd boarded the *Lightbringer* and resumed her position as Shiplord. She had died shortly after the *Lightbringer's* launch. But that didn't make her betrayal any less heinous. Keelraiser now refused to even refer to her by name.

Yes, *her.* You couldn't tell a rriksti's sex by looking at it. Alexei, who had lived among them on the surface for months, insisted that they really were male and female, two days out of eleven, or was it three days out of thirteen? Jack defaulted to *it,* rather than risk referring to the wrong rriksti by the wrong pronoun on the wrong day of the week. But he made an exception for Eskitul, the dark mirror of bright Kate. It really pissed him off that she had died before he could sort her out.

Well, he'd settle for sorting the *Lightbringer.* The *SoD* still had a couple of nukes left.

But would he ever get a chance to use them?

He pictured the *Lightbringer's* trajectory on a mental map of the solar system. It had burst out of Jupiter orbit at an angle that took it away from the plane of the ecliptic, after a narrow shave with the Io flux tube. He knew this from tracking it with the *SoD's* radar. OK, he was a bit obsessed. So was everyone on Earth, of course, and they had the James Webb telescope, whose infrared sensors had portrayed the *Lightbringer* as a hot comet rising from Jupiter, gouting 1,600,000° water plasma from its business end as it continued to burn.

And burn.

And burn.

After escaping Jupiter's gravity well, the *Lightbringer* had thrust for a solid week, bending its trajectory back towards the plane where the sun's planets resided.

Back towards Earth.

It was now 55 million kilometers away, coasting towards the asteroid belt, well launched on its mission of death.

"The question is," Jack muttered, "how much reaction mass have they got? Obviously a lot, if they can afford to throw it at us …"

"In human units," Keelraiser said, "a metric fuck-tonne.

Oh, I don't know, Jack! I'm not a propulsion technician. I barely even knew how many water tanks we had on the *Lightbringer,* until they exploded."

Jack sighed. "Sorry. I was just wondering …"

"If we could catch up?"

"I swear, you can read my mind or something."

"No," Keelraiser said, "it's just that we think in the same way. It's interesting, in and of itself, that two beings born on different planets can be so much alike …"

Jack nodded. His mouth felt dry again.

"… but it means, of course, that you already know what I'm going to say."

"Not a chance in hell," Jack acknowledged. The *Lightbringer* had a four-month head start. It was travelling at a hair-raising velocity of 97,000 kilometers per hour. Jack continued to lie awake during his sleep periods, playing with orbital dynamics, and imagining tricks that could wring more delta-V out of the *SoD,* but he rationally accepted that it was hopeless.

Especially if the *Lightbringer* was going to make a habit of shooting motorized icebergs at them.

"Here's what I was thinking," he said to Keelraiser, snapping his fingers. "You should be our weapons officer. You know, I started off flying Tornados. Have you ever seen a Tornado?"

He meant on television. All the rriksti had seen a lot of television. There had not been much else to do during their journey from Imf. That, too, was how they'd learned English. Keelraiser had wound up with an upper-class British accent straight off the BBC. There hadn't been anyone in Jack's RAF squadron who sounded that posh. He tried not to hold it against Keelraiser, reminding himself that everyone on TV had talked like that in the 1950s and '60s.

"The Tornado's got a pilot and a navigator," Jack explained. "The navigator is also the weapons officer. He drops the bombs." But the command was given by the pilot. Jack had dropped bombs on the wrong people once or twice. Faulty intelligence, a fat-fingered navigator—excuses could be made, but Jack took responsibility. Somewhere in Iraq, broken families still hated his guts, even if they would never know his name.

"The *Cloudeater* is not armed," Keelraiser said. "It's just a shuttle. Do you mean you are putting me in charge of the *SoD's* railguns?"

"Er. No. But seeing as the main threat at the moment is remote-controlled icebergs ..." Keelraiser didn't seem as pleased as Jack had thought it would. "You did a fantastic job with that maser, plus you've got a better telescope, so I'd like to make that your official responsibility."

Keelraiser twisted its head and shoulders sideways, like a horse shying. This was how the rriksti shrugged, as far as Jack could make out. "We should talk about how we're going to leverage the *Cloudeater's* life-support capabilities. I'd like to show you something."

It floated out of the cockpit, its coattails flapping.

"What are you wearing, anyway?" Jack said in amusement as he followed. He had never before seen Keelraiser in anything but tatty shorts or a spacesuit.

Keelraiser turned to face him in the narrow corridor. It wore a tailored jacket, long in the back and square-cut in front, open over its chest, with pleated Bermuda shorts. The whole ensemble was bright orange, except for some navy blue circle patches on the lapels.

"My uniform."

"Aha."

"It seemed appropriate for the *Cloudeater's* last flight."

"Surely not its *last* flight ..." Jack had a vague ambition to land the *Cloudeater* at some symbolic location such as Heathrow or JFK. That's what the shuttle was made for, after all: de-orbiting on a planet with an atmosphere. However, that was all so far in the future he hadn't really thought about it. First, they had to *get* to Earth.

"The *Cloudeater* is now welded to your low-tech disaster of a ship," Keelraiser said. "That's rather permanent-feeling."

"Oh, I wouldn't put that much faith in my welds ..."*Low-tech disaster?* Well, yes, from Keelraiser's point of view. It must feel like lashing a Prius to the deck of a fifteenth-century sailing ship. Still, no need to rub it in.

"While I'm being pessimistic," Keelraiser said, reverting to its usual self-aware, ironic tone. "About one-third of the civilians are quite sick."

"Yeah, I know."

The rriksti required a diet rich in heavy metals, which had been in short supply on the surface of Europa. After ten years, the refugees were chronically malnourished. Cancer also stalked them, owing to cumulative radiation exposure, although that wasn't always the death sentence you might think.

"I've discussed it with Cleanmay, and we've decided to turn the *Cloudeater* into a sickbay," Keelraiser said. Cleanmay was a rriksti doctor. A doctor without a hospital or any medical equipment to speak of. "We haven't got many treatment options. Still, the sick would be better off in a proper rriksti environment."

They reached the passenger cabin, which was the length of economy class in a 747, but twice as wide and high. A proper rriksti environment. Hot, steamy, and gloomy. Imf must be a proper tropical paradise. Jack reminded himself that the environment also included X-rays sleeting invisibly through the *Cloudeater*. The rriksti basked in X-rays like humans basked in sunlight. It wouldn't be healthy for Jack to hang out in here too long.

"Well, that sounds like a plan," he said. "Rip out some of the seats …"

"The whole middle row." Keelraiser slapped the back of a seat upholstered in the same shade of orange—Jack now noticed—as its uniform. The movement sent Keelraiser rebounding to the ceiling. "We'll break them down for raw materials. Plastics, aluminum alloys—you can find a use for those, can't you?"

"Well, sure."

"Will you help?"

"Now?" Jack suppressed a sigh. He had a thousand things to do in preparation for their burn out of Europa orbit. With more icebergs potentially coming their way, he was even keener to get moving.

But none of his tasks would take as long as getting the passengers settled, and the sick required extra care. This was *your* idea, Kildare, he told himself. Don't half-arse it.

"OK. Shall I go fetch our laser saw?" He wasn't joking. The *SoD* had run out of all the things they really needed, such as duct tape—but hey, they had a laser saw! The eggheads at NASA had got the mission requirements about 80% wrong. Jack could write a book on Shit You Really Need In Space. In fact, he had.

"No need for that," Keelraiser said. It raised both hands to the back of its neck. The snaky black bio-antennas whipped out of the way, the seven-fingered hands flashed down, and two short swords stopped dead in an en-garde position. Skeleton-leaf blades trapped oily puddles of light from the LEDs. Keelraiser floated away, laughing with its hair.

"Now I'm very jealous," Jack said. "They never issued *us* anything like that."

"The cutting edges are just a few tungsten atoms wide."

"Bet you keep those locked up."

"Yes. They're not the sharpest things in the universe. Carbon nanocables would be … cuttier? Is this correct?"

"'Cutty' *ought* to be a word."

"But it's more elegant to carry a sword than a piece of string. At least that is what our commanders thought."

"I'd have to agree."

"I used these to chop up the *Cloudeater's* mobility pods," Keelraiser said, referring to the small orbital transfer vehicles they had sacrificed for parts. "Now for the seats." It held out one of the swords to Jack, who took it carefully. The off-white hilt felt smooth, yet sticky, like rriksti skin. "Let's race," Keelraiser suggested. "You start from that end. I'll start from this end."

Jack grinned. "You're on."

*

On the bridge, Giles Boisselot frowned at his laptop. The Excel spreadsheet on the screen had three columns: a list of Rristigul words for heavy metals, the rrikstis' own translations of these words, and Glies's glosses, including alternative translations where he thought the rriksti might have made a mistake. Arsine? Or did they mean arsenic?

For a xenolinguist, Giles made a good gardener. So he had concluded after months of struggling with Rristigul, the language used by the Darksider rriksti on the *SoD*. There were two rriksti nations, broadly speaking—the Lightside and the Darkside, who lived, obviously, on the light side and the dark side of Imf. Perhaps the Lightsiders spoke a less fiendish language. Giles would never know, because the Darksiders had obliterated them in an all-out planetary war. Then for an encore they had come to invade Earth.

The trouble with Rristigul was not the 15 different declensions of nouns, nor the three tense-sensitive cases used for pronouns, nor even the fact that the meanings of words changed depending on frequency as well as amplitude. No, it was the fact that the Darksiders were so infuriatingly dishonest, even in matters, such as the naming of heavy metals, which could make the difference between life and death for them.

File name: SHIT WE NEED.

Jack had started the list. By now it was book-length. They had all added to it as their margin for survival frayed thinner and thinner. Four months spent orbiting Europa had *not* been in the mission plan.

Nor had 306 rriksti.

Rescuing them from Europa had been Jack's idea. He'd said it was the least they could do, after the rriksti helped to refill the *SoD's* water tanks. Alexei backed him up, as he always did. Skyler's opinion did not matter. Giles flattered himself, half-seriously, that his own opinion did matter. He approved of the decision, as he recognized that Jack was acting, consciously or unconsciously, on the Golden Rule: do as you would be done by. This at least moved interstellar relations back in the right direction, after the disastrous start they'd got off to. Furthermore, Giles had begun to grasp the importance of reciprocity in rriksti culture. But the question remained:

How the fuck are we going to get home?

It's nice to have plenty of reaction mass, but that will not keep us alive for two years, not if we don't have—say it with me—all this Shit We Need.

Sighing, Giles scrolled down to the end of the list. Someone had made a new entry. He smiled. Then he touched the intercom.

"Jack?"

Alexei answered. "He's still on the *Cloudeater*. What's up? Another iceberg?"

"No, no. Is everyone safely aboard?"

"Aboard, yes, safely, no comment. It is complete chaos back here."

"Are you going to hook up the plumbing now? Or later?"

While he waited for Alexei's response, Giles scanned the internal monitoring feed, flipping through grainy videos from all the different cameras mounted inside the *SoD's* modules. Each and every camera showed rriksti. Rriksti, and more rriksti. Their luggage littered the floor of the main hab. Hydroponic tanks and trays had leaked in transport. Several rriksti knelt up to their elbows in a large tank, wrestling with Imfi fish. Giles spotted Alexei at last, in the Potter space under Staircase 5, standing on poor dead Qiu Meili's desk, driving rivets into the hab wall. The plan was to rig nets to stop all this crap from shifting around when they burned.

"I will do the plumbing later." Alexei's lips moved on the screen, and his voice came through the intercom. They'd patched their rriksti headsets into the ship's internal comms.

"Rivets?" Giles said.

"We're out of duct tape."

Giles sighed. He glanced back at his laptop screen. The DUCT TAPE!!! entry was highlighted in yellow, sandwiched between 'nitrogen' and 'antibiotics.' "We really need that resupply flight," he said.

"Send them some more pictures of your feet," Alexei said.

Giles looked down at his feet. *His* feet? He wiggled his toes.

He was a quadruple amputee. He had not started out that way. His hands and feet had been severed, just for fun as far as he knew, by Ripstiggr, the commander of the *Krijistal*.

Ripstiggr now held the distinction of being the individual Giles hated most in the universe, narrowly edging out the new director-general of the European Space Agency (ESA).

After the amputations, while Giles was unconscious, the *Krijistal* had sealed his stumps with skin caps. They had stuffed him into poor Hannah's spacesuit and cast him out of the *Lightbringer*.

At first, the skin caps had looked like rounded clubs, the pale color of rriksti skin. Jack had made him a pair of strap-on hooks so he could perform basic tasks. No one had been more surprised than Giles himself when his stumps started to grow. Day by day, those mushroom-colored clubs had sprouted nubs that turned into fingers and toes, on the ends of wrists and ankles which still continued to elongate.

The rriksti had *not* been surprised. They had apparently known this would happen. On Earth, research into limb regeneration was in its infancy, but the rriksti were fifty to a hundred years ahead of humanity in most arenas. And that very much included medical technology.

When Giles pressed for information, the rriksti doctor Cleanmay had speculated that the guys on the *Lightbringer* must have done a quick and dirty analysis of his DNA, and used cells from his fingernail and toenail matrices to 'program' the skin caps, in the hopes that their regeneration technology would work, probably, mostly, sort of.

Mostly. Yeah. Sort of.

Giles's small, bony new hands had *seven* fingers each. His little flipper-like feet (still growing) had *seven* toes.

But whether it has five or seven fingers, a hand is a hand. Right? Even if the word in Rristigul is *shka,* and we just call them hands to make it seem mostly, sort of, OK.

They had, of course, sent pictures of his amazing new limbs back to Earth.

Giles regretted that more than he regretted losing his hands and feet in the first place.

Because the director-general of ESA—the second-most-despicable person in the universe, let's remember—had got hold of those pictures, and leaked them to the media, to make it look as if the rriksti were miracle-workers.

An outrageous deception!

Giles knew well how tempting it was to believe in salvation from beyond. That's what had brought him out here. But as it turned out, the rriksti themselves needed salvation at least as badly as humanity did. *Quelle dommage!* What a pity God did not exist, Giles thought.

CHAPTER 4

Jack discovered that Keelraiser's tungsten-bladed sword was a joy to use. It went through the aluminum frames of the seats as if they were made of butter.

They started at opposite ends of the cabin and worked their way towards each other. Jack soon got into the rhythm of it. He swung and hacked, bracing his feet against each seat in turn while he demolished the one behind it. Air cushions embedded in the seats popped, unleashing a strange, wild odor. Air from Imf, trapped inside the upholstery all these years.

Swing and hack. Swing and hack. Sweat shook loose from Jack's body in airborne rivers. Some of the seats wore the face of the late Eskitul. Some of them became *Krijistal*. Some of them took on the faces of the fucking idiots on Earth who'd approved this mission in the first place. And some became the NASA project managers who'd half-arsed their design evaluation processes, leaving Jack to command a low-tech disaster …

He backed over a seat and hit nothing with his legs. A single row of seats remained in the middle row. The rest drifted in pieces around the cabin like orange-and-gray asteroids.

"I won," Keelraiser said, sheathing its sword. Until now, Jack had thought that the rriksti didn't sweat like humans. Turned out he'd just never seen one of them work this hard before. Keelraiser's pale face dripped like a seashell just pulled out of the surf. Its cheeks glowed pink, and it had dark circles under its arms. It mopped its face with its sleeve.

Jack ducked an airborne seat chunk closing in on his head, and laughed. "Think we might have got a bit carried away there."

"It was fun," Keelraiser said. "But you chopped them up too much. That is why you lost."

"I did not lose."

"Lies, damned lies, and English." Keelraiser had found a water bottle somewhere. It closed its small lips around the nozzle. Its throat worked as it drank.

"Gimme some," Jack said, realizing how thirsty he was.

"No," Keelraiser said, still drinking. *When you talk with your hair, you can talk with your mouth full.* "It would poison you."

Jack hated that rriksti food and drink was toxic to humans. It made him feel vulnerable. Irrationally, he refused to be beaten by some stupid Imfi beverage. "We've got to share everything now, you know," he said, making a grab for the bottle.

Keelraiser plunged away through the air. Jack gave chase. Keelraiser threw a chunk of seat at him. They pelted each other, dodging and diving. Keelraiser's laughter pealed like the noise of a sat-upon concertina. Yeah, it was childish, but now that everyone was safely aboard, couldn't Jack stop being the mission commander for five minutes and just be himself? Freefall was *fun,* something he forgot for long stretches at a time through focusing exclusively on the dangers of space.

He caught Keelraiser by the legs and pinned it to the floor. There was no 'down,' as such. The floor was just one side of the battle theater they had made of the passenger cabin. Jack hooked his toes and fingers around severed seat supports, spreadeagling himself on top of Keelraiser. "Why orange?" he gasped, referring to the seats.

Keelraiser panted under him, his torso rising and falling. Its coat had fallen open to reveal the ribby breadth of its chest. It had no nipples. Gusts of salty breath blew into Jack's face. "Darkside Space Force colors. Orange, indigo, and white. This craft started its life as a commercial passenger shuttle."

"So it *was* a Concorde!"

"Yes, something like that. A Concorde that flew to the moon and back. It was commandeered when the last war but two broke out. In those days, the military had enough money to employ people to design carpets and soft furnishings ..."

"We've got plenty of those."

"So they refitted it as a stylish and patriotic troop transport. Then it got reassigned to the *Lightbringer*. When we reached Earth, I would have flown support missions, taking the Darkside infantry to carry out their terror operations on Earth, and resupplying their bases." Jack could feel Keelraiser's heartbeat thudding, belying its calm voice. "I was looking forward to it."

Jack fell silent, thinking about that nightmare scenario. It could so easily have happened. But now the rriksti infantry were all dead. The war on board the *Lightbringer* had done for them. And there were no more shuttles. Only the *Cloudeater* remained. The *Lightbringer* might still wreak havoc but not half as much as it had been designed to. Humanity owed Keelraiser an incalculable debt.

He stared down (up) into Keelraiser's eyes. "You were looking forward to it, but then you changed your mind."

"I changed my mind."

Jack took his right hand off the seat support he was holding, so that Keelraiser—like his shuttle—was now only secured by the minimum three points. He picked up one of Keelraiser's seven-fingered hands. The six fingers were arranged in two groups of three, with a gap between them. The two middle fingers were the longest. He remembered something, a moment from their first meeting that had been eating at him ever since. He put one of Keelraiser's fingers into his mouth.

Still as stone, Keelraiser stared up (down) at him.

Jack moved his tongue around the tip of Keelraiser's finger. The fingernail was blunt, heavy, like the claw of a dog. The salty residue on Keelraiser's skin tasted pungent. The delicate first joint contracted, hooking the fingertip behind Jack's teeth.

Jack pulled back.

"Why did you do that?" he said. "The very first day we met. You put your finger in my mouth. Why?"

"To see if you'd bite," Keelraiser said quietly. He rolled his head to the side as if seeking an escape route. Jack caught himself thinking of him as a *he*. Of course, he *was* male, two days in eleven or whatever. Jack had been wrong about that at first, too.

"I suppose I don't come off as very civilized," Jack said ruefully. He moved to let Keelraiser up.

Keelraiser writhed, jerking one arm up and behind his neck.

Jack saw the blade coming, like a gray leaf falling where there was no gravity to bring it down, but he had no time to dodge.

CHAPTER 5

Skyler took off his spacesuit in front of a dozen rriksti who weren't too traumatized by the killer iceberg drama to laugh at his genitals. Apparently this hilarious sight never got old for them.

Shooting them a friendly middle finger, he went aft to the engineering module.

This had formerly been the private kingdom of Hannah Ginsburg, the *SoD's* propulsion specialist. Skyler gazed at the reactor and turbine controls on the curved side walls. Pumps, thermocouples, and SCRAM controls, oh my. The engine controls took up another section of wall. A laptop was duct-taped, open, above the tankage pressure display. Skyler touched the trackpad and saw one of the checklists sent by Mission Control. Jack and Giles had been following these step-by-step instructions to monitor the reactor and turbines. But to Skyler, the checklists were not reassuring. They made Hannah's absence as real and tangible as a punch to the gut.

Everyone said she was dead. Had to be dead. The *Krijistal* on the *Lightbringer* had kidnapped her, and look what they did to Kate and Giles.

Yet during his lonely nights in the rriksti bunker, Skyler had hoped against hope that she might be alive. That he might even see her again someday.

He glanced at the fragile, faded origami Star of David floating above the hexagonal array, and the photo of Hannah's family above the dollar meter. Her sister, brother-in-law, and two kids. They looked crunchy, wholesome. California nice. Had they been notified of Hannah's death? Did they still cling to hopes as faded as an old photograph?

Skyler sighed, letting his desolation roll over him. If he was going to be the *SoD's* new reactor and propulsion specialist—such, incredibly, was the plan; they were so shorthanded now that *Skyler Taft* had to look after the freaking reactor—he'd better get to work.

He drifted over to the laptop on the wall.

But instead of starting on the checklists, he checked that the laptop was connected to the *SoD's* Ka comms system, and opened Google Chrome.

During his months on the surface of Europa, he'd been totally cut off. No idea what people on Earth were saying about their mission. Jack had been very stingy with news, claiming that Mission Control had clammed up on them.

Well, that's what the internet was for, wasn't it?

This far from Earth, every click took 66 minutes, round trip.

Skyler didn't care.

He typed in the search box: "Hannah Ginsburg." *Return*.

Then he studied Reactors for Dummies for an hour and six minutes.

At last his results came back.

Every result on the first page was a video.

He clicked on the first one.

Another hour and a half passed.

Jack's voice came from the intercom, pulling him out of a vortex of shock and horror. "Alexei?" Jack said.

"Yeah?" Alexei said, from somewhere else on the ship.

"Can you meet me at the storage module airlock?"

"Oh Jesus," Alexei said. "I have to find somewhere

dark for the mushrooms. There aren't enough nets. And I still haven't secured our own hydroponics."

Jack laughed huskily. "OK, sounds like you're busy. Carry on."

Skyler blurted, "I'll be right there."

He flew forward into the storage module, just as Jack dropped out of the airlock. Jack hadn't succumbed to the convenience of rriksti spacesuits. He still wore his Z-2. It was the one with the red piping.

"Clear out," Jack said, waving his arms at the rriksti that were exploring the storage lockers, lab, and machine shop.

Skyler flew over to him and unlatched the back entry port of the Z-2. He assumed this was why Jack had wanted someone to meet him, although a rriksti could have done this simple task.

"I need a bit of help," Jack said.

As Skyler helped him to doff the suit, he tried to decide how to broach the subject of the videos. Jack had to have seen them. He'd lied to Skyler—by omission, but still. What the hell was going on?

Jack emerged from the suit, and Skyler forgot about the videos. It was that bad.

"You're bleeding!"

Blood swelled in zero-gee worms from cuts on Jack's face, arms, and chest. Globules broke off like icebergs calving from red glaciers, and set off on wobbly journeys towards the intake ducts of the ventilation system.

"Get the betadine wipes," Jack said calmly, backhanding blood out of his eyes. "Gauze. Mupiricin ointment. And don't let the blood get into the fans."

Skyler flew across the storage module to the first aid

locker. This gave him an opportunity to see the rrikstis' reaction. It was strange. They did not freak out. They did not ask Jack if he was OK. They did not even rubberneck. They hastened in good order towards the forward keel tube, as if Jack's order to 'clear out' had belatedly sunk in.

"Ixnay on the gauze," Skyler said, rummaging in the first aid locker. "Here's the mupiricin." He also took out the suture kit.

Jack had got his t-shirt off. It was already so saturated, it wasn't much use as a rag. Skyler gave him a towel and used another one to mop the blood out of the air. All the towels were so filthy that they crunched as if starched. "Is there anything to drink?" Jack said. "Such as neat whiskey?"

"Ha ha. Gatorade?"

"Is there any left? Brilliant."

There were fewer than a dozen capsules left. These capsules were clever gimmicks, developed especially for the *SoD*. Place one into a bottle of water and shake. Skyler presented the bottle to Jack with a bartender's flourish. "That's a lot of blood, man."

"I know. I'm never going to get it out of my suit."

Skyler opened a new betadine wipe and swabbed Jack's arms, trying to be gentle. Trying very, very hard not to think about what the *Krijistal* had done to Kate. And Giles. Was it starting again? Had they misjudged these rriksti, too?

Jack drank half the Gatorade at once. He reached for Skyler's headset and pulled it off. "Giles! Is Gatorade on the Shit We Need list? If not, add it …"

"You need stitches on some of these cuts," Skyler said.

"OK, do it," Jack said curtly.

Skyler tore open a suture pack and got to work with the attached needle. For some time the only words exchanged were "Ow!" and "Sorry."

Most of the cuts on Jack's chest and face were shallow, like long paper-cuts. The bad ones were on his forearms.

Defensive wounds.

What the hell *happened?*

"I'll do this one on my face myself," Jack said. "It's not as if I can get much uglier. But I'm the one with advanced medical training …"

Skyler clamped the mirror into the vise on the lab bench. Jack stitched the deepest cut on his face, which ran down his left cheek to his jaw.

"Fucking tricky doing this backwards … Want to have a go, actually?"

Skyler was starting to feel like he might throw up. He kept seeing Hannah in Jack's place. If the supposed good guys had done this to Jack, what had the bad guys likely done to her? True, she had looked uninjured in the videos. But she'd been wearing jeans, long sleeves … He clamped his teeth shut and forced himself to push the needle through the skin of Jack's cheek.

"This would be easier in Medical," he said, meaning: in the official sickbay, in the main hab, in gravity. Everything's harder in zero-gee, and that includes stitching up someone's face.

"I know, but I'd rather everyone didn't see." Jack was shaking. Skyler could feel it. "Those fuckers who were in here will probably tell all their friends, anyway."

"Jack, what *happened?*"

*

Jack stared at the blood spots on the towel he was holding. He couldn't look at Skyler. Much less look in the mirror. Basically, he wanted to die of embarrassment.

"I fucked up," he said.

"Um …"

"I just fucked up."

"OK."

Skyler got ready to make another stitch, his face strained with concentration. Jack held onto the lab bench to keep himself from drifting away. He knew he would have to come up with a better explanation, but every stab of the needle further fractured his understanding of what had, actually, happened.

Ow. *Ow.*

Keelraiser cut me up.

Ow.

Those blades are so sharp, I didn't even feel it at first.

Then it was just—blood everywhere. I'm blocking with my arms, trying to defend myself, but he keeps coming. Screaming, *Why don't you hit me back? Why don't you hit me back?* Well, I'm trying, Keelraiser, but I'm not the one with a tungsten-bladed sword, am I?

Fortunately, he wasn't out to kill me.

Just messed me up.

Then kicked me out.

Ow. *Ow.*

Jack had the shakes, something he hadn't experienced since he was in Iraq. Struggling to hide the shameful reaction, he made a consequential decision without even thinking about it. "We were doing a bit of redecorating," he said, "and I wasn't careful enough. Moral of the story, don't play with pointy objects."

"Redecorating ... with scalpels?"

"More or less."

Skyler snipped off the thread. He put the suture kit back in its box. The strained look around his eyes tipped Jack off to what must be going through his mind.

Skyler thought Keelraiser had gone ape.

(Had Keelraiser gone ape?)

Skyler was afraid they were going to have a repeat of the battle for the *SoD*. Only this time, it would be 306 against four.

(Were they going to have another battle?)

No. Of course not. Don't be daft. I'm rescuing them from Europa, aren't I?

"It's OK," he said as forcefully as he could manage. "I fucked up, but it's going to be OK. You see, what happened ..."

(Oh, *this* is what happened!)

"... I offered Keelraiser the job of weapons officer. Tail-gunner kind of thing. And I think it was a bit insulted by that, so ..."

Skyler shared Jack's preference for 'it' as the generic rriksti pronoun. "Did it try to heal you?"

Hope and relief glimmered in Skyler's eyes. Jack realized that Skyler had hit on an explanation that made sense to him, which did *not* imply mass slaughter round the corner. So even though that wasn't what had happened at all, Jack said, "Yeah. Yeah, and as you know, I'm really not into that."

"But I thought Keelraiser wasn't extroverted," Skyler muttered, spotting the hole in his own explanation.

"Well actually it is," Jack said. Lying his arse off. Just like a rriksti. "And you know they think they're doing us a tremendous favor when they offer to heal us. They get quite huffy if you say no, don't they? So we'll just give old Keelraiser time to cool off." Two years would be about right, Jack thought. He was also reconsidering the plan to hook up the two ships' plumbing, although he knew that would be pure spite. "I suspect I'm persona non grata on the *Cloudeater* at the moment, but that's OK. There's no reason I need to go over there."

"Better to stay out of those X-rays, anyway," Skyler muttered. He put away the first aid kit. Then he met Jack's eyes. "I need to show you something."

Jack gestured wearily: go on. Skyler went aft. While he was gone, Jack checked the first aid locker for painkillers. As he had already known, they were out of everything. Rot in hell, Mission Control.

Skyler floated back into the storage module. As soon as Jack saw the laptop in his hand, he guessed what Skyler wanted to show him. "You found the videos?"

"The *Lightbringer's* got its own damn YouTube channel," Skyler said, his voice breaking. He clicked. Hannah Ginsburg's voice emerged from the laptop's tinny speakers.

Jack reached over and clicked the video off. The cuts on his arms throbbed with every movement. "I've already seen it."

"There are like twenty of them."

"I've seen them all."

"Why didn't you *tell* me?"

Skyler was white as a sheet. He was clearly struggling with fierce emotions. Jack had felt the same way when he first saw the videos. But for Skyler, it must be far worse. He'd had an unrequited crush on Hannah for years. Jack felt a deep pang of sympathy for him. "We just didn't know how to tell you. I sincerely apologize."

"Do you think they did the same thing to her that Keelraiser did to you? Or what they did to Giles?"

"It doesn't look like it, does it?"

"You can't really tell," Skyler said, staring at the paused video.

"You can't, but listen. Keelraiser thinks they must have made her Shiplord after Eskitul bought it. There are clues in some of the other videos, and you can see a scar of some kind on her forehead. That's where the implant would be."

Skyler bit his knuckles so hard Jack worried he would break the skin.

"The point is they're probably treating her like a princess. So it isn't really as bad as it—"

"It's obscene," Skyler said. "It's grotesque, it's disgusting." He shut the laptop, hard.

Jack wondered if he should just give him the rest of the videos, to save him the trouble of downloading them later. He and Giles had downloaded them all over the last four months. Mission Control must have seen them, too. The flipping things were on Youtube, as Skyler had discovered.

CHAPTER 6

Hannah Ginsburg floated through the bowels of the *Lightbringer,* wearing her spacesuit. By the light of her chest-lamp, she saw rows of tanks stretching away along both sides of the corridor. The *Lightbringer* was only five kilometers long (ha! *Only!*) but it could seem as vast as the universe. It *was* her universe now, enclosed within a 1.5-meter steel hull.

The hull, however, had a big-ass hole in it. So most of the ship was in vacuum. That's why she wore her spacesuit. It was a rriksti suit, fitted to her body. They'd built a fishbowl helmet into it, just for her.

She consulted the display projected on her left optic nerve. It came from the chip embedded in her forehead, which had semi-successfully set up an interface with her brain. Most of the stuff it offered her was useless, as she couldn't speak Rristigul. The maps, however, came in handy.

"Zghersh 23," she read. The chip had figured out how to transliterate Rristigul into the Roman alphabet. It also rendered rriksti numbers as Roman numerals, although it did *not* convert base 14 into base 10. She had to do that in her head. So, she was looking for Zghersh, which meant Dormitory, 31. The dull green arrows superimposed on her vision told her that it was *that* way. She dimmed her chest lamp to get a bit more contrast behind the arrows. The rriksti saw colors differently with their dark-adapted eyes. They perceived imperceptible, to her, differences in dull, sludgy shades, while pastels all looked white to them.

Not that there were any pastel hues on this ship. The

Lightbringer was a warship, built for epic meanness, an interstellar killer cloaked in asteroid steel. Its interior proportions echoed the kinks and dents of fossils. A saurian bulkhead loomed out of the darkness. Hannah turned the corner into Dormitory 31.

Tank 35d8.

Base 14 to base 10 ...

9,402.

Hannah peered at the tall, rectangular door of the tank. It looked just like a high school locker, except bigger. The occupant's telemetry had flatlined yesterday. Happened. Even rriksti technology sometimes went on the blink after 70 years.

She banged on the tank with her gloved fist.

It lit up. Green light spilled down the corridor.

Inside, a rriksti floated in a loose, relaxed posture, like a giant fetus. You couldn't tell by looking at it whether it was dead or alive. Hannah cleared her throat and said: "Acquire Tank 35d8 telemetry."

The chip didn't need her to talk out loud to it, because it was in her head, sealed behind the skin of her forehead, talking directly to her brain via nanoscale filaments that had grown through her skull like grass roots growing through pavement. But they were not made for each other. She came from Earth. The chip came from Imf. Vocalizing helped her to form a clear picture in her mind—*tank, telemetry;* the chip could understand that. One picture is worth a thousand words, after all. The fact she was standing right here in front of the tank in question also helped.

The chip established a wireless connection with the tank and painted graphs on her field of vision. Hannah had done this enough times to know which one was the brain activity monitor.

"We got a deader," she said. The chip converted the electrical impulses in the speech center of her brain into radio-frequency transmissions. The comms unit in her helmet boosted the signals. "Come on down here, because I am *not* doing this by myself."

"Be right there," said a rriksti voice on the other end of the radio.

While she waited, Hannah gazed at the dead occupant of Tank 35d8. She wondered what its name was, whether it was male or female, and why it had signed up to invade Earth. Had it left a family on Imf, knowing it would never see them again? How did you *do* that?

Pot, meet kettle. Hannah had done something similar herself. She'd volunteered to go on the *Spirit of Destiny,* knowing she might never see her family again. Some schlemiel by the name of Richard Burke, director of the *SoD* project—Hannah loved Burke dearly, and missed him—had persuaded her that she had, lurking somewhere in her engineer's soul, a spirit of adventure.

So she'd said goodbye to her sister Bethany, and David, her brother-in-law, and Isabel and Nathan, her niece and nephew, who were all the family she had. Bethany had been relentlessly negative about the whole thing, but Izzy, sweet Izzy, had been so proud of her ...

Hannah blinked—bad idea to cry in zero-gee. "Hurry up," she yelled, just as Gurlp and Joker rounded the corner, flying on their wrist rockets.

"See how swiftly we obey," Joker said. His real name was something else, of course. Hannah had nicknamed him Joker because she actually did think he had a sense of humor, kind of dry and sarcastic, like Jack Kildare, the pilot of the *SoD*. Jeepers, at this point she would even be glad to see *Jack*. But he was dead, of course. They all were. The *SoD* had been abandoned in Europa orbit without water or power. Of the eight-person crew, she was the only survivor.

Which didn't say much for Earth's chances.

"Authorize recovery," Gurlp said.

"What's the magic word?" Hannah said.

It was Joker who said, "Pleeeease." Gurlp said nothing.

"I authorize recovery of this organism," Hannah said. The chip transmitted the authorization protocol to the tank. The cloudy green liquid drained away, leaving Soldier 9,402 floating in the vacuum. The door popped open, and the corpse floated into Gurlp and Joker's arms, dripping.

They took it back to the Land of the Living, a two-kilometer journey through the sleeper decks. In her roamings Hannah had discovered that the numbers on the tanks actually went up to 16,000 (in base 10). *Sixteen, freaking, thousand* soldiers of the Darkside had signed up for the voyage to Earth and gone willingly into the Long Sleep. Of course, a lot of the numbers in the middle were missing. They had been vaporized or blown into space when Eskitul turned the ship's muon cannons on its own midsection.

Hannah had conflicted feelings about Eskitul. She admired the late Shiplord's noble resolve to prevent the *Lightbringer* from conquering Earth. But she also resented her quite a lot for dying and sticking *her*, Hannah, with the job.

Because what was the use of being Shiplord when you couldn't speak the language, so someone had to hand-hold you through the most basic operations, and your neural patterns confused the heck out of the mini-computer implanted in your forehead, so that even if you could read Rristigul, it wouldn't work properly *anyway?*

They hauled the corpse through the service airlock, into the kitchen. Hannah doffed her suit to the tops of her shoulders. Heat and steam filled the cavernous room. It was hot and steamy everywhere in the Land of the Living, now that the *Krijistal* had enough spare water to keep the atmosphere tropical, the way they liked. The floor exerted a comfortable 0.5 G pull on her feet. They used mass attractors to create artificial gravity. It's hard to cook in zero-gee.

During the *Lightbringer's* ten years in a parking orbit around Europa, the *Krijistal* had huddled on the bridge to save air. After they got the power back on, they'd reoccupied the kitchen, the laundry room, the industrial-scale hydroponic farm, and the other service areas below the bridge. Oh, call it what it is: the servants' quarters. The rriksti made no bones about being basically a feudal society. There's a reason Hannah's title was Ship*lord*.

She knew her un-lordly behavior annoyed and upset them. That's why she did it.

She sat on a kitchen counter that was neck-high on her, watching the cook, Figgrit, and his assistants clean and dry the corpse of Soldier 9,402 and put it into the dehydrator.

Ah, the dehydrator. No well-appointed rriksti kitchen would be without one. A van-sized box painted with a red sun in an orange and pink sky, its front hinged down like an oven door. The whole set-up made Hannah, a Jew, think icky thoughts about Auschwitz. But this was how the dead were always treated on Imf, apparently. They slid Soldier 9,402 inside the dehydrator on a giant tray, and Ripstiggr showed up to do the funeral.

"This brave soldier gave his life for the Darkside," Ripstiggr orated. "His sacrifice shall be recorded in the annals of Imfi victory, which span four thousand eight hundred and twenty-seven years, and shall continue until the sun stops flaring."

It was really amazing how much platitudinous rriksti eulogies sounded like platitudinous human eulogies. All Soldier 9,402 needed was a flag draped over the top of the dehydrator.

"In death, he shall sustain the living."

Well, until you got to the *cannibalism* part.

"He looks pretty soggy, actually," Ripstiggr said, veering off-script. "Make sure you run the dehydrator on the highest setting, Figgrit."

The cook backed out of the circle of rriksti and went to change the setting.

Hannah, standing outside the circle, said, "Is that an approved part of the liturgy? What would the Temple say?"

"It's perfectly allowable to personalize the service," Ripstiggr said, hair dancing.

"Oh, sorry, the Temple doesn't even know you exist. You got your clerical certification over the Imfi version of the internet. It probably has spelling mistakes in it."

Joker's hair quivered, a sign of amusement inadequately concealed. Ripstiggr stalked across the circle and backhanded Joker in the face. The black-haired rriksti staggered back and crashed into the refrigerator. Unfortunately, Hannah knew Joker would not hold a grudge over being disciplined so violently. Ripstiggr hit his people all the time, and they loved him for it.

"Where was I?" Ripstiggr said. "Ah, yes. In the name of Ystyggr, Lord of the Visible and the Invisible ..." He raised his arms, spreading the stiff blue-gray sleeves of his priestly robe like wings, so that he seemed to become a snake-haired vulture-man, nine feet tall, his silver bio-antennas glittering in the low light—beautiful, terrible. "Let's eat!"

When *Ripstiggr* made a joke, it was OK to laugh. Everyone's hair danced, and they piled out of the kitchen to go up the curving staircase to the bridge. Hannah brought up the rear, bracing her hands on her thighs as she climbed. The staircase went around the mass attractor installation, approaching closer to it in the middle, so that the gravity felt stronger. By the time you got to the top, your orientation had changed 180 degrees. The floor of the kitchen was also the floor of the bridge, with a king's ransom in super-compact iridium and other very dense elements sandwiched in between.

A wave of weakness overtook Hannah on the last few stairs. She dragged herself to the top, feeling nauseous. She hoped it was just the shifting gravitational field doing it, but when she coughed, she saw flecks of blood on the dark gray palm of her glove.

Aw, crap.

Coming down with *another* bout of radiation sickness.

Just another day on the *Lightbringer*.

CHAPTER 7

Burn minus 5 minutes.

Carefully, Jack bled some of the housekeeping turbine's steam into the drive tubes. This should have been Hannah's job, but there was no Hannah anymore, and Jack had severe doubts about Skyler's ability to fill in for her. The poor guy had been thrown in at the deep end. No one could be asked to ullage a spaceship on his second day on the job.

Anyway, Jack had his own set of engine controls on the bridge. He goosed the ship into a plod. The maneuver gently jostled liquid water from the bioshield tank into the pipes.

"Oh man, Sparky is kicking out the jams!" Skyler said on the intercom. "The fuel cells are full! The primary heat exchanger is maxed out! Jack, do something with this load before the back of the ship falls off!"

"Sit tight. We're going to burn it."

The big steam turbine growled like a Formula One race car. The whole ship vibrated. A tang of ozone from the generator blew through the fans on the bridge. Back in the main hab, everything was tied down, or someone was holding onto it. Best we can do.

Burn minus 50 seconds.

As Jack glanced from one set of instruments to another, the stitches in his face and arms pulled painfully. Everyone seemed to have bought his story about dicking around with alien pointy objects. Why? Did they assume he was lying? Or that he was telling the truth? Which was worse, from the point of view of confirming the inarguable defects in his character?

Burn minus 30 seconds.

What *had* happened, anyway? Why had Keelraiser attacked him? The only explanation he could come up with was that he must've pushed Keelraiser too hard. Pushed it right over the edge into rriksti ultraviolence mode. Not that that really explained anything … But he was deeply reluctant to think about what, specifically, he might have said or done that triggered it.

Fortunately, he had the best possible excuse to put the whole wretched business out of his mind.

309 other people were counting on him to get them safely out of Europa orbit.

"Star sights valid," said Alexei, in the left seat.

"Gyroscopes spun and locked. Thrust is stable." Kate was gone, so Jack said her part for her. "Burn on my mark."

The two of them could fly the *SoD* alone, since they didn't have to mess with the comms at the same time. Earth was 67 minutes away by radio, round trip. Much too far to be any help. All the telemetry for this burn would have to come from the *SoD's* own sensors. However, Jack had decided to leave the channel to Mission Control open for the time being. He had repurposed some rriksti clingfilm (not quite as good as duct tape) to tape the TRANSMIT switch down in the 'on' position.

Why? Because fuck 'em, that's why. *If we die, I want them to at least notice.*

Burn minus 0:05. He poised his sore hands above the flight controls. "Five seconds, mark. Four. Three …"

Alexei smirked. "Jack, do you feel a need …"

"… a need for speed?" Jack finished the quotation. "I

sure do."

Burn minus zero.

He punched in the throttle command. Way away at the back of the ship, the MPD engine opened its throat and let out a silent roar. Water flashed into steam. Tremendous pulses of radio energy ionized the steam into plasma. Secondary electrical coils hammered the plasma out of the engine bells. The back of the ship did not fall off.

"Full throttle," Jack said with studied calm.

The *SoD* rose out of Europa's gravity well on the wings of Oliver Meeks's genius.

And Meeks had got his inspiration from an alien ship's drive.

What goes around comes around.

The *Cloudeater* clung to the truss like a butterfly perched on a metal twig, inert.

What's Keelraiser doing over there? Jack wondered, with a tiny fraction of his mind.

0.10 gees of thrust gravity.

0.12.

0.13.

The welds held.

*

Burn plus one hour 15 minutes. Jack undid his harness and rose into the air to stretch.

Technically, he should under no circumstances have left his seat while the ship was still burning. But he'd throttled back the drive to 25% after they escaped Europa's gravity well, and this was his only chance to take a break before he'd have to precess the axis of the ship to bend their trajectory towards Jupiter. Anyway, his brain had fused with the flight controls to such an extent that he'd know in his gut, he felt, if a single indicator moved in the wrong direction.

He pissed into a bottle. This particular bottle had a funnel and a suction pump attached. He and Giles had made it a couple of months ago when they were bored.

"You should patent that," Alexei said.

"That's how I'll make my millions," Jack deadpanned. The joke was that it didn't work all that well. Splashback happened. Whatever. The bridge couldn't get much dirtier than it already was.

"Future best-selling penis enlargement device. Use at own risk," Alexei said, yawning away the tension.

Crumbs, dead insects, used wipes, slagged electronic components, connectors, syringe wrappers ... thrust gravity had pulled a truly shocking amount of rubbish loose from the crannies where it accumulated. Since they were still burning, all of it stuck to the aft wall in a lumpy carpet. Weighing a couple of pounds, Jack fell slowly through the air and sank in up to the tops of his feet. He kicked rubbish into the air. Some of it actually was dead leaves.

"Anything from Mission Control?" he said.

"Nope."

"Fuck them, anyway." Jack bounded back up to the couches and stuffed the piss bottle into the nearest cup-holder.

"Oh, no," Alexei said quietly.

Jack looked at where he'd put it. In the cupholder for the center seat. Kate's seat. Her empty seat. "Hmm," he said. "Whoops." He moved it.

Alexei and Kate had been in a relationship. What kind

of relationship? Jack still wasn't sure. But he knew it had involved sex, and he had a feeling it had also involved love. He hadn't asked how Alexei was coping with her loss. Didn't want to hurt him by reviving memories of Kate's horrible death. The *Krijistal* had brutally beaten and then shot her, right here on the bridge of the *SoD*. She had died in Jack's arms. The only way to deal with *that* would be to murder every single *Krijistal* on the *Lightbringer*.

If wishes were booster rockets …

Alexei went aft to see how the passengers were holding up. Jack settled into the foot tethers at the left seat. He switched on the camera. "Well, hey there, Houston," he said. "Sorry. Forgetting my manners. Mission Control, this is the *SoD*, presently 550,000 kilometers from Jupiter."

He smiled. The expression looked truly frightening—a lopsided Frankenstein grin, pulled askew by the line of stitches running through his beard and up to his cheekbone. And that was just the dim reflection in the camera lens. Richard Burke, the big cheese at Mission Control in Houston, should fall off his chair when he got this. Jack hoped he did.

"We've been feeling a bit forgotten recently, Mission Control. I sent you our flight plan. All we got back was a one-sentence acknowledgement. I suppose it's understandable. Hannah's the star. We're the boring, depressing show with crappy ratings. But *really,* Mission Control? Is that how you treat a five hundred billion dollar investment? Is this thing even *on?*"

He reached forward and rapped his knuckles on the camera lens. He then glanced down at the antenna status display to make sure that he was, in fact, transmitting. Jupiter radiated a blizzard of electrical interference. The closer they got, the worse it got. In a little while, they'd lose comms with Earth altogether, but for now it looked good.

"I hardly even dare to ask how the *Victory* project is coming along. But I ask about it every time, so I may as well. Any chance of an update? It would be appreciated." Jack scratched a scab on his chest. It came off. *Ow.* He flicked it at the camera.

The *Victory* was their resupply ship. At least it would be if it ever got built. They'd been shown plans for a smaller, faster version of the *SoD*. The *Victory* would be unmanned, of course. It would catch up with the *SoD* somewhere around Mars and deliver the stuff on the Shit We Need list.

Except Jack had a feeling it was never going to happen, because both Houston and Star City had gone ominously quiet about the project.

Alexei came back. He tapped Jack on the shoulder, holding out a laptop.

"Right. While we're on the topic, here are the latest items on our wish list."

Alexei had scrolled down to row 1209 of the Shit We Need spreadsheet. Jack started reading from the cursor position.

"Welding rods. High-capacity rotary torque sensors, part number 1003XP. Pressure sensors, part number B234a, the ones that go up to 3000 psi. Ibuprofen. Mucipiricin. Gatorade."

Alexei was hovering over him for some reason. Jack frowned up at him and read on.

"Rheostats for the LEDs, part number ZY1. Number

600 screws. Gay porn videos ..."

Jack's eyes bulged. He looked up at Alexei. His friend's face was red with suppressed laughter.

Jack cleared his throat and returned his gaze to the camera. In the same authoritative voice as before, he continued to read: "Bukkake is OK, but no BDSM please. Beautiful butts a must." There were a lot more specifics on the screen but he couldn't go on. He improvised, "Additionally, *straight* porn. Sexy librarians, traffic cops, rock chicks, desperate housewives, we're not fussy. Thanks, Mission Control, I know you'll understand. It's a matter of life and death to us. *SoD* out."

Alexei sagged against the aft wall, weak with laughter.

Jack thumbed the intercom. "All right, guys. Who added porn to the Shit We Need list?"

Although he had been the victim of the joke, he was teetering on the edge of a laughing fit. Alexei's honking laughter was more infectious than the flu.

"It was me," Skyler admitted, from Engineering. "I just put it in as a joke ..."

"Skyler, you horndog! I always thought you might be gay."

"I'm not gay!" Skyler yelled.

Gallic guffaws on the intercom resolved into Giles's voice. "I found his entry and fixed it for him. Ho ho ho. Did you send it to Mission Control, Jack? I am very proud of you."

Still laughing, Jack vacated Alexei's seat and clambered back to his own. He used Kate's empty seat as a stepping-stone. "What's buk-whatsit? Is it Japanese?" *Japanese* made him think of perverted comics. Tentacle porn. *Alien* porn. "No actually, I'd rather not know." He dropped back into his seat, feeling great. He gulped cold tea from his squeeze bottle. It was really just tea-flavored water at this point. Tea was item #2 on the Shit We Need list. Would've been #1 if not for coffee. Remembering the tea-vs-coffee argument, he chuckled. "You got one thing wrong, Skyler."

"What?"

"You put porn at the end of the list. Should've put it at the top."

"Um, no. I *need* my coffee."

"Heads up." Alexei had just taken the star sights. "We're about to cross inside Io's orbit."

Jack sobered quickly. "OK everyone, strap in. This could get ticklish …"

*

Back in Engineering, Hriklif said to Skyler, "What is porn?"

Skyler made a sad face at the rriksti. Hriklif was an atomic engineer. It had come over to make sure Skyler didn't break anything. Yes, it knew about *fusion* reactors, not fission reactors like the *SoD's,* but that was still more than Skyler knew. He felt better having Hriklif here. But it did have a tendency to ask awkward questions.

They were standing on the aft wall, floating on their tiptoes, like you do in a swimming pool when you're almost out of your depth. Hriklif was sturdy for its kind, six and a half feet to Skyler's 5'8". The hexagonal array's yellow glare turned its dark blue bio-antennas green.

"Haven't you ever seen porn on TV?" Skyler tried to dodge the question.

"Yes, yes, I know, it is human beings having sex on

camera. Not good for language learning. We change channel."

"Hmm, I see your point."

"So what is it for?"

Skyler sighed. He always seemed to end up apologizing for the warped emanations of human culture that we put on TV. "Don't you guys have porn?"

"Of course we do. But only on weekends."

"Okayyyy." Skyler had no clue about rriksti sex and reproduction, despite having lived among them for months. Alexei had taken more of an interest in that side of things when they were on the surface.

He schooled himself not to glance at Hriklif's baggy shorts. He didn't even know what sex the atomic engineer (sometimes) was, much less what it kept down there. Then again, did it matter? Hriklif knew what all these frightening displays meant. *That* was what counted.

"So why do humans need porn?" Hriklif wasn't letting him off the hook.

"Well, people watch it to get their rocks off … when they haven't got anyone to have sex with." Skyler shrugged.

"I have not had sex since we left Imf."

"I haven't had sex since we left Earth. Booyah."

"But weren't there females on this ship when it left Earth?"

A fresh wave of loss rolled over Skyler. "Yup. Our first commander was a woman, so was our hydroponics specialist … and of course, our propulsion specialist."

Hriklif said, "Yes. Hannah."

Just the sound of her name felt like lemon juice on a cut. Skyler had spent all night looking at those videos. "You guys would have had a lot in common," he said, past a lump in his throat so big it felt like he'd swallowed a golf ball of pure grief.

"Did you want to have sex with her?" Hriklif said, gently.

"I loved her."

Skyler braced for Hriklif to ask some really awful question such as *What is love?* But the rriksti just parted its lips in that weird all-purpose expression of theirs, which could mean *Oh shit,* or *Gotcha,* or *Ha ha; you just made a funny.* It was maddening not to know which.

CHAPTER 8

Hannah's dinner consisted of mashed potatoes without milk or butter, a kale and sprouted lentil salad dressed with salt, and a hunk of sourdough bread with ten drops of olive oil. The *Krijistal* had stolen her sourdough starter from the *SoD,* as well as tons of hydroponic equipment, seed potatoes, and seeds. So she had her own little garden. Figgrit could cook vegetables to toothsome perfection; she baked the bread herself. The one thing the *Krijistal* had forgotten was dietary fat. They had brought *one* jug of olive oil, thinking it was something for the plants. So Hannah Ginsburg was looking positively svelte these days.

Of course, regular bouts of radiation sickness also helped in the weight-loss department.

Feeling more nauseated by the minute, she choked her food down. Eating was not just a nutrition thing, but also a power play. The *Krijistal's* plates held sad little piles of pressed suizh cubes, which were basically alien tofurkey, and boiled *mirip* leaves. They had had—were still having—serious trouble ramping up their hydroponics production. After ten years, there'd been little enough left to eat on the *Lightbringer,* and the crew had doubled since then, as Eskitul had brought thirty deserters back with her and *they* were still around, although she was not. They were toughing it out on half rations. So she got to gloat over them. Look at *my* delicious meal! Don't you wish you could chow down on these yummy Russet Burbanks? What a shame they'd make you sick ...

The rriksti required a diet heavy in metals, but many of the fat-soluble vitamins in terrestrial vegetables poisoned them. Instant vitamin toxicity—puking, diarrhea, dehydration—it wasn't pretty. Their big eyes sadly tracked her fork's progress from her plate to her mouth.

The tables turned, however, when Figgrit brought out the meat course. Sliced into strips, cooked medium rare, the roast filled the bridge with a tantalizing odor. Hannah's mouth watered. She folded her hands in her lap, knowing where that roast came from. Last week's dead soldier. Or maybe day before yesterday's.

The bridge of the *Lightbringer* had a domed ceiling. Variable polarization built into the structure of the dome, and the hull sections above it, made it optionally transparent. Now, with the bridge oriented away from the sun, stars filled the dome. There was no other light on the bridge apart from some dim candle-like lamps on the dining tables, and the LED displays in the drive chancel. The constellations shone as bright as the glow-in-the-dark stars Hannah had once given Isabel for the ceiling of her bedroom. She gazed up, trying to see if she could pick out Alpha Centauri, so as to wish Biblical plagues on its cool red cousin.

The smart hull also allowed X-rays through. She estimated she was taking about 0.5 Grays a day. That's one reason she got sick all the time.

The other reason ...

Figgrit's assistant approached her, having served Ripstiggr and the other higher-ranked *Krijistal*. It tonged up a small slice of meat and laid it on her plate.

You need protein, Hannah-banana.

You don't have a decent B12 source. Lentils won't cut it in the long term.

So she shredded the slice of human flesh—no, *rriksti* flesh, they are *not* human, but it still feels like cannibalism, dammit—into tiny pieces, and mixed them into her mashed potatoes. She swallowed the mixture without chewing.

Ripstiggr laughed at her with its hair, while it tore apart its own slab of metal-loaded, radioactive meat with its sharp teeth.

Hannah sighed loudly. "Y'know what goes with red meat?" She raised her cup of water. "This isn't it."

The rrikstis spoke in a frequency range of 800-2,600 KHz. Their bio-antennas converted signals from the language-processing regions of their brains into radio-frequency signals. Hannah, of course, vibrated the air with her vocal cords to produce sounds at a nice low 800 to 2100 Hz, which the rriksti could not hear. The Shiplord chip gave her a single, weak bio-antenna. It was meant to be used by someone with iron hair, and only carried over short distances without a boost, but it worked for casual dinner conversation.

"I've always liked to pair steak with pinot noir," she went on. "I'd settle for a good merlot, but not cabernet sauvignon. It's way too hit and miss."

That's what she said, but she'd have sold her soul for a $5 cab sauv from Walmart.

"Can't wait to try this *wine* stuff," said Joker, on her right. "You'll have to point us to the best vintages when we get there."

OK, she'd walked into that one.

When the meal was over, Ripstiggr rose. They had some customs that paralleled human ones, e.g. the boss gets the best seat, and dinner's not over until he says it is. Ripstiggr stalked down the table to her and demonstrated another human-analog custom: he took her hand and raised her to her feet. It was almost courtly. He then tucked her arm through his own, so that no one else would see her swaying and almost falling down as they walked.

"I feel like crap," Hannah muttered as they left the bridge.

"Lie down."

She didn't have to be told twice. She collapsed on the bed, hitting the wrist-button to doff her suit as she did so. She wore the suit as clothes most days, taking advantage of its radiation-shielding, but again, it didn't block stupid X-rays. It flowed away, leaving her naked. She shrugged the backpack straps off her shoulders, and sprawled facedown on the quilt. It smelt salty, and felt like a furry hug. It was made from the wool of an Imfi animal called a *zlok,* which looked like a dog-sized yak. She'd put a bit about it in one of her videos.

This was the Shiplord's cabin. The décor was schizophrenic: Eskitul's watercolors adorned the walls, and Ripstiggr's piles of electronic junk cluttered the floor. Hannah had not added any personal touches of her own. That would feel like admitting she lived here.

But she *did* live here, and she wanted to keep on living, so she lay still while Ripstiggr knelt over her and laid his hands on her sweaty, radiation-reddened skin.

A cool, refreshing sensation spread from the alien's seven-fingered hands, taking away the pain and nausea. She tasted garlic, and drifted away on the waves of relief. When Ripstiggr rolled her over to do her front, she flopped willingly on her back, eyes closed, imagining that she was lolling in gentle surf.

Hannah had a fairly comprehensive knowledge of the laws of physics, but she had no idea how the fuck this worked.

Ripstiggr, the seventh-level priest of Ystyggr, insisted it was faith healing. He used the word *extroversion,* extroversion apparently being a Very Good Thing in the cult of Ystyggr, akin to the standing of love in Christianity and Judaism.

Yeah, nope. Hannah wasn't about to accept that the rituals of an alien cult, centered on a god whom *even Ripstiggr* admitted was imaginary, could cure radiation sickness and cancer.

Maybe if she were a doctor or a biologist, instead of a rocket scientist, she'd be able to work it out in a jiffy. Certainly, she knew very little about biology. She just had to hope that all would become clear when she understood Rristigul better. For the time being, she reluctantly contented herself with:

It works.

Minutes, which felt like languorous hours, passed. Ripstiggr worked over her body methodically, restoring her to health from the inside out. As the process weaved towards completion, the cool sensation segued into a pleasant tingling in her extremities.

All over, actually.

The trouble with this faith healing business?

It made Hannah ridiculously horny.

She writhed on the bed, enjoying the sensual feeling of the fur sliding against her skin. Then she opened her eyes.

Ripstiggr stood over the bed. His arms were folded behind his back, so that his chest puffed out. The posture looked domineering, but she knew that it actually signified awkwardness.

Hannah smiled lazily up at him. "Come on," she said. "Don't be shy."

Ripstiggr knelt by the bed and parted her legs. His long fingers danced into her crotch.

He never touched her sexually unless she asked him to. He was a gentleman in his own way, wasn't he? Kind of.

Somewhere in the back of her head, she thought about a man she'd never see again. Skyler. Sweet, funny, handsome Skyler. But he was dead now, like all the others, so she stopped thinking about him, because *this* was *happening* and it felt ... so ... *good.*

She scooted away before she could climax. Sat upright. "Take that shit off."

"Your wish is my command, Shiplord."

"Oh, stop it."

Opening his mouth in a rriksti smile, Ripstiggr shed his loose shorts and smock. (The priestly robes had already vanished somewhere, which showed how casual he was about the whole 'faith healing is a gift of Ystyggr' shtick.) Naked, he looked even more human ... and *less.*

The rriksti had a loose pouch of skin between their legs. Both sexes looked superficially identical, unless they were in musth, when a male's pouch got, *ahem,* bulgier. But arousal changed things down there. Touching Hannah had turned Ripstiggr on. So his pouch had retracted into a wrinkled nest of hairless skin, from which protruded a penis the approximate shape and size of a HB pencil.

The jokes wrote themselves.

Hannah didn't crack wise out loud, because she guessed that rriksti males were probably as sensitive about the size of their equipment as human ones, and anyway, she'd seen what happened in musth—alien sex was no laughing matter *then.*

But even on the nine days out of eleven when they weren't male or female, in their own understanding, rriksti could get aroused. They could want. They could need, maybe even as badly as Hannah did.

So she pulled Ripstiggr down on the bed and gave him a blow job.

"Now me," she said, and flopped on her back again, so she could eke out the afterglow of the healing with multiple orgasms, courtesy of Ripstiggr's long fingers, and yes, his tongue.

"You're beautiful when you climax," he said when it was over.

"Spare me the flattery," Hannah said. The comment reminded her of something a guy she picked up at a bar might say. No, Hannah wasn't new to this business of screwing the wrong males. Back on Earth, she'd had a terrible habit of getting drunk and going home with strangers. An alien was new territory, even for her. But on the other hand, Ripstiggr was no longer a stranger ...

He got up and stalked to the safe in the corner. Eskitul had decorated it with a painting of a gloomy purple forest on Imf. Only Ripstiggr now knew the combination. He unlocked it. China clinked. Hannah's mouth watered.

He came back to the bed, bringing two cups full of *krak,* the booze they brewed in a still that was *also* locked up, unfortunately for Hannah. The small drink was his. The big one hers.

Hannah snatched the cup and inhaled the potent fumes. This was the miracle that kept her going: 200 proof ethyl alcohol brewed by aliens. It had exactly the same chemical composition as moonshine brewed by a naughty propulsion specialist in the turbine room of the *SoD*. No, it wasn't a quality merlot. But it didn't poison her, either. It did the job, for a high-functioning alcoholic.

Sipping, she relished the warmth burning into her stomach. It drove her anxiety away, although it couldn't completely erase her self-disgust at what she'd just done. "A great dinner, a great screw, and a drink. What more could a girl ask for?" she said, wryly.

"You forgot the faith healing experience," Ripstiggr said. He tickled her bare hip casually.

"So I did, and also, this definitely isn't 250 milliliters."

"Hell with milliliters. We use *wergs*," Ripstiggr said. "But actually, you're right. It is only eight wergs."

"Huh? How come?"

"You haven't earned the other two wergs yet."

CHAPTER 9

Burn plus 1 hour 27 minutes.

Io flashed past, a malevolent speck in the distance. Jack opened the throttle again, chucking the exhaust down the throat of the MPD engine as fast as possible.

Io posed unique dangers to spacecraft. A flux tube curved from this volcanically active moon to Jupiter's poles, carrying a monstrous electrical charge. The *SoD* fled beneath the flux tube, gaining speed all the time as it fell towards the gas giant.

"OK," Jack said to Alexei, unable to hide his elation. "We just broke our own record for closest approach to Jupiter."

"Closest human approach, but what about closest rriksti approach?" Alexei grinned like a skull. He had his e-cigarette clamped in his teeth. "The *Lightbringer* went lower than this."

"I wasn't forgetting about that." In fact, Jack had modelled this burn on the *Lightbringer's* escape burn. He was gambling that the *SoD* could stand up to anything the alien ship could take.

Lower and lower they plunged, into a storm of radiation. Highly energetic particles pelted the *SoD* and the *Cloudeater* like invisible machine-gun fire. This was too much for even rad-hardened circuits to bear. Fragile external sensors on both ships began to glitch out. From Engineering, Skyler and Hriklif warned that circuit-breakers were red-lining.

"Remember when you and Kate fought about whether to raise or lower our perijove?" Alexei said, no longer smiling.

"Yep," Jack said.

On their initial approach to Europa, Jack and Kate had argued about whether they should swing closer to Jupiter or stay at a 'safe' distance. Their fierce disagreement now seemed comically trivial, like disagreeing about whether to have one sandwich for lunch or two. This time around, Jack planned to skim the tops of Jupiter's clouds—an idea that would have made him flip out a few months ago.

That was before he knew just how tough the *SoD* was.

This time, he calculated they would hit perijove—their point of closest approach to Jupiter—a mere 10,000 kilometers above the top of the gas giant's atmosphere.

Closer and closer.

Faster and faster.

Jupiter filled the forward camera feed entirely, like a divine fingerpainting experiment. God: Let's see what I can do with just hydrogen and helium ...

Jack roused himself from his trance of concentration. He leaned over, framed the screen with his old Nikon, and clicked.

"What the hell are you doing?" yelped Alexei.

"What does it look like? Taking pictures."

*

42 minutes post-burn.

The comms console beeped. Alexei wearily downloaded and buffered the transmission.

"Wow," Jack said. "They called back."

Light takes just as long to get anywhere as radio signals. Right now, Mission Control's network of tracking and data relay satellites would be seeing the *SoD* skimming out of Jupiter's orbit. 33 minutes ago, when this signal originated, they would have just seen the *SoD* reappear around the gas giant's limb.

But in real time, the excitement was over. The thrust

gravity fairy had flown away. Rubbish spun sluggishly in the air as the fans scattered it back to the corners. Back in the main hab, the rriksti were settling in for the long haul.

Jack had been putting off going back there to see how chaotic it was. He floated in his straps, staring at the velocity calculation which he had just redone by hand for the second time, to make sure the computer wasn't messing with his head.

585 million kilometers away and 33 minutes ago, Mission Control said, *"Ty che,* guys?" What the hell? "You scared the shit out of everyone here."

"Hi, Pavel!" Jack and Alexei said, waving at the screen.

The *SoD* consortium had started out as a grand multinational effort. Now it was down to a bare-bones US-Russian alliance. *Alliance,* in this context, meant the same thing as *international cooperation* had in the old days: the exact opposite of what it said. Houston and Star City often did not seem to be on the same page.

Now, veteran mission controller Pavel Berezin slumped at his desk, elbows propped on his belly. A cigarette burnt in his fingers. People moved between messy desks in the background, stopping to wave at the camera, or make devil horns behind Pavel's head. Discipline at Star City mission control was not what it used to be.

"Come on, guys," Pavel said sorrowfully. "Don't *do* this crazy shit. It would be a hell of a thing for you to survive first contact, and then kill yourselves on the way home …"

"This ship survived three HERFs," Jack said, referring to the high energy radio frequency attacks the *SoD* had weathered on the way out. "I had a reasonable degree of confidence that we could survive a dash through Jupiter's radiation belt. But do continue to yell at us."

"At least we got their attention," Alexei said.

"D'you think maybe Houston didn't share our flight plan with them?"

"You sent it on the secure link, right?"

"Yeah, with the NXC's encryption." Jack hadn't wanted to tell the *Lightbringer* exactly what they would be doing and when. He assumed the *Lightbringer* was reading all their transmissions, encrypted or not. It had a freaking quantum computer, after all. But there was always a chance that it couldn't break the NXC's supposedly ultra-secure crypto.

Now that the burn was over, however, there was no harm explaining what they'd done.

In fact he wanted the *Lightbringer* to hear this.

Anything you can do, we can do better …

He put on the comms headset, muffling the voice of Pavel, who was now chatting about football. The *SoD,* of course, could transmit and receive simultaneously, on parallel frequencies.

"Privyet, kak pazhivayesh?" Jack gave his basic Russian an airing, before dropping back into English. "It sounds as if you may not have had prior notification of our flight plan. So I'll just quickly hit the highlights. The idea was a powered fly-by of Jupiter with the goal of achieving maximum acceleration. We performed a continuous burn at full throttle to escape from Europa's gravity well. Quarter throttle down to Io's orbit, then full throttle again. We stayed at full throttle whilst rounding perijove, and burned for a further hour and two minutes, for a total burn time of eight hours and twenty-one minutes. This

maneuver had a threefold purpose. One. Limit exposure to Jupiter's radiation belt. Two. Ensure that we would fly beneath the Io flux tube."

Nyah nyah nyah nyah. I didn't graze the Io flux tube.

"Three. This is sometimes called an Oberth maneuver. When you fall into a planet's gravity well, and then *accelerate,* you end up going quite fast. So after completing this maneuver at burn plus four hours and 13 minutes, we left Jupiter's orbit, travelling spinwards. Our present velocity is ..." He gulped. "Thirty kilometers per second." 108,000 kilometers per hour.

"Are you serious?" Alexei hissed.

"Yeah," Jack whispered back. "We haven't dropped as much speed as I thought we would."

They'd whipped past Jupiter at an astounding 61 kps. Climbing out of Jupiter's gravity well, they'd lost a lot of that speed. Still, they were travelling twice as fast as they had on the outward leg of their journey.

"Going forward," Jack continued, "we will coast for fourteen months."

The timescales involved in spaceflight could make you cry. Jack's only comfort was that the *Lightbringer* had to obey the laws of physics, too.

"At the end of that time, we will perform a powered fly-by of Mars."

Because that was what the *Lightbringer* would be doing, based on its current trajectory and speed. There was nothing else it *could* do and still reach Earth.

The *SoD* might have another option. But Jack was keeping that in his back pocket for now. He'd wait to see how Mission Control reacted to this first.

"Our estimated time of arrival at Earth is April 27th, 2023."

Making a total journey time five months shorter than the outbound leg, thanks to the very high coasting speed the *SoD* had achieved. But still too long. Too goddamn long.

The *Lightbringer* would still reach Earth first, by a margin of two or three months.

Jack started to feel a familiar sense of helplessness. No matter what he did, it wasn't going to be enough. He couldn't save Earth. They'd have to save themselves. The *SoD* still picked up terrestrial television broadcasts. Every talking head had become an expert on orbital defense platforms, space-to-space weapons, and next-generation kinetic kill vehicles. Jack was iffy on the concept of orbital defenses. Planets are sitting ducks, absent hardcore science-fictional kit that would be far beyond anything Earth could develop in the next fifteen months. The *Lightbringer* wouldn't even need to repair its muon cannons and railguns and all the rest of it. Little had the Darksiders guessed, 70 years ago, that humanity's space capabilities would advance so little during the 20th and 21st centuries, all they'd need to do was drop *rocks* on us …

Jack just had to pray the TV pundits knew more than he did. But he couldn't muster much optimism, especially when he thought about his parents. John and Helen Kildare lived on their own in southern England. They were in their seventies and completely defenceless.

Then again, Warwickshire would probably be as safe as anywhere else on Earth when the *Lightbringer* arrived …

He took his helplessness and frustration out on Pavel. "Look, scratch everything I said. The *SoD* may arrive at Earth in April 2023, but there won't be anyone left alive on board. We are running out of everything. We cannot survive for another twenty months without that resupply ship! *Where is it?*"

CHAPTER 10

Jack immediately regretted his outburst. It wasn't Pavel Berezin's fault their resupply ship had not been built, much less launched. The problem was money, beyond a doubt. Who do you blame for that? Everyone on Earth?

He floated out of the left seat so Alexei could take his place. Pavel, who of course hadn't heard Jack's rant yet, was now talking in Russian.

"What's he saying?"

"Russia has qualified for the 2022 World Cup," Alexei translated.

"England?"

"Lost to Brazil in the qualifiers."

"Balls."

"Also, the Cup is moving from Qatar to Belgium."

"A likely story!" Jack yawned. He'd been awake for twenty hours straight. "I'm going aft." He flew into the keel tube and sank feet first towards the blaze of light from the main hab.

He emerged into the axis tunnel that ran the length of the main hab. LED growlights and fans festooned the outside of the lattice. The axis tunnel was in zero-gee; everything else whirled around it. Jack hung weightless, watching his little world blur past, ten storeys below.

Growing crops on board a spaceship was a piece of cake, contrary to the scientists' pessimistic predictions. Plants loved the controlled environment. On their way to Europa, the crew had feasted on fresh fruit, potatoes, legumes, and leafy veggies, supplemented with fish.

Successive unplanned power-downs had taken their toll

on the hydroponics. The *Lightbringer* had also stolen a lot of seeds and nutrients, adding insult to injury. But during their long stay at Europa, Jack, Giles, and the *Krijistal* deserters had restored the garden to close to its former glory.

Then they'd harvested a final crop and cleaned out 90% of the trays and tanks, to make room for crops from Imf.

In their bunker on the surface of Europa, the rriksti had grown *suizh* (looks like pampas grass), *jgzeriyat* (Jurassic-looking fleshy ferns), and *yfrit* (think Little Shop of Horrors, shortly before things got interesting), as well as several kinds of edible fungi. They'd also raised *apé,* which looked like coelacanths. They had a composting system based on water tanks populated by genetically engineered bugs. The bugs ate poop and all kinds of rubbish, the fish ate the bugs, the people ate the fish, and round we go again. They'd transported as much of this stuff up to the *SoD* as the *Cloudeater* could carry.

As the hab spun at 3 RPMs, Jack gazed down at rows of tanks that blurred together into snaking, forking patterns. The rriksti must have been working straight through the burn to get things in order. Jack's fears of spills and chaos had been unfounded.

But what really wowed him was the radiant jewel tones of the Imfi vegetation. He'd never before seen it under proper lighting. The perpetual twilight in the bunker hadn't done the plants justice. Leaves, flowerheads, and fronds painted the floor of the hab with hues of aquamarine, peridot, amethyst, and opal …

Alexei shook his shoulder.

"What?!"

"You fell asleep."

"Jesus. Sorry about that." Jack uncurled, stiff muscles cramping. His mouth tasted like dirty socks. You had to be *really* tired to fall asleep in the air. "How long?" It was dark.

"Only a couple of hours. Come on downstairs."

Jack yawned hugely. It didn't seem to be as dark as it usually was during lights-out. They had the growlights set to go off for six hours out of every 24: a 'night' for the plants, rather than for the men, who staggered their sleep shifts. "Who's on the bridge?"

"Skyler."

They slid through the lattice onto Staircase 1. The tops of the staircases rotated slowly around the axis tunnel. It was like stepping onto an escalator. Ten storeys down. Jack trailed after Alexei, still half-asleep. "What was the story about the flight plan in the end?"

"Star City never saw it. There was some mix-up with the crypto."

"That's what I thought." Jack was done with Mission Control. They couldn't even coordinate their own internal communications. Zero chance they could pull off a resupply flight. The *SoD* was on its own.

As they neared the bottom of the twenty-storey staircase, Jack and Alexei grew heavier. A pleasant salty scent reminded Jack of the rriksti bunker. It already felt warmer down here than it used to. He breathed deeply, and rubbed his eyes. "Why does it look like the plants are glowing in the dark?"

"Because they are," Alexei said gleefully. "I wondered how long it would take you to notice!"

Amazed, Jack descended the rest of the steps, into a

fairy forest.

Even the tanks glowed.

Nene, one of the rriksti from the surface, came out of the Potter space under the staircase, carrying a pail full of fireflies.

Alexei gave Jack his headset. Jack put it on in time to hear Nene say: "—amazing! We have never seen this before, either!"

Electric blue water slopped from the pail as Nene gestured excitedly. Jack took the pail before it could spill. The rriksti had turned this Potter space into a rough and ready biotech lab for breeding their smart bugs. Krill-like shoals of bugs floated in the pail, illuminating the water inside.

"You've never seen this before, either?" Jack asked.

Nene's hair danced. "No! Sharzh has no UV in its spectrum."

Sharzh was what the rriksti called Proxima Centauri, their sun.

"It flares constantly in the X-ray portion of the spectrum, but only at very short wavelengths. Our bunker on Europa, of course, blocked out UV, but allowed X-rays in. So this is a real-life experiment! This is the very first time plants from Imf have ever been exposed to UV light."

"Chlorophyll ought to work the same everywhere …?" Jack said. In fact, the rrikstis' lives depended on the assumption that it did.

"Oh yes, yes. The plants absorb in the red end of the spectrum. UV, no UV, this is irrelevant. But even though a thing is irrelevant, it can be beautiful." Nene clasped its hands in front of its flat chest. Its eyes shone like huge black gems in its triangular face. "To me this is very beautiful. To you, too?"

"Yes," Alexei said. "To me, too."

"Maybe that's the definition of beauty," Jack said. "Superfluous loveliness."

Other rriksti wandered along the avenue. Their heads were above the level of the suizh-tops. Jack heard them twittering and chirruping in their own language on his headset. They were all equally awed by the glow-in-the-dark veggies. Rristigul usually struck him as an unlovely mashup of babbling brook sounds and German, but right now it sounded like birdsong. Well, human voices sounded nicer, too, when their owners were not upset or afraid ....

"It's fading," Nene said in disappointment, though no dimming was yet visible to human eyes.

"Bio-fluorescence," Alexei speculated. "That only lasts for a short time after dark."

"Like coral!" Jack said. He looked up. Twenty storeys overhead, the plants on the other side of the hab hung upside down, a night sky full of jewel-hued stars. The rriksti had chosen a layout of interlocking arabesques rather than a boring grid. Jack imagined he was gazing at constellations never seen by human eyes; perhaps the constellations you could see from Imf ...

"That is the jgzeriyat! Oh, I want to see it up close!" Nene said. "Quick, before it fades—"

They ran around the circumference of the hab. The luminous forest seemed to slope uphill, an illusion of spin gravity. Nene bounded ahead. Alexei chased it, laughing. Jack slowed down. He swung the pail of bugs, watching the glowing water bulge as the low gravity warred with surface tension.

Keelraiser *has* to see this.

On an impulse, he handed the pail off to a passing rriksti. He headed for the aft stairs, climbed back to the axis, and flew through SLS to the storage module. He was in a tearing hurry to make it up with Keelraiser before the bio-fluorescence faded and his chance was gone—although, rationally, he understood that this would be a show they saw every lights-out period, and they would get used to it.

The storage module teemed with rriksti working at the machine shop and the lab. They evidently weren't interested in glowing veggies. Philistines. Jack took his Z-2 down from the wall. Then he saw Brbb and its best mate, Difystra, floating in front of the airlock.

Barring his way.

"Excuse me?" Jack said, raising his eyebrows.

"You want to visit the *Cloudeater*," Brbb said.

"Yes, I do."

"Not a good idea."

"Sorry, Brbb; this is my ship."

"But the *Cloudeater* is not your ship."

Brbb could be a bit of a prick sometimes. That was why Jack had defaulted to prickishness himself. But now Brbb's posture suggested a preemptive cringe. Quite a feat when you were an eight-foot skeleton with a mane of blue snakes on your head. Brbb explained reluctantly, "Keelraiser is there."

"So are thirty-odd sick people," Jack said, pretending not to get it. "Everyone's been going back and forth. Why shouldn't I?"

Difystra opened its mouth, showing its sharp little rriksti

teeth. "You have to leave Keelraiser alone."

"Why?"

Brbb traced one of its middle fingers down its own left cheek, mirroring the line of stitches on Jack's cheek.

"Look, if you think he'll get the jump on me again ..." Jack's urge to reconcile with Keelraiser was withering as he spoke. But he still wanted to assert his right to visit the *Cloudeater*. "I can assure you I won't make the same mistake twice."

"No! That is not correct!" Brbb exclaimed, its hair thrashing. "Everyone must leave Keelraiser alone. We are shunning him."

*

"Skyler!" Giles said. "Have you seen the plants? They are biofluorescing!"

"Saw it," Skyler said distractedly.

Giles floated onto the bridge. Some of his rriksti friends trailed after him. Silver, gold, and bronze (Skyler hadn't got their names), the *Krijistal* deserters who'd been helping him in the garden. "What are you doing?" Giles said.

"Mmm," Skyler said. He was sitting in the left seat, as the center seat scared him. He had his laptop strapped across his knees. "Gimme a minute."

He heard Giles going into the curtained-off corner of the bridge they were using as a nap room. Lockers opened and shut. "Where are the cards?" Giles said.

"Somewhere, I guess."

"Want to play gin rummy?"

"Not right now." Skyler clicked *Run*.

Technically, he shouldn't even have had this laptop

anymore. Back in April, he and Alexei had discovered malware triggers on half the electronic devices on board. The GRU—Russia's dreaded military intelligence agency—had installed malware on the *SoD* during construction. What did the malware do? Don't know, don't want to know. Alexei had tried to delete the trigger, which had resulted in its automatically copying itself to every other device in wireless range. So they'd smashed them. With hammers.

Skyler's laptop was also infected. But a laptop was not something to lightly destroy when you were millions of miles from the nearest Best Buy. So he'd just moved the trigger to its own directory, to get it out of the way of accidental clicks.

Now he was *very* glad he'd hung onto the laptop.

Because it also contained the decryption program that the NXC had given him, lo these many moons ago, before he told Director Flaherty to get fucked.

A mix-up with the crypto.

Something about that explanation just bugged Skyler.

He was no longer a spy. The NXC had turned him into an asshole—or maybe he'd been an asshole to start with. Either way, he didn't want to be one anymore.

But it wasn't so easy to unlearn the habit of suspecting everyone and everything.

Why would Pavel Berezin waste fifteen minutes of comms time rambling about soccer, excuse me, football? Mission Control might be in a shambles, but they sure didn't have money to burn.

So Skyler had downloaded the transmission to his laptop, to see if there was anything else in there. And it looked like there was.

The decryption progress bar moved slowly across the screen.

Behind him, Giles found the playing cards. He and the *Krijistal* started a game of gin rummy. Skyler frowned. Why did they have to do this on the bridge? Cards always wandered off in zero-gee, no matter how clever you got with rubber bands.

Waiting for the decrypt to complete, he turned sideways in his seat and watched the game. The one with gold bio-antennas was Rockshanks. Their names were easier to remember when they translated them into English. Silver was Cruiggr or Creiggr, and bronze Skyler couldn't recall. Solkine? Solkane? The distinctive salty smell of rriksti body odor pervaded the bridge. By some biological accident, this smell appealed strongly to the human nose. Skyler liked it, because he was human, but it also made him feel uneasy. He had not slept well the whole time he was on the surface. And then there was whatever happened between Keelraiser and Jack. The worst of it was that Jack was obviously lying about it. Redecorating with pointy objects? How dumb do you think we are, Kildare?

To be sure, Giles's *Krijistal* buddies looked fairly unthreatening right now, tossing the playing cards around and kicking their big flappy feet in amusement. When Skyler first met the rriksti he had thought they looked like goblins. Now that he was used to them, the proportions of their faces and bodies pleased the eye, like Modiglianis, and their snaky bio-antennas conjured thoughts of dryads and naiads. But these classical allusions, it had to be remembered, meant nothing. They were *aliens*.

And they were way too good at cards.

A chime pulled him back to his laptop.

Decryption complete (1 of 2).

A .txt file.

To: SPIRIT OF DESTINY

From: Thomas Flaherty, Director, National Xenoaffairs Council

Skyler's guts churned at the sight of his former boss's name.

But the text clearly hadn't been written by Flaherty himself. Impersonal, it stated that the NXC assessed with high confidence that the squids had broken NASA's 4096-bit encryption *and* the NXC's own AES-256 encryption.

"Squids?" Skyler muttered. "Is that, like, a technical term?" He might not think the rriksti were the most charming creatures in the universe, but *squids,* come on. That was just derogatory. "Hey Giles. The NXC thinks the *Lightbringer's* been reading our mail."

"Quelle horreur," Giles said.

"So it says they've developed a new crypto solution. Details forthcoming. So *that's* where all the money went."

Skyler chuckled cynically, Giles laughed with him, the *Krijistal* who understood English opened their mouths wide in appreciation, and Jack burst onto the bridge. Wild-eyed, he shouted, "What are these cunts doing here? Get them off my bridge."

He dived towards the curtained-off corner.

But Giles moved first. He tackled Jack with his little regrown arms. "Skyler!" he screamed. "Don't let him—" A grunt cut off the rest of the sentence as Jack peeled Giles off, not very gently.

Skyler froze.

The three *Krijistal* did not.

They pushed off and arrowed past Jack, flipping to block his way. Jack struggled with them. Punches were exchanged, which resulted in all four of them caroming away from each other like billiard balls.

Giles had not wanted Jack to get into the nap room. Why not? What was in there?

Skyler forced himself to move. He dodged the melee and flew through the curtain. There was a sleeping-bag tied to the side wall. He started opening lockers, scared of what he'd find. Dirty clothes spilled out like pigeons. Did Jack and Giles *ever* do their laundry?

A gun floated out, wrapped in a grubby t-shirt.

Skyler flinched. He caught the gun reflexively. It was one of those blasters they'd used during the battle for the *SoD*. Looked like an AR-15, except bright red. The rriksti sure did love bright colors. They'd never got the memo that tools of slaughter are supposed to be gray or black.

Skyler stuffed the blaster back into the locker it had come out of, and found two more alien guns wedged into the back. These were the even nastier Super Soaker type. He had one in each hand when Jack ripped the curtain down. "Gimme those," Jack said.

Giles, behind Jack, shouted, "No. Don't!"

The rest of the Krijistal arrived on the bridge. Brbb's blue bio-antennas whipped furiously. Skyler did not have his headset on but he could see it was shouting at Jack, who spun in the air and shoved it hard in the sternum. Newtonian physics sent Jack backwards. He collided with Skyler. He had a bruise rising on his cheek, Skyler saw for the first time.

"Gimme the goddamn guns."

"No," Skyler said, holding the Super Soakers out of Jack's reach. He hated guns. He used to have one of his own but he'd left it on Europa, accidentally on purpose, after he almost murdered Alexei with it. He couldn't believe this was happening. "Why do you need them? Who're you going to shoot?"

"No one! I've just got to show them who's boss."

Brbb's voice boomed from the intercom. The rriksti could hijack the PA when they really needed the humans to hear them. "You were breaking the rules!" it said.

"Huh?" Skyler said.

"I don't know what fucking rules it's talking about," Jack said. "I wanted to visit the *Cloudeater*. Why not? Perfectly innocent. Why shouldn't I? This lot tried to stop me from reaching the airlock."

Giles pushed past Jack, getting between him and Skyler. With his regrown hands and feet, he looked like a grotesque dwarf. But he stared Jack down. "I *thought* you would end up going for the guns. I wasn't wrong, eh? I wish I had been."

Jack flushed red at the contempt in Giles's voice. "I wasn't actually going to shoot anyone."

Skyler wished he believed that. He suspected that Jack himself believed it, which still didn't necessarily make it true. He stuffed the Super Soakers back into Jack's locker.

"I just can't have them behaving like this," Jack muttered.

"Who started it?"

"They did, obviously!"

Difystra took the intercom. "No. The commander started it. He was breaking the rules."

"My ship, my rules," Jack snapped. But Skyler could see that being called *commander* placated him. He drifted up to

Difystra, who flinched. Jack wiped a thumb across the *Krijistal's* lips. "Sorry about that."

Skyler couldn't see what he meant, until Difystra opened its mouth to reveal a gap where one of its needle-sharp front teeth should have been. "Do not worry. It will grow back."

"Your teeth grow back? That's convenient," Skyler said. Like sharks, he thought.

"Hurt me more than it did you," Jack grumbled, cradling his right hand. His knuckles were gashed and bloody.

Giles said with forced lightness, "You've got to stop colliding with pointy objects, Jack; we are too short on medical supplies!"

Jack snarled at him, which Skyler thought unfair. Giles had had the foresight to see this coming and head it off. A casual game of cards on the bridge? *Now* it made sense.

Skyler's laptop chimed. He lunged for it with Pavlovian alacrity.

"Something up?" Jack said.

"Just a second …"

"It's something from the NXC," Giles said.

Jack made shooing gestures at the *Krijistal*. "Out." They filed off the bridge. Jack and Giles gathered behind Skyler's seat.

Decryption complete (2 of 2).

"I found encrypted files in that video of Pavel talking about soccer," Skyler said. "It's called steganography. Hiding files inside other files."

The second file was an .exe file. Skyler installed it and clicked around. "It's a new decrypt tool. OK. They said they've developed a new crypto solution, called AES-512. This must be to decrypt messages encoded with that."

"Don't you need a key, too?" Jack said.

"That was in the first file."

"So now we've got the software, but nothing to decrypt with it," Jack summed up. "Well, maybe they'll send something soon. Now if you're OK here, I'd better go catch up with Brbb."

"And do what?"

"And apologize, of course." Jack sighed. "We've got to get along, no matter what. We're all in this together."

CHAPTER 11

Gurlp set the stage. In civilian life, Gurlp had worked in the movies. Well, not really movies. Portals, or 'ports.' As far as Hannah could discover, 'ports' were radio plays with immersive virtual sets, fed directly into your brain via stick-on chips. They didn't work with her brain, but the rriksti were crazy about them. Not surprising, in Hannah's opinion.. Life on Imf must have been a crapfest even before war broke out. No wonder they craved escapist entertainment.

It was hard to believe the bad-tempered Gurlp had ever been a civilian, much less a set designer. But she knew her stuff. She slapped some of Eskitul's watercolors onto the walls of the primary life-support chancel, dragged in a priceless 500-year-old couch, tossed some bits of electronic junk on the coffee table in front of it, and left. The effect was exquisite. It looked as if Hannah and Ripstiggr had just happened to sit down for coffee in a room lined with mouthwatering high-tech machinery.

The viewers would never know it wasn't coffee in their mugs. Hannah had *krak,* those last two wergs of her daily ration. Ripstiggr had water, as there was nothing else.

"Greetings, Earthlings!" Ripstiggr said to the camera. He had made this catchphrase into his trademark. Freaking Marvin the Martian. Hannah remembered watching that cartoon when she was a kid.

Now the children—and adults—of Earth were hooked on the Hannah Ginsburg Show. This broadcast would be sent Earthwards as an analog signal multiplexed into a carrier wave, targeted at the northern hemisphere, set to repeat every hour on the hour for 24 hours, so that everyone on Earth with a satellite dish could pick it up, not that they'd need to, as the *Lightbringer's* transmissions always went viral on the internet, according to Ripstiggr.

Hannah had told them that frequency-hopping digital broadcasts were no good. She'd also told them how to encode the audio sideband in the human-audible range. Did it matter that they'd threatened to hurt her if she didn't cooperate? Did it matter that they would've figured it out on their own in the end? It was still her fault. Her show.

Anyway, the *krak* tasted fine, and she listened with keen interest to Ripstiggr's commentary on the biggest news stories from the week of August 20th-27th, 2021. This was the closest she ever got to finding out what was happening on Earth. Yet another "ancient kingdom" had been resurrected in what used to be China's Hunan province. After the collapse of the Communist regime last year, the once-mighty PRC had shattered like a mirror, each fragment reflecting the true China, so it claimed. Ripstiggr offered some pseudo-deep thoughts on how the ancient history of the Middle Kingdom might be repeating. On the other side of the world, Texas threatened to become the next state to secede from the US. Hannah speculated miserably about what was happening to her country. It seemed to be fracturing like China. Ripstiggr, of course, urged a peaceful resolution to the crisis.

Hannah was drunk. She snuggled against Ripstiggr's side and said, "C'mon. They want to hear about Imf."

Ripstiggr patted her shoulder. This was all calculated to show that a human need not fear a rriksti's touch. Hannah wondered what would shock the audience more, if they knew the truth: that she actually loathed and feared Ripstiggr … or that these long fingers had been inside her vagina half an hour ago?

"Hannah and I were chatting about Imfi funeral customs today," Ripstiggr said to the camera. His hair stirred like snakes, but he was the snake-charmer, playing his flute. "We thought we'd show you this video to give you a taste of our culture. Raw video footage from Imf is quite rare, as we use more advanced data storage formats these days." He meant the format used for 'ports.' Everything got encrypted into data-rich signals that mimicked rriksti brainwaves—the same as the I/O protocol of the Shiplord chip, actually. "This comes from the region known as the Lightside, which is comparatively less developed."

The video played on a large screen set up behind the couch. Hannah turned sideways to watch it.

EXT—a desert on the Lightside of Imf—day

Redundancy alert! It's *always* day on the Lightside. Imf is tidally locked to Proxima Centauri. So you have the Darkside, where it's always night, the Lightside, where it's always day, and the twilight zone, a region of howling winds and drenching rains, which the rriksti talk about as if it were freaking California. Everyone wants to move there. I guess it must be nice in contrast to this.

Henna-red rocks stretch to the horizon, cracked like clay in a kiln. You can practically feel the heat rising off the screen. It gets up to 100° Celsius in the middle of the Lightside, directly below the glare of Prox b. Even here, at the edge of the Lightside, the temps are Sahara-hot. But people live in the Sahara, and they live here.

In the middle distance, a town spikes up from the desert like a high-tech hedgehog made of mirrors. Those spiky roofs are actually solar cells, permanently angled towards the sun's red light. A water pipeline connects the town to a spaceport on the horizon. Technology has made life on the Lightside much more comfortable.

A motorcade crawls towards us. Each 'car' has three large, fat wheels that squish and inflate as they pass over the jagged rocks. Their hexagonal solar-panel roofs double as parasols. The hexagon is to rriksti as the square is to us: fingers -1, a good shape to build with. As the motorcade approaches, we see just how fast it's going. *Whiz!* A spearhead-shaped chassis races over our viewpoint, smearing the camera lens with red dust.

EXT—a graveyard on the Lightside of Imf—day

The motorcade arrives at a flat plain covered with stone tables. A silvery geodesic dome sports a sign subtitled 'Café (Vomitoriums for Customers Only).' This subtitle may be Ripstiggr's little joke.

Rriksti disembark from the cars, clad in reflective white burnouses. One is hoodless, its face seamed and reddened from professional exposure to the elements. It is a priest. Its robes are much fancier than Ripstiggr's. It supervises the unloading, from the last car, of a coffin.

The mourners carry the coffin to a vacant stone table. They open the lid. We zoom in on the pale, dead face of an elderly rriksti. You can tell it's old because of the frosted-glass translucency of its skin. Rriksti don't get wrinkles. They get thin-skinned.

CUT to the mourners. As the priest orates, they tear off their hoods in grief. Their hair thrashes, and flakes of skin waft from their faces, to be blown away in snow-like eddies on the wind. "They are weeping," Ripstiggr explains, in voice-over. "We do not cry with our eyes. We cry with our whole bodies."

"In other words," said Hannah, "you *shed*."

While the video played, Gurlp wasn't recording, so she could say what she really thought.

So could Ripstiggr. "Lightsiders are so emotional," he commented with distaste, as the mourners fell into each other's arms, shedding like crazy. Their body language clearly expressed devastation. Hannah did not find their grief excessive. It reminded her of her parents' funeral. The Ginsburgs had died too young, in a car crash, leaving her and Bethany to be raised by their grandmother. And if this scene touched her emotions, she had to assume it would also touch other human beings. They would feel kinship with the rriksti. A cross-species emotional bond.

"Just to be clear," Hannah said, "these Lightsiders are the ones you guys nuked to oblivion."

"That's exaggerating," Ripstiggr said. "Lightsiders always exaggerate."

"To be precise, you smashed them in a brutal war that dragged on for centuries, and escalated to tactical nuclear exchanges, and was ultimately ended by orbital bombardment of the largest Lightsider cities."

"Yeah."

"So that town we saw probably isn't even *there* anymore."

"It's there," Ripstiggr said. "It's just ruined. On the other hand, who knows what's going on nowadays? It's been seventy-six years since we set out, and ten years since we had any news from home."

Hannah knew better than to respond to this. The *Lightbringer's* inability to establish contact with Imf worried Ripstiggr, maybe more than anything else he had to deal with at the moment.

On the screen, the mourners trailed away towards the café, leaving the coffin open. Close-up, once again, of the deceased's face. Subtitles explained that the heat and the dry wind would mummify the corpse, a process explicitly likened to ancient Egyptian burial practices. Small white flags streamed around the perimeter of the graveyard, and small birds gathered out of nowhere to peck the mourners' tears out of the air.

Hannah said, "Are you going to show the part where they come back 77 days later, slice bits off the corpse, and ceremonially eat them?"

Ripstiggr's hair twitched. "Don't be stupid," he said.

Hannah sensed that Ripstiggr was getting tired of her snark. She withdrew into herself, eking out the last few swallows of her drink, rebuilding the flimsy wall between herself and reality.

After the video, Ripstiggr wrapped the broadcast up with some general comments about how the meeting of cultures was always fruitful and beneficial for everyone involved. He then gave an updated estimate of the *Lightbringer's* ETA: "We'll arrive in Earth orbit on the twenty-second of February, 2023. The whole crew is looking forward to this so much. But maybe Hannah is the most impatient of all! After all, for her, Earth is home."

Cued, Hannah smiled at the camera. "That's right. I absolutely cannot wait. If you're watching, Rich, hi! And also my sister, Bethany ... Hi, Bee-Bee!" She waved at the camera, and leaned forward. "The kids must be so big now. Hi, Isabel ... hi, Nathan."

Could they see the desperation in her eyes? Did they guess that far from being a happy passenger on the *Lightbringer,* she had an alien computer in her brain and a metaphorical gun to her head?

"Oh, and I don't want to forget David. Dave, you better start laying in microbrews, because maybe what I'm looking forward to most of all is a nice cold beer!"

"Perfect," Ripstiggr said, sliding his hand down her arm in a distracted caress. She was wearing one of the camera-ready outfits they'd printed off for her: blue jeans and a long-sleeved blouse.

She stood up and went to change. These clothes did not offer any radiation protection at all.

CHAPTER 12

Tom Flaherty, director of the National Xenoaffairs Council, and in the estimation of some (not all of them his enemies) the most powerful man in America, paced the deck of a car ferry churning through the Gulf of Mexico, off the Louisiana coast.

The August sun baked the crust of salt on the deck. Hot wind whipped away the smell of aviation fuel.

Squinting through the glare, Flaherty tried to count the small boats chasing the ferry. They'd scattered when his helicopter arrived. It was almost like they thought a Coast Guard chopper might open fire on them. Flaherty grinned humorlessly. In the not-so-distant past, he had had to order some of the paramilitary units under his command (the SWAT teams formerly attached to a bunch of superfluous federal agencies now folded into the NXC; a beefed-up SAD and SOG, the special ops units attached to the CIA, ditto) to shoot at civilians. But the Coast Guard? Not yet. He prayed not ever.

That said, the Coast Guard was all he had out here today, versus a motley flotilla of shrimpers, yachts, and Jesus God what is *that* thing?

Flaherty stopped at the rail next to a Coast Guard officer. "What is that thing?"

"Too damn hot for Kevlar," the man said. Flaherty uh-huh'ed. His own loose navy t-shirt concealed a bulletproof vest. Wore the thing every damn day, never got used to it—nor the Sig Sauer in his hip holster, either. He had started out as a field agent in the CIA, his weapons a keen intellect and a folksy aura that fooled the people who mattered. Pre-MOAD (that's how Flaherty still thought of the *Lightbringer:* the MOAD, the Mother Of All Discoveries), you could get ahead with brainpower. Didn't need firepower. He missed those days.

The Coast Guard officer went on, "That boat looks like a destroyer got shrunk in the wash?"

"Yeah."

"Superyacht. Belongs to some tech guy."

That was the trouble with the Earth Party. Too many tech guys.

"I'm told it's got its own missile defense system."

"Hope it ain't got its own *missiles.*"

Flaherty walked forward, stumbling as the ferry met the ocean swell. The Coast Guard men positioned here and there along the rail twitched when he passed them, like iron filings at the approach of a magnet.

Flaherty's chopper stood on the foredeck, which was marked out as a helicopter pad. Kuldeep Srivastava, Flaherty's personal assistant, sat in the side door with headphones on. Kuldeep had worked for the NXC before it was the NXC. Flaherty had hired him back last year because he needed someone who wouldn't bullshit him or cringe in his presence. He veered over to the chopper.

"You should go inside. Don't tell me you can hear a damn thing out here." The ferry's engine was noisy, the sea was noisier, and someone on one of the pursuing boats had a bullhorn. They were yelling their usual pacifistic war-cries.

"It's OK," Kuldeep said. "I've already watched it three times, anyway. Now I'm just listening for ..." He rocked one thin, dark hand from side to side. "Nuance."

"And also, you're scared we might have to take off suddenly."

"And also that."

Beyond the prow, twin towers poked from the dazzling horizon.

*

By the time the car ferry reached the New Hope launch facility, the fastest of the pursuing boats had caught up. The tech guy's superyacht tore defiantly across the ferry's bow. Garishly dressed people lined its top deck. They threw paper airplanes at the ferry.

Now named the *Gulf Commander,* formerly the *Caribbean Fantasia,* this ferry used to run passengers and cargo between Puerto Rico and the Dominican Republic. Refurbished from stem to stern, it served as a floating R&D facility and dormitory for refugees from Kennedy Space Center. Its roll-on, roll-off car deck had become a transport barge for rocket parts and tanks of fuel.

Leaving the crew to unload, Flaherty strode up the gangway with Kuldeep in tow. They were going to see Richard Burke.

Flaherty had promoted Burke, the director of the *SoD* project, to director of NASA. Burke had chosen the name of New Hope for this launch facility. Flaherty thought *Last* Hope would have been more appropriate, but he kept that to himself. He valued Burke, after all, for his dogged optimism.

The Vehicle Assembly Building was the larger of the twin towers that represented America's new hope / last hope. The other tower, actually a scaffold, supported a Falcon Heavy rocket in two Strongback cradles.

"Stick around and you can watch the launch," Burke said, gesturing out his window in the VAB.

"That's what I came for," Flaherty said, although it wasn't. He'd come to see for himself just how bad the security situation was. The VAB's elevation above the sea gave him a good view. A smudge in the distance was the Louisiana coast. The Earth Party flotilla stood off at a distance of half a mile. A single Coast Guard cutter threw up spray.

"If this one goes down …" Burke said. "Every launch is crucial, but this launch is more crucial than others."

"I hear you."

Flaherty took a turn around Burke's spartan office. He stopped in front of a picture on the wall facing Burke's desk, where the NASA director would see it every time he lifted his eyes from his work. A publicity shot of the *Spirit of Destiny's* crew, taken the last time all eight of them were together on Earth before entering pre-launch quarantine. The rainbow of different-colored jumpsuits proclaimed the mission's international character. The crew's smiling faces made Flaherty's eyes humid, and he wasn't a sentimental man. How did Burke stand to look at that every time he glanced up from his computer screen?

Kuldeep sat on the corner of Burke's desk, talking about the latest transmission from the *Lightbringer*. Sounded like Burke had already watched the new video himself. His interest was understandable. Apart from the intrinsic whoa-shit factor of the videos, Hannah had been a favorite of Burke's. A protégée even, going back to their days working on the Juno probe.

But obsessing over the Hannah Ginsburg Show was

Kuldeep's job. It was not Burke's.

Flaherty needed Burke focused on his own job.

Saving humanity.

He took the crew picture down from the wall, slid the photo out of the dusty frame, and laid it flat on Burke's desk. The other two men fell silent, gazing down at the photo as if they'd never seen it before. Plucking a Sharpie from Burke's kid-made pottery penholder, Flaherty drew fat black Xs over the faces of Katharine Menelaou, Qiu Meili, and Xiang Peixun.

"They're gone."

He hesitated, then X'd out the face of Hannah Ginsburg. Burke started to speak but stopped, shaking his head.

"She is gone."

Flaherty circled the faces of Jack Kildare, Alexei Ivanov, Giles Boisselot, and Skyler Taft.

"These are the guys who're gonna save the world."

Gotta think positive.

"You hit the jackpot with them, Burke. Would be nice if we could say the selection process worked like it was supposed to, but in all honesty, there was an element of chance in all four of these selections, right? Doesn't matter. We got four guys who went through hell and came out stronger. It's a credit to your judgement, and to the enduring power of the human spirit."

Burke said, "We always strive to select people who score well on the Antonovsky scale—" a measure of the ability to stay mentally healthy under stress— "but what these guys are going through is off the charts. So why don't we tell them the truth?"

Jesus H. Christ.

"Can't risk it, Burke. If the squids find out, we're cooked."

"So AES-512 *isn't* secure, after all?" Burke's tone was gentle but probing.

Flaherty looked to Kuldeep to get him out of this. Kuldeep embarked on a numbingly boring explanation of how the new AES-512 crypto worked, and how it was *probably* secure, even against a quantum computer, but no one could be sure, because there weren't any quantum computers on Earth to test it against, but the eggheads at the NSA said that it *should* hold up, for at least the next couple of years ... and all they had was twenty months, anyway.

The truth was, Flaherty would rather not have given the *SoD's* crew AES-512 at all. He'd ginned up worries about their existing crypto on purpose to put a chill on communications. Burke had convinced him that they had to have a secure channel to exchange technical data. Fine. Flaherty got that. He just didn't want anything else being exchanged.

It was hard enough keeping the media in the dark. Helped that New Hope was way out here in the Gulf, but all it would take was one person on one of those boats with a good phone camera, who knew what they were looking at. The guys on the *SoD* could surf the internet, too, after all. That's how they'd found out about the Hannah Ginsburg Show.

Well, hopefully they had less time to waste online these days, with a spaceship full of squids ... Three *hundred* of the fuckers. Jesus.

Burke steepled his fingers in front of his moustache. It

was still brown, but the hair on his head had gone completely gray. "The squids are going to see what we're doing," he pointed out, "regardless of what we tell the boys on the *SoD.*"

Flaherty said, "There's a big difference between what the squids can deduce observationally, and what they would know if we spill top-secret information over the radio."

"So you're saying AES-512 is *not* secure."

Flaherty would have torn his hair, if he had enough of it left. "We're up against technologically superior aliens here. We do not know what they can or can't do, but that doesn't excuse us from handling classified information in a responsible manner."

Burke nodded grudgingly. He would do as he was told, Flaherty thought. Institutional obedience went deep in the man. But it was plain to see he was uncomfortable with the deception they were weaving. He had an emotional attachment to NASA's old ethos of transparency and openness.

Too bad. The world had changed. The *Lightbringer* had changed it, without even crossing the asteroid belt yet.

"How's the family?" Flaherty said.

"They're settling in in Houston." Burke grinned, evidently grateful for the change of subject. "You know, I've been trying to convince Candy to move to Texas for years, starting in 2012, when I was first assigned to the *SoD* project. It was always no. The kids' schools. Our church. The dogs … When they stopped picking up the garbage in Santa Monica, she changed her mind inside a week."

California had seceded in May, making good on years of threats. Uncollected garbage, wildfires raging unfought, and the Earth Party's plan for a statewide universal basic income had dominated media coverage, but from NASA's point of view what hurt the most was the loss of the Jet Propulsion Laboratory in Pasadena. Nearly all the JPL staff had joined their colleagues in Houston, but there was no replacing those R&D facilities.

"I was like oh, shit," Kuldeep said. "There are JPL refugees sleeping in their cars in the JSC parking lot. At least you guys have a house in Houston, right?"

"Yup," Burke said, making no big thing of the irony that he wasn't there. He was stuck in the Gulf of Mexico.

Because Florida had followed California, declaring independence in June. And maybe Flaherty should've told the president to declare martial law, maybe they should've opened fire on the pacifists rampaging through downtown Miami—but he'd blinked. He had fucking blinked, because a voice in his heart cried that American soldiers don't shoot at American citizens. And there went the Kennedy Space Center and Cape Canaveral.

It could not have happened at a worse time.

Even the Russians were too horrified to gloat.

Flaherty had found himself on the receiving end of furious phone calls from Moscow and Tokyo, the USA's only remaining partners in the space business. President-Emeritus Putin had threatened to cut NASA out of the *Victory* project altogether, but that was just bluff. Even the two new launch pads at Baikonur could not make up for the loss of Cape Canaveral.

Hence New Hope, a launch facility built of string and sealing wax on three fixed-leg oil rigs.

Welcome to the USA, Flaherty thought. We're running low on states, but we got plenty of second-hand drilling platforms.

Faint shouts came in through the open window along with the sea breeze. Three platforms made up New Hope: the VAB platform, an intermediate platform, and the launch platform. Hard-hats clambered over the scaffold on the launch platform, connecting the Falcon Heavy's leads and hoses to generators and supply tanks.

Of course, the sea-launch idea had been kicking around for thirty years. But New Hope avoided the fatal flaw of the original Sea Launch platform, which was the need to transport rockets horizontally and then jack them up to the vertical, requiring extra structural reinforcement that constrained their capabilities. Here, rockets were stacked in the VAB and crawled across to the launch platform in their upright position. The crawler sat on the intermediate platform, looking like something out of Star Wars. Sea water corroded everything.

A faint hissing noise came in through the window.

"They're purging the fuel and LOX tanks," Burke said. "In about an hour we'll start the automated countdown sequence. If you want to go out and take a look, now's your chance."

"I'll take you up on that," Flaherty said.

"I'm gonna stay here and distract the launch director from his job," Kuldeep said.

"Nothing for the launch director to do right now," Burke said. "It's all computerized."

CHAPTER 13

"So," Kuldeep said, as the door closed behind his boss. "Beer."

Richard Burke said wearily, "No alcohol at the facility, although I did hear a rumor that the *Gulf Commander* may have brought a case of Coors."

"Sounds good," Kuldeep said. "Maybe later. But I was talking about the new video."

Kuldeep Srivastava had started his career at the CIA almost twenty years ago. Got fired five minutes before the Miscellaneous Reports Desk turned into the NXC. Kuldeep had not looked back. His combination of SIGINT (signals intelligence) and HUMINT (human intelligence) skills turned out to be in high demand in the computer games industry. He'd bounced around from startup to startup, making truckloads of money for other people, getting more and more cynical about humanity … but the cynicism had flaked off like dirt in the shower when the *Lightbringer* started its voyage towards Earth. Kuldeep took for granted that the alien ship was coming to destroy humanity. The only thing that puzzled him was that people were actually debating this.

So when he got a call from Director Flaherty, he'd jumped at the chance to return to the NXC. Now he worked among people who *got it*. The view that the *Lightbringer* represented an existential threat to Earth—a minority view, for which more than one former friend had labelled Kuldeep an extremist nutjob—was not a 'view' at the NXC; it was a fact. It felt great to work among people who grasped the danger and were trying to do something about it.

However, they were failing hard at countering the Earth Party's narrative that the squids were lovable interstellar visitors.

Kuldeep was working on that.

Find cracks in the narrative and exploit them to induce cognitive dissonance. Same thing he used to do as a game designer, in reverse. Instead of building a seamless player experience, he was looking to screw with the player experience created by the Earth Party social media bubble.

Naturally, he focused on the Hannah Ginsburg Show.

"Beer," he repeated. "Hannah referred to beer at the end of the video. Remember?"

"Yeah."

"I believe that's a coded signal for something else."

Burke frowned. "What's your theory?"

This was a bit touchy, as Burke was Hannah's former boss. "Well, here's the thing. Hannah is an alcoholic."

"What the heck? She is not."

"A high-functioning alcoholic. Sorry, but we've established it with a high degree of conviction through background interviews."

Burke shook his head. "She used to refuse drinks at office parties."

Because she needed to fool you, Kuldeep thought. He said, "Well, all I can tell you is what her sister, Bethany Ziegler, told us. She said that Hannah promised her she would get help. This was after an incident at their house where Hannah drank too much and endangered their younger child. So Hannah's alcoholism has been a major issue in her family."

"I don't believe it," Burke said.

"And now Hannah is asking her brother-in-law to lay in supplies of booze? It doesn't fit."

"You think it's code for something else? 'Lay in supplies of ammo'?"

"It's just wrong."

"So what's she telling us?"

"That something's wrong," Kuldeep said. "The whole situation is fucked. We know this. But this still strikes me as important. Hannah's trying to warn us that all is not as it seems."

Burke looked down at the crew photograph that still lay on his desk. He touched the X over Hannah's face. "I've never believed Hannah could be a traitor."

Kuldeep winced. The word sounded strangely old-fashioned. "We call it self-alienation. It's the same thing happening with those knuckleheads out there." He gestured at the window. "Smart people are not immune. In fact they're often more vulnerable."

"I don't believe it," Burke repeated.

Key word, *believe*. Burke didn't *believe* Hannah was alienated. He didn't *believe* she was an alcoholic. That and $1.50 would buy you a Coke. They had to operate in the world of facts. And it was a fact that Hannah Ginsburg's funny, informative video blogs were converting millions of people to the *belief* (there was that word again!) that the squids were friendly.

"Have you made any progress finding her family?" Burke asked.

"Unfortunately, no," Kuldeep said with real regret. Hannah's family had dropped off the map. After California declared independence, the NSA's ability to monitor the population of the Golden State had taken a hit. People were cutting up their credit cards, throwing away their smartphones. "We're still trying."

If they could find Hannah's family, that might give the NXC a leg up in the battle of the narratives. Bethany Ziegler had seemed all too eager to smear her sister, the Earth Party heroine—

A gunshot cracked outside.

Kuldeep dropped to the floor and crawled under Burke's desk. His face wound up inches from the knees of Burke's wrinkled slacks. The man hadn't moved.

"They're going to stop this launch if they can," Burke said. "And if they do? The boys on the *SoD* will die."

*

Outside the VAB, the sun slammed down on Flaherty's head and shoulders like a griddle wielded by some mad grandma. He walked away from the insulated aluminum silo. Coast Guard officers fell into step. Flaherty did not avail himself of a Secret Service protection detail, although he could've. The day he let the Secret Service control his movements would be the day he lost touch with local law enforcement, and that would be fatal. If he was Caesar, the various special ops units were his praetorian guard, but the police, the National Guard, the Coast Guard—they were his legionaries. *They* were holding the rump of America together.

Flaherty had been caught flatfooted by California and stunned by Florida. He'd been ready for Montana, but who gave a shit about Montana? Right now he was concentrating on Texas and Louisiana.

In other words, New Hope.

"You got any more boats coming?"

"Sorry, sir. All our assets are in operation blocking the port of New Orleans."

"I hear ya." The NSA had picked up chatter about using a New Orleans ferry to ram the New Hope launch platform.

Swell licked against the legs of the platform, swallowing the sound of their footsteps. The clatter of generators on the launch platform got louder as they crossed the intermediate platform in the afternoon shadow of the crawler.

A speedboat dashed out of the flotilla, towards the platform. The Coast Guard officers dropped into firing stances. No nonsense, no drama. They trained their sub-machine guns on the speedboat, tracking its approach. Flaherty wondered if it would dare to zip *under* the platform. There was plenty of clearance, but that would be crossing an unspoken red line. He sweated, wondering if this would be the next Paris.

Late last year, French riot police had opened fire on an Earth Party 'walk' that had besieged the Élysée Palace. When the smoke cleared, France had become the first country in Europe with an Earth Party government. The intermediate steps—media outrage, snap elections—had become optional since, and could be skipped.

At the last possible moment, the speedboat's pilot yanked the helm over. The people on the deck launched a volley of party poppers. If it was dark, those would have been firecrackers, or laser pointers aimed at the Coast Guard officers' eyes. Extremely fucking dangerous.

The officers lowered their weapons. "These fools are playin' with fire," one said.

Flaherty watched the speedboat flee back to the flotilla. "They sure are."

The youngest Coast Guard officer, just a kid to Flaherty, pushed up the bill of his cap. "What they tryin' to *do,* sir?"

The kid reminded Flaherty of Lance Garner. When Lance died, it had felt to the childless, unmarried Flaherty like losing a son. The memory softened his normally gruff voice. "They're trying to stop this launch."

"Why, sir?"

"They think it's an act of war." Japan had the same problem at Tanegashima. Russia did *not* have the same problem at Baikonur. Just shoot 'em. Works. But you can't do that in America. Can you?

Flaherty gazed up at the 80-meter obelisk of the Falcon Heavy, reminding himself of the precious payload it carried up top. An engine exhaust assembly, built at JSC in Houston. A critical component of the big deception that might save Earth.

"They think *what's* an act of war, sir …?"

Flaherty realized no one had bothered to tell this Coast Guard recruit what the New Hope launch facility was, anyway.

"Son, this facility is sending up parts for the *Victory*. We're building a new ship in orbit, so we can send the *Spirit of Destiny* the shi—the stuff they need to get home. Four launches just to get the pieces of the engine up. This's the last one."

"I kinda thought this was …"

"What?" Flaherty's secret weapon was his unthreatening

appearance. Just a middle-aged black guy, overweight, sweating in the sun. Caesar wasn't no Hollywood action star, either.

"Star Wars. Y'know. Nukes in space, to stop the *Lightbringer.*"

Flaherty took the hysterical guffaw that rose up in his throat and he turned it into a knowing smile. "We're doing what we can." And that was the truth.

None of the Coast Guard officers laughed out loud at the very idea of 'nukes in space.' In fact the same idea got thrown around all the time by hawkish pundits. It was completely futile but people couldn't help their ignorance. You had to have a top-level security clearance to know the hard upper limits on Earth's capabilities—so many tons per launch, so many launches per month, so many highly-skilled engineers, so many factories. And even if you had those numbers at your fingertips, you would not grasp the utter futility of Earth's position unless you also knew that a majority of the launch sites, skilled technicians, IT geniuses, et fucking cetera, had gone over to the other side.

"Look out!" The senior officer jostled Flaherty, yelling, "Lady's got a gun!"

A motor dinghy had pulled out of the flotilla. In the prow stood a human being of possibly female gender, dressed in blue and green robes like some Greek goddess. On her head, a wig of the type Flaherty had begun to see more often. Silicone snakes down to her waist. Imitation is the sincerest form of flattery. "That ain't no lady," Flaherty said. "And that ain't no gun."

The alien cosplayer raised her 'rifle'—just a big water

pistol—and shot a red stream up at them. It splashed Flaherty's jeans. Dyed water? Pig's blood.

The Coast Guard officers, nerves frayed to the limit, shouted at the cosplayer to go back to California.

"Sometimes I think America's not worth saving," Flaherty muttered.

And those were the worst times of all.

CHAPTER 14

After dark, floodlights lit up the pure white stalk of the Falcon Heavy.

T-00:02:00.

The hoses, leads, and pumps had been disconnected. The Strongback cradles had opened, and the support scaffold had retracted, leaving the rocket standing proud on the launch platform.

A light breeze licked Flaherty's face. 3 mph, nothing to worry about. He had other things to worry about. He and Kuldeep stood on the deck of a Coast Guard utility boat, half a mile from the launch platform. One more UTB and an 80-foot cutter had arrived from New Orleans to help clear the blast area. But they were simply outnumbered by the Earth Party flotilla. The Coast Guard vessels dashed back and forth, slewing their spotlights over the sea. "Clear the blast area! Clear the blast area NOW!" The civilian boats just snuck between them, flocking back towards New Hope. Already there had been one collision. The cutter had had to stop and rescue disconsolate boaters in silicone wigs.

Flaherty laughed out loud— "Worse than herding cats! At least cats got a sense of self-preservation."

Kuldeep, life-vest up around his ears, looked at him sadly. Kuldeep was a fine young man with a lot going for him, but he was no Lance Garner. He didn't get Flaherty's sense of humor. Few did.

"Clear the blast area!" bawled the Coast Guard officers.

T-00:01:30. Flaherty had the launch countdown loaded on his wristwatch. Getting close to the point of no return.

The clattering and rumbling from the launch platform mingled with the noise of all the boat engines. Sound travels well on a calm night at sea. Partier voices sang, a capella, "We will overcome." A recording from the launch platform droned, "Clear the area! Clear the area RIGHT NOW!" Burke and his team were under cover in the VAB, watching their computers.

T-00:00:45.

Flaherty's earpiece beeped. Burke said desperately, "The blast area is not clear. We are going to have to abort."

"No! No, you will NOT abort." But Flaherty could see they were not going to clear the blast area in time. "I'm gonna get the Navy to help us out," he said. "This is intolerable." Caesar had wrapped his tough hands around Roman seapower. He couldn't've defeated Pompey without it. The American story was not ending, Flaherty swore to himself. It was beginning now. "Those Marine reserves at Belle Chasse are just sitting on their asses. We need some of their Super-Hueys out here."

As he spoke, the tech guy's superyacht heaved into range of the UTB's searchlight. A banner stretched along its rail said ONE GALAXY UNDER KEK.

"It's not safe!" Burke said.

Another buzz cut into their conversation. "Sir," said the cool voice of an NXC sniper on top of the VAB, "I have acquired a drone."

A drone.

This was what Flaherty had been afraid of all day.

A drone.

That was how they'd lost the July launch that carried the turbine for the *Victory's* engine. A fast-moving drone had zipped into the blast area and shot a bullet into a tank full of rocket-grade kerosene. The resulting explosion had destroyed the rocket and damaged the scaffold. You could still see the scorch marks on the VAB. Payload was a write-off. It had set the orbital construction schedule back by 40 days.

Tell Burke to abort?

They'd built another turbine. They couldn't build another engine exhaust assembly. There wasn't *time*.

"Go," Flaherty said. "Just go!"

Tracer rounds sizzled from the top of the VAB.

"Go!"

Flaherty plunged into the pilot house of the UTB. He shouldered the pilot aside and swung the helm over, pointing the bows straight at the superyacht.

The drone's operator had to be aboard this floating techno-nightmare.

"Go!"

T-00:00:03

The Falcon Heavy's first-stage engines ignited. Fire bloomed over the launch platform. Toxic clouds of exhaust rolled down to the sea, engulfing the flotilla.

The UTB rammed the superyacht,. Its prow crashed into the larger boat's hull with a shuddering boom. Flaherty pitched face first over the wheel.

T-00:00:00

The Falcon Heavy lifted off, rising into the night sky on a pillar of smoke as straight and perfect as the column that the Israelites followed, believing it was God.

*

48 hours later, Skyler decrypted the first AES-512

transmission from Earth. The other three men hovered behind him. As the progress bar crawled across his laptop screen, the tension ratcheted up until Skyler felt like his skin no longer fit his body.

"OK, let's see what they've sent us." *Click.*

A wall of text met their eyes. The crypto had stripped out the formatting.

HOUSTON / STAR CITY MISSION CONTROL to *SOD*

At the bottom of the screen were numbers and tables. Jack stuck his arm over Skyler's shoulder, reaching for the trackpad. "Let me see what that says—"

"Wait, let me *read* it!"

"It's about the *Victory!*"

For a second, long-repressed hopes escaped from control. Jack actually tried to grab the laptop from Skyler. Then he apologized. All four of them read through the file at the same time, shoulder to shoulder, huddled around the screen like cavemen around a fire. Alexei, the slowest reader in English, complained every time Skyler tried to scroll down.

At last they got to the good bit.

The huddle exploded. The men flew backwards across the bridge until they rebounded from the walls. They high-fived, bounced off each other, and spun around, cheering. If the rriksti in the main hab could hear in the human-audible range, they would have thought the men had lost their minds.

At last, Jack returned to the laptop. Pink with happiness, he crooned, "Fast unmanned ship. A mini-*SoD*. It'll launch in December, do a parabolic slingshot around Mars, and catch up with us a couple of weeks after *we* pass Mars, in

November 2022."

"You're kidding," Skyler said, his elation crushed. November 2022.

They wouldn't be getting the Shit We Need until the end of next year.

Jack shrugged, undaunted. "This is as good as it gets. The December launch window is the only one left. There was one in May, but they missed that one, obviously."

"And now we know why," Alexei said, sobering. "This is unbelievable! I thought NASA would contract with California and Florida to continue using their facilities."

"That's what we all thought," Jack said.

"Not me," Giles said. "You can't negotiate with the Earth Party. There is no leadership to negotiate with. And anyway, they want Cape Canaveral and the California launch facilities for themselves."

"For their moon base," Alexei grunted.

Camp Eternal Light Limited (CELL), the two-year-old moon base established by Earth Party-affiliated entrepreneurs, got glowing TV coverage. The fawning reports seldom mentioned any technical facts or figures. But CELL definitely received regular supply flights.

The men on the *SoD* had assumed that if two launches a month were winging towards the moon, there must be plenty of spare capacity for *Victory* construction launches.

Not so. The rest of Mission Control's transmission summarized the difficulties that NASA and to a lesser extent Roscosmos and JAXA had been having. They'd kept the truth out of previous, unsecure transmissions as a counter-reconnaissance measure against the *Lightbringer*. Now, in unvarnished English, Richard Burke revealed that

NASA was down to a single launch platform on an off-shore oil rig, and the Coast Guard had just fought a running battle with a bunch of crazies trying to sabotage their launch schedule.

"Hippies gone wild!" Jack said.

"You make the same mistake as everyone else," Giles said. "You underestimate the Earth Party." Skyler knew that Giles had identified with the Earth Party himself, before he was abused and mutilated by the very aliens he had hoped to welcome to Earth. Hatred for his former ideological peers hardened his voice. "The combination of cutting-edge technology and primitive religious impulses is very powerful."

"Religious impulses?" Jack scoffed.

"Of course," Giles said. "Look what they are doing. They are sacrificing rockets to the *Lightbringer.*"

Twelve people drowned. Two killed by sniper fire, Burke wrote. *Dozens more in hospital. Tom Flaherty, remember him? Our favorite Fed. He rammed a Coast Guard tug into a yacht the size of the Flatiron! Wound up in hospital with broken ribs. Man's a hero.*

Skyler had trouble processing the idea of Director Flaherty in hospital. Flaherty was supposed to be invulnerable. Lance was dead, but Flaherty was Teflon.

Then again, a wounded-hero rep could be an ace in the game of inter-agency politics ...

The events of two nights ago had finally pushed the president to declare martial law, Burke wrote, lapsing into a bureaucratic mode that carefully obfuscated who had done the pushing. From now on, a USN detachment and a Marine Corps air squadron would enforce a cordon around New Hope. Good news for NASA.

But the bigger story here, Skyler thought, was that the NXC had finally got its dirty hands on the prize of prizes: the US military. His sympathy for Flaherty evaporated. A couple of busted ribs weren't much to pay for *that*.

There was a moment's silence after they reached the end of the file. Then Jack scrolled back up and studied the *Victory's* flight parameters.

"So," Skyler summed up. "We're getting our resupply flight. This is good. On the other hand, American democracy is dead." He made a performance of knuckling his eyes. "Excuse me while I cry for my country. I know it's not a big deal to you guys."

"Good thing I only burnt down to 60% of reaction mass," Jack said. "We'll need to burn more water at Mars to make this rendezvous than I'd originally budgeted. It's going to slow us down, too. Bugger."

"Skyler?" Giles said, plucking at his sleeve with one small, seven-fingered hand.

"Yeah, what?" Skyler said.

"Am I correct that this file came packaged inside a video?"

"Yeah. It's called steganography. This file, the payload, was encrypted using AES-512, and then hidden inside another video, the carrier file. That's all the *Lightbringer* would see." Despite himself, Skyler snorted at the thought of the *Krijistal* decrypting and watching this particular video. Not much use for language learning …

"And what was the title of this video, *mon ami?*"

Skyler cleared his throat. "Well …" He dragged it out until the other two were paying attention.

"Busty blonde Russian chicks?" Alexei said.

"Sexy librarians," Jack speculated, eyes gleaming.

"Hot interracial gay sex," Giles said.

Skyler let out a howl of laughter. He clicked on the video and sent his laptop spinning across the bridge like a frisbee. Startled, Jack caught it. "No!" Skyler shouted. "None of the above! Do you think the NXC actually gives a fuck about your wants and needs? Think again, suckers!"

Jack looked down at the screen. *"Our Wild Planet.* Oh, David Attenborough. I used to watch his stuff when I couldn't sleep."

Skyler folded his lips between his teeth. The news from America had shaken him more than he wanted to acknowledge.

Jack passed the laptop to Alexei, flew to Skyler, and took hold of his shoulders. "C'mon, Sky," he said, giving him a gentle shake. "It's not the end of the world. Er, not until year after next, anyway."

Skyler managed a stiff smile. It embarrassed him that Jack had to tell him, in almost as many words, to man up. He resolved not to give Jack any further reason to think he was a wimp. He waited until Jack's hands dropped from his shoulders, and then said, gesturing at Jack's face, "What happened this time?"

Jack had a purple blossom on his jaw, balancing out the pink scar on the other side of his face. He brushed it with his fingers. "Oh, just Brbb again."

Giles said, "The rules require reciprocity. I do not understand anything else about them, but I understand that much."

"That much even I've figured out. You ought to see *Brbb's* face." Jack grinned.

"What was the issue?" Skyler said.

"Oh, the *Krijistai* keep going on about wanting shorter days. They'd turn this ship into a miniature Imf if we let them," Jack said, rolling his eyes.

*

Six months later. Same place. Same time …

Good one! There is no time in space! We measure weeks in kale harvests, and months in corrosion damage.

Anyway, Skyler was alone on the bridge, so it was either Monday or Wednesday or Friday, although he couldn't have told you off the top of his head if it was January, February, or March. He floated in the center seat, one bare foot thrust through a tether, wearing nothing except underpants. Too damn *hot* for clothes these days. Humidity coated his skin. He was reading *Nuclear Reactors for Dummies* on his laptop, and biting the peace symbol that floated from his neck on a thong. He checked the telescope when he remembered to.

He was meant to be scanning the sky nonstop for icebergs. The *Lightbringer's* improvised missiles had gotten smaller but meaner, laced with explosives as well as debris. They sailed in at the rate of one every 16.1 days on average, although there was no regularity to it. Lulls could last a couple of days, or a month; either felt equally long.

Mercifully, the icebergs were more frightening than dangerous. They could be seen a long way out, and thus deflected. The *SoD's* crew usually found out about them from the *Cloudeater,* in the form of coordinates and single-sentence reports on successful deflections. That's the only way they knew Keelraiser was still alive over there.

Yet the cold war between Jack and Keelraiser, or whatever the hell was going on, continued, so Jack insisted on duplicating the *Cloudeater's* scans with the *SoD's* own inferior technology. Everyone was supposed to keep their eyes glued to the optical telescope when they were on bridge duty.

Skyler approved of vigilance, of course. But in practice, he wasn't great at repetitive and mindless tasks. Boredom left him prey to dark impulses, such as: Why don't I check YouTube and see if there's a new episode of the Hannah Ginsburg Show? He hated those videos and yet he couldn't help watching them. They made him sad and mad and horny all at once—a terrible combination.

He tried to exercise willpower by focusing on his study materials, but *Reactors for Dummies* evoked Hannah's memory, as well. Everything circled back to her.

All right. Time for some weapons-grade displacement activity.

He closed his laptop, checked the telescope once more, and went to take his guitar down from its bungee-cord cradle on the aft wall.

His guitar? Yeah man. We long-distance spacefarers *groove,* you dig?

The guitar was made of off-white bio-plastic, a tip-off that it came from the 3D fabber in the *Cloudeater's* cargo hold. Awesome machine. Input your specs, and out pops whatever you need, as long as it's made of bio-plastic.

The guitar sounded OK, though. He'd ended up using aluminum-alloy for the strings, printed on the *other* 3D fabber, which did metal parts.

He slipped the shoulder strap over his head. "The void waits, it's ravenous," he sang, fingerpicking chords. He used his right elbow to trap the guitar against his body in the absence of gravity. "How many corpses can it take? The vacuum wants to swallow you." Am, Dm, G. "How long before you break?"

Skyler used to compose doggerel about his love for Hannah, using other people's tunes. For a while her loss had put him off music. But now, for the first time in his life, he was taking the guitar seriously. His exposure to rriksti ballads had been an inspiration. They'd been a spacefaring people for long enough to develop a whole musical tradition around the ultimate frontier. Judging by their lyrics, the longer you messed around in space, the more you got to hate it. Surprise, surprise.

"Yet in your heart you know that you're not destined for this death." C, Cmaj9, Am. "And you pray for salvation with every breath." There was no such word as *salvation* in Rristigul. They had *kmanif,* which translated as 'self-perfection,' according to Giles's dictionary, which was now up to 20,000 words.

As he sang, Skyler heard a low-pitched grinding noise. He stopped. Listened. Only the noise of the fans …

With a mental shrug, he went back to trying out different chord progressions.

After a while, he noticed a yellow light flashing on the mechanical systems console. He flew over to have a look. By now, of course, he knew what all the consoles controlled, and what the various alerts they generated meant. This one didn't seem very important. But he didn't know how to shut it off.

Call Jack?

Maybe just to be on the safe side.

CHAPTER 15

"Jack? Jack, can you come up here for a minute?"

Jack heard Skyler's voice in his headset. "Iceberg?" he said sharply.

"Nope. It's just ..."

"Hang on a sec and I'll be there," Jack said, frowning up at Brbb.

A froth of ripe blue suizh framed Brbb's head. Now on its third planting, the rriksti staple had grown to twice Jack's height. Pale blue feathery fronds and seedheads of turquoise berries drooped above them like a forest canopy. Every plant represented calories in the bank and CO2 sucked out of the air, nature's great two-fer. Apé rubbed their nacreous bellies against the sides of the tanks. Jack sometimes liked to just sit here and watch the fish, revelling in the calories they represented, like a king in his counting-house counting out his money.

That is, when the *Krijistal* deserters weren't getting on his case about this and that and the other rule he supposedly wasn't enforcing properly.

"What's the problem, Brbb?" He already guessed, but he believed it was good for them to be made to *say* what they bloody *meant*.

Brbb's pupils were pinpoints, nearly invisible. Rriksti did not have enough facial mobility to squint. "We need to make the days shorter," it said.

Jack sighed. He looked up, through the suizh, up, past the blaze of light around the axis tunnel, to the other side of the hab, where more jungle, and a village of tenement-style shelters built from structural aerogel and curtains, hung upside down. A cat's-cradle of irrigation hoses and power lines stretched over the whole mess. Six months into its voyage, the *SoD* had become a flying slum. But so what? Everyone was still alive, *alive*. Jack felt prouder of that than of anything else he'd achieved in his life. They'd only had two deaths since leaving Europa, and both of those had been cancer patients, so it was sad but expected. Extroversion wasn't magic.

Near the rriksti village, a patch of green vegetation sprawled along the aft wall. The terrestrial crops were flourishing, too. Make the days any shorter, however, and the all-important potatoes would begin to suffer.

"Ever heard of sunglasses?" Jack said.

A couple of months ago he'd unearthed his own Ray-Bans. He couldn't even remember why he'd brought them from Earth. Probably just for the coolness factor. Anyway, they added a touch of distinction to his outfit, which otherwise consisted of ragged shorts. He lowered his sunglasses, like Tom Cruise in *Top Gun,* and smirked at Brbb. "My ship, my rules."

Brbb drew back its fist and swung at him. Jack had known this was probably coming and he dodged under the blow, aiming a punch of his own at Brbb's midriff. His sunglasses fell off. His fist connected, as if with a suede-covered brick wall. Brbb pistoned its other fist at the side of his head. *Six* knuckles. A rriksti fist was the size of a cricket glove. The blow landed on Jack's shoulder. Shaking off the pain, he went in for the clinch. You had to get these buggers down on the ground, where superior human mass could tell. Rriksti had wiry muscles, belying their frail appearance, and they were *fast*. But Brbb, despite being taller than Jack, with a longer reach, weighed less, and could not muster as much raw stopping power. Jack ended up kneeling astride its chest, working its face over with his fists. He waited for Brbb's hair to move, or its fingers to flutter away from its eyes, before letting fly, forcing it to protect its face again.

The other *Krijistal* stood around, ready to drag the suizh tanks out of the way if necessary. They would not intervene, as this was an argument, not a fight. At least that's how Jack understood it. Brbb had tried to dictate to Jack, Jack had shot it down, Brbb had expressed dissent with its fists, and now Jack was asserting, for the second or third time this week, that yes, he was the commander of this ship and his word was law. *So. There.* The rriksti rules of engagement, in his still-hazy understanding, allowed for differences to be hashed out by violence, regardless of the actual rights and wrongs of the issue. So instead of going round and round in rhetorical circles, they went round after round on the filthy floor of the hab. Brbb's hair whipped, stirring leaf mould and *suizh* husks into the air.

Jack heard an odd noise.

There wasn't usually much to hear in the main hab, apart from the roar of the fans and the more distant rumble of the housekeeping turbine. Hundreds of rriksti made remarkably little noise. Of course, in the mid-kilohertz range, it was a different story. Jack was accustomed to a certain level of background chatter in his headset, which picked up some of the rrikstis' signals in Rristigul as well as their English-language signals to the humans. But his headset had come off in the fight. He froze, listening to the quiet.

Brbb took advantage of his distraction to throw something at his face. His Ray-Bans. One earpiece had snapped off. After all these years!

Jack saw red. He jumped off Brbb, scuffed back, and before it could rise, delivered a vicious kick to its groin. He knew now what they kept down there. It wasn't quite like kicking a human in the balls, but close enough. Even though Jack was barefoot, his toes delivered enough pain to make Brbb curl up like a spider pulling its legs in. Gone, gone were the days when Jack Kildare had scorned fighting dirty. He picked up his broken sunglasses and put them in his pocket. He retrieved his headset and put it on. He panted, "Now we won't have any more nonsense about the fucking lights for at least twenty-four hours, will we?"

The first thing he heard was Alexei saying, "—get hold of Jack," and then Nene saying, "Jack? I'm afraid the forward toilet is broken."

"Again?" Jack picked up a long-handled gaffer hook leaning against the nearest stand of suizh. That would show Brbb he was seriously pissed off. Jack did not flatter himself that he really understood the rriksti rules of engagement, but he grasped that arming oneself meant one was ready for bloodshed. Jack wasn't, but hopefully it would send a message. The gaffer hook would also come in handy to unclog the toilet. "I'll be right there," he told Nene, glad of the excuse to cut this short.

He walked diagonally forward, brushing through the froth of suizh and jgzeriyat, still out of breath from the fight. His shoulder hurt. He told himself he would be all right. The nutrient solution dripping from the irrigation hoses gave off a briny smell. With all this water around, spills were inevitable. Wet leaf fragments and other rubbish squidged under his toes, the consistency of mud. He passed a rriksti child painstakingly scraping the stuff off the floor, for recycling. They couldn't afford to lose a single molecule of the vegetation's heavy metal content. Jack smiled at the child, and wiped sweat off his face with a bare forearm.

"Hey, Jack, just wondering if you could come have a look at this?"

"I said I'll be right there, Skyler," Jack snapped, as he reached the forward toilet, in the Potter space under Staircase 2.

Nene stood in front of the open door, keeping out a crowd of rriksti who were desperate to go. Jack edged between them. Their hair undulated, red and bronze and gold and silver and black, transmitting apologies into his headset. "Sorry. Sorry." It was the one English word every rriksti had learned to say. "Sorry." The apologies blunted Jack's exasperation, reminding him that they weren't slovenly by choice. And they hated pissing into buckets. Much as Jack sympathized, he wished they would.

"What seems to be the trouble?" he said dryly, easing Nene aside. He peered into the reeking hole in the wall which had once been a $31 million commode equipped with the same suction system used on the ISS, plus a water-sparing flush mechanism similar to an airplane toilet. The commode was still there ... shit-encrusted, the seat long gone. But it was walled in with bales of the rough toilet paper that the rriksti insisted on manufacturing for themselves, and a bag for *used* toilet paper—Giles's wheeze to get them to stop flushing the stuff. Some of them perversely played dumb, as if it were beneath them to let on that they understood what the bag was for. "Let me guess," Jack said. "Someone's been flushing the toilet paper again."

"I don't *think* so," Nene said, wringing its hands. Short for a rriksti at just 6'3", Nene had dark red bio-antennas and a face more rounded than the rriksti norm. It almost had apple cheeks. Jack could see, in certain lights, that it was cute. Alexei swore it was female two days in eleven. All the same, Jack still thought of Nene—of all of them, in fact—as *it*. This was deliberate. He couldn't allow himself to start imagining that they were just humans in alien suits, as he knew all too well they weren't.

Half-hearing Nene's demurral, he moved past it, breathing through his mouth, to have a go with the gaffer hook. Giles had invented this gizmo and printed its pieces off on the 3D fabber. It had a glove at the bottom of the handle with spaces for seven fingers. Jack, naturally, only used the first five. Pressure pads allowed intuitive operation of the hook, which converted into a four-way grabber.

He smiled in triumph as he drew a compacted lump of alien shit up through the U-bend. "Problem solved."

Nene helped him scrape the tarry mass into the toilet paper bag. "You see," it said, "the trouble is that the flushing mechanism hasn't been working. There isn't any water."

Jack froze. "No *water?*" he said, and heard that weird noise again.

*

Jack flew onto the bridge. Skyler looked around. "Hey, sorry about that. The computer threw up a mass trim alert. But it's OK now. Panic over."

Jack wasn't so sure. He dived into the center seat and punched up the external camera feeds. The cameras on the outside of the rotating hab showed nothing except space. Light from the distant sun reflected off the hull. He switched to the feed from the aft-facing cameras mounted on the 'bottom' of the rotating hab, where a 46-foot steel disk crammed with bearings connected the hab to the truss tower.

"Did you hear that funny noise?" Skyler said. "It was weird. Almost subsonic. It's stopped now."

"Yeah, I heard it." Jack pored over the camera feeds. He saw a bloom of white all around the edge of the bioshield. He cranked the magnification. It looked like a snowfall had dusted the bioshield.

Snow.

In space.

Jack let out a howl. He rocked back in his seat—in zero-gee, this movement threatened to turn into a backwards somersault—and clamped his hands over his face, as if he could un-see the sight that spelled doom for everyone on board.

CHAPTER 16

Jack's surrender to despair lasted for all of a microsecond. He rocked forward and checked the rotation rate of the hab. As he'd expected, it was rotating slightly faster than before—3 RPMs had turned into 3.12 RPMs. That's what would happen, when the hab got *lighter*.

"What is it?" Skyler shouted. Jack's despairing howl had launched him out of his seat. He turned, gripping the EVA suits that hung against the aft wall. "What's going on?"

"Put down your suit," Jack said tiredly. "There's nowhere to go." And that was exactly the trouble. Nowhere to go. They were so alone out here, the English language needed a new word for it.

"Everything OK?" It was Alexei, on the intercom. Rriksti voices murmured nervously on the channel.

"Come to the bridge," Jack said. "Giles? You, too." He switched off the intercom.

"OK, hit me," Skyler said, tense.

"That noise was the hab's bearings. I didn't recognize it straightaway." Jack could have kicked himself for that. And for fixing the toilet first. And for not being able to be in three places at once. On the other hand, he knew nothing would be different even if he'd reacted immediately. By the time they heard that grinding noise, it had already been too late. "Remember how the mass trim control system works?"

Skyler licked his lips. "It's like ballast tanks in an oceangoing ship. There are two water tanks, one on either side of the hab. The computer feeds water from one tank to the other to balance the hab."

"So what do you think would happen if one tank was completely empty, and the other was full?"

"First of all, you'd get friction in the bearings. *Oh.*"

"Yup."

"If there's an imbalance, the computer pushes water through the cross-connect until the tanks balance."

"Or until both tanks are empty." Jack pointed at the external camera feed. The sinister bloom of snow on the bioshield. "Guess what that is."

"Oh, shit," Skyler said. "Our water."

"Bingo."

"Something holed one of the tanks."

"Must've."

Skyler actually went white. You'd think a man who had not seen the sun for three years couldn't get much whiter, but fear turned him into a spectre. "The *Lightbringer*," he said.

"Yup. Looks like they got us."

"I thought Keelraiser was scanning for icebergs!"

Jack had no wish or reason to defend Keelraiser, but he heard himself saying, "It must have been tiny. Kinetic energy is mass times velocity squared. A pebble would do it, at this speed."

Skyler flew to the life support console. "It says both tanks are full!"

"That's what it's said for the last year. I should have noticed something was off."

"The sensors are fucked," Skyler surmised.

Alexei and Giles flew onto the bridge. Several rriksti, including Nene, jammed the keel tube behind them. Jack shot out of his seat. "Close the door," he shouted. Alexei did not do it. Jack had known he wouldn't. He turned the crank himself, spraying insincere smiles through the gap until the heavy steel pressure door hid the rrikstis' blank faces. Questions shrieked tinnily from Alexei's headset when Jack physically removed it from his head. There was then a lot of shouting, which gradually cohered into a shared understanding that they now had no drinking water except for what remained in the algae tanks, the irrigation hoses, and the sewage lines.

The four men stared at each other in silence. They all understood what water meant in space.

Life.

And what *no water* meant.

Death.

"We can reclaim a little bit of water from the hydroponics," Giles said. "But not much. The nutrient solutions have precise molarity and isotonicity. We make a different solution for each tank, in a narrow range of concentrations for nitrates and other nutrients. If we extract water from the solutions, the increased concentration of salt and nitrates pulls the water out of the cells of the plants. They die. Then we die."

Alexei gave a death's-head grin. "Looks like I picked the wrong week to quit smoking."

Jack laughed. "Looks like *I* picked the wrong week to quit doing amphetamines."

Alexei, dressed in a rriksti outfit that looked like two shopping bags with the 'handles' over his shoulders, which, he swore, kept him cool in the heat and humidity, plucked his e-cigarette out of a pocket and blew vapor into the air. He had, of course, gone to extreme lengths *not* to quit smoking—or rather, vaping. He grew his own tobacco plants. The vapor swirled towards the vents on the ceiling, and Jack thought about all those particles of precious water vanishing into the air circulation system, contributing to the general humidity, ending up as a corrosion hazard, useless to man or rriksti.

"The dehumidifiers," he said, snapping his fingers. "If we crank them up, we can wring quite a lot of water out of this fucking sauna. Yes, the rriksti will scream bloody murder. They'll just have to cope."

"That buys us maybe one more day's water," Giles said. "Then what? We start throwing them out of the airlock?"

The words hung in the air like a turd in zero-gravity.

Skyler broke the silence this time. He was back on his laptop, running calculations. "What I want to know is who designed this fucking ship? I mean, I cannot believe this didn't happen before. Why did they put the potable water tanks on the *outside* of the hab? Why, why?" He did a nasal, nerdy voice. "We need extra shielding for the rotating hab. Hey, I know! Water makes great shielding! Wow, that's genius! Let's use the waterRRRRRR!" Skyler's eyes popped; he mimed wringing the necks of the engineers whose rushed, half-arsed design decisions were now killing them.

Everyone laughed. Jack smiled at Skyler, grateful for the moment of levity. "Right, we've got to conjure up 1.8 million liters of water from thin air," he said. "Ideas?"

"There is plenty of water in the bioshield tank," Alexei said.

"Tritium and oxygen 14!" Skyler said. "Tasty."

"We're already glowing in the dark," Jack said, shaking his

head.

It was true they had plenty of water in the propulsion tanks. Unfortunately, it wasn't drinkable. Their big burn out of Jupiter orbit had left the *SoD* with 6.6 million gallons of H2O in the bioshield tank and the four external tanks, respectively, as well as another million or so in the plastic bags attached to the bioshield. But as Skyler had pointed out, that water was extremely radioactive. It had been sitting out on Europa for billions of years, getting bombarded by neutrons, which mutate good old hydrogen into stable nuclides of tritium. Little rocks of cancer in every drop.

Yet now the others were all jabbering about the water in the ETs. Jack rubbed his fingers together nervously. He was afraid they were getting blasé about radiation. They weren't rriksti. They couldn't rely on extroversion. Even the rriksti couldn't rely on it. The magic in their fingers was just too failure-prone. Too *weird*.

"Jack, the rriksti drank Europan water for ten years!" Alexei said.

"After processing it through a DIY mass spectrometer the size of a house," Jack pointed out.

"It was just a big box."

"Yes …" A *really* big box, made of cast iron, lined with magnets. Shoot water plasma in at the top. Leave the radioactive nuclides behind, run the rest through a fuel cell, and you get pure, neutral, non-radioactive water. But the flipping thing had weighed a metric fuck-tonne. On top of that, it had been badly radioactive from all those years of shoving Europan ice down the chute. So *that* got left behind.

But—

"The algae tanks!" Jack shouted. "That's it!"

At the same time, Alexei said, "We could build something that works the same way. It doesn't have to be the size of a house."

"It only has to be the size of an algae tank!"

"That's what I'm saying," Alexei said, cool as a cucumber, as if he'd never even thought about freaking out. Jack could have hugged him.

"God, this is a great team," he said five minutes later, when they had roughed out the specs. They could science their way out of this yet. Take that, *Lightbringer.* You and your high-speed pebbles.

Giles nodded. "I believe it will work. But how *fast* will it work? Normal requirements are fifty liters per person per day. The rriksti require slightly more drinking water than we do. It takes almost one month to process sewage. And with no flush water, we cannot process the sewage, anyway. What will they drink until the apparatus produces drinkable water?"

Giles had a point. "Damn. Alexei, how soon d'you think we could get it up and running?"

"A few days?" Alexei shrugged.

"Yeah, that's what I thought."

"Such precision," Giles said.

"I have a degree in physics, you know," Jack retorted, thinking: How many people will die in *a few days?* Fuck it, fuck it. "Right." Before morale could deflate again, he turned to Alexei. "Water rationing. And when I say rationing I mean *zero.* Tell them we're going to fix this. But until then, they'll simply have to suck it up."

Alexei grimaced. "Got it. No sugar-coating. I give it to them good and hard."

He drifted to the door and turned the crank. The pressure door retracted into the wall. Rriksti arms and hands reached through the gap, and Alexei vanished down the keel tube, his demeanor shifting to match the rrikstis' jerky, quick movements, mirroring their agitated state. Jack wondered if he'd just made a mistake.

For Alexei was no longer quite the same man Jack had considered his Russian brother from another mother. Six months among the rriksti (not forgetting Alexei's additional months among the rriksti on Europa) had changed him, more than any of the other men.

Most notably, Alexei had mastered the rriksti communication style. So whatever he promised, he was going to leave that promise on the bridge. He was *not* going to give it to them good and hard. He'd pour his energies into calming their fears, and it might be ages before he got around to explaining about the water.

On the other hand, was that necessarily a bad thing? It would give Jack time to take actions that might be unpopular.

Jack pulled Giles close. He held him by the spindly wrists that sprouted from his elbow joints. "Good thing we never hooked up the plumbing to the *Cloudeater*."

"Yes," Giles said. "If we had, they'd have lost all their water, too."

"They've got about two hundred thousand gallons in their potable water tanks. I want you to go over there and ask for it."

"Why don't you?"

"Jesus, Giles. I'd be breaking the rules. I don't know why but I do know I'm not supposed to go over there. Brbb would go after me in its self-appointed role as rule enforcement officer in chief. I do *not* need another punch-up today, on top of everything." He touched his shoulder. The fresh bruise from Brbb's fist still stung.

Giles pursed his lips. "It is possible that we do not fully understand the particular rules that have been applied here," he said carefully.

"Possible? I just told you I do *not* understand the rules. But … Look, just do it, Giles. Please."

"All right," Giles said. "I'll arrange it with Cleanmay. We'll run hoses from the *Cloudeater's* potable water tanks to our irrigation lines."

Giles forced his way down the keel tube, and Jack flew to the curtained-off end of the bridge. Ducking under the lines of floating laundry, he dug out his blaster and fastened the holster belt diagonally across his shoulder. The blaster was too big to wear on your hip, even in zero-gee.

"Skyler, you have the bridge until I get back."

Skyler nodded, absently biting the straw of his squeeze bottle. Jack gestured at it. "What's in there?"

"Water." Skyler held it out. "Want some?"

"Water," Jack echoed. He shook his head. "I meant how much?"

"Oh. Maybe twelve ounces."

"You and your imperial measurements. Make it last. That's your ration for today."

He flew down the keel tube, his mind already jumping ahead. First step: remove some of the electromagnets from the drive turbine …

CHAPTER 17

"Right, we're going to have to make examples. Might as well start now," Jack croaked. The crisis had dragged on for four days. The men had cut their own water rations to 1.5 liters a day, while the rriksti were getting a quarter of that. "If you'd like to do the honors, Brbb?"

"Your wish is my command," Brbb said, taking the piss, Jack thought, but also enjoying this. *Definitely* enjoying it.

Maybe I should do it myself.

Too late for second thoughts. Brbb headed forward, delivering a flurry of kicks along the way to the four rriksti who'd been caught siphoning water from the algae tanks.

Brbb's mates held them in a full-Nelson grip, so that their arms floated above their heads. When kicked, they jerked. Brbb's mates cranked their joined hands back, applying pressure to the thieves' throats.

Jack gestured for the *Krijistal* to escort the prisoners out of the turbine room. Before following them, he grabbed his blaster and slipped the holster belt over his shoulder.

"I'll stay here and monitor the tank," Alexei said, without meeting Jack's eyes. Alexei had argued against making examples. But the water thievery was getting outrageous. Jack couldn't let it go on. It wasn't fair to those who were *not* stealing.

They floated out of the turbine room and through the engineering module. Skyler manned the turbine and reactor controls. He looked away as the unhappy procession passed through, and Jack gritted his teeth against a surge of anger. Yes, that's right, Taft, avert your eyes! We all know you haven't the guts to lay a finger on a rriksti. Humans, on the other hand ... you've no problem killing your own kind, have you?

The whole point here is *not* to kill anyone, Jack rehearsed to himself. We have to punish some of them so that we won't have to kill anyone.

The water thieves shrieked as the guards stuffed them into the keel tube, their hair swirling wildly.

Through the storage module. Through SLS. The two *Krijistal* guarding the algae tanks shot Jack a rriksti salute, which was like a Vulcan salute turned backwards, so it resembled the charming British gesture for "up yours." It often made Jack smile but not now. He reflected that it had been quite the feat for four half-dead rriksti to steal water from under these guys' noses, and wondered if Brbb and company had accidentally-on-purpose *let* them steal it, so that they'd have someone to make an example of. They'd entrapped a whole family: three adults and a child of maybe twelve.

Jack slapped the lean rump of Difystra, speeding it through the keel tube into the main hab. They all trooped down Staircase 6. From high on the stairs, Jack scanned the jungle, counting empty patches, brown patches, and yellow patches. Giles was dripping the water from the *Cloudeater* into the hydroponics, but people had got thirsty enough in the last couple of days to start drinking nutrient solution. They were killing their own crops. That would have consquences down the line, but right now it didn't seem to matter.

The hab seemed deathly quiet, devoid of life. But as they paraded through the jungle, rriksti peeked between the fronds of suizh. A crowd of silent spectators had coalesced by the time they reached the walking track that ran around the hab's circumference.

This was the one place they'd kept free of vegetation. It was a lane through the jungle, about four feet wide.

Brbb addressed the prisoners in English. "You have committed a crime worse than murder, and you will pay for it!"

As Brbb spoke, a rope-end whipped past, bouncing along the track. Brbb stepped nimbly aside.

Jack glanced up.

Another rope swung towards them, rotating with the hab. Its top end was tied to the axis tunnel.

Jack swallowed a gasp of bittersweet recognition. On the way to Europa, he and Alexei used to play a game with a rope tied like this. Jump on, rise up, jump off, win imaginary money.

Surely Brbb wasn't going to play *games* with the water thieves?

Rriksti—who the fuck knows how they think?

Jack counted one rope swinging past every six seconds, making four in total. Brbb delivered a lengthy lecture in Rristigul. Flakes of dry skin drifted from its scalp as its hair shot this way and that, making its points. It then seized the nearest prisoner, waited for a rope to approach, and seized that. Brbb and prisoner rose swiftly off the path. When you attach a weight to the end of a rope and swing it around, it becomes a bola.

There was a loop in the end of the rope.

Brbb stuffed the prisoner's head through the loop and jumped off the rope, sticking the landing.

The loop was a *noose*.

The prisoner rose higher and higher, a twiggy silhouette, spinning by its neck. Shrieks pierced Jack's ears. He snatched his headset off. Paralyzed with horror, he watched the rope, with the prisoner on the end, wrap around the axis tunnel. He hadn't expected anything like this and didn't know what to do. The prisoner collided with the lattice with a meaty crunch. The screaming continued. It was coming from the crowd.

Oh Jesus, Jack thought. How could I forget they are *Krijistal?* They're the exact bloody same as the guys who murdered Kate and kidnapped Hannah and cut off Giles's hands and feet. It's just sheer chance that these ones got left behind.

"I thought you were just going to beat them up," he shouted.

Brbb regarded him in disappointment. "This was a serious crime," it said.

Jack took off running towards the aft stairs. Maybe the hanged rriksti was still alive. "Don't touch the rest of them," he shouted over his shoulder.

*

At the same time, Giles was reclining on the bridge, working on his dictionary. It was something to do when one was dying of thirst. After his initial struggles with Rristigul, he'd adopted a mechanistic approach to the language. Noun by noun, verb by verb, he was building up a lexicon of rriksti concepts, which in turn adumbrated a shadowy picture of the strange culture of the Darkside.

Word of the day for February 7th, 2022: *Krijistal.*

A real bitch, this one. He listened to his collection of recorded snippets featuring the word, his fourteen fingers folded over his belly, trying to ignore the ache of thirst in his throat. He reminded himself that the rriksti in the main hab did not even have 1500 milliliters of luke-warm H2O to get them through the day.

The intercom snarled to life. "Giles!"

"What is it, Jack?" Giles said calmly.

"Need you to spin down the hab."

"Pardon?"

"Spin. Down. The. Hab!!"

Jack was in a rage. Hoping to calm him down, Giles said, "Why?"

"Because I fucking said so," Jack shouted. "Look, we were going to spin it down anyway, to mend the tanks. We'll just do it ahead of schedule."

Giles could hear rriksti voices on the channel. He could hear *screaming*.

"Bien," he said. "Consider it done." He added, "I am not sure I actually know how to spin down the hab."

"It's self, fucking, explanatory. Do it now." Click.

Giles flew to the right seat. He found the controls of the hydrazine-fuelled rim thrusters and stabbed the button marked ANTI-SPINWARDS. The thrusters began to fire against the direction of the hab's rotation, slowing it down.

CHAPTER 18

Alone in the turbine room, Alexei checked the levels of O2 and H in the fuel cells. Getting there ... but not fast enough.

They'd emptied out one of the algae tanks. Hauled it back to the turbine room. Six feet by four, it *barely* fit through the keel tubes. Then they'd sealed the tank, turning it into a vacuum chamber. Inside: magnets from the drive turbine, cold cathodes, a radio-frequency generator.

Ionizer at one end of the tank. A copper pipe with a grid inside. High voltage running through it.

The jury-rigged apparatus filled the center of the turbine room, above the rusty turbine cabinets. They'd had to re-route all the plumbing back here to feed LH2 and LOX from the reactant tanks into the apparatus, instead of into the fuel cells where it would normally go. That meant they couldn't use the fuel cells, and *that* meant brown-outs, because the mass spectrometer was gobbling most of the electricity from the housekeeping turbine. And *that* meant everyone was cold.

As well as thirsty.

And their skin was falling off from the low humidity. They were literally shedding. Full-body dandruff.

Alexei coughed, his throat scratchy. Flakes of riksti skin swirled like snow in the air, left over from Brbb's brief invasion of the turbine room. He hated to think what was happening in the main hab right now. All he could do was hope that Jack would restrain Brbb's violent tendencies, without resorting to violence himself. The rriksti could be incomprehensibly brutal, but there was also a sweetness in them.

A gentleness. Alexei saw that. He wasn't sure Jack did.

Wearily, he stared at the arc of green gas shooting through the algae tank. Oxygen, minus one electron, glowed like the Northern Lights. Hydrogen was invisible. So was the evil stuff, the tritium from Europa. *That* stayed in the tank. The oxygen and the good, clean hydrogen spurted out the other end, into the fuel cells, but it was so slow, so goddamn *slow*. They were still waiting for the fuel cells to overflow into the algae tanks, so they could start giving water to people.

The turbines made a lot of noise, so Alexei didn't notice that Nene had entered the room until she floated down into his field of vision. He smiled, happy to see her.

She hugged a shawl around her shoulders against the cold. Her normally porcelain skin looked ashy. Alexei reached for his headset. He'd taken it off because he didn't want to hear how the business with the prisoners turned out. Shame on you, Alexei Dmitrovich.

"It sings," she said.

"What sings?"

"The mass spectrometer. I can hear the radio-frequency resonance from the tank."

"Of course you can," Alexei realized. "For you, machinery sings." It must be so cool to be a rriksti. He felt fifteen years old around them sometimes. Especially, it had to be said, around Nene.

"They wanted me to heal those prisoners," Nene said. She drifted down and sat on the algae tank, hooking one foot around the intake piping. The spectral green glow from the tank lit her face from below. She was a doctor. A different kind of doctor from Cleanmay, the rriksti who ran sickbay on the *Cloudeater*. Cleanmay was the kind of doctor we all understand, an expert typist, not much use to the sick without shedloads of fancy machinery. Nene was a fifth-level cleric (her words), certifiied by the Temple of Ystyggr on Imf. OK, maybe *doctor* was not quite the right translation. But it was the best Alexei could come up with..

"I refused to help them," she said. "They are sadists. They would have had me heal the prisoners, so they could punish them again. I refuse to play along with that anymore."

Alexei smiled, proud of her. That must have been a difficult decision. "Good for you." He hesitated. "Did Jack back you up?"

"Yes, yes. He doesn't like it, either."

That relieved Alexei more than he wanted to admit. To hide any hint that he had doubted his friend, he hunted for his squeeze bottle. It still held 400 milliliters of his daily ration.

"They will probably die," Nene said. "But probably we will all die, anyway. They'll just die faster."

Alexei whirled, bottle in hand. "No," he said forcefully. "We will *not* die." He slapped the tank full of ionized gases. "This is working! It just takes a little more time, then there'll be water for everyone."

She hunched her shoulders. *No, I don't want to be cheered up*, her long, sad face said.

Alexei considered himself an expert cheerer-upper. He held out the bottle. "Have some water. Straight from the dehumidifier, everyone's breathed it; it is really disgusting."

"No. That's *your* water." But her eyes followed the bottle.

Alexei clamped the straw in his teeth and sucked, filling his mouth with stale water. He badly wanted to swallow it, but he didn't. Holding it in his mouth, he floated over to Nene and took her by the shoulders. He pulled her closer, felt no resistance. He pressed his lips to hers and opened his mouth, parting her lips by force so that the water trickled into her mouth.

Her hot, sharp tongue chased the last drops past his teeth. Alexei convulsively clutched her. Their bodies, though fully clothed, seemed to fuse together. Rational thought left the building.

"I've wanted to do this for so long," he muttered into her cheek.

Her hair—her bio-antennas, those amazing whip-like tendrils, the color of rubies—caressed his skull and shoulders. "I remember when we first met," she said through his headset. "You and Jack tried to shoot us. That was your way of saying hello. We thought: oh, they are just like rriksti, after all! Then, gradually, I found out that you are *not* like rriksti." Alexei moved his right hand up and down, stroking the bony nape of her neck. Her skin felt like the most expensive and delicate leather, supple as silk, although it was so dry. He almost hated to touch it with his rough, damaged, astronaut's fingers. "But strangely, now that I know how different you are, I like you even more."

"I could teach you Russian," Alexei suggested. "I'll teach you how to say 'leave me alone; you stink.'"

"But I don't want you to leave me alone!" Her hands fastened on his back. Fourteen points of heat digging into his skin.

"This is crazy," Alexei muttered. He was talking to himself, rather than her—trying, one more time, to talk himself out of his obsession with this beautiful, strong-minded ... *alien*. "We're not even from the same planet."

"So what? I want you. Is that correct?"

Alexei laughed breathlessly. "Oh yes, that's correct, honey."

*

Jack floated in the axis tunnel, glaring at Brbb. One of the water thieves also floated in the tunnel. Jack had untied it. It had been hanged by the neck and slammed into the lattice at car-crash speed, but it still wasn't dead. Rriksti are tough. Blood trickled from its ears and foamed on its lips. Same color as human blood. Blue on the inside, red when it got outside of the body. Jack was sick of seeing it.

The other three thieves were still wrapped around the outside of the axis tunnel. Brbb's mates had hung them from the ropes while Jack hurried up here to save the first one.

Down below, rriksti crowded the walking track. Their upturned faces looked like daisies in the jungle, blurring around.

"All right, fun's over," Jack said. "Get your lads up here. If you all work together, you should be able to save them."

"Make Nene do it," Brbb grumbled.

Nene had refused to help, on principle. Jack respected its ethical stand, while finding its refusal inconvenient, not to mention a bit heartless. However, Nene wasn't the only rriksti with sorcery in its fingertips. "You'll just have to do it yourselves," he told Brbb. "Hurry up!"

"All right," Brbb muttered. Its hair swirled. "If this ever got back to the Temple," it said darkly, "Nene would have her clerical certification suspended."

"Your Temple is four and a half light years away," Jack said. "Thank God." He drifted forward to check on the nearest thief hanging outside the tunnel. The child. Its eyes were half-open, unseeing. Was it already too late? "Your culture stinks," he informed Brbb.

"This was a *serious crime,*" Brbb said. It clearly thought Jack a moral retard. The feeling was mutual.

However, Jack was in no mood for a punch-up, especially not if it turned into eight on one. That's why he had thought of a different, cleverer way to spike their grisly agenda. He glanced out of the axis tunnel, and sighed in relief. The jungle was sliding past at a noticeably slower rate. Giles had done it.

"We're spinning the hab down," he told Brbb. "So no more hangings today, I'm afraid."

Brbb startled. It spreadeagled itself on the lattice and stared down at the jungle.

"Hope you tied down everything that won't fly well," Jack said, enjoying Brbb's dismay. He'd ordered the civilians to tie everything down at the beginning of the crisis, knowing they would have to spin down the hab sooner or later. The hydroponic tanks and trays had already been covered with watertight lids, to deter theft, not that it had worked.

As the RPMs ticked down, Jack reached through the lattice to free the child and the other two thieves. "Mostly dead, or all dead?" he muttered to himself. Brbb's slipknots defeated his fingers. "I need some help here! Where are your mates?" he shouted in frustration.

"There," Brbb said, pointing.

As the hab's rotation slowed to a crawl, the jungle stayed on the floor, but all the people on the walking track and around its borders rose into the air. They rose in knots. Each knot had one of Brbb's friends inside it. Rriksti fists rose and fell. The civilians were punching the shit out of the *Krijistal.*

As spin gravity lost its hold, the mobs broke up in confusion. The civilians dived for handholds. Their victims floated unmoving in the air.

Jack clutched his head, gut-punched by horror for the second time today. He saw too late what a terrible mistake he'd made. *Two* mistakes, in fact. He'd set the *Krijistal* to lord it over the civilians as rule enforcement officers … and then he'd forthrightly criticized Brbb's methods, giving the civilians the impression that it was open season on them.

Jesus. He couldn't have fucked up worse if he'd tried.

"Nene!" he shouted. "NENE! This is an order! Need your help, NOW!"

Brbb spidered down Staircase 6 to help its friends. Smashing Jack's face in could wait, presumably.

Nene emerged from the keel tube with Alexei. Jack noticed that the man and the rriksti were holding hands, but assigned no importance to the fact. The shrilling of Rristigul in his headset was getting unbearable. The combination of an unannounced spin-down and mob violence had pushed the situation to the edge of chaos. "Sorry, Nene. You've got to help the *Krijistal.*" He pointed down.

Nene ignored his pointing finger. It gazed at the mostly-dead water thieves. "Do you actually understand what they were planning to do to these poor people?"

"Yes!" Jack said. "They were going to heal them, then

punish them, then heal them again, and punish them some more! It was a standard feature of law enforcement on your utterly vile planet! As the ranking cleric, you were supposed to help with the healing bit. Well, the whole thing's gone sideways I'm afraid. The civilians mobbed them—" he pointed at the *Krijistal* floating around the tops of the suizh plants. "I don't know how badly they're hurt, but I need them! I can't keep order without their help, precisely because they are such bastards! So save their lives, if you don't mind—NOW!"

Alexei headed for the stairs. He, having served in the Russian air force, saw Jack's point. Nene stayed put. "What about them?" Its bio-antennas indicated the thieves.

"Oh Jesus," Jack said. "I don't fucking know!"

Keelraiser should've been here. Jack shouldn't have had to be managing this crisis alone, or rather mismanaging it.

"Here, here's what we'll do about them." He pulled his blaster off its strap.

He had to take the *Krijistal's* side to stop the situation from spiraling into chaos. He couldn't let his own squeamishness stop him from doing what a commander's got to do. But he was damned if he'd go along with the sadistic rriksti concept of justice. On sailing ships in the old days, captains used to shoot thieves and mutineers outright. One of Jack's own ancestors on his mother's side had captained a privateer in the American Civil War.

Holding onto the lattice with his left hand, he aimed and shot at the first thief. Then the other two adults. The child last of all. Born in space. Born to die in space. The invisible beam drilled a hole in each bloodied forehead.

It's easy to shoot well when your targets aren't moving. Pink steam—body fluids superheated by the laser—jetted out of the holes. Each corpse moved away, like tiny rockets spitting bloody exhaust. The ones still hanging by their necks floated away from the axis tunnel, ropes gradually unspooling. Jack felt like crying.

"There," he said. "Problem solved."

Nene had left the axis tunnel while he was shooting. The rriksti did that. They either hit you or they walked away. Nene was already halfway down the stairs.

"Jack?" Skyler spoke in his headset. "Hriklif's been monitoring the mass spec, and it just told me—"

"What's gone wrong now?"

"Nothing!" Skyler said. "The fuel cells are full. We can start giving people water!"

CHAPTER 19

One of the outside water tanks was fine.

The other one had a spray of holes in it so small that Jack and Alexei only found them after forty-five minutes' fingertip inspection.

Jack poked a gloved finger into the largest hole. "Pebbles," he said over the radio. *"Several* pebbles. The water leaked away bit by bit, and the stupid bloody computer kept pushing more water through the cross-connect."

He pushed off the hull with his fingertips and gazed into space. The *SoD* seemed to hang immobile in the darkness. But they were actually rushing towards the sun at 103,000 kph. And somewhere ahead of them ... *far* ahead of them ... was the *Lightbringer*.

You nearly got us this time. But we're still alive. His breath sighed in his helmet. *Still alive.*

Alexei opened the damaged tank's external valve port, which had not been touched since the *SoD* was built in Earth orbit three years ago. *"Blin!"* he swore as a cloud of dust rose into his face.

"Holy shit," Jack said. "The bladder."

Alexei explained to the rriksti, "The tanks were self-sealing. They had elastomer bladders. But all that time we spent around Europa must have wrecked the molecular bonds of the elastomer. So when it had to seal ... it just crumbled."

"What is elastomer?" said Brbb.

"A non-smart material," Jack said bleakly.

"Every day," Brbb said, "I am more amazed that you ever reached Europa."

Jack swung a mock punch at Brbb. It darted away, its hair dancing in the psychedelic coating of its spacesuit. "With your permission, shall we patch the tank now?"

"Yes," Jack said. "Alexei and I will be down there, making sure this doesn't happen again."

The two men flew 'down' from the rim of the main hab to the bridge module. Both of them, like the rriksti, wore tethers. Alexei had abandoned his Orlan EVA suit for a rriksti spacesuit. Jack still hadn't given up his Z-2, but he was regretting his stubbornness. Dried blood stiffened the sleeves of his suit liner. Scratchy. And the lingering smell of his own blood cast a shadow on his mood.

He hooked one boot through a grab handle on the outside of the bridge module, and shook out a 3-meter sheet of insulation backed with reflective silver Mylar.

"Why do you think they gave us this stuff?" Alexei said.

"Fuck knows. I used a bit of it to insulate my camera when I took pictures of Jupiter. Remember?"

"You should take pictures now." Alexei pointed at the rriksti swarming above the rim of the main hab. The colors of their suits vibrated against the blackness. Sparks sputtered. Jack felt a pang of worry—was he *really* letting Brbb use his precious welding kit?

Yes, he was, and it was all right. Something had changed between him and the *Krijistal*. Perhaps they were gratified that he'd upheld their judgement on the water thieves. Or perhaps their experience of being set upon by the civilians had humbled them. All of them had recovered from the brutal beatings they received, thanks to Nene, but it had been touch and go for Difystra and a couple of the others. Anyway, their attitude towards Jack had changed, as if they accepted his authority at last.

Jack was not happy with the high price they'd all paid for this relative peace and harmony. But he might as well enjoy it while it lasted.

"If Mission Control could see this, they'd kill us," he said lightly. "They're very unhappy that we even brought the rriksti along in the first place."

"We had no choice," Alexei said.

"No, of course we didn't. It's easy for *them* to say from millions of miles away that we ought to have left them to die."

Alexei was silent for a moment. Jack thought he might be about to hear something from his friend, some kind of confession or ... he didn't know what. Something that would bridge the awkwardness between them.

Instead, Alexei began to sing. "It's a hard knock life for us ..."

Jack joined in before he remembered where the song came from. "It's a hard knock life for us!"

"Instead of kissing, we get kicked!" Alexei took the other end of the insulation sheet. Floating into space, he used his wrist rockets to maneuver around the outside of the bridge module to the *SoD's* radar dish. The wrist rockets—rriksti tech, although there was no reason NASA couldn't have developed something similar, if they didn't have their heads up their arses—puffed out compressed CO_2, allowing Alexei to change direction in freefall. He landed on the far side of the radar dish. Grasping its mounting, he said, "Glue gun."

"Catch."

"Fuck!" But Alexei made the catch. Jack had known he

would. He glued the Mylar to the edge of the radar dish, pleating its inner edge as he went, so that it formed a skirt around the dish's edge, doubling its size. "It's a hard knock life for us ..."

"Instead of treating, we play tricks!" Jack improvised, as he unfolded another Mylar sheet from his satchel.

They needed two sheets to go all the way around the outside edge of the first piece. This turned the radar dish into a huge cone, reflective inside. It wobbled above the bridge module like an upside-down umbrella.

"Now we've just got to shove a large current into it," Jack said happily.

The *Krijistal* had finished patching the tank. Jack double-checked their work. "Well done. We can start refilling the tanks."

Two by two, they waited out the airlock cycle and doffed their spacesuits on the bridge.

"Were you really singing a Broadway song?" grinned Giles, who'd been monitoring their EVA. "I thought I was the gay one."

"No, you're the one who thinks Slayer is the greatest band in history." Jack flipped him a rriksti salute. "Spin the hab up again. Slowly, we don't want to waste the hydrazine. Once *that's* gone, it's gone."

Naked rriksti filled the bridge, bouncing around in the air. "Hydrate!" Brbb cried, shooting a stream of water into the air from a squeeze bottle.

"Christ!" Jack shouted, fearing for the electronics. One of the other rriksti caught the whole stream in its mouth. Their laughter crackled from the intercom.

"Gimme some!" Alexei said, joining in the horseplay. Jack

smiled wistfully. It was good to see everyone cheerful. But the contrast with his own mood reminded him of the task still hanging over his head. This wasn't over yet, for him.

He pulled on shorts and gathered his Z-2 under his arm. "Right. I'm going aft …"

He thought no one heard him, but Giles caught him up at the keel tube. "Where are you going?"

"To the Cloudeater."

"That's what I thought. I wonder if I should tell you …"

"Oh come on Giles, now you've got to."

"OK. The newest word in my dictionary is *Krijistal*. We thought it's a word for special forces. Chuck Norris, right?" They both smiled at the old joke. "But the meaning of Rristigul words varies depending on the amplitude and frequency, as you know. They sometimes talk on more than one distinct frequency at the same time, and this locates the word on a spectrum of meaning. So in one sense *Krijistal* does mean Chuck Norris. In another sense, it means something close to 'rule enforcer,' as you've been calling them. But the basic, single-frequency meaning of the word is just *military*. So there are not eight *Krijistal* on the *SoD*. There are nine. The ninth is Keelraiser."

"Ah," Jack said. "Good to know. Thanks, Giles."

He flew aft through the axis tunnel. In SLS, water gushed out of the overflow spigot for the algae tanks. Rriksti jostled joyfully, collecting the precious liquid in plastic sacks. As Jack passed, they seemed to cringe. A babble of Rristigul washed through his headset and then fell silent. He'd saved their lives, but at what cost? Were they grateful to him, or did they resent him for handling the crisis so badly?

In the storage module he donned his scratchy, smelly Z-2 once more.

"Where's Keelraiser?"

They'd done a nice job with the passenger cabin of the *Cloudeater*. Two long rows of cots occupied the center of the cabin, where Jack and Keelraiser had ripped out the seats. Thirty-odd patients lay strapped to the cots, hooked up to IVs. Their dark eyes followed Jack yearningly.

"Somewhere in the crew area, I assume," said Cleanmay, the rriksti doctor. Its phrasing conveyed that it did not give a flying rat's posterior about Keelraiser's whereabouts.

"Thanks."

"Do you want help?"

Jack hesitated. Was Cleanmay offering to help him deal with Keelraiser? Was it trying to tell him he was putting himself in danger?

The doctor motioned towards the back of his Z-2, and Jack realized it had only been asking if he wanted help doffing it.

"Yes, thank you."

Cleanmay unlatched the rear entry port. Hot, damp, salty air flooded in. Jack had actually been going to keep the Z-2 on, but he realized it was better this way.

He pulled on the shorts he'd brought with him and jammed his headset on. Carrying the Z-2, he flew forward over the left block of passenger seats. The door to the crew area was a wall. He had to wave his hands all over the place to trigger the autorip sensor, and when it opened, he was staring at *another* wall that shouldn't have been there.

He pushed on it.

It hinged forward, and a dirty white blade sliced down like a guillotine.

CHAPTER 20

Jack sprang back, heart racing.

A guillotine? No, just a shelf.

Furniture blocked the corridor on the other side of the door. Ropes and glistening wodges of clingfilm suspended disassembled panels of feather-light plastic, like a rriksti-sized spiderweb with dirty dishes and cups caught in it. Jack's feet dislodged the rubbish as he shoved through the barricade.

The autorip sealed behind him with a squelch.

He breathed shallowly in the briny humidity. The indirect red lighting made the ceiling of the corridor glow, as if a red sun had just slipped beneath the horizon. The furniture Jack had dislodged drifted around the corridor, bumping gently into the walls. Apart from that, a stale, crypt-like silence reigned.

He found himself shaking. The sick, electrified feeling in his gut reminded him of long-ago combat missions in Iraq. He also remembered something that had never happened: his planned quest into the bowels of the *Lightbringer,* in search of an unknown alien menace … Before he and Alexei could put that plan into action, the alien menace had made itself known by stealing the *SoD's* water and killing Kate.

Ahead of him, a slit yawned in the wall. Keelraiser floated out of the computer room. It wore shorts and a frayed tank top. It was not holding a gun or a tungsten-bladed sword or anything. "Come in," it said without any sign of surprise.

It floated back into the computer room. Jack squeezed in after it, gritting his teeth. He had to tug on his Z-2 to get it through the door.

This 'room,' scarcely bigger than a wardrobe, was actually the operator's chamber of the *Cloudeater's* quantum computer. Noisy fans sucked away the humidity. There was hardly enough room in here for one person, let alone two. Jack held his Z-2 in front of him like a shield.

"Well, it's over," he said cheerfully. Who was he kidding? It wasn't over. Nothing was over. And his hearty tone was a complete pose.

"You handled it well," Keelraiser said.

"I fucked it up completely. I killed four people."

"Yes, I heard about that."

"How?"

"Everyone was talking about it."

Jack recalled that rriksti voices went through walls, unless they were specially coated with radio-frequency shielding paint. They had a very different concept of privacy. So even Keelraiser, locked up in here like a prisoner, would have heard the scuttlebutt.

"Those were the only deaths throughout the whole crisis," Jack said. "So yeah, I think I could have handled it a little better."

Keelraiser's hair danced. "Brbb was apparently very impressed. That lot all think you've really got the right stuff now."

"Oh, brilliant. I *thought* that might be why they're finally playing nice. Wonderful. That makes me feel a lot better."

The crisis had left Jack charged up like a battery with strong emotions. Fear was only one of the faces emotion could wear. He rubbed one hand over his face, struggling to cope.

SHIPLORD

"Are you all right?" Keelraiser said.

"What would you have done?"

"Me?"

"You're *Krijistal*. It just means military, right? You've had the training. You know the rules."

"I *broke* the rules. No one cares what I think," Keelraiser said crisply.

"I just feel like utter shit about this."

"Come back and talk to me when you've murdered thousands."

Stung and embarrassed by the repulse, Jack glanced away. He tried to make out what was on the screens. It all looked like smudgy brown and pink shadows to him. Rriksti eyes detected contrast at far lower lighting levels than human ones could.

Pulling himself together, he said, "Did you get any camera footage of the projectiles? I know they'd have been too small for your telescope to detect."

"Yes. I've gone through my external camera footage frame by frame. Three projectiles hit the main hab, and another seventeen passed by at distances from one to seven meters. None were larger than one centimeter in diameter. Based on their sphericality, they were ball bearings."

"Ball bearings!"

"Yes."

Jack laughed hollowly. "Have they run out of icebergs, or what?"

"They've changed tactics. The icebergs didn't work. This … almost did. It would have worked, if not for you."

"Well, it won't work twice. I've turned our radar dish into a paraboloid jammer." Jack's voice gathered energy as he described the hack he and Alexei had implemented with the Mylar-backed insulation sheets. It was based on the DIY radar jammers that speeders on Earth used to thwart the cops. "It'll swamp their radar with a more powerful signal, like shining a spotlight into their eyes. I only wish I'd done it before. I *thought* of it before, but the trouble is, if I'm using the *SoD's* radar set as a jammer, I can't use it for anything else."

He would be blind. Completely dependent on the *Cloudeater's* instruments. That's why he had resisted doing this so long.

"But I think we've no choice now. We can't survive another hit like that."

"There's not much targeting involved. These projectiles were just dumped in our path."

"But what'll come next? It might be worse than ball bearings. All in all it seems a good idea not to let them paint us with a targeting laser."

"Agreed."

"So that's what we've done, but now we've got no radar. So I'll need to use your radar …"

"It is strange talking to you. I haven't talked to anyone since we left Europa."

"…to track the *Lightbringer*, as well as for telemetry when the *Victory* comes within range."

"Yes, the *Victory*. It's on course to make a tight swing around the planet you call Mars."

"So you have been listening to our comms. I suppose you can hear everything we say to Mission Control through the radio hook-up."

"Yes. It's something to do."

"You must have been bored, stuck in here."

"There's always television."

"The news is crap. It's all the *Lightbringer,* all the time."

"The internet is worse."

"You've actually been browsing the internet? It still takes fifty minutes per click."

"I've got nothing but time."

There was a short silence.

"We can't go on like this," Jack said, and at the same time Keelraiser said, "I've even been emailing … what? What did you say?"

"I can't go on like this," Jack repeated, "not knowing what the hell happened. You broke the rules. All right, but which rules? What rules?"

"The rules," Keelraiser said. "It's a religious thing, for God's sake. Do you know what the *Krijistal* are?"

"The Darkside military …"

"A religious order. The cult of Ystyggr is the Darkside military is the *Krijistal,* and I should frankly never have gotten in, but having got in, I was bound to abide by the *Krijistal* code of conduct. Which says, among other things, that one shouldn't attack an opponent who is unarmed."

"Hey, we've got that rule, too," Jack grunted.

"There you go, then." Keelraiser's mouth was shut in a tight smile—not actually a smile, of course, but a sign of tension in the rriksti. "It wasn't reciprocal, was it?"

It most certainly had not been. *Why don't you hit me back? Why don't you hit me back?* Jack loosened his arms from the bundled-up Z-2 he held in front of him. Nerve-endings thrummed as his adrenal system responded to the vibes of tension and hostility he was getting from Keelraiser. He caught himself gauging how much room he'd have in this confined space to swing his fists, and realized in horror that part of his own motivation for coming here, hidden even from himself, which was why he'd subconsciously dreaded it so much, had been to hit Keelraiser back. It deserved to pay for locking itself up in here and leaving Jack to handle the crisis alone.

This realization absolutely gutted him, not least because it revealed how habit-forming his ritual exchanges of blows with Brbb and company had become. He had come close to accepting that violence was the only way to deal with the rriksti. Considering this idea consciously for the first time, he repudiated it. He opened his arms, letting the Z-2 float free. "I just want to know *why* you did it!" he said desperately.

Keelraiser caught the spacesuit before it bumped into the screens. "Though I am native here and to the manner born, it is a custom more honour'd in the breach than the observance."

Jack laughed, diverted by the Shakespeare quote. "Benefits of sixty-five years of watching television."

"Only about eight. I slept most of the way."

"How old are you, anyway? Do you count the years you spent asleep?" Jack knew that the *Lightbringer* had been equipped with cryosleep facilities. That's how the infantry had got here. They had ended their journey without ever waking up, when the *Lightbringer's* midsection exploded. More senior crew, like Keelraiser, had slept and woken off and on, according to their preference. Eskitul, apparently, had spent a full third of the journey awake, watching TV.

"We decided not to count the years of hibernation," Keelraiser said. "That makes me one thousand, three hundred and twenty-seven years old."

"Rriksti years are like one of those currencies where you need to be a millionaire just to go shopping." Jack knew the conversion, though. Eleven Earth days to a rriksti year. So Keelraiser was forty. It jolted him to realize Keelraiser was younger than he was, if only by a couple of Earth years.

Handling the Z-2, Keelraiser said, "Why did you bring this in here?" Its long fingers delved into the suit's thigh pockets. Before Jack could respond, Keelraiser plucked out the only item in either pocket: a scrap of blackened metal. "What's this?"

Jack's jaw tightened. "Right, I was going to show you that."

"Is it a silicon device?" That was how the rriksti referred to human chips, to distinguish them from their own semiconductors, which were made of *diamond,* thank you very much.

"Yup."

Keelraiser set the device between its teeth. "It tastes good. A bit burned."

"It's a tank sensor."

"Oh." Keelraiser removed the ruined sensor from its mouth. The device floated above its palm, a tiny lump of carbon that had nearly cost 310 lives.

"I recovered it when we repaired the tanks. It's completely slagged." Jack flushed as he relived that bleak discovery. "We'll have to investigate why it failed high, but it must have been fried in the first or second HERF you hit us with. Or maybe the third."

"We were trying to stop you from reaching Europa," Keelraiser said. "It makes me shed to remember it."

"At least you're not still trying to pretend the HERFs were just your way of saying hello," Jack snapped.

Keelraiser's hair washed around its face. "I'm sorry!" it shouted. "Yes, we tried to kill you! No, we did not succeed! I'm fucking sorry, and I don't know if I'm sorry for trying, or sorry that we failed! There you go! I'm being *honest* with you!"

The last words scaled up to a high, squealing note that went straight through Jack's head. This sometimes happened when the rriksti were not careful how they tuned their voices. It was nails on a blackboard, a jackhammer digging into your brain.

Jack lost it.

CHAPTER 21

That fucking noise just really set Jack off. He grabbed Keelraiser by the hair and dragged it out of the computer room.

Nothing hurt the rriksti quite as much as grabbing their hair. It was completely out of bounds. Keelraiser screamed and screamed.

Out in the corridor, Jack switched his grip to Keelraiser's arm. Kicking off from the wall, he towed it down the corridor and over the ruined barricade in front of the door. The wall ripped. They shot out into the hospital.

A mosaic of rriksti faces turned their way. Jack glimpsed Brbb at the far end of the passenger cabin. It must have come rushing over to make sure he wasn't violating any rules. Until this moment, Jack hadn't been absolutely sure what he was going to do, but now he understood that he had no choice. As the *Krijistal* started towards them, Jack braked by dragging a foot against the ceiling. He let go of Keelraiser, freeing his right hand, and grabbed its vest in his left hand. He pushed it in the chest, open-handed, and then drove an upper-cut at its face. His fist thudded into Keelraiser's cheek.

It's not easy to beat someone up in zero-gee. You can't put your weight behind your punches when you weigh nothing, and you can't get the bugger down on the ground when there is no 'down.'

However, Jack had mastered certain rriksti tactics. He wrapped his legs around Keelraiser's slender waist, so that it couldn't float away, and punched it hard in the face several more times.

"If I have to walk around looking like Joseph's fucking

Technicolor Dreamcoat, you can, too, dickface."

Every time his fist connected with Keelraiser's flesh he got a jolt of emotional and physical satisfaction. At the same time he hated himself for doing this. He hated himself even more for enjoying it.

He waited for Keelraiser to fight back—he'd left its arms free on purpose, so that it could have a go if it wanted—but concluded after a couple of minutes that it wasn't even going to try.

Blood glistened on Keelraiser's lips, black in the dim light. It must have cut the inside of its cheek on its own teeth.

"Oh, look at that," Jack said heavily. "You're bleeding."

He kicked Keelraiser away.

Even the goddamn patients sat up and applauded.

Rriksti applause was a combination of high-frequency whistles, which Jack couldn't hear, having lost his headset in the fight, and foot-stamping, which couldn't be done in zero-gee. But he got the gist from the heels of seven-fingered hands going up and down, thudding into pillows.

He looked around for his headset. Brbb gave it to him. If rriksti had any amount of facial mobility, the blue-haired giant would've had a shit-eating grin on its long face. "—took you long enough," it said.

"I know," Jack said. "What can I say? I'm human."

Difystra and Fewl, two of Brbb's mates, laid Keelraiser out on a cot. They fastened the straps around its limbs with an efficiency that recalled cops restraining a suspect. Laying their hands on Keelraiser's head and abdomen, they froze in stiff-backed postures. Other rriksti crowded around to join in. They were healing Keelraiser, whether it liked it or not. Within a few minutes its bruises and cuts would hurt less, if not vanish altogether, as the magical antioxidants secreted in their palms speeded up cellular-level tissue repair, or whatever the fuck really happened when they got extroverted. Jack had initially thought it was some kind of New Agey energy transfer thing, and liked it no better since he had come to understand that it was both less and more than that.

He said to Cleanmay, "Sorry about that. Didn't mean to disturb the patients."

"Not at all," the rriksti doctor said. "This kind of thing is great for morale."

"Are you serious?"

"Why wouldn't I be?"

Shaking his head, Jack went forward. He left a table jammed in the auto-rip so that it couldn't close again, to show them all that the crew area would no longer be used as a moral leper colony with a population of one. He drifted into the cockpit, and settled into the commander's seat.

The illusion of variable polarization sealed around him. He seemed to be floating in space, unprotected against the vaccum. The sun rushed toward him like a car with one broken headlight, the illusion of toppling motion no lie at all, given how fast they were travelling, but inconsequential on the scale of the solar system, let alone the universe.

Jack's heart thudded, saliva collected in his mouth, and sweat started out all over his body. He felt trapped in himself, as if he were a tin can, with walls as impermeable as the hull of the *SoD*, hurtling, like the ship, through a hostile black void.

A speck floated across the sun. Jack reflexively reached out and caught it. It was that slagged tank sensor. How had it got up here? Well, things floated.

He put it between his teeth and bit down. The taste of metal filled his mouth. He imagined what it would be like to be a rriksti, to think this tasted good, to feel his sharp teeth crunch into the transistors.

CHAPTER 22

Hannah prepared for the weekend with care. She selected her hiding-place and began moving food and drink into it a couple of days in advance. Wander through the garden, pocket a few potatoes. Hang out with Figgrit in the kitchen, leave with a handful of jerky. She had a mismatched collection of bottles. She filled them all with water.

Just water, sadly. She'd have to go without booze for the weekend. She accepted the trade-off. Every week, Ripstiggr promised her extra *krak* if she would stay put, but she didn't think it was worth it. Two dry days out of eleven; she could do that, just about.

On Saturday morning, although it wasn't Saturday really, of course, she awoke to a pregnant silence. As she got dressed in her spacesuit she heard, now and again, an ominous hoot.

She sauntered out of her room. There were not many people on the bridge. Those that were there pretended to ignore her—this in itself a deviation from their habitual ironic genuflections—while grinning sneakily at her when they thought she wasn't looking. The expression she thought of as a grin was a drop-jawed gape. 'Sneaky' was when you could see those sharp rows of needles they had for teeth.

"Any new mail for me?" she said to Gurlp, in the comms chancel.

Gurlp wasn't a fan of the weekend either, so she was in an even worse mood than usual. "Check your notifications," she snapped.

Hannah sighed. Whenever she told the chip to show her notifications, a feed of subject lines scrolled over her left eye almost too fast to read. It didn't help that the chip transliterated them, because Rristigul written in Latin script was still gibberish. "Gurlp, I get hundreds of notifications every day. *Thousands.* The ship sends me status updates on every little freaking system that I don't care about, and if there are comms notifications mixed in there, I have no way of filtering them out." She remembered when she had started doing Twitter, on Richard Burke's orders. "It's worse than Twitter."

"What is Twitter?"

"A old social media platform." Hannah rode out a pang of longing for the world she had lost.

"Oh," Gurlp said. "Twitter is defunct. Now is Yell, Barf, Emojigram, Spark, and HiThere, among others."

Back in the early 2010s, technology platforms had exhibited centripetal tendencies; now they all seemed to be fracturing. Even mighty Google had split up into a dozen different browser/search engine combos.

But people still sent email. They even sent email to the *Lightbringer.* The comms team filtered them out of data traffic intercepts by flagging terms like *Lightbringer, Proxima b,* and *Hannah Ginsburg.* Hannah was allowed to read the ones addressed to her, after suitable redactions had been made. It made her miserable but it was a better way to spend the weekend than staring at the walls and listening to those distant, throaty hoots.

"Come on, Gurlp, just forward them to my inbox."

"Fine."

"Thank y—"

"I teach you how to filter notifications."

Gurlp walked her through the gibberish that webbed

her vision. Since Gurlp couldn't see what Hannah saw, she had to spell the Rristigul words and get Hannah to find their matches, as if Hannah were a toddler matching triangles and squares. That's about how intelligent Hannah felt right now. But at last they managed to set up a filter consisting of one word, 'Hannah.'

"Now you only see notifications with your name in subject line or body of email."

"This is awesome! You rock, Gurlp."

"Now you don't bug me anymore."

"Love you too, girl," Hannah said wryly to the blue-haired, seven-foot alien. "Stay safe."

"Is no danger."

Hannah left the bridge with a spring in her step, for a change. It felt great to have done something useful with the Shiplord chip, even if she had needed help to do it.

Her mood dimmed as she descended the curving staircase. Two rriksti dashed past, knocking her into the wall. They grinned at her with glaring eyes. One stuck out his tongue and waggled it like Gene Simmons. Then they charged away.

Down in the service corridor, she met more rriksti who gave her a wide berth, but turned to watch her after she passed. Their eyes seemed to glint redly. She told herself it was just the lighting down here, an indirect red glare from behind the walls that made moiré patterns on the ceiling, like red reflections on water, emulating the sky of Imf before a storm.

She was relieved to reach the garden. The gravity eased off to about 0.2 gees as she entered the hall full of hydroponic tanks stacked up to the ceiling. No sense wasting mass attractors on plants, when they grew just as well in minimal gravity—or did *not* grow just as well, if you lacked sufficient nutrients, which was the problem here.

But it wasn't Hannah's problem. She climbed a ladder past several layers of starveling suizh plants, wrinkling her nose against their rotten-cheese smell. At the top, she trotted along the catwalks into a maze of yfrit. These sugarbush-like plants had large, spiky leaves that looked ashen in the perpetual gloom.

She would've liked to retreat to her own garden, an area in the corner of the hall, enclosed in blackout tarps, where jury-rigged UV lights shone on a little patch of Earth. But that would be the first place they'd look for her.

She parted the leaves, bounced on her toes, and jumped inside a large yfrit plant.

These ugly vegetables usually cradled gigantic flowers with edible seeds in the middle, but this one did not, because Hannah had wedged a table inside it, upside-down.

She sat on the overturned table, hugging her knees, with her weekend supplies piled up around her in a rampart. She remembered playing boats like this with Bethany when they were little. An overturned coffee table their boat, the carpet their sea. Pretzel crumbs scattered on shag-pile waves ...

"Man, I would donate a kidney for pretzels and orange juice right now," she whispered, although it was really Bethany she missed. That plump, giggly girl had grown up into a plump, neurotic woman, who still counted on big sister Hannah to protect her from the pirates ...

Yfrit smelled of bubblegum, which was not so terrible. Nibbling on a raw carrot (leucine! Vitamin K!), Hannah glanced through her fan mail.

Far away, the distant hoots crescendoed.

*

They found her much sooner than she had expected.

Admittedly, she rarely escaped discovery for the *whole* weekend. For the *Krijistal* it was a game, with Ripstiggr as ringleader. He could find her with minimal effort. There just weren't that many places to hide in the bridge, the servants' quarters, and the associated life-support facilities. But Ripstiggr understood that Hannah had reservations about the whole business, and went easy on her. So she usually got left alone until Sunday afternoon-ish.

This weekend, maybe Ripstiggr figured enough was enough. She'd been on the *Lightbringer* for a whole year. (A whole *year?* Oh my God. But it was true.) Time for her to stop playing coy.

Or maybe he was just really feeling it this week.

Or maybe it was the other guys, the low-ranking squirts, setting the pace.

Anyway, she heard them skirmish into the garden only a few hours after she nestled into her hiding-place.

Hooonhh. Hooonh.

Those terrible hoots. The throaty noises tightened her chest. She sat up straight, tense.

Shrieking and carolling in their own language, they spread out. They were searching the ground-floor level of the garden. "Hannah! Haaaaannah!"

Hannah bit her lips. Just when she'd been reading a *really interesting* email! Well, it sounded like they were pretty drunk. Maybe they'd give up and go away …

The rriksti weekend, of course, hinged on booze. They

spent two days getting absolutely hammered, and that's why Hannah was tempted to participate properly, of course she was. Had the ship been maneuvering, had there been any conceivable possibility that the crew would be called on to do their jobs, Ripstiggr would never have allowed these Dionysian revels—so he took pains to assure her. But they were just zooming through deep space, same as yesterday, same as tomorrow, so it was OK to give their biology its due. In fact it helped to keep them psychologically healthy by recreating the cycle that governed life on Imf. *Sure* you don't want to play, Hannah?

Nope. Me: human. You: rriksti. You go on and have your fun. (Although, saying that, she felt bad for Gurlp and the handful of other abstainers.)

Krak, Hannah. All the *krak* you can drink …

No. No. No.

Breathing shallowly, she squatted on her table. Scuffling noises filtered up through the vegetation. They were right below her.

The structure she was perched on began to shake.

Someone was climbing up.

Hooonhh!

With trembling hands, Hannah stuffed her supplies into her backpack. She might be able to evade them. Sneak out of the garden and run to one of her other hiding-places. That would be unsporting, but maybe if she did that, Ripstiggr would get the message that, nope, she *still* wasn't into alien parties.

Yet, despite the impulse to flee, she stayed where she was, like a rabbit hiding in long grass, hoping the dogs would pass her by.

SHIPLORD

The catwalks shook. Tall ripples glided across the water covering the yfrit plant's roots.

The wall of foliage around her ripped from top to bottom, and a rriksti face appeared. Oh, *great*. It was Hulk, as she nicknamed him. His mouth gaped. His eyes widened. He let out a bellow in Rristigul—presumably, "Found her!"—and at the same time, from his throat, not his bio-antennas, issued a wordless hoot.

Hooonh.

The rriksti were mute, but they didn't have to be. Lacking vocal cords, they could not form words... yet they could make sounds by driving air through their larynxes. The first time Hannah had heard these hoots she had found them absolutely terrifying.

Matter of fact, she still did.

Because the rriksti only hooted when they were in musth.

Hulk pushed the yfrit leaves further apart. He leaned into the central cavity of the plant, reaching for her. Hannah cringed away to the far corner of her table. Hulk made a grab for her ankle.

"Leave me alone!" she cried. "I am *Shiplord!*"

"Eskitul used to play," Hulk said. "Not with us, admittedly."

"I'm not playing with you, either!" She threw a carrot at him, realizing that he would interpret this as playing.

He caught it neatly and made lewd gestures at her with it. The carrot was quite a big one but it was dwarfed by the tent-pole in his shorts.

More rriksti approached. The tower shook and swayed. *Hoonh, hoonh.* The hoots reminded her of the time she'd seen a Down Syndrome man lose his shit on the LA Metro. His primal howls had seemed to express some need so great he could not put it into words.

All life on Imf was governed by 11-day cycles. The planet took 11 days to go around Proxima Centauri. Being tidally locked, with zero axial tilt, it had no seasons. But a slightly elliptical orbit caused variations in the weather. Twice a week (a "year" in Rristigul), when the planet was furthest from its cool red sun, the atmospheric pressure dropped, causing the perpetual gales to die down to a breeze. Hannah was no meteorologist, but she figured it was kind of an 'eye of the storm' thing. The skies cleared, birds sang, flowers bloomed ... and rriksti got horny.

She had asked Rripstiggr why they had a two-day weekend, when Imf must logically reach peri-Sharzh *twice* per week, not once.

"You cannot run an advanced industrial society with a four-day work week," Ripstiggr had said. "So we moved to the eleven-day week, with a two-day weekend. People adjusted."

OK.

Hannah was never going to adjust to this. That's what she'd said to Ripstiggr and she'd meant it. Right? Yes, she had.

As the other rriksti closed in, Hulk turned to fight them off. Maybe they'd end up scrapping and forget all about her. Happened, when you were several drinks over the limit.

While Hulk wasn't looking, she scooted backwards and scrambled out of the other side of the yfrit plant—

—straight into Joker's arms.

"Oh boy," he said. *Hooonh*. "My turn at last."

Hannah struggled. "I like you, Joker, but not in that way!"

It wasn't getting through. *Nothing* got through when you were drunk and horny, as Hannah knew all too well. Joker clasped her to his chest, too excited to even try to get her out of her spacesuit. His boozy breath washed over her face. His penis pressed against her lower ribs.

"*NO* fighting on the hydroponic towers!" Ripstiggr's yell cut into their heads. Joker's bio-antennas whipped around. "There are too many people up here! Get down to the ground before the whole thing collapses!"

He stalked towards them along the catwalk, resplendently bare-chested. Joker let go of Hannah and fled.

"Good," Ripstiggr said. "Now it's just you and me."

The game was over. This was how it always ended. Well, there had been that one time when another rriksti got to her first. She hadn't stopped crying for days afterwards. Ripstiggr had torn that rriksti to pieces (literally), and since then it had been understood that although the others might play the game, they were to let Ripstiggr win.

Now he was here, she was safe.

Safe?

Safe from the other rriksti.

But not from her own desires.

CHAPTER 23

Hannah had not really been hiding from Ripstiggr, of course. She'd been hiding from herself.

Now she'd lost the game. She stood and waited for him to come to her. He stepped behind her and pressed the button which made her spacesuit flow away. Suddenly naked, she shivered, despite the heat.

Ripstiggr embraced her from behind. She knew immediately he'd dropped his shorts. She turned around, pushing him away a little so she could look at his penis.

No more Mr. Microdick. The biological phenomenon she called musth—a word borrowed from the periodic testosterone rises in bull elephants—was basically a 24-hour hard-on. That No. 2 pencil had swollen into a rod with a bulgy tripartite tip, so long and thick that you could hardly imagine it fitting inside a human woman.

It did, though.

She felt weak in the knees just looking at it.

Now now, Hannah. Don't drool.

She'd always had a thing for, ahem, *larger* men. That was part of the reason she used to pick up guys at bars. Like a gambler heading back to the track again, she'd always hoped she might strike gold. Or rather, girth. And length.

Love? Romance? Those were for people who didn't have a drinking habit to hide.

With Ripstiggr, she no longer had to hide anything. It was liberating. And if the price to pay was her self-respect? Right now, it seemed worth it.

She reached out and wrapped her fingers around his

amazing schlong. For a fleeting second she remembered Skyler… but he was dead. She was alive. And hurting, and empty. She needed to be filled.

Ripstiggr shivered like a horse at her touch. Stooping, he grasped her butt and effortlessly picked her up. She wrapped her legs around his waist and clung to his shoulders for balance. The distant look in his eyes cued her to anticipate the magic. Within a few seconds, cool waves of bliss started to spread from his hands into her ass. Two birds with one stone. He was pepping her up, and getting her ready. With the best will in the world, she couldn't handle that girth without a bit of prep work.

As the refreshing magic worked on her, the very touch of the air on her crotch became a torment. She reached around and felt for him.

"Naughty, naughty," Ripstiggr crooned. Her un-ladylike ways were catnip to him in the sexual arena, apparently.

"I hate you, you know," she informed him, belatedly reminding herself of why she shouldn't be doing this.

"My Shiplord. Why are you so cruel?" He set her down on her feet and dropped into a kneeling position, which put his face at the level of hers. "Allow me to worship you." His hair danced—he couldn't help laughing at his own joke. His hands pumped more magic into her body. He stared into her little, brown, human eyes, and she knew he was exulting in his power over her. She felt dizzy. The black foliage in the reddish twilight, the catwalk, the disconsolate hoots of rriksti retreating from the garden, all faded, leaving only the feelings.

But the feelings were her enemy.

Ripstiggr was her enemy.

Even if she had allowed herself to be degraded to the point that she enjoyed this, she still hadn't asked to be here, and Ripstiggr was still the inhuman monster from another star system who'd kidnapped her and killed her friends!

Gathering the shreds of her dignity, she pushed him away.

"Wouldn't you rather be with a rriksti female?" she said shakily, stalling.

"There are only five other females on board, and Gurlp doesn't play. Anyway, I like you best."

"What if I say no?"

Ripstiggr seemed to think about it. *"Krak?"* he offered. "Might help you to get in the mood."

Hannah reached through the yfrit leaves, grabbed her backpack, and ran.

*

She stopped at the far end of the garden just long enough to don her spacesuit. The smart material flowed up to her neck and stopped, pushing insistently at the base of her skull. She reached back, uncrumpled the helmet built into the suit, and pulled it over her head. For a scary instant it was like wearing a plastic bag, and then her air supply inflated the fishbowl.

Glancing over her shoulder—half fearing Ripstiggr would pursue her, half hoping for it—she slapped the sensor next to where the water pipes ran into the wall. There was a hatch there so they could service the plumbing for the hydroponics. Backpack bouncing on her back, breath rasping, she scrambled along the top of the bundled conduits. Gravity oscillated as the tunnel curved around the mass attractors. She popped out of another hatch in the wall of the pantry, under the depleted shelves.

Movement caught her eye. She froze, then relaxed. Figgrit was screwing one of the female *Krijistal* up against the pantry wall. Rriksti females went into estrus on the weekend, same as the males went into musth. It mystified Hannah why, after all these years, there were no rriksti babies on the *Lightbringer*.

She tiptoed across the otherwise empty kitchen and slipped out of the airlock, into the wilderness of the sleeper decks.

*

Now where was that email again?

Aha. Here.

Subject: *From A Friend*

Dear Hannah,

You don't know me, but my name is Iristigut. I may be able to help you. If you have any questions about the Lightbringer, *or anything else, please reply to this email. (To reply, just give the verbal or neural command 'Halb,' meaning 'Reply,' followed by your text, and then 'Sgrat,' 'send.')*

Yours sincerely,

Iristigut

P.S. By the way, to search old emails, give the command 'Ilvigt,' search,' followed by your search term.

Floating through the damaged deck levels aft of the bridge, Hannah frowned at the biophotons induced by the chip's electrical stimulation of her brain, which were currently arranged into words. These particular words puzzled and intrigued her.

Iristigut sounded like a genuine rriksti name. It actually rang a bell, although she couldn't place it.

It might have come from some nutjob on Earth. But the nutjobs *asked* questions (invariably redacted by Ripstiggr's censorbot). They never offered to *answer* them.

However, the real revelation was that the *Lightbringer's* messaging system worked a lot like Gmail.

"Ilvigt 'Iristigut,'" she vocalized—and gasped as the chip presented her with a long list of identical subject lines. She opened and read a few at random.

This Iristigut character had been emailing her pretty much every day for a year.

Hope blazed up, tempered by regret that she hadn't seen any of these emails before.

"Halb." She mentally visualized the words, as if typing, and the chip formed them out of biophotons. "Hello, Iristigut. This is Hannah. Questions, I got them. Starting with, who are you? Sgrat."

Maybe she had a friend on board. Maybe one or more of the *Krijistal* shared her reservations about the weekend bacchanals. Maybe ...

Drifting upwards, she twisted the dials of her wrist rockets to float over the glacier that had gushed from the forward potable water tank, and then frozen when the ship depressurized. All the water tanks had shattered on that terrible day eleven years ago. *Muon* cannons? If you say so. She couldn't imagine what else could have caused such devastation.

Calling up a map of this deck, she hurried aft.

She assumed at this point that the rriksti would not pursue her. She'd made her wishes pretty clear, after all. She couldn't stay out here forever—her suit only had a few hours of air tanked up in the life-support backpack, and she'd left all her supplies behind—but if she stayed away as long as she dared, that would give most of them time to score, taking the edge off their frustration. Only a few of them would get to score with the females, but the guys were not above screwing each other. Biology must have its due, after all.

Grimacing, she flew on through the maze of dormitories, and along broader halls dotted with groups of tables and chairs for when the sleepers, one day, awoke. As she turned a corner she glimpsed a dim gleam of light far behind her.

Oh hell!

"Hannah," she heard in her head. It was Ripstiggr's voice. "Hannah …"

She opened the nozzles of her wrist rockets and dived down a side corridor.

A reply from Iristigut popped up at the top of her notifications.

Hello, Hannah! I am so glad you answered my email! If you don't mind, I would rather not tell you anything more about myself. But I promise that I am your friend, and I would be happy to answer any other questions you may have. I want to help you.

Sincerely,

Iristigut

Reading, Hannah almost crashed into a wall. She caught herself with her feet and bounced off. "Halb," she visualized. "Yeah, hey, Iristigut. Do you know anywhere on the *Lightbringer* I can hide where I can lock the fucking door?" She needed to literally lock herself away from temptation. "Thanks in advance. Bye. Sgrat."

She burst out of the darkness into light.

The light of the sun coldly drenched the corridor.

Above her, empty space gaped.

She floated at the bottom of the crater ripped in the *Lightbringer's* side by the explosion of the primary water tanks.

High overhead, jagged teeth of hull plating curled back from the crater's rim, dotted with work lights placed here and there by the repair crew.

They'd been working to fix the damage ever since the *Lightbringer* left Europa, but it sure didn't look like they'd accomplished much.

Knowing how dangerous this was, knowing that the *Lightbringer* was charging through space at thousands of kilometers per second, and that one mis-vectored leap could carry her out into the void, where her life would depend on the CO_2 reserves in her wrist rockets, she flew up the side of the crater, grabbing onto sheared-off structural members and warped deck plating. Tangles of wiring she avoided, although she was pretty sure none of that stuff was live.

What region of the ship are you in?

Iristigut was answering her emails so fast, he couldn't be far away.

If you are amidships, you might try the gunnery deck. It escaped major structural damage, and its door would stand up to anything. Search for 'Libzig Afraf' on the map.

Libzig Afraf, Libzig Afraf …

"Hannah! Where *aaare* you?"

Glancing down, she saw them at the bottom of the crater, like black fish darting at the bottom of a sunlit pool.

Libzig Afraf. There it was!

On the far side of the crater, natch.

Hannah took a deep breath and kicked off. She flew diagonally across the crater, just a few meters this side of where the hull would have been.

"There she is!"

"Hannah, hey, Hannah, don't be a party pooper!"

She flew into the shadow of the overhanging hull plates, and plunged into the black mouth of a burrow in the hull's thickness. The arrows pointed her at a door, not an autorip, a solid steel door, which stood ajar, which had actually been *propped* ajar with a portable generator, because the repair crew had been working in here, but no one was here now, because it was the weekend. Hannah kicked the generator off its magnetic feet. It floated into the hall. She floated through the door, and swung it shut.

Ahhh. Peace at last.

She was in a tiny antechamber, so low, by rriksti standards, she could touch the ceiling with her fingers and the floor with her toes at the same time. Offcuts of thin steel pipe floated around her.

As she turned to float into the next room, the door started to open.

It wasn't locked!

"Halb! Iristigut, how do you say 'Lock this fucking door'? Sgrat!"

A rriksti arm reached through the opening door. Hannah whacked it with a length of pipe. This had been a game before, but now she was genuinely scared. She couldn't tell one rriksti from another when they wore their spacesuits. They were back to being the octopus-headed monsters that had boarded the *SoD* and stolen everything that wasn't nailed down. Well, they looked a *little* bit different right now. Fun fact: rriksti spacesuits do not hide massive hard-ons.

She slammed the door. Rebounding, she jammed the length of pipe she held against the door, and braced its other end against the opposite wall. The door shook and shuddered. Hannah hung on. The pipe prevented it from opening more than a crack.

"Oh, Hannah," Ripstiggr said in her head. "When I catch you, I'm going to give you *such* a spanking."

Her stomach liquefied.

The command is 'If thelele.' I'm sorry! I should have told you that straight away.

"If thelele," she said, staring at the door. Yes, this door, right here. Come on, chip. "If thelele!"

A *thunk* travelled up the pipe to her hands. Doubtfully, she let the pipe float free. The door vibrated. They must be kicking it, banging on it. They wouldn't get anywhere. It was well and truly locked.

Grinning broadly, Hannah transmitted: "I am Shiplord, boys. Woot."

"You can't stay in there forever," Ripstiggr growled. "If you come out and say sorry, we'll let it go. If you don't …"

Hannah made a face as Ripstiggr enumerated the graphic acts he would perform on her. Tuning him out, she floated into the next room. She was trembling with shock. Her bravery had carried her further than she expected. She read the rest of Iristigut's email. He / she had given her a whole list of useful phrases, including how to *unlock* the door. She would need that at some point, as she couldn't stay in here forever. It was just a pocket of vacuum inside the *Lightbringer's* hull.

A row of flexible tubes hung from one wall, where a heavy-duty housing had been removed. Looked like they were replacing the pipes ...

... oh. Of course. This was a *gunnery deck*. Those pipes must be the legendary muon cannons that had almost destroyed the *Lightbringer,* or some of them anyway.

Hannah followed the flexible tubes across the deck to an enormous armor-plated cabinet. It reminded her of the *Lightbringer's* fusion reactor, which she had seen once, when she was first brought on board.

Proton-lithium-6 fusion, as developed by the rriksti, used muons to catalyze the reaction. It followed that they generated muons for the cannons using the same technique employed in the reactor. The nitty-gritty of that technique remained a mystery to Hannah, which frustrated her, because once, long ago, she'd been a nuclear propulsion specialist.

When Ripstiggr first brought her on board, he had asked her to be their propulsion technician. But then he'd gone and killed Eskitul, and suddenly there had been a more urgent vacancy for Hannah to fill.

She stroked a glove over the generator cabinet. A thin fur of ice crystals melted at her touch, becoming floating droplets of water. She licked her lips, realizing how thirsty she was. She would have to head out and face the music. But first ...

"Halb. Hey Iristigut," she visualized. "Any chance you could explain how this muon generator works?"

*

"You were very naughty, Hannah."

Spank.

"You had everyone worried. You might have gone over the side. What would we do if we lost our Shiplord?"

Spank. Ripstiggr's palm came down again with a loud cracking noise on her bare buttocks.

"I said I was sorry," Hannah gasped, face down across his lap. He was sitting on the beast-footed chair in the Shiplord's cabin. She clawed at the carpet with her fingertips as he spanked her again. It hurt.

"Yes. If you *hadn't* said sorry, I would be using the *kuvr*. It is a sort of whip."

Muons decay in 270 milliseconds. She reread Iristigut's last email, printed in bright biophotons on the carpet. *Thus, muon cannons are short-range tactical weapons. They were installed on the* Lightbringer *as anti-boarding defenses …*

Spank. This time, after hitting her, Ripstiggr laid his other hand on her butt. Cool bliss flowed into her hot, stinging flesh. Just as she started to relax, thinking it was over, Ripstiggr withdrew his hand and spanked her again, harder than ever.

She leapt like a fish, yelping.

Her confused nerve endings had interpreted the slap as a pleasurable stimulus.

"This is what we call a punishment cycle," Ripstiggr said.

Spank. Relief. *Spank.* Relief.

After a few rounds of that, she was wriggling on his lap, out of her mind with desire. In between spanks, she fumbled with the drawstring of his shorts.

He stopped spanking her. "Wasn't really a punishment cycle," he whispered. "Real punishment would really hurt.

I was just playing with you."

"I know." She sat up and straddled his lap.

"All the same, don't do that again. OK? It's bad for morale."

"OK." She had completely lost interest in the conversation. She stood on her tiptoes and lowered herself down, inch by inch.

"Hoooonh," Ripstiggr grunted, from his throat.

The key application of muon generation is in nuclear fusion. By applying a gauge field to increase the range of the strong force, we extend the lifetime of muons …

The golden skeins of text broke up as Hannah squeezed her eyes shut in ecstasy.

CHAPTER 24

On October 23rd, 2022, an observer on Mars might have seen a strange new star flash across the sky.

A month later, they would have seen another one.

From 36 million kilometers away, the second star did not look like a star at all. It was, in fact, the drive plume of a spaceship: the *Victory*.

The *SoD* was in the middle of a test burn for their own Mars flyby. Given their absurdly high coasting speed, Jack would have no choice but to use the *Cloudeater's* drive as well. They had to wring the maximum deceleration out of this maneuver. But since the two ships had never blasted together before, they had to get their thrust vectors aligned before cranking up the power.

"Gimbal your engines out some more," he said brusquely over the radio. The *Cloudeater's* thrust was off-axis, so both ships had to gimbal their engine bells to compensate. The *SoD*, as the more massive component of the stack, determined their center of gravity. Right now, Jack was trying to line up their center of propulsion with that center of gravity. *A little bit this way, a little bit that way, and if I get it wrong those bloody welds will break when we go around the curve.*

"How is this?" Keelraiser said over the radio.

"Better …"

Keelraiser was no longer in disgrace. It had resumed normal communication with the other rriksti, making life easier for everyone. But Jack could never forget that he'd liberated Keelraiser from social purgatory by literally beating it to a pulp. He felt that there were dangerous loose ends there, floating around like fallen power lines, and avoided them by avoiding Keelraiser itself.

So he'd been nervous about how this would go. But soon they were working together as smoothly as in the old days, and Jack forgot to walk on eggshells.

"Come and see this," Keelraiser said abruptly.

"What?"

"Come and see this. It's interesting."

"Define interesting," Jack said, with a glance at Alexei.

Alexei cleared his throat and let out a shout. "Oh my God! We're all going to die!"

Jack cracked up. That one never got old. But after the test burn, he left the bridge and crossed over to the *Cloudeater*. "What is it?"

Keelraiser's withdrawn, distant demeanor chilled Jack's anticipation. Hriklif, who'd been collecting engine performance data during the test burn, sat beside Keelraiser in the cockpit. Keelraiser threw a meaningful look at the atomic engineer.

Uneasily, Jack said, "OK, Hriklif, you can go." He folded his arms, floating, waiting.

Even when they were alone, Keelraiser did not meet Jack's eyes. It gestured at the radar imaging screen. "That is the *Victory*. It's lining up for its Mars flyby."

"Yeah. Time for NASA's programmers to earn their pay." Jack spoke with mordant humor. If the programmers faceplanted, and the remote-controlled *Victory* failed to execute its flyby properly, the *SoD* would pay the price. That distant blip contained the Shit We Need ... at this point, the Shit We Really, REALLY Need.

"*Look* at it," Keelraiser said. "Quick, before it turns

end-on to us again."

They'd only ever been able to observe the *Victory* head-on, as it had been travelling towards them since it launched. To be precise, at the extreme distances that separated the ships, they'd only ever been able to observe its drive plume. But as the *Victory* vectored towards Mars, they'd be able to see it in profile for a few short hours.

Jack floated behind the pilot's seat and into the illusory void. Mars queened it over the black velvet night. Near the planet's limb floated a red speck.

"Infrared imaging," Keelraiser said.

The speck seemed to hurtle towards them. It elongated into a blur. The familiar drive plume of its MPD engine, now seen sideways-on. As Keelraiser cranked up the magnification, the *Victory's* heat signature grew bigger on the screen, but it also grew shorter.

"It's turning," Keelraiser said. "Can you see it?"

About to answer that he could see it fine, Jack finally understood what Keelraiser was driving at. The heat signature was shaped like an exclamation mark.

"What's that?"

"The forward region of the ship is emitting heat," Keelraiser said.

"Yes, obviously. It's using waste heat from the reactor to …"

"To do what, Jack? To keep the computers warm?"

Their eyes met for the first time in months, not in understanding, but in shock and doubt.

*

Two weeks later, the *SoD* hurtled into its own Mars flyby.

Jack had once dreamt—hadn't every astronaut?—of going to Mars. But right now he had so much on his mind that he didn't see Mars at all. He didn't see its austere beauty, even when it grew to fill the sky, as large as the Earth seen from the ISS. All he saw was a planet-sized brake.

"Hey Jack." Alexei was staying chill. "What did one Martian say to the other Martian?"

"Wait …" Jack watched the thrust indicator climbing. "Wait … OK. I've got a good one. 'Spaceships are like buses. You wait four billion years and then three of them come along at once.'"

"Nooo," Alexei said. "'I'm hungry.'"

"What?"

"'I'm hungry.'"

"That's it?" Jack started to laugh. "That's not funny."

Alexei cackled. "No, it's not funny! Hee hee hee!"

After 14 months of this they were both easily amused. But the truth was the joke cut a bit close to the bone. Imaginary Martians were not the only hungry ones.

The ruddy light of Mars shone through the portholes onto a bridge stripped down to the steel and aluminum bones. Naked dials and unhoused buttons glittered. The housings had been unscrewed to allow access to electronic components … and their copper and silver content. There'd been plenty of components that had failed in the HERFs, but had never been removed because they had no replacements. Jack had let the rriksti have them. He owed them more than that, and did not complain even when some of the housings vanished, as well. Even the paint was gone off his radar altimeter—it had turned out to have lead in it. Yummy, yummy.

The missing paint made the numbers hard to read. He had not used this instrument once since they left Earth. "God, I hope this is accurate …"

Altitude: 150 kilometers. He touched the rosary that he wore always, these days, around his neck.

"Gimme a star sighting."

Alexei read out the numbers. Jack bit the inside of his cheek. They had to come out of this with rock-solid positioning. Every tenth of a degree mattered, and he didn't trust NASA's numbers. He didn't trust NASA at all right now. Or anyone on Earth, really.

He radioed up to the *Cloudeater*. "Let's punch it harder."

There were only two things they could control: thrust and attitude. And thrust was a dangerous tool that might turn on them. The *SoD's* truss had not been designed to take the strain of a welded-on shuttle and its thrust. No choice, though; got to do this.

"On my mark." Jack poised to precess the axis to angle the *SoD* into a steeper dive towards Mars. The paint was also gone off the metal keyboard he used to control the reaction wheels. He went by touch.

Hriklif, co-piloting for Keelraiser, radioed down. "By the way, we are in the thermosphere. That is not space out there anymore."

"I know," Jack snapped.

"If we go much lower, the bridge will melt off."

"Wouldn't *that* be interesting," Alexei said, rolling his eyes.

Jack recognized that Alexei was telling him to chill, and he was right. With a deliberate effort, he freed up a fraction of his mind from the maneuver. After all, he'd done this before.

He reached for the radio, winked at Alexei, and spoke.

"Hey, Mission Control. You keep bugging us for information. How about this?"

He fumbled for the camera feed. "Alexei, are those loons still out there?"

"They are," Alexei said grinning. He touched the intercom and spoke in broken Rristigul. To Jack, he said, "Bridge camera two."

"Got it."

Jack switched the feed to Bridge Camera 2. A moment later, the view of Mars on the main screen turned into a view of a psychedelically EVA-suited rriksti. Its tendrils whipped in the wind of the Martian thermosphere. It gave a double rriksti salute.

Jack snorted in amusement. "Do that again," he said. He patched the camera feed into the comms transmission. "Here you go, Mission Control. You're going to love this. Pictures of Mars, taken by rriksti lunatics who decided to do the flyby *outside* the ship ..."

*

In New York, in the back seat of an armored SUV screaming along the center lane of the Brooklyn Bridge, Tom Flaherty wondered whether to laugh or explode at the pictures Richard Burke had just forwarded to his phone. "What *is* this shit?"

Far away in Houston, Burke said, "Beats me. Kildare says they are squid selfies with Mars in the background."

The SUV slewed to a stop in the middle of the bridge. "I don't need this. Tell Kildare to quit fucking around and do his job." Flaherty was looking forward very much to the day when Jack Kildare would not be needed to do his job any longer.

Pocketing his phone, he threw his legs out of the SUV's door.

A tsunami of voices crashed over him. Chanting, singing, shouting.

The fierce urgency of now, as a smart politician had once put it, elbowed the *SoD* to the back of Flaherty's mind.

NYPD cars and Humvee ambulances barricaded the bridge, facing Brooklyn.

The Manhattan side of the bridge was completely empty, as no one was trying to *leave*. Enormous banners draped the skyscrapers at the south tip of the island. Legible from the bridge, they said things like "JOIN THE PARTY," "PARTY POOPERS OUT!" and of course "ONE GALAXY UNDER …" Fill in the blank. The deity of choice varied according to fad. The banner Flaherty could see now featured a picture of the Flying Spaghetti Monster, which had mystically grown arms and legs. In other words, it had turned into a squid.

Slipping on sunglasses, Flaherty walked towards the barricade, followed by his Secret Service detail. Yes, his Secret Service detail. He had finally given in. But he didn't let the men in black cramp his style. Police officers looked around from their huddles to greet him. He bumped fists, slapped shoulders. My legionaries.

Helicopters clattered high overhead. Radios squawked. Steam wafted from paper cups of coffee. Those takeout cups with the Greek design—one little piece of New York that hadn't changed.

Everything else had.

Flaherty swung up on the step of a prisoner transport van. He looked across the line of crowd control barriers in front of the vehicles, at a mass of ordinary Americans who had woken up this morning and decided they *had* to be in Manhattan, because the aliens were coming. Because they were scared. Because New York, New York, is the very heart of it. Join the Party.

This particular crisis had started with a meme purporting to come from the *Lightbringer,* which promised that the alien ship would actually land in Central Park. Despite the fact that it was an obvious rip-off of the movie *Independence Day,* thousands believed it.

The ETA of the *Lightbringer* was still three months away, but every park in Manhattan had turned into a shanty town. When looting threatened to rage out of the NYPD's control, Flaherty had decided they had to stop the influx.

Yet the thin blue line of riot shields behind the barriers looked terribly fragile, in contrast to the tidal bore of humanity pressing onto the bridge.

A flurry of paper airplanes fluttered towards the barricade. Jumpy police officers reached for their weapons, then relaxed.

As if the paper airplanes had been a signal, the crowd surged forward. Barriers scraped across the asphalt. The riot cops threw their weight against the crowd.

Flaherty saw to his horror that the walkers were squeezing onto the bridge like toothpaste squeezed through a tube ... but this tube had holes in the sides: the gaps between the struts of the bridge. People climbed up on the guardrails, whooping in excitement, hundreds of feet above the water, their silicone wigs blowing in the wind.

*

"Hriklif. Calm down. It's OK."

The rriksti engineer had been getting very jumpy as the *SoD* thrust deeper into its flyby. Jack suspected Keelraiser was, too, although it would never say it. He racked his brains for something to say that might help.

"Have you ever seen dirt track racing?"

The *SoD* vibrated. The bass rumble of the drive turbines combined with the scary sound of creaks from the truss tower. Martian gravity, atmospheric drag, plus the combined thrust from the *SoD* and the *Cloudeater,* added up to one hell of a structural stress. They might come out of this with bent truss members. But they were not, not, *not* going to die.

"Where was I? Right. Dirt racing."

When Jack said dirt racing he was thinking of the motocross track near Bristol where he and Oliver Meeks had spent many happy Saturdays when they were in uni. Jack hadn't been able to afford a bike of his own, but Meeks, who came from a well-off family, had had a top-of-the-line Yamaha.

"When you're riding into the curve, see, you're typically going far too fast to make it around the curve. So you set up a skid and you accelerate radially to the curve."

In his mind's eye he saw the dirt flying up from the wheels, Kevlar-clad knees scraping the ground. He smelt the exhaust fumes, and chip fat from the van that always set up near the little grass-edged track. He heard the spectators screaming, straining to see which riders made it round the curve.

The *Lightbringer* had made it around.

The *Victory* had made it around.

The *SoD* had to go lower and faster than either of them.

"So that's what I'm doing. Skidding. We're just trying to stay in the groove as long as we can …"

*

The noise from the other side of the barricades redoubled. The Secret Service guys tried to hustle Flaherty back to the SUV.

"Mr. President!"

Oh yeah. That's me.

"Mr. President, we need to get you out of here!"

Meaning they thought the barricade would break. But they were wrong. Flaherty's legionaries would not break.

He stiff-armed the SS goons away and strode between the cop cars. A SWAT team had arrived, fresh from skirmishing with looters on Fifth Avenue. Better late than never. They took cover behind their BearCat, aiming their MP5s at the walkers. Flaherty could remember when the MP5 was the most bad-ass, reliable assault weapon on the block. But the last ten, twenty years, H&K's quality control had gone to shit. The new MP5s were under-engineered, liable to overheat and fail in rapid-fire situations. Flaherty had seen it in Montana, in Louisiana, and in Washington DC, where walkers had occupied the Mall and stormed the White House. The whole world had assumed that was going to be America's Paris, the moment when the country fell into the Earth Party's hands. But Flaherty's legionaries had not broken. They had fallen back in good order and the mob had captured a figurehead who was not president anymore, Flaherty himself having been secretly sworn in overnight.

Since then he'd been trying his damnedest to minimize cop-on-citizen confrontations. But here he saw no choice. No more people could fit into Manhattan.

No more people could fit on this damn *bridge!*

A chopper circled low overhead. Not the NYPD. One of those 'independent' news organizations. Not satisfied with being the news, the Earth Party now wanted to make the news, too.

Thousands of paper airplanes swirled out of the chopper's side door. The downdraft from its rotors immediately scattered them into a multicolored cloud.

Flaherty knew what was going to happen before it happened.

The 'attack' compressed the nerves in someone's trigger finger, and when the guy next to you starts firing, you start firing, too.

Gunfire hammered the air. Flaherty threw himself flat on the tarmac, thanking God he wore his Kevlar today. He craned to see past the Secret Service guys crouching over him.

Men and women standing on the guardrail of the bridge jerked, collapsed, and fell like un-aerodynamic paper airplanes, all the way down to the East River.

Their screams came thinly over the racket of gunfire and helicopter rotors.

"Mr. President. Please. Come on."

The Secret Service hustled him back to the SUV.

"DC wasn't our Paris, and this ain't, either," Flaherty grunted. "It's our own personal Tiananmen Square."

*

"*O Gospodi,*" Alexei muttered. "If I have a bomb I can

drop down crater of Mount Olympus!"

But Jack wasn't looking at Mars. He was seeing Meeks screeching up to the finish line, tearing his helmet off, his black hair sticking up, his face alight with happiness. *OK Jack, your turn…*

Meeks's motocross obsession hadn't lasted long, of course. Bikes didn't deliver enough speed or danger. He'd moved on in short order to auto racing, and then started building his own cars, culminating with the rocket-powered suicide machine that slammed him into the side of a Welsh quarry and disabled him for life.

OK Jack, your turn …

*

On the way back to Trump Tower, which he had inherited as a New York base of operations, Flaherty found a paper airplane on the floor of the SUV.

A message was written on one wing in a girlish hand with heart-dotted i's.

The weekend is coming!

Flaherty snarled, recognizing a direct quote from Hannah Ginsburg. In the latest episode of the Hannah Ginsburg Show, she and her squid buddy had discussed what a fun-loving people the rriksti were, and how they devoted every weekend to partying. Hannah had closed out the transmission with this quote: "Get ready, everyone, because the weekend is coming!"

Kuldeep insisted on reading layers of meaning into this, like he did with all the transmissions. But Kuldeep sometimes overthought things. To Flaherty, the message was simple.

We will annihilate your civilization and enslave your people.

The squids had already made headway on the first half of that, despite not having reached Earth yet. New York had ceased to function as a center of finance and culture. Wall Street had relocated to the secure data centers Flaherty's people set up in the Midwest. Broken windows and steel shutters lined Fifth Avenue.

But even with a hundred people lying dead on the Brooklyn Bridge, and the Coast Guard fishing more bodies out of the East River, Flaherty refused to give up.

Instead, he'd double down.

On the *Victory*.

Jack Kildare wasn't going to have it all his own way much longer.

CHAPTER 25

The bridge hadn't melted off, the welds hadn't given way, and most importantly Jack hadn't smeared the *SoD* across the side of Olympus Mons, so all in all, not *that* interesting a maneuver.

As he rose from his seat, Alexei stopped him. "One to ten."

"Oh, God. I don't know." Jack interrogated his own body. Various muscle aches presented themselves for inspection, as did the pain in his lower spine which he'd been ignoring for weeks. "Six?"

"Do something about it."

"Yeah, yeah. OK."

Once upon a time, the crew had gone through rigorous weekly medical examinations. Now their medical examinations consisted of: *One to ten? I guess about six.*

And their treatments consisted of this:

Flat on his stomach on the floor, in the main hab, beneath an oak-sized yfrit plant, amid the sound of water dripping from irrigation pipes. Jack closed his eyes and braced himself against the waves of cool relief rolling through his back. Brbb squatted beside him with one hand on his lower back. Difystra and Rockshanks, two of Brbb's friends, knelt on Jack's other side, pressing their palms to his kidneys and nape respectively.

All the *Krijistal* were very extroverted.

"Spine cancer again," Brbb said. "No worries. Feel the wrath of Ystyggr, despicable little cancer cells!"

Brbb's voice seemed to come from a long way off. Jack still found it embarrassing and shameful to submit to this procedure, as if he were letting them see something that was no business of theirs: the seeds of cancer sprouting here and there in his body, as a result of the staggering amount of radiation he'd absorbed in the last three years. It *wasn't* any business of theirs. But he couldn't say no to a cure for cancer, for God's sake.

He drifted off on the cool tide of relief, and woke with the taste of garlic in his mouth. He'd gone to sleep on his front but now he was lying on his back. He felt a thousand times better, but still drowsy.

Someone, squatting beside him, said, "They are completely misrepresenting our culture. Parties every weekend! Fun for one and all! What planet do *they* come from?"

Still half asleep, Jack heard only the cross, intense tone of voice, not the words. He prised open his eyes and thought that the person squatting beside him was Oliver Meeks. The shock of black hair, the busily gesticulating hands, the sharp pale jawline—seen from beneath, it *was* Meeks, in the act of taking life by the throat and turning it upside-down to see what it had in its pockets.

Then the illusion broke like a soap bubble, and Jack realized that in the dim sulfurous twilight, the person he'd taken for his dead friend was Keelraiser.

"Oh, I know I'm being an elitist. But honestly. Most of us do *not* behave like that. You've known us for years. Have you ever once seen the faintest suggestion that we might feel an urge to abandon our duties and have—have *orgies?*"

Jack propped himself on his elbows. The really embarrassing thing about accepting extroversion was that one tended to wake up with a stiffy. Glancing down at his underpants, he said ruefully, "No, but I have. Felt the urge, I mean. Hang on until I take a cold shower ... oh wait, there are no cold showers. Right. Where were we?"

"Five million kilometers from Mars," Keelraiser said, getting to its feet. "Our positioning looks good. We will overhaul the *Victory* in thirteen days, although the rendezvous will ultimately depend on successful attitude adjustments by both craft."

"Perfect!" Jack jumped to his feet. "We did it." He raised his hand for a high-five, but Keelraiser backed away.

"That's all I came to say."

Confused, Jack watched Keelraiser stalk away between the saurian stands of yfrit and gnarled bushes of jgzeriyat.

This was the first time Keelraiser had left the *Cloudraiser* since the spring of 2022.

Had it really just come to the *SoD* to report on the success of their maneuver? It could have done that over the radio.

Maybe the ice was beginning to crack. Maybe Keelraiser, too, had a nagging sense of loose ends that needed to be sorted out.

Or maybe it had just come to have a look at the garden.

If so, it must have had the surprise of its life.

This was what a rriksti food garden *should* look like.

Something out of the Cretaceous.

Jurassic Park, the Lost World, fountains and mountains of foliage, all sunk in a gloom that leached the amazing colors from the vegetation. The plants had recovered from the trauma of the water crisis.

It helped that they were no longer exposed to UV light.

Now, orangey-red filters covered the growlights overhead. A torn filter flapped in the breeze from the fans, letting a single star of bright white light shine out. You could have stood a spoon up in the humid gloom, but Jack wouldn't have had it any other way.

He walked aft, through the rriksti village. The shelters were no longer needed as refuges from the light, but the rriksti still lived in them for privacy's sake. Wouldn't you?

Their numbers had shrunk from 306 to 288 in the last six months. Jack nursed every one of those deaths like a personal slight.

It had taken him far too long to work out that the *SoD's* powerful growlights were killing the Imfi vegetation. Yes, Brbb had kept asking him to make the days shorter, but he hadn't understood why. Nor had Brbb, to be fair. It had just been repeating what the smarter civilans told it to say. At last, the penny had dropped: the crazy growth rates of the plants were causing endocrine imbalances. The beautiful bio-fluorescence phenomenon was a symptom of over-stimulation. On the third or fourth generation, the plants had stopped flowering, which meant no more seeds.

The experiment of raising Imfi plants in a terrestrial environment had come to a screeching halt. They'd made filters for the growlights out of recycled upholstery (those Darkside military colors!), and cranked up the heat and humidity even more, coddling the surviving plants until they recovered.

It had been a hungry couple of months. And the crop losses had exacerbated the underlying problem of nutrient shortages.

Jack stopped in the village to chat with the Mars documentary crew, who were editing the footage they'd filmed during the burn. What do you do when you're dying of malnourishment? If you're a rriksti bureaucrat, you make art. Films ('ports'—whatever), poetry, drawings ... they'd even organized a band. Skyler played lead guitar.

Jack came to a circus tent made of stitched-together suizh textile. He lifted the flap and ducked into the light of 'day.' The men had removed two banks of growlights from the axis tunnel and set them up on an aluminum-alloy scaffold above the kitchen table. (Those chopped-up seats really were coming in handy.) Water and electrical lines looped overhead. Towers of spinach and kale, root vegetables, and legumes framed the pantry shelves like bleachers. At the table, Giles was chopping carrots and watching TV on his laptop.

Their original television had had an LED display; that had been eaten. Jack drew the line at letting the rriksti dismantle any of the screens on the bridge, but he saw no harm in letting them have the europium-doped phosphors out of the TV. Everything on the air was crap now, anyway.

He squatted and knocked on the side of one of the fish tanks underneath the table. A tilapia nosed the glass. "Hello, Finny. Shall we have you for lunch today?"

"It is not fish day," Giles said. "I assume we didn't crash into Mars?"

"You assume correctly." Jack straightened up and glanced at the laptop. It had an LCD screen so it was safe from being eaten. He didn't recognize the chyron at the bottom of the screen. The images, however, produced a scowl of recognition. "This must be that video Keelraiser was talking about."

"Tokyo Rose has nothing on la Ginsburg," Giles grunted.

"Don't let Skyler see it." Jack popped a chunk of carrot into his mouth. "I was thinking, though. We should have a party."

"A party?"

"A proper blow-out. After all, we're really at the end of the line. If we make the rendezvous, we'll live. If we don't, we'll die." By *we*, here, Jack meant the rriksti. "So we might as well lift the rationing restrictions and let them eat all the things."

Giles looked at Jack's rosary.

"Nope, they're still not getting this."

"I'm not sure the timing is right for a party," Giles said. "It would be depressing. We have so little of everything left. Perhaps we should wait until we get the Shit We Need."

"Yeah, you could be right," Jack said. He felt a bit intimidated by Giles's calm confidence that they could pull off the rendezvous. It wasn't the technical aspects he was worried about. It was that glimpse of the *Victory's* longitudinal profile he had seen on the *Cloudeater's* radar, which had never been explained. When he asked Mission Control about it, their silence had been deafening.

CHAPTER 26

Twelve days passed in tense anticipation as the *SoD* crept up on the *Victory*. Jack finessed their position, using the *SoD's* hydrazine-fuelled reaction control thrusters and the *Cloudeater's* off-axis thrust. The *Victory* matched his every move. Those NASA programmers were doing an amazing job, despite the five-minute lightspeed delay to Earth …

And pigs roosted in treetops.

Whoever was flying the *Victory*, it wasn't a computer. Jack felt pretty certain of that now. The other men shared his conviction.

By December 13th, the *SoD* was just a few hundred kilometers behind the *Victory*. Their lateral separation had narrowed to thirty klicks.

Jack brooded over the *Cloudeater's* radar returns. On the forward wall of the cockpit, the sun shone bright, almost the same size as when seen from Earth. Earth was a notation bobbling behind the sun, like a small person jumping up and down, trying to be seen. A red polygon winked off to the left, hurtling away from Mars, towards Earth.

"There it goes," Jack sighed. "Decelerating like a motherfucker."

"That's not the *Victory*," Skyler said, behind him.

"No, it's the *Lightbringer*. Remember, the ship that's on its way to snuff out humanity—" Jack turned to look at Skyler, and brought his forefinger and thumb together— "like *this?*"

"I haven't forgotten," Skyler said. "I think about Hannah every damn day, which is actually none of your business."

The alien behemoth was now widening its lead on the *SoD* by the minute. The *Lightbringer* would cut in front of the sun, as seen from the direction of Mars and Earth's orbits. The *SoD* had lost any chance of overtaking it when they swung the *other* way around Mars to meet the *Victory*. The two human spaceships would pass behind the sun, and arrive at Earth five long months from now.

Unless ...

Jack still believed they could have their cake and eat it. But he kept that to himself for now. He felt bad about reminding Skyler of his loss, and didn't want to get his hopes up.

"OK, here we go, the *Victory*." Glancing at the handy English labels that Hriklif had put on the consoles, he threw the optical telescope display up on the wall.

Now that they were practically alongside the *Victory*, they could observe it in near-photographic detail. The resupply ship was a mini-*SoD*, about half the size of the original, with one big difference: no rotating hab. A tapered truss tower ended in externally mounted tanks and the bell of an MPD drive. At the forward end of the ship, the truss tower housed a stack of small modules, like a sleeve full of tennis balls. Lacking a bridge, the ship looked headless.

"Now here's the IR view. We're getting a temperature reading of about twenty degree from all those *cargo containers.*"

"Very weird. Very weird indeed," Skyler said. The sarcastic snap was back in his voice, and Jack smiled.

"Remember we're not doing this for money ..."

"We're doing it for shitloads of money!" Skyler finished. *Spaceballs* had become required viewing on the *SoD*. The men savored the simple, now almost quaint idea of doing crazy shit for *money*. The rriksti just thought Dark Helmet was hilarious.

Alexei radioed over from the bridge of the *SoD*. "It's about time."

"OK. Coming."

Jack and Skyler retraced their steps through the cabin of the *Cloudeater*. Jack averted his gaze from the patients in hospital. Their eyes felt like midges biting him, desperately sucking hope. He couldn't let them down.

On the bridge of the *SoD*, Alexei had been dripping thrust out of the RCS bundles, making final positioning adjustments. Jack took over the controls. The *Victory* was now so close they could see it on the external camera feed. The two ships were like top-heavy scooters laden with live chickens, pigs, and furniture, edging towards each other in an ungainly shuffle, while racing at full speed towards the sun.

Jack took a deep breath. "Ranging."

Using the comms laser—the same comms laser with which he'd been feeding telemetry to the *Victory* for weeks—he triggered a squirt and fed the figures into the targeting computer. 2.2 kilometers.

All four men waited in tense silence.

Jack shrugged. "Powering up the rails."

A low growl started up, almost below the threshold of hearing, and rapidly climbed the scale. The lights dimmed as the *SoD's* railguns sucked power from other systems throughout the ship.

"You have five seconds to come out with your hands up," Jack drawled. He was starting to enjoy himself, despite the nerve-shattering tension, or because of it. "Five ... four ..."

Sitting alongside the *Victory*, they were in perfect position to fire a broadside at the smaller ship.

"Three ... two ..."

Of course, the *Victory* had no way of knowing the railguns weren't loaded with actual slugs.

"One. *Zero.*"

Alexei had loaded some tracer rounds earlier. Jack mashed his finger on the firing button. The bright streaks of fire sped towards the *Victory*.

The radio shrilled.

"For fuck's sake, you maniacs. Don't shoot!"

Grinning, Jack gestured for Alexei to respond.

"This is the *SoD*. *Victory*, who are we talking to?"

"Is that Alexei Dmitrovich? *Ty zhiv? Kak dyela?*" The voice on the other end of the radio broke into a stream of Russian.

Alexei made a face of astonishment. "I know this guy!" he hissed. "It's Grigory!"

"Grigory who?"

"Nikolov. Remember, Jack, he was on the ISS with us. Now he's here!"

*

Yet Alexei's astonishment could hardly have exceeded Jack's when they completed the docking maneuvers, and *three* astronauts floated out of the supposedly unmanned *Victory*.

One Orlan suit—that woud be Alexei's old buddy Grigory.

One Starliner, the new suit NASA and Boeing had developed to replace the Z-2.

And another Starliner with a Rising Sun patch on the

shoulder.

The *Cloudeater* was already docked on one side of the *SoD's* truss tower, so the *Victory* had had to squeeze in on the other side. It had spat out a bouquet of cables with clamps on the ends, powered by cold gas thrusters. Jack had known NASA could build something like wrist rockets, if they ever got off their duff ... The cables had flown through the void, camera-guided, and clamped onto the *SoD's* truss tower. It had been a fun ride for a few moments until the two ships' velocity vectors clicked into alignment. Then the cables were winched taut, snuggling the *Victory* nose-down against the truss tower, with its tail sticking over the bioshield.

"Come on in," said Jack to the three astronauts, floating inside the *SoD's* truss tower, underneath the belly of the *Victory*.

They'd debated how to handle this, and decided on a charm offensive. Keep Grigory ... sorry, Grigory and his two friends ... off balance. Give them a chance to explain themselves.

"Airlock's this way."

As soon as the last of the newcomers entered the airlock, Jack radioed to Brbb. "Coast's clear."

"Roger," responded Brbb. The *Krijistal*, their suits stealthed black, flitted through the truss tower on their way to the *Victory*.

"Be careful," Jack warned. "This might not be all of them."

The *Krijistal* rapidly explored all five of the *Victory's* modules and informed Jack that there was no one else on board. "But there are lots and lots of boxes!" Brbb said happily.

Jack could hear the other *Krijistal* ululating in Rristigul on the channel. Brbb's voice filtered through the clamor. "We are opening the first box ... Yes. YES. Arsenic ... cadmium ... mercury ... copper ..."

Thank you, God. Jack touched his rosary through his suit, offering a silent prayer of gratitude. "That's fantastic, Brbb," he said. "Right. You sort out the cargo. I'll sort out the crew."

Grigory and his friends had a lot of explaining to do. But they had apparently brought the Shit We Need—including the Shit We Really, REALLY Need: micronutrients for the rriksti. That made Jack feel a lot better about the situation. He dropped into the airlock, waited out the cycle, and flew into the storage module.

Surrounded by rriksti, the American astronaut was in the act of clambering out of his Starliner.

Hang on.

Her Starliner.

"Linda!" Jack cried in joyous disbelief.

Trim, elfin-faced, her short dark hair tied back in a ponytail, his old colleague Linda Moskowitz hadn't changed a bit. They'd been in the same NASA class, the Peacocks of 2004. Jack went to hug her.

The look on her face warned him off just in time. Braking his untoward flight, he saw the scene afresh through her eyes.

Rriksti had crowded into the storage module to greet the newcomers. To Linda, they must look like ... well, aliens. And he, Alexei, Skyler, and Giles, probably looked even more horrific—long-haired, gaunt, wearing funkadelic tights. There was no question that they *smelled* worse than the rriksti. The expressions on Linda and Grigory's faces said that whatever warnings they received had not sufficed.

Christ, I could have at least shaved, Jack thought, rubbing his bearded chin. He knew this wouldn't have occurred to him if one of the newcomers wasn't a woman. Linda's femininity reminded him how long it had been since he or any of the other men even tried to uphold the standards of human civilization. Their stunt with the railguns kind of made the point.

The Japanese astronaut unzipped his Starliner and pulled his helmet off. "Hey, long time no see!" he yelled happily.

"Koichi!" Jack exclaimed.

Without the slightest hesitation, Koichi Masuoka flew towards Jack. Remembering that the reserved Japanese astronaut never had gone in for hugs, Jack stuck out his hand. The mid-air handshake ended up with them bobbing up and down like opposite ends of a seesaw, bumping into the ogling rriksti. Everyone laughed, breaking the ice.

"So you made it here after all!" Jack said.

Koichi had been penciled in for Hannah's slot on the *SoD'S* crew until China's rivalry with Japan got him kicked off the mission.

"Better late than never!" Koichi grinned. "How was Europa?"

"Hardly worth getting out of bed for."

The exchange reminded them all of the dark background to their reunion: the four lost members of the *SoD's* crew, and the spiraling political chaos on Earth, including the disintegration of China into 105 separate states, at last count.

Jack shook off the clouds of gloom that threatened to

close in. "Well, come on into the main hab. We've organized a welcome party for you!"

He'd been afraid this would go badly. But the *Victory's* crew had brought the Shit We Need. That was bigger than any political complications that might be lurking in the background. And it was just so damn good to see their familiar faces.

"A party, Jack? Oh, you shouldn't have," said Linda, retrieving her poise.

"Well—we're hoping *you've* brought the food," Jack said with a grin.

It remained to be seen why Mission Control had deceived them by presenting the *Victory* as an unmanned ship, and insisting on radio silence.

But Jack decided not to bring that up right now. "Small world!" comments helped the conversation to flow, and soon they were talking as easily as if no time had passed since the *SoD* left Earth.

The three *Victory* astronauts—no newbies, after all—masterfully played down their undoubted shock when they saw the jungle in the main hab. Giles gave them a quick tour. "You have already seen these," he said when he caught them staring at his hands and feet. "Everyone on Earth has seen them, no? It is not interesting. A cheap technological marvel. Look around and you will see something *really* marvellous: plants from Proxima b! You see, because there is no UV in the spectrum of Proxima Centauri, one of the biggest catalysts for mutation is absent. So evolution has proceeded slowly. It is as if we live among plants from the Cretaceous period on Earth ..."

Yes, the prehistoric appearance of Imfi vegetation was

no accident. The rriksti themselves had reached the evolutionary pinnacle of sapience thanks to the mutagenic effects of X-rays, which they'd understandably come to believe were emanations from God.

They settled on the hill, which was Jack's new favorite place in the hab. Spinwards of the village, the rriksti had repurposed some of their flat-panel shacks to build an artificial hill. It was hollow. Underneath: a cave crammed with edible fungus and apé tanks. Up top: another fungus, as hard as rubber, which covered the 'ground' like rubber barnacles. The rriksti liked to eat it and Jack liked to sit on it. He looked up at the rips in the upholstery filters, shining like stars, and his heart swelled with pride. He loved his ship, and he loved Grigory and Linda and Koichi for getting here, and he even loved the dysfunctional space agencies of Earth, which had organized this miracle.

Grigory got them all arranged in a circle, as if they were sitting in a meeting room, rather than on a carpet of alien fungus in a spaceship.

"We," he said, "are humanity's last best hope."

CHAPTER 27

Grigory Nikolov was a barrel-chested cosmonaut in his fifties. He sported one of those moustaches that only old-school Russians could carry off. He also seemed to be completely immune to self-consciousness or embarrassment. In a quasi-oratorical voice, he intoned, "Only we can save the human race from annihilation." He prodded Jack's knee, holding his gaze. "Only this ship can do it." Prod. "Only *you* can."

Jack scooted back, averse to being prodded, and sensing a set-up. "Well, first of all it's nice to know that the threat's being taken seriously. We've been screaming about it for the last year and a half. It has felt sometimes as if no one's listening. So—good to know that our warnings have been heard."

"The level of cheerleading for the squids in the media is just unreal," Linda said. Her mouth twisted as if she'd tasted something sour. She gazed down at the rriksti village. Angular silhouettes flickered in and out of the dimly lit doors. Jack could smell suizh toasting on jury-rigged hot plates, and hear insects popping in the microwave.

Koichi said, "So it's really just us now. The space agencies. People on the inside of the *SoD* project. *We* know what happened to you. We have failed to get the truth out."

Linda said, "Thank God a few folks in government appreciate the threat." She smiled at Skyler. "Your guys have kept the money flowing, for which many thanks."

Skyler's face wore the Fed mask Jack hadn't seen for many months. "I guess there wasn't enough money to put a radio on that thing?"

"Oh God," Linda said, "yeah. Yeesh. The thinking was, better safe than sorry. Know what I mean?"

Jack dropped his gaze to his ankles, hoping to hide his dubiety. 'Better safe than sorry' was so illogical, he could almost accept it as an example of NASA's typically excessive caution. He resisted the suspicions returning to roost in his mind again, but queasiness settled in as he faced the undeniable fact that Grigory, Linda, and Koichi were lying to them. So much for auld lang syne.

"So as I say, this is our last chance to save our species." Grigory's keen eyes, under heavy gray eyebrows, peered into the gloom, and then returned to Jack. "Those railguns still work, eh?"

"Yes."

"Good. And the ... secret munitions?"

Evidently not such a secret anymore. "Yes, we still have three plutonium rounds."

"Good," Grigory repeated. "Now please listen carefully. We are to fly the *SoD* to the moon."

Jack interrupted. "To the *moon?* What the hell for?"

"To save humanity!" Linda said.

"CELL is our last hope," Grigory said.

"You must be joking. The Earth Party's vanity project?"

"It's an ark," Koichi said. "It can preserve the human species. That's our primary goal—our *only* goal. Nothing else matters."

Jack seriously wondered if they were pulling his leg, until he saw the fiery determination in Koichi's eyes. The Japanese astronaut always had given 200% to achieving his goals. He was serious about this. So were Grigory and Linda.

Jack shook his head, still more incredulous than angry. Objections crowded his mind, creating a traffic jam on the way to his mouth. He settled for saying, "You're acting as if we've already lost. We haven't."

Grigory said, "And you think you can win?" His indulgent smile pricked Jack's pride. "You can defeat the *Lightbringer* all by yourself, maybe?"

Jack was about to launch into a explanation of why he believed he *could* do exactly that, when they were interrupted by rriksti flooding onto the hill and sitting down to eat. At first the interruption annoyed Jack. But after a moment he realized it was just what he needed: a reminder of the good turn the *Victory* crew had already done the *SoD,* and its passengers.

Bowls brimmed with rubbery chunks and greasy slabs, dollops of gelatinous pudding, mountains of crispy seed-pods, and what looked like black popcorn, all flavored with heavy metals from the *Victory*. This was the first really nourishing meal the rriksti had had in years, and it warmed Jack's heart to see them eat. Grigory mustered his courage to try a piece of 'popcorn.' Feeling mischievous, Jack bided his time before telling him that it was actually a microwaved genetically engineered poop-eating insect.

"Don't worry," he added. "Here comes Giles with something for us. Ratatouille, if I'm not mistaken." He stage-whispered, "It's the only thing he knows how to cook."

The party grew rowdy as the *krak* flowed. Scraping the last chunks of ratatouille out of his bowl, Jack watched Grigory, Koichi, and Linda pick at their own food. Their small talk had dried up. Their eyes flickered in every direction at once, and they froze every time a rriksti approached them, although it was only ever to say thank you. Jack didn't feel the least bit bad for them. He'd been thrown in at the deep end, and learned to cope; they could, too.

Out of sight in the jungle, the band started to play. They'd designed an amp for Skyler's guitar with a radio oscillator that transposed its notes into the rriksti frequencies. The resulting wall of sound evoked Led Zeppelin.

Jack waded through the coruscating chords, stepping over people sitting on the floor, to get some more *krak*. He spotted Keelraiser helping itself to microwaved bugs.

"There you are." Jack was a bit drunk. "Come and meet the new guys."

He introduced Keelraiser as the pilot of the *Cloudeater*. Grigory, Linda, and Koichi simply stared at the tall, black-haired rriksti as if it came from another planet. Well, it did, of course, but for fuck's sake. None of us would be here today without Keelraiser. At least treat him like a human being. No, that doesn't sound right. Oh, fuck it.

"So, regarding this fly 'er to the moon scheme," Jack said to Grigory, tipping some *krak* from his own cup into the Russian's. "I *have* always thought I'd like to walk in the footsteps of the Apollo astronauts.. But I would hope it goes without saying that it's completely out of the question, under the circumstances."

Keelraiser said, "Did I miss something?"

"They want us to fly the *SoD* to the moon. Honestly, I wonder what Mission Control's smoking these days."

"Who are you talking to?" Linda said.

"My partner in crime," Jack said, nodding at Keelraiser.

"We're going to nuke the *Lightbringer*. So you see, there won't be any need to dig in on the moon. That's a complete non-starter anyway, for a hundred reasons I could name if you want to talk life-support technicalities. So we'll just save Earth instead. *Much* simpler."

Grigory laughed. He sounded genuinely tickled. "How? We won't even reach Earth until the *Lightbringer* has been there for months, raining death and destruction on the planet!"

Jack grinned, his eyes narrowing to lazy slits. "I suppose your orders are to go back the same way you came?"

"Yes. We will perform a powered flyby of Venus, utilizing the Oberth effect. I think you are familiar with that type of maneuver?" Grigory said smugly, reminding Jack of the way he'd bragged about his Jupiter flyby last year.

But that was nothing to what Jack had in mind now. "I'm actually considering a different Oberth maneuver. It would be highly doable to swing around the *sun.*"

He had not told Keelraiser about this idea he'd been chewing over in his spare moments. Now he wished he had warned it. He dared not glance at Keelraiser to see its reaction. Keeping his gaze on Grigory, he explained, "Faster, simpler, shorter. Get it just right, and we'll reach Earth at the same time the *Lightbringer* does."

"Jeepers creepers, Jack!" Linda exclaimed. "Inside Mercury's orbit?"

"Nope, between Mercury and Venus."

Linda shook her head. "You'd need SPF 5 billion."

"Ever heard of sunglasses? Seriously, though, we can rig a sunshade. That's not a big deal."

Koichi said, "Neutrons."

"Neutrons, yeah," Jack conceded. "Nasty little buggers."

"The closer to the sun you go, the higher the neutron flux." The Japanese astronaut talked fast, as if determined to have his say before he was cut off. It reminded Jack of Hannah, who used to do that, too. And of course, Koichi and Hannah had worked together closely while they were building the *SoD's* MPD engine. "Free-flying neutrons have a halflife of about 15 minutes, so a quarter of them have decayed by the time they get to Earth orbit. But down around Mercury, not only is the flux higher, but they are younger neutrons! And what does neutron flux do to ships and people?"

"Oh, why don't you tell me, Koichi," Jack said. He was more disappointed than he wanted to admit that the *Victory* crew had not immediately seen the genius of his plan. "I can see you're dying to."

"Neutron flux causes elements to change into other elements. *Radioactive* elements!"

"Big fucking deal, to be honest with you." Now Jack did look at Keelraiser. It was leaning back on its sharp elbows, gazing up at the upholstery-rip stars, listening—or pretending to listen—to the music. "We have a cure for that. I'll save the details for tomorrow, as I wouldn't want all of your heads to explode at once. But just take my word for it, radiation sickness is not a major issue."

"How can you say that?" Linda exclaimed.

Jack stood up. "There's a reason I don't have two heads at this point."

He reached for Keelraiser's hand and pulled it to its feet. "Come on."

"Where are you going?" Grigory demanded.

"To relieve Alexei."

"Where is Alexei Dmitrovich?"

"On the bridge, of course."

Jack stomped down the hill, pulling Keelraiser by the hand. The stickiness from the microwaved insects Keelraiser had been eating formed a seal between their palms. Jack let its hand drop as he veered aside to top up his squeeze bottle with *krak*. The alien booze, fermented from suizh, was a rare treat.

"I suppose I fucked that up," he said, returning to where Keelraiser was waiting for him beneath a birch-sized stand of yfrit. "But I don't care. Jesus. Take the *SoD* to the moon!? You might as well park a nuclear-powered aircraft carrier in the garden and use it to keep the lights on."

"Perhaps it's the *Cloudeater* they really want," Keelraiser said.

"Yeah. But why would they give it to them? That moon base is the Earth Party's project. There's no love lost between them and the space agencies."

"Follow the money," Keelraiser said. "Is that correct?"

Jack snorted. "Probably. Well, it's out of the question, anyway. Hopefully I can persuade them to see sense."

"It might be easier if I weren't there," Keelraiser said, delicately.

"Because they can't handle talking to aliens?"

"Well …"

"You're quite right, they can't." Jack boiled over again. "How flipping rude can you be? They didn't even have the decency to say 'you're welcome' when people thanked them!"

"They don't have headsets."

"No, that's not it. I passed my headset around so they could hear. The issue is that they don't see you as human."

Keelraiser laughed.

"You know what I mean," Jack grumbled. Linda's word, 'squids,' kept echoing in his head. The crew of the *SoD* had encountered the rriksti with open minds. But maybe that was no longer possible. Humanity had divided into two camps—*for* the *Lightbringer's* false promises of interstellar friendship, and *against* the 'squids.'

They walked forward. Keelraiser said, "I had thought of doing a parabolic swing around the sun. But I didn't think you would want to risk it."

"You know me."

They passed the band. It was not the rriksti custom for bands to perform facing their audience, as long as they were in bio-antenna range. The twenty-one musicians stood in a circle among the suizh plants, their hair swaying in complex patterns. They had no musical instruments. The entire range of signals that comprised their music, from spine-chilling sobs like a bagpipe to the droning low notes of an organ, came from their bio-antennas. The complexity of rriksti radio-speech allowed for a range of tonal colorations equal to a full orchestra. Skyler sat on a stool with his suitcase-sized amp at his feet, picking his guitar. He was singing. His strong tenor melded with the wall of sound in Jack's headset, evoking ordinary human emotions of yearning and hope against a galactic panorama of loneliness.

"Sky's gotten to be really good," Jack said. "I think this's one of his songs." It awed him to reflect that this musical fusion wouldn't be possible without the same high-tech accomplishments that brought the *Lightbringer* to Earth. But Grigory, Linda, and Koichi were blind and deaf to the wow factor he had wanted to share with them. All they wanted to think about was the bloody moon.

They climbed Staircase 3. On the way up, Jack pinged Alexei. As they reached the axis tunnel, Alexei emerged from the keel tube, followed, to Jack's great surprise, by Nene.

Jack peered up the keel tube. "Anyone else up there? Were you having your own private party?"

"Kind of!" Alexei said, grinning. "Is there any food left?"

Jack quickly filled him in on his conversation with Grigory and the others. "The whole moon business is dodgy as hell. And they didn't have a logical explanation for the radio silence thing. See what you can find out."

"Leave it to me."

Jack flew onto the bridge, followed by Keelraiser.

After the twilight in the hab, the lights on the bridge seemed shockingly bright. Jack closed the pressure door. Better safe than sorry, as Linda had said. With the door closed, the bridge also became radio-proof: the thickness of the steel plate at the top of the main hab, and two layers of hull, blocked bio-radio speech. So they had privacy in both the human and the rriksti senses.

Jack turned a slow somersault in the air. He was drunk enough that the bridge seemed to revolve around him like a fairy carousel.

"Do you want another fight?" Keelraiser said.

"No. Do you?"

"No."

CHAPTER 28

"Have some more *krak*," Alexei said, topping up Grigory Nikolov's cup. His plan was to get Grigory drunk and see what came out.

"I should report you for drinking on the job," Grigory teased with a gleam in his eye.

"To who?" Alexei said. He sipped the sweetish, potent liquid in his own cup and glanced around the hill. The party was winding down. Full-bellied rriksti lay in groups, listening to the music, chatting and cuddling. Linda Moskowitz and Koichi Masuoka had also lain down, although not together. They looked to be asleep. Alexei judged it safe to say, *"Pobeda?"*

The *Pobeda* would have been the Russian spaceship that met the *SoD* near Earth on its return, hijacking it and confiscating its expected cargo of alien goodies. Alexei had had orders to help with that. The malware installed on the *SoD* had also been a part of the scheme. He wasn't sure what ditch the *Pobeda* project had died in, but it couldn't be a coincidence that *Pobeda* meant *Victory* in English.

"Just a joke," Grigory said. "The *Pobeda* is dead, long live the *Victory!* If we lose our sense of humor, we're doomed."

"Yes. So are you hijacking us?"

Grigory snorted. Peering with bleary eyes into the jungle, he said, "Is there anything here worth having? All I see is plants."

"And aliens," Alexei said, squeezing Nene's hand, a gesture hidden from Grigory, as she was sitting on Alexei's other side.

"You must be crazy to bring all these squids."

"It's a crazy universe."

"Exactly! Look at me. I should have been retiring next year. Me and the wife had plans to buy a little place on the Black Sea. I'd have spent my days fishing. Instead I'm trying to save the human race." Grigory shook his head. "Everything's changed, Alexei Dmitrovich."

Alexei nodded. He wondered if Grigory had changed. They'd had problems with each other on the ISS. Grigory was an old-school cosmonaut who made no secret of his belief that Alexei's generation was Westernized and sissified. He was also in with the GRU clique who'd drafted Alexei into the *Pobeda* project.

Still, it felt great to have someone to speak Russian with again. Feeling guilty about leaving Nene out of the conversation, Alexei snuggled an arm around her back and drew her against his side. They'd been together for almost a year now and were getting sloppy about keeping their relationship private. After all, they had nothing to be ashamed of, did they?

"The government is relocating to Arkhangelsk," Grigory said. "We survived Napoleon and Hitler, we'll survive the squids! That's what they say, anyway."

The fatalistic way Grigory was talking resonated with Alexei's own thoughts. The *SoD* now had no hope of overtaking the *Lightbringer*. Arriving at Earth two months after the *Lightbringer* would begin its deadly work, they might—*might*—have a chance to disable the alien behemoth in orbit. If successful, they could save the portion of humanity that had hidden in bunkers above the Arctic Circle. It killed him that that was all they could hope to do. But you can't fight the laws of physics.

Grigory leaned forward. "You've got to help us, Alexei Dmitrovich. We need to work together."

Alexei tilted his head on one side. "Are we *still* trying to one-up the Americans?"

*

Jack floated on the bridge, parallel to the ceiling. He'd let himself get quite drunk. It took his mind off his disagreement with the *Victory* crew, and allowed him to enjoy a rare glow of contentment.

"So what's the absolute best film in history?" he said.

It was always safe to talk about movies. Keelraiser had viewed vastly more films and TV shows than Jack had, starting from well before Jack was born, but they had some shared favorites. The original Dr. Who. *The Life of Brian!* Jack couldn't believe he'd never mentioned Monty Python to Keelraiser before. He even used to have a Flying Circus sticker on his laptop, the one Alexei had smashed because it had the malware trigger on it.

They'd got a lot of conversational mileage out of that, but now the joking mood had departed from Jack. Tipsy, not sleepy, but relaxed, he floated in flat circles, noting the corrosion damage on the ceiling wiring.

"I would have to say *The Passion of the Christ,*" Keelraiser said.

Jack opened his eyes wide. Keelraiser drifted nearby, at an angle to him. "You're kidding! That gorefest? *My* all-time favorite is *Independence Day.*"

"That gorefest?"

"Er. Well."

"It's different when it's aliens taking a beating?"

"Yeah, exactly. That's it." Jack rolled over in the air. He

reached out and prodded Keelraiser in the chest. "I was extremely disappointed that you didn't swoop down into the sky over Manhattan with guns blazing. I mean, *that's* what I was training all my life for ..."

"Really?"

"Not really. I wasted my youth chasing girls and generally having a good time." Jack remembered when he'd turned the corner and left time-wasting fun and games behind. He could pinpoint it. The turning point had come on a beach in Wales, the night he got into a fistfight with Meeks about the merits of, yes, *Independence Day*.

He remembered that eerie moment after their Mars flyby when he'd mistaken Keelraiser for Meeks. He gazed at Keelraiser's profile. In the brighter light of the bridge, it was impossible, of course, to mistake it for a human. But there was no denying that the dead man and the living rriksti had certain traits in common. Obstinacy, quirkiness, and what Jack most admired, the self-belief it took to go *your* way when the chips were down and the whole universe seemed to be against you.

Yet Keelraiser had served in the Darkside military. That didn't seem to fit with its extreme independence of mind. Jack well remembered how military camaraderie and routine had fogged his own mind during his Iraq deployments, to the point that he'd had to get home before he was really able to think about what it meant to kill people.

"How did you end up joining the military?" he said.

Keelraiser arched its back. "Oh God, talk about wasting one's youth. I was determined to get into the *Krijistal*. The last war but three had just broken out. My father was in the service. He actually held rather a high rank, which I suppose would correspond to admiral."

"Your dad was an admiral?!"

"The ranks do not translate exactly. But yes, we were a prominent military family. I had three half-brothers and two half-sisters in the service—"

"Gosh, it's very good of you to slum it with the likes of us." Jack pretended to tug his forelock.

"Stop it," Keelraiser said, laughing with its hair. It aimed a mock punch at him. "What I am trying to tell you is I was completely unqualified. I failed the entrance trials three times."

"And then your dad pulled strings?"

"No. I did get in in the end, by other means."

"Why did you fail the first three times?" Jack couldn't stop himself. Curiosity gripped him like a fever.

"Because I'm not extroverted."

"I know, but ..."

"Extroversion is a key qualification for the *Krijistal*. It's meant to be non-negotiable, although obviously, introverts like me do slip through the cracks."

Jack sighed. He turned in the air to face Keelraiser. Their bodies were aligned in the same plane. "Aren't you extroverted at all? Really? Not even the tiniest bit?"

Keelraiser reached out. Jack held still in the air. Keelraiser laid the tip of one finger in the hollow of his throat.

"Do you feel anything?"

The heavy, claw-like fingernail pressed gently into the notch at the top of Jack's collarbone. His pulse beat against Keelraiser's finger. A shuddery thrill ran through his body.

"Well, I can't really tell," he said.

Keelraiser reached out and pushed its other hand into

Jack's hair, taking care not to dislodge his headset. It grasped a handful of the blond—and now more than a few gray—strands. "Now?"

Jack had grabbed Keelraiser's hair when they fought. Now Keelraiser was doing the same thing to him. It was a test of courage, and a challenge. He reached out and slid his fingers in among the gleaming black bioantennas. They ranged from the diameter of an electric cord, around the face, to the fat ones at the top of the skull that were thick enough to wrap your hand around. They felt velvety, hot and stiff, yet supple. He'd remembered that strange, enticing texture, and yes, it really was like that. He let the bio-antennas comb through his fingers like seaweed underwater.

Keelraiser opened his mouth in a nervous rriksti grin. He let go of Jack's hair. "Do you know how you look to me? I—I mean humans, in general."

"How?"

"You're so cute. Small and compact and… simply irresistible."

"I'm going to try not to take that personally." Jack chuckled. "If you think us smelly, hairy men are cute, what about Linda? She's *very* cute, isn't she?"

"Is Linda female?"

"Er. Didn't you notice?"

"I couldn't really tell the difference," Keelraiser admitted.

"We're actually very different." Jack yawned. "Up here …" He pointed to his head. "And down here." He pointed to his groin. Then he took Keelraiser's hand and placed it on the outside of his shorts.

The long fingers pressed lightly. "It's hard to tell …"

"Try squeezing a bit."

The gentle pressure felt like erotic lightning shooting through Jack's body. It ripped the scab off a need so deep it was like a wound.

"It's the weekend, you know," Keelraiser said. He sounded nervous. His eyes were wide and expectant. Jack noticed that he was thinking of him as a *he* again, but so what, honestly? No one would ever know …

His mind belatedly caught up to the conversation. "What? It's not the weekend. It's Tuesday. I think it is anyway."

"Never mind," Keelraiser said. He cupped Jack's shoulder with his other hand, bringing him closer. His fingers slipped inside the elastic waistband of Jack's shorts, which were now far too loose for his waist.

"Oh! … That feels good." Jack involuntarily arched his back. "Do that … some more …"

"Like this?"

"Yeah, a bit more … sort of harder, if you know what I mean …"

Keelraiser didn't seem to understand quite how this worked. His fingers enclosed Jack's cock and stayed there without moving. "What will happen if I do this?"

Jack closed his eyes. His arousal was still building. The point of no return loomed. He was suddenly afraid of losing control. "Nothing," he said, making a promise to himself. "Nothing will happen."

"Do you want me to stop?"

"No, don't! I mean …" Jack caught Keelraiser's wrist. "This is fine. This is nice. Don't move! If—if you could just sort of hold me …"

CHAPTER 29

"No, no," Grigory said. "We're not trying to put one over on the Americans. Things are too serious now to play political games."

"Then why do you want to fly the *SoD* to the moon? Do you mean we're *not* going to point the railguns at CELL, land the *Cloudeater* near the base, and force all the Americans to leave so that we can take over?"

This was the scenario that had sprung fully-formed into Alexei's mind the moment Jack told him about the *Victory* crew's 'idiotic' plan. Jack was English. He did not always see these things coming.

Grigory tugged his moustache. "You haven't been on Earth since 2019, Alexei Dmitrovich. You don't understand how bad it is."

Alexei shrugged. "Am I right?"

"Let's not divide the pelt of a bear we haven't killed yet. First things first." Grigory paused. "Have you still got the trigger for *Zmeyka?*"

Alexei raised his eyebrows at the change of subject. *Zmeyka.* The 'Little Snake.' That had been the GRU's codename for the malware.

"No," he said, greatly enjoying the look on Grigory's face. "I destroyed it."

"You're joking."

"With a homemade sword. And a hammer, just to make sure."

Grigory shook Linda. Koichi uncurled, too, and sat up. "He says he's destroyed it," Grigory said in English.

"How unpatriotic of you, Alexei," said Linda. Her

teeth caught the dim light as she smiled.

Alexei's mind reeled. It looked like *Grigory* was the unpatriotic one here. No one was meant to know about the malware! When Alexei shared the trigger with Kate, he had been conscious of committing high treason. It had troubled him deeply, though not as much as he was troubled by resentment of the *siloviki* who manipulated people's lives for the sole purpose of getting rich.

But Grigory was one of that gang, or rather, he licked their boots. He'd never disobey an order from the GRU. *That,* Alexei felt certain, hadn't changed.

Yet here was Linda Moskowitz, a sassy American woman, murmuring, "Guess we got nothing to worry about, then," and Koichi Masuoka, a son of Nippon, saying, "Except the squids," and lo and behold, Grigory Nikolov, that old cuss, the terror of the ISS, was pointing a gun at Alexei's stomach.

Alexei recognized the squared-off barrel of a PYa Grach, the same weapon he himself had carried when he was in the air force. Small enough to fit in that satchel Grigory had brought with him.

Damn it! We should've searched their bags!

But if Grigory, growling in Russian about Alexei's *duty*, thought Alexei would do as he was told like a good little soldier boy, he was wrong. Alexei grabbed Grigory's wrist and forced the barrel of the gun away. Alexei had been living in 0.3 gees, working like a farmhand; Grigory had had a year in freefall for his muscles to deteriorate. Using the low gravity to his advantage, Alexei spun Grigory around by the arm and flipped him head down on the hill. Rriksti scattered. Alexei didn't see where Nene went. He was trying to decide whether to break Grigory's trigger finger.

Cold steel ground into the back of his neck. "Get the fuck away from him. *Now.*"

Linda.

Alexei slackened his grip. He sat back on his heels, every movement a parody of exaggerated caution. Linda moved with him, keeping her gun pressed into his neck.

Grigory jerked his clothes straight and faced Alexei. "What are you, some kind of animal? Or have you turned alien like Hannah Ginsburg? Human on the outside, squid on the inside?"

Alexei didn't dare to move anything except his eyes. His headset lay out of reach on the fungus. He spotted Nene, standing on the top of the hill, wringing her hands. He mouthed, "Run," and wondered if she understood. There were still a lot of other rriksti around, staring curiously. They clearly did *not* understand. They thought this was the human version of a *Krijistal* punch-up.

Alexei knew better. He knew this was the *siloviki* exacting their long-awaited revenge. Except the usual suspects had changed—that was where his assumptions had led him astray. "You're not with the GRU anymore, are you, Grigory Abramovich?"

"Oh, I am!" Grigory said. "And she's with NASA, and he's with JAXA, and all of us have the same goal: saving humanity. My question is, are *you* with us?"

"Of course I am," Alexei said.

"I wonder. Looked like you were getting very friendly with that squid. That's disgusting, Alexei Dmitrovich. You should be ashamed of yourself. Better to fuck your hand than one of those things."

Alexei bit back a foul-mouthed response. Defending Nene's dignity would get him nowhere right now. He had to find out what the *Victory* crew wanted from him. "This is stupid, pointless. We're all on the same side. Why do you think we're not?"

Linda said, "Oh, because you loaded up your ship with *squids?*"

She dug the gun into the base of his neck, toppling him face-first onto the fungus. He poked up his head and saw that Nene was gone from the crest of the hill.

"It's your call, Grigory," Linda said. "Wanna take him back to the ship? Or leave him here, or what?"

"Kill him," Koichi said.

Grigory swore in Russian. He sounded distressed at the thought of killing Alexei. But not *that* distressed, evidently, because his legs entered Alexei's field of vision, spread apart in a shooting stance, and then the world went away.

*

Aboard the *Victory,* Giles and the *Krijistal* were having their own party.

Giles had come aboard to help them unload the Shit We Need. Heh, not really. Brbb had tipped him off earlier—bring some *krak* ... By the time he got there, the party was well underway. The *Krijistal* floated through the five linked modules of the *Victory,* already sloshed, to judge by the way they were bumping into the walls of boxes that lined the modules.

"Giles!" Brbb greeted him with a flash of teeth. The teeth looked black. They must have been snacking on metals from the single box of Shit We Need they had got around to unpacking.

"You could have waited for me," Giles said, doffing his spacesuit.

"We did wait!" Brbb trapped Giles against the wall of the cockpit and kissed him deeply. "See? No one has disrobed yet!"

The bitter taste of metal made Giles cough. He broke the kiss to gulp from his bottle of krak. That made him cough again, and all the *Krijistal* laughed, but they weren't laughing at him. They were laughing with him. They accepted him the way he was, and welcomed his participation in their weekend games. Maybe, Giles thought, there was a God after all.

He was looking forward to tonight.

They'd never had real privacy before.

Snatched moments in the shacks of the rriksti village, with their paper-thin walls, could not compare to having a whole spaceship to themselves.

Giles also intended to take advantage of the privacy for another purpose.

He winked at Brbb, and hooked his MP3 player up to the *Victory's* PA system.

Slayer thundered through the spaceship.

"It is a shame you can't hear it," Giles said, nodding to the beat.

"No, I think it is probably a good thing," Brbb said. "The other humans say your taste in music is shit."

Giles pounced on him. "Is my taste in aliens shit, also? Mmm?"

As they spun in a freefall embrace, Brbb's spacesuit flowed down to the top of his pelvis, exposing his hot, slightly sticky skin. His erection pressed against Giles's thigh. "What luck the *Victory* arrived on the weekend," he said.

"Why is there sometimes a weekend, and sometimes not?" Giles said.

Brbb cringed away. "That sounds like philosophy. Ask someone else."

"No, no," Giles said, laughing. "I'm just being a xenolinguist. Language and culture are two sides of a coin. You speak of the weekend as the end of an eleven-day cycle, but in fact, sometimes a month goes by without any weekends."

"Sometimes work comes first," Brbb said.

"And some people—in fact, everyone else on board, no?—never seem to have a weekend at all! How can that be, if it's a biological cycle?"

"They just don't know how to have fun," Brbb said.

Difystra put in, "He's messing with you, Giles. Is this correct?"

"I fear so," Giles said.

"We've got implants." Difystra reached out and flicked the back of Brbb's neck with a long finger. "Everyone has them."

"Everyone who crewed on the *Lightbringer?*"

"Everyone, everyone," Difystra said. "Fertility control. It's better this way. We're not slaves to our biology like they were in the Dark Ages. So if we want a weekend, we have a weekend. If not, we don't! Isn't technology great?"

"So being drunk and insanely horny is a choice," Brbb said. He gave Giles a soulful look. "Unless I can blame you. Can I? Yes. It's all *your* fault."

Giles groaned. "Work calls," he said. "We'd better start unpacking the boxes before the others start to wonder what we're doing."

"Later."

Sometimes Giles deplored his own commitment to duty. But there it was. He couldn't have fun as long as a task remained undone. "No, we'd better make a start, at least …"

"Oh, all right."

Drunkenly, to the strains of Giles's heavy metal playlist, they started to open the Shit We Need boxes.

*

Skyler swayed on his stool, lost in the music. He knew he was being antisocial, but fuck it. He was pissed as hell about being lied to, *again,* by the very people they counted on for support. It was on the newcomers to explain themselves. Wasn't on him to make nice.

Without warning, a harmonic shriek drilled into his ears. Skyler snatched his headset off. Ears ringing, he thought for a second that someone had hit a bum note. Interstellar fusion, as they grandly dubbed their new genre of folk music, had to be structured around the harmonics that hurt human ears—like composing without the E string, for example. Not that hard, but sometimes someone forgot, and hit it.

But the musicians seemed agitated, staring aft in confusion, although Skyler could see nothing amiss. Their bio-antennas were doing something he'd *never* seen—flattened straight down their backs, giving them strange, snake-headed silhouettes.

Skyler slid off his stool and put his guitar down on the amp.

The musicians twitched. One or two fell to their knees.

Static burped from the headset in Skyler's hand.

Hriklif, on the far side of the circle, took one tottering step towards him, and collapsed.

Skyler took off running. As he dodged through the towering stands of suizh, he jammed his headset on. "Jack! Jack, come in!" No response. In fact he could not hear a single thing in the headset, not even the usual background chatter of Rristigul.

He burst out of the jungle on the edge of the village.

And tripped over a body.

Catching himself on his hands, he flew over in an inadvertent handspring. He landed in front of the long table that had served as a buffet. Rriksti sat and lay on the floor, shaking, twitching, obviously in such pain that they couldn't move. Every one of them had its hair flattened down in a single mega-dreadlock, like an antenna folded away.

Skyler shook the nearest one. "What's wrong with you? What happened?"

Bio-antennas whipped, but Skyler heard nothing. That's when he realized his headset wasn't working.

The goddamn thing had crapped out on him.

Or *burnt* out.

He blundered through the village.

A single form lay on the hill in a contorted, frozen posture.

"Alexei!"

Skyler leapt up the hill. Shook Alexei. Checked his pulse. Prised up his eyelids to see the whites.

And found twinned red blisters on the back of Alexei's neck.

The marks of a taser.

The three *Victory* crew members bounded aft through the choking heat. They forced their way through vegetation that Linda would describe to her son, if she ever got to talk to him again, as *like the weeds in your aquarium after Mr. Turtle died.* Grigory, in point position, swept his taser high and low, squeezing the trigger every time something moved. They hadn't anticipated this stroke of luck. The taser worked like a magic wand on the aliens. Discharge voltage, Mister Squid he take dirt nap. Didn't even have to hit them with it. The 50,000-volt arcs wriggling between the electrodes flashed eerily in the gloom.

They hurtled up the aft stairs. Clambering into the axis tunnel, Linda gasped for breath. Was it starting? *Duh.* It had already started. But none of them knew how fast it would go.

They got to the storage module. There were some squids swarming around. Grigory tased them. The three humans got into their suits. Linda checked the atmospheric monitor in her heads-up display. *Whoa* boy.

"You kids go first," Grigory told them on the suit-to-suit comms. Linda hated leaving him behind in the storage module, but only two of them could fit into the airlock at a time.

Outside, the delta-winged alien shuttle blocked out the sun. Linda and Koichi crabbed around the outside of the *SoD's* truss tower. They had to get back in the *Victory*. There, they'd be safe. Batten down the hatches and wait until it was over.

The truss towers of the *SoD* and the *Victory* came together in a V. You could think of it as the bottom of a deep valley with the stars at the top. Linda scrambled across the gap, holding onto one of the cables that secured the two ships together.

The airlock of the *Victory's* foremost module opened.

A beam of light shone out of the hatch and raked across Linda's face, blinding her.

A blow hammered into her helmet.

Koichi dragged her away from the ship as blows rained down on them both. It wasn't just one squid, it was hundreds of them ... well, at least two ... with their head-lamps in the middle of their chests and their tentacles swirling in the vacuum like industrial mops.

Dizzied by the blow to her helmet, Linda reached into the thigh pocket of her Starliner. She dragged out her specially modified Glock and fired. The gun kicked, propelling her backwards against the truss tower. The squids scattered. "Die, motherfuckers, die!" Linda screamed with the passion of a woman dispossessed of home, planet, and now, it appeared, ship as well. Koichi was shooting, too, upside down, knees hooked through the lattice.

But the squids had only been startled. They closed in again, and now there were more of them. Linda and Koichi battled their way back to the *SoD's* airlock. More squids arrived from the *Victory* to join the attack. Out of ammo, Linda pistol-whipped the nearest ones with the butt of her Glock.

Somehow the two humans crammed themselves back inside the airlock and closed it against the monsters.

"Least they didn't have ray-guns," Koichi panted.

"Same fucking difference." If they couldn't get back to the *Victory,* they were dead. Linda shook the dizziness off, tasted blood in her mouth. She'd bitten her tongue.

"They're in our ship," Koichi told Gregory, back inside. "We saw four of them. There may be more. They attacked us."

Grigory swore in Russian. "We're not safe here, either."

Tased squids drifted around the storage module like garbage. The taser didn't kill them, it just put them down for the count. Who knew how long the effects would last? And in a few minutes, the other squids, the aggressive ones, would pile in through the airlock.

"Get batteries for the taser," Grigory said. "Extra oxygen tanks."

The same people who built the *Victory* had built the *SoD*. The *Victory* crew knew where everything was stored. Although the crew of the *SoD* had ignored orders and betrayed their own humanity, they'd not cut any corners when it came to inventory maintenance.

Burdened, they flew back through the secondary life-support module. Linda felt a yearning to stay right here. It was so peaceful, with the huge algae tanks spinning their contents in the normal, bright, *human* light. But they weren't safe here, either.

They flew on through the axis tunnel, between the fans and the growlights swathed in handmade orange veils, towards the bridge.

CHAPTER 30

Skyler carried Alexei to Medical. It seemed to take weeks. He kept having to stop and pant for breath. Along the way, he shouted for help. No one heard him, unsurprisingly as his headset was dead. He was so out of breath that his shouts came out as croaks.

He dumped Alexei on the stretcher tucked into the Potter space under Staircase 4, and switched on the high-powered LED light above it. He knew that tasers don't knock you unconscious. Alexei had stopped shaving his head because they'd run out of anything to use as a razor. Parting the greasy dark hair, Skyler found a swollen gash. He began cleaning the wound with a wet rag. There was nothing else to use. He hoped the *Victory* had brought the medical supplies they needed, although he very much doubted it at this point.

A rriksti stumbled into the pool of light. Nene. Its bio-antennas spasmed. Same thing was wrong with it as with all the others. It crumpled to its knees beside the stretcher. Its arms fell limply across Alexei's body. It rested its face on his stomach.

"Hey, Nene," Skyler said. "Can you do anything for a knock on the head?" He laughed bitterly.

Nene levered itself upright and stumbled to the whiteboard on the wall. Grabbing a marker, it scrawled in capital letters. At first Skyler was so taken with this unprecedented behavior—a rriksti writing!—that he neglected to read the words.

CO_2 CONCENTRATION 4.2%.

Skyler's mouth dropped open. He lunged for the monitor

built into the wall and clicked up the atmospheric sensor readouts. "No, it isn't."

YOUR COMPUTER IS WRONG. I HAVE AIR QUALITY SENSOR, MANY SENSORS INTEGRATED INTO MY ROBE. Nene touched the garment Skyler thought of as a smock. THIS IS STANDARD GARB FOR CLERICS.

"Oh shit," Skyler said. "Oh shit oh shit oh shit." So that's why he felt so out of breath. "There's gotta be something wrong with the valves …"

*

On the bridge, a voice abruptly crackled from the intercom. "Hey Jack! It's Linda."

Jack startled violently. He sprang away from Keelraiser. He smoothed down his shorts, heart pounding with embarrassment.

Nothing had happened, he told himself. "Nothing happened," he said to Keelraiser.

"Nothing happened," Keelraiser agreed, floating in the air with his eyes closed.

"Why've you got the door shut?" Linda said over the intercom. "Ha, ha. Can I come in and hang out?"

Jack frowned at the solid plug of steel that blocked the keel tube. "Should I let her in?"

"It's up to you," Keelraiser said.

"Oh come on, Jack. I know you're in there," Linda said playfully.

"That just sounds really off somehow." Jack flew to the intercom. "You OK, Linda?"

There was a pause. Then Linda seemed to break down. "Jack, they tried to kill us! When we tried to go back to our ship—just to, to get some stuff—they attacked us! They *hit* us!"

"Who did?"

"The squids! Can you let me in, *please?* I don't feel safe out here!"

"They wouldn't have hurt you," Jack said unsympathetically. His instincts were yelping at him that something was wrong here.

"They *hit* us!"

"It's their way of showing affection."

"They're monsters!"

Jack yawned, oddly as he wasn't sleepy at all. "All right, I'll ping them and ask them to stop monstering at you for a while." He moved to the comms console and set the radio to the EVA frequency. "Hello Brbb? Come in."

He knew it had to have been Brbb and company, because he'd asked them to weld the *Victory* to the truss tower. Those bungee cables didn't look very secure at all.

A furious stream of Rristigul erupted from the headset. Jack ripped it off and fell backwards, clutching his ears.

Keelraiser leapt for the console and muted the piercing harmonics. His hair stabbed the air as he spoke in Rristigul, piggybacking on the open channel.

"Bad news, I'm afraid," he said to Jack, tossing the headphones in his direction. "You'd better talk to Giles."

Jack held the headphones sideways to his face. "Giles?"

"I am on the *Victory*," Giles said. "With the *Krijistal*. I estimate that we have now opened a representative sample of the *Victory's* cargo. It is all stuff for *them,* Jack—those *salauds*. Sorry, I know they're your friends. Life-support supplies, personal items, MREs. There is no Shit We Need. I exaggerate. There were two or three boxes containing our items, in the forward module, near the airlock. Those held a small amount of the micronutrients and medical supplies we requested. But there is no more. Those things were only there to—to pass a cursory inspection. *Merde!*" Even the even-keeled Giles could not relate these horrific facts with equanimity.

"Oh my fucking God," Jack said. "Well, I suppose we can eat the MREs." He drew a shuddering breath. "All right, Giles. Stay where you are for the moment. I'll get back to you shortly."

Anger boiled in his veins. He leant to the intercom. "Linda, I think we'd better talk. Stand by. I'm opening the door."

Keelraiser said, "Are you sure that's wise?"

"I want to know exactly what's going on here." Jack flew to the aft wall, braced his feet on the bulkhead, and turned the crank.

The door opened a crack.

When the crack was the width of a human body, a hand shot through it.

The hand was not Linda's. It was large and hairy.

It held a gun.

The gun fired into the bridge. In the confined space, the noise was worse than any rriksti harmonics.

Jack spun away from the pressure door, reflexively ducking for cover.

Grigory forced his bulk through the gap and levelled his gun at Jack, keeping his aim steady even as he drifted across the bridge under his own momentum.

Behind him, Koichi burst onto the bridge, bringing his

own weapon to bear on Jack.

Keelraiser dropped from the ceiling of the bridge like a spider. He pounced on Koichi and wrestled him.

Jack saw this blurrily past the gun barrel aimed between his eyes. It *did* concentrate the mind.

"Jack, we can do this the easy way or the hard way." Grigory kept one eye on the melee as he drifted towards Jack, holding his gun level in a two-handed grip. "I am relieving you of command."

Jack took a deep breath. He noted that ceramic fragments and dust were swirling around. Grigory's gun was loaded with frangible bullets which would not damage the ship. But at this range, they'd damage *him*. Terminally. "Why?"

"It's been decided that you're no longer fit for command."

"This is sort of coming out of the blue."

"You've been asking for it for the last year and a half!" Linda screamed. She had a gun, too. She was pointing it at Keelraiser and Koichi, trying to get a clear shot as they wrestled.

"I don't want to do this, Jack," Grigory said. "I would like you to join us. I would like to have your skills, your experience. But we cannot trust you anymore. Call that squid off before it kills Koichi! He's your friend, no? Are you going to let it kill him?"

Something crackled. Grigory glanced away for a second. Koichi fell away from Keelraiser, frozen in a rigid, unnatural crouch.

Linda fired her pistol.

Jack flung himself into a backwards somersault, straight through the curtain in the corner. He wrenched open his personal locker.

When Grigory came through the curtain he came face to face with a Super Soaker.

"I picked this up on Europa," Jack panted. "It'll vaporize your brain and leave your skull full of radioactive ion soup. Want a demonstration?"

He pushed Grigory back out through the curtain.

Keelraiser held a taser. He was bleeding from one arm, but seemed not to have noticed. "This is a torture weapon," he said through the intercom. Jack's headset was not working. "Banned on Imf."

Linda fired at Keelraiser again. Ceramic shards rebounded from the comms console housing.

Jack swung the Super Soaker to cover her. "Drop your weapon, Linda!"

"Don't shoot me. I have a kid," Linda gasped. Then, strangely, she yawned.

From the intercom, Skyler's voice crackled. "… CO_2 is way up …"

CHAPTER 31

"We were ordered to stand off until the sterilization protocol was complete," Grigory said.

"Uh huh," Jack said. He unscrewed the air compressor from the wall of the secondary life support module. It had to be the valves. What a coincidence that the valves should fail at the exact moment when the *Victory's* crew came on board. Behind the air compressor was a cavity filled with plumbing. Jack held the compressor away from the wall while Alexei—groaning, still recovering from being tased and hit on the head—peered into the cavity and examined the valves. "Sterilization protocol?" Jack said.

While they worked, a long line of rriksti edged through SLS. They were moving everyone across to the *Cloudeater* as fast as possible. Still reeling from the effects of the taser, whose electromagnetic pulses had deafened and tortured them, the civilians were now also sliding into narcosis as the CO_2 concentration in the air pushed 6%. The *Krijistal,* spacesuited, flew up and down the line, keeping everyone moving. There weren't enough suits for everyone, never had been. Spare oxygen tanks could only do so much good, especially as the weaker civilians were too confused to breathe into face masks. At 8% they would start dying. Gotta get this fixed, *now.*

"It was meant to be quick and painless," Grigory said. "They would have gone peacefully to sleep."

Skyler was on the bridge, but because they were all in their EVA suits, he could listen in on the radio. "Oh yeah, carbon dioxide toxicity, that's a real painless way to die. And what about us? What was supposed to happen to us?"

"We were also supposed to die, of course," Alexei said. "Jack, there is nothing wrong with these valves."

"I tried, damn it!" Grigory said. "I tried to save you, Alexei Dmitrovich! But you chose the squids."

"Are you sure?" Jack said to Alexei, ignoring Grigory.

"Yes. See here, the purified, oxygenated air comes out of the algae tanks. It is fed into the air circulation system. This pipe feeds old air into the tanks. It's working fine."

"Shit," Jack said, at a loss. He rounded on Grigory, Linda, and Koichi, who floated in a huddle, with Keelraiser pointing two blasters at them, one in each hand. "It's not the valves. What is it? *What is it?*"

"Dunno," Koichi said. He sounded exhausted, his voice as colorless as recycled paper. "We just clicked where it said to click."

"The malware," Skyler said.

"Yeah," Jack said.

"I see," Alexei said. "The Americans found out about the *Pobeda* project, so we had to cut them in."

Grigory bristled. "They wanted to send drones. We convinced them that *Zmeyka* was a more elegant solution."

Alexei suddenly slapped his palm with his socket wrench. "He asked me if I still had the malware trigger. I said I destroyed it."

"I've got a copy!" Skyler broke in.

"You have?" Alexei said. "I thought we destroyed them all."

"Um, it was like, I really need this laptop. So yeah. I know it was dumb—"

"Not that dumb!" Alexei said. "The trigger is also the

off switch. It's got to be!" He broke into Russian.

While Alexei and Grigory snarled at each other in Russian, Jack replaced the air compressor. A comatose rriksti floated out of the queue and caught on the algae tanks like a flag, barely living.

"Try the output," Keelraiser said.

"It can't be the output," Jack said.

But it was.

At the other end of the string of algae tanks, the exhaust air from the tanks entered a feedback loop. This was supposed to return air to the tanks if it still had too much CO_2 in it. But the feedback loop had turned into a dead end. *All the air was going back into the front of the loop, blocking any stale air from being processed by the algae.*

Jack disconnected the exhaust pipe and pointed it at the rriksti caught on the tanks. "It was the CO_2 sensor." He was so angry his vision tunneled. "It wasn't you lot this time," he said to Keelraiser. "It was them."

"What's wrong with the sensor?" Alexei said.

"Stuck on eleven." Jack dug a gloved hand into the wiring and ripped out the electrical leads. Then he prised the CO_2 sensor out with his screwdriver, and approached the rriksti on the tanks. It was blinking and starting to recover as sweet, oxygenated air blew into its face. "Here," he whispered. "Have this."

The rriksti took the sensor delicately from his fingertips. It shrugged, and crunched it between its teet.

"Copper," Jack whispered. "Silver, germanium." His own mouth watered sympathetically as the rriksti savored the metals in the chip.

"They are saying we didn't get the Shit We Need," it said.

"Right. We only got a tiny bit of it. Effectively nothing. But if it's any consolation, we'll start yanking the semiconductors out of everything when we're finished here. You can eat those."

"Um," Koichi said. Just the tiniest grunt of disagreement, but it set Jack off.

"What else am I going to do? I can't trust the computer anymore. There was probably something else coming after this. *Wasn't* there?" the *Victory* crew didn't know, of course. They hadn't designed the malware. They'd just clicked where it said to click. "So the computer's got to stay off. We'll have to do everything manually. Shit, shit!"

Alexei grabbed his arm. "Not necessarily."

"We can't take the risk of something like this happening again."

"Grigory confirms it. There is an off switch. It's in the trigger. And Skyler has a copy."

"Skyler," Jack said, "can you fix this?" No matter what he said, he needed the damn computer. The *SoD* was dead in space without it.

"Theoretically, yeah," Skyler said. "Actually? I'm gonna have to call the NXC."

CHAPTER 32

Flaherty got goosebumps as he listened to Skyler Taft's voice, transmitted across the immense distance between the *SoD* and Earth. The spooky thing was Skyler sounded the same as always. Flaherty could close his eyes and imagine they were standing on a stoop in Arlington, Massachusetts, chatting about aliens.

Flaherty knew he'd screwed up, back in 2019, when he subbed Skyler in for Lance at the last minute. He had had no alternative. But a sensitive Harvard Ph.D couldn't fill the shoes of a balls-to-the-wall redneck. The mission had suffered for it, the NXC had suffered for it, and Skyler himself had probably suffered most of all. When Skyler screamed at him from Europa to get fucked, Flaherty had shrugged—he'd known that was coming.

Now Skyler was relating a bitter tale of betrayal and failure.

Skyler's betrayal.

Flaherty's failure.

The unelected president of the United States felt every one of his sixty-two years as he listened to Skyler's ultimatum.

"Tell me how to disable the malware," Skyler said, "or Linda, Koichi, and Grigory get it." He laughed, faintly. "I have to tell you, Jack wouldn't do it. He's got a, what do you call it? It's on the tip of my tongue … Oh yeah. A moral compass. I, obviously, haven't."

The self-lacerating assertion revealed just how badly the NXC had damaged Skyler Taft.

"I killed Oliver Meeks. Surprised? Did Lance tell you he

did it? Nope, that was me."

"I did not know that," Flaherty said to Kuldeep, who was listening with him on speaker.

"So I've already crossed that line. Also, I don't give shit one about these guys. Jack and Alexei know them from the old days. Jack is like, we'll just make them clean the toilets until they say sorry. Are you kidding? These people tried to murder us all, and we're gonna let them walk around like nothing happened? I would be very happy to feed them to the fish. I don't give a fuck about their families or whatever. And I know where the guns are." A staticky pause. "So, Tom. Ball's in your court. Want to keep them alive? Tell me how to disable the malware. You have 24 hours. Out."

The recorded transmission ended.

Kuldeep said, "This is the guy Lance picked to work with him after I got fired, right?"

"Right," Flaherty said. "Lance had a real eye for potential."

"I thought he was this wimpy scientist dude. He sounds bad-ass."

"He's gone over to the squids, body and soul," Flaherty said. He glared bleakly at the computer which had been playing the recorded transmission, seeing that dumb peace symbol Skyler used to wear.

"Yup," Kuldeep said. "That came across loud and clear. He's self-alienated. Just like Hannah."

Flaherty roused himself to do what had to be done. "Call Moscow," he said to his chief of staff, who was hovering obsequiously at the door. "Get hold of whoever it is in the GRU who knows this shit. ASAP, before they get put in front of a firing squad. Got it? Tell them to write it down, step by step, no mistakes, and send it by secure courier to Houston for transmission to the *SoD.*"

"You're doing what they want?" Kuldeep yelped.

Flaherty gazed at him bleakly. "Son, what happened to *your* moral compass?"

"On it, Mr. President," said the chief of staff. "Will there be anything else at this time?"

"Yeah. Get the plane fueled up. We're going to Florida."

*

On the bridge of the *SoD,* Skyler, Jack, and Alexei watched Mission Control's reply come in. It was packaged in a clip from a nature documentary, as usual. Skyler downloaded it to his laptop and decrypted it.

Jack let out a whoop. "That looks right! Is it?"

Skyler swiftly read through the payload file. "Yup," he said huskily. "It's instructions for switching off the malware." Relief flooded him. He leaned back and pulled his hair out of its ponytail, trying to cool the sweat that clung to his scalp. "I guess they believed me."

"It was a great performance," Alexei said.

"Oscar-winning," Jack said.

Skyler glanced at them. He wondered if his performance had been *too* good. Maybe he shouldn't have referred to the murder of Oliver Meeks. He knew Jack was still sore about that, although Skyler had apologized from the bottom of his heart.

And Alexei was rubbing his shoulder, where a starburst of faint scars commemorated the place Skyler's frangible bullet had gone in. Skyler had apologized for that, too.

But apologizing was never enough, was it? No matter

what he did to prove his loyalty, they'd still see him as the Fed he used to be. He'd put himself on the line to save the *SoD,* and even that wasn't enough.

"So what *are* we going to do with them?" he said.

Jack shook his head tiredly. He had been up all night, Skyler knew, fixing the output of the algae tanks and monitoring the air quality until it returned to normal. The rriksti were moving back in today. "I don't know. There's no good solution."

Yes, there is. Throw them out of the airlock, Skyler thought. Because that was the really sad thing. He *hadn't* been lying on the radio. He'd seen the fury and defiance on the faces of Grigory, Linda, and Koichi, and he believed they would try again if they got the ghost of a chance. He'd feel better if they were sleeping with the fishes.

But he couldn't say that out loud, or Jack would think he was trying to be some kind of badass. He glanced at Alexei, hoping the Russian would say it for him. No such luck. Alexei held his tongue, clearly unwilling to pass a death sentence on his old friends.

"Well, I'd better get to work on this," Skyler muttered, turning his attention to the file of instructions.

"And we've got to get to work on the sunshade," Jack said to Alexei.

"Sunshade?" Skyler said.

"For our parabolic swing around the sun!" Alexei said, grinning.

"Parabolic swing around the *sun?*" Skyler said. "What happened to Venus?"

"Right," Jack said. "I must have forgotten to mention it.

I, ah, thought of a way to shave two months off our travel time. So, yeah. We'll be rigging a sunshade!"

"Um. How?"

"Vapor deposition." Jack's eyes sparkled.

"Use the plastic bags that had the water in them for a mold," Alexei said. "Cut it in half and double it."

"Too bad we can't put anything in between the layers," Jack said. "It would be nice for ions that hit the first layer to have time to decay before hitting the second layer."

"Foamed lead would do it."

"What lead? All the mass we have is either structural, edible, or electrical."

Nothing got these two pumped up like the prospect of death-defying maneuvers, Skyler thought sourly. He listened to them argue for a few minutes. Then he broke in. "Guys. We have to decide what do about the *Victory* crew."

Jack sighed, clearly wishing the problem would just go away. "At the moment they're in the main hab. Got a couple of the *Krijistal* guarding them. I suppose that'll do for the time being."

"So they get to kick back and guzzle our food and water for the next five months—"

"Three months."

"That'll really teach them a lesson," Skyler said sarcastically.

"Yeah," Jack acknowledged. "Uh, we could make them clean the toilets?"

*

Driving out from Miami-Dade, Flaherty's convoy got held up at three separate roadblocks. Brothers with nines tucked into their warm-ups searched every vehicle and patted everyone down, even Flaherty. A hundred bucks in crumpled greenbacks for every twenty miles of road. The Secret Service paid up. They were trying to keep a low profile.

In the new Republic of Florida, an armored SUV and a pair of Humvees did not attract as much attention as you might think. Burnt-out cars littered the shoulder. If you travelled by highway in Florida these days, you travelled with a shotgun on the passenger seat, and preferably a coupla guys manning the sub-machine gun in the bed of your pick-up. The President of the United States on a diplomatic visit barely registered.

But once they got past the final checkpoint, outside the Cape Canaveral Air Force Station, everything changed. The Air Force had left Cape Canaveral after independence. The Camp Eternal Light Limited (CELL) consortium had taken over. New space-themed murals adorned the buildings, and hybrid cars filled the parking lots. The last Whole Foods in Florida, probably, occupied the former PX. The base had become a residential campus for CELL employees, as if Google had picked up and moved to Cape Canaveral, which wasn't that surprising as many of these people used to work in the cocooned world of high-tech. Flaherty wondered how long their private security would keep out the rising tide of lawlessness. Even odds, he thought, whether the dam broke, or the *Lightbringer* got here first.

They drove over the speed bumps and into a traffic jam behind a rocket in its upright position, mounted on a crawler. The rocket inched along ICBM Road at five miles an hour until it turned off towards one of the launch pads along the water. Traffic spilled out of the bottleneck and dispersed to the other launch pads. More rockets reared up from behind the trees like futuristic church steeples, pricking the cloudless winter sky.

You had to hand it to CELL. If these guys had been in charge of the American space program, we would've had cities on the moon by now, men on Mars. Liberated from federal safety regulations and reporting requirements, CELL had pushed their launch tempo to an average of five launches *per day*.

Not all of those launches went up from Cape Canaveral, of course. CELL also controlled the former ESA facility of Kourou, the former military launch sites on the West Coast, and the pay-to-play pads at Baikonur. They'd get the New Hope sea launch facility, too, now that Texas had declared independence.

Stepping out of his SUV, Flaherty smelled a heady blend of sea air and rocket fuel. As time got shorter, CELL seemed to be pushing even harder, racing the calendar. The frantic atmosphere of haste contrasted with the methodical, by-the-numbers pace he remembered from NASA launches. Ground techs swarmed over the scaffold cradling a 300-foot rocket in the middle of the pad. Fuel tankers idled in line to unload into the underground tanks. Geeks strode around barking into headsets. Amidst this organized chaos, bewigged Partiers queued for the Portapotties and milled around food trucks selling tacos and pho. It was clearly not possible to keep the freaks out entirely, given that CELL had grown out of the Earth Party and relied to this day on its goodwill. If the base ain't happy … well, a drone could take out a CELL rocket just as easily as a NASA one. Flaherty smirked to himself, relishing the pickle his enemies were in.

"Passenger terminal's over there," said Kuldeep, consulting his phone. "That's gotta be it."

Before they got there, James Coetzee intercepted them, flanked by aides in chinos and headsets. They did the good to see you thing. "Nice launch facility you got here," Flaherty said. Translation: we still got the airpower to bomb this place to shit if we feel like it. Coetzee smiled cynically. In fact, the very fact he'd emerged from his bat-cave to greet Flaherty confirmed that CELL was still nervous about American airpower. Coetzee was CELL's biggest shareholder. The rocket towering overhead bore the logo of his aerospace company.

The wind blew the smell of kerosene over them. Flaherty scratched his ribs. Coetzee said, "This flight is scheduled to take off at twenty-three hundred. Two stages to LEO, rendezvous with Sky Station scheduled for tomorrow."

Sky Station was the space station assembled by CELL to support its Moon supply flights. It made the old ISS look like a tin can, just as the CELL consortium made the old *SoD* consortium look like a prototype.

"The passengers will relax and acclimatize," Coetzee continued, "and then board the Moon shuttle. They'll be settling into their new homes at Camp Eternal Light one week from now." He paused, and then spiked the ball. "You're more than welcome to accompany them, Mr. President."

Flaherty grinned. "Surprised to see you're still here yourself, James. How much longer you planning to stick around?"

"I'm a big believer in hands-on management," Coetzee

smoothly evaded the question.

"Until the squid-heads realize you're fucking them over?"

"I'm more worried about the crypto-fascist gangsters running Miami," Coetzee said.

"You should be more worried about your own base. Some day soon they're gonna wake up and realize the 0.001% is bailing on the movement."

The nearer the *Lightbringer* came to Earth, the more obvious it became—to Flaherty, anyway—that the shotgun marriage between Big Tech and the Earth Party was headed for the rocks. The tech guys, the aerospace moguls, and the celebrities had no intention of hanging out with the masses in Times Square to await the coming of the squids. They were running away.

Flaherty threw out a question that had been on his mind for a long time. "Did you ever really believe the squids were coming to save us? Or was it just the excuse you needed to ramp up your private space program?"

"It isn't a question of belief, Mr. President. I deal in facts. And that offer stands, if you would like to avail yourself of it."

Flaherty shook his head, losing interest in the conversation as they neared the passenger terminal. His mind filled with the deeply unpleasant duty he had come here to carry out. On the other side of the world, his Russian counterpart was doing the same thing at Baikonur.

The passenger terminal was in fact a bus, where the passengers who would travel in the capsule atop this rocket would receive their final safety briefings and suit up for the trip. Kuldeep said, "Can I just go in?"

Coetzee sent a couple of his aides with Kuldeep, no

doubt assuming that the American officials had come to see 'their' passengers off in person. Godddamn, when the asshole found out the truth, he was going to gloat like a banker who just foreclosed on his worst enemy's house. But there was no way to stop him from finding out. Anyway, their working relationship demanded disclosure. Like it or not, the United States and CELL needed each other, like estranged family who still shared a home.

"How's your supply chain doing?" Flaherty said, instinctively looking for something he could beat Coetzee with.

"Amazingly solid," Coetzee claimed, with a rare grimace. Flaherty filed that away. As a future bargaining chip, he could offer CELL production time at the few factories in American-held territory capable of manufacturing rocket boosters. Then he caught himself. Future? The future was only 70 days long. CELL wasn't even manufacturing first stages anymore. Just throw them up, land them, refurbish them, repeat until they break.

He glanced up at the sky, in the nervous gesture that had become universal among all humans, rich and poor. You could go nuts thinking you saw things in the mild winter sky.

"How's it going with that secondary build at Shackleton?" he said, for something to say.

Why ask? Coetzee reeled off a canned press release. Everything was *great,* it was *amazing,* he was *so proud* of the CELL team. While he was in the middle of that, Kuldeep came back down the steps of the bus, herding a group of individuals with backpacks.

Flaherty quickly walked over to them. "Hello, folks. I

guess you didn't expect to see us again so soon."

They gazed at him, nervous as hell. He took a moment to go over their details in his mind.

Stephen Sheridan, NASA researcher, and Rufus Moskowitz-Sheridan, age seven. Stephen held the kid's shoulders in an ostensibly reassuring grip, but it looked like the son was supporting the father, not the other way round.

Naoyuki and Yurika Masuoka—Flaherty mentally congratulated himself on remembering *those,* and remembering furthermore that Naoyuki, Koichi Masuoka's elder brother, was a materials scientist. The old lady, Fumiyo, was Koichi's mother. At 81, she would have been the oldest person to travel to Camp Eternal Light. Two teenagers stood silently beside Naoyuki and Yurika. He couldn't remember their names, dammit.

"Folks, I have very sad news for you today, and there's no easy way to say this." As he spoke the next words, he was more aware of Coetzee hovering than of the civilians whose lives he was about to destroy. "The *Victory* mission has failed."

Stephen Sheridan blustered denials: no, it's not possible, Linda never fails at anything she sets out to do …

The Japanese family just seemed to cave in on themselves, like the petals of a flower folding.

Coetzee and his people took over, as Flaherty had maybe subconsciously hoped they'd do, so he wouldn't have to confront the devastated family members alone. They wanted confirmation of the *Victory* mission's failure. Technical details. Data data data.

Kuldeep said, "The ships are hundreds of millions of miles away. We don't *know* what happened. What we have is a long transmission from Skyler Taft, rated R for language, in which he threatened to kill our astronauts. If the mission had succeeded, he would've been dead. Draw your own conclusions."

"You said it was a sure thing," Naoyuki Masuoka said in precise, accusatory English.

"What else were we gonna say?"

Linda Moskowitz's son squeezed between the grownups towards Flaherty. His hair stood up in slept-on cowlicks. He had a chocolate-milk mustache. "Mr. President? Is my mom dead?"

Flaherty had got the instructions for disabling the malware from its unfortunate creators at the GRU. He had had them sent to the *SoD*. He therefore believed Linda was still alive, because he believed Skyler was too well-brought-up to break his word. But it was all *belief*. He had criticized Richard Burke in the past for treating his hunches as facts. Now he was the one falling back on hunches and hope, while Coetzee smugly bragged about living in a world of facts. The shoe was on the other foot and no mistake.

He managed to smile at the child. "Your mom's doing fine, Rufus. She'll be coming home real soon."

The kid didn't know any better than to be reassured. The sweetest grin transformed his face. Flaherty rocked, hands in pockets, thinking, Strike me down now, Lord.

Kuldeep said, "Unfortunately, this means we're required to cancel your trip to the moon at this time."

CELL personnel were already collecting the launch pad lanyards from around the family members' necks. The American and Russian governments had offered the *SoD* to CELL in exchange for a beefed-up role in the consortium. CELL had jumped at it. They wanted the alien tech in that shuttle, of course. The smart materials. The advanced 3D printing technology. The *fusion reactor.* Damn, Flaherty wanted that shit himself. But it wouldn't do Earth any good after the *Lightbringer* came. So—donate it to the Ark, as James Coetzee liked to grandly call his moon colony. In exchange, CELL had agreed to take a select group of top American and Russian officials ... and the families of the three *Victory* astronauts.

No *SoD?* Deal's off. Take a powder.

"You folks got lucky, in my own opinion," Flaherty said to the families. "These bottle rockets ain't the least bit safe."

Hefting backpacks, the Secret Service got the family members moving towards the presidential convoy.

"You're coming with us to someplace that's *really* safe," Flaherty assured them. "So safe I can't even tell you where it is yet."

James Coetzee walked along with them. He murmured in Flaherty's ear, "The offer still stands."

Flaherty turned on him. "You got seven empty seats on that rocket." He flung out an arm, indicating the gaggle of squid-heads eating pho on the grass beyond the Portapotties. "I recommend you offer 'em to those guys."

They got into the SUVs and drove away from the end of the world, back to America.

CHAPTER 33

The sun is hot.

About five and a half thousand degrees on the surface.

Even when it reaches Mercury, the sun's light is still hot enough to melt lead. If you put the Statue of Liberty down on Mercury's surface, by noon you'd have a swimming-pool.

The *SoD's* hull is made of steel, so's the *Victory's;* the *Cloudeater* is made of tougher stuff but it's not highly heat-resistant. Why would it be? It wasn't built to go anywhere near a star. Nor were we, for that matter.

Steel loses half its rated strength at 700° C.

So we're using aluminum for the *SoD's* sunshade. Higher thermal conductivity, you know—

Actually, Jack was just using it because they'd got it.

Those chopped-up seat frames kept on coming in handy.

Broken down in the *Cloudeater's* upcycler, reformed into slugs of pure aluminum, vaporized by tireless rriksti striking arcs between pairs of them, the seat frames designed by military decorators on Imf now formed a 60-meter aluminum bubble floating ahead of the *SoD* on tethers. On Earth, manufacturers built expensive vacuum chambers for vapor deposition. Out here? All the vacuum you could want, for free. Plastic bags pieced together made a fine mould. That said, the bubble was uneven and not exactly spherical. Good enough? It'd have to be.

They cut the bubble in half. Maneuvered one half inside the other. Then someone had to crawl in between the two halves, putting in spacers. Jack volunteered. He wanted to check the thickness of the bubble for himself.

In between the two curving sheets of metal, in total darkness, his feeling of being trapped came back, stronger than ever. Trapped in himself, trapped in this shoddy gizmo, trapped on a vector that would take them insanely close to the sun.

He touched his rosary through his suit. Am I really going to do this? Is this what You want me to do, God?

No reassurances popped into his mind, supernatural or otherwise. Instead, he thought of Keelraiser. *What will happen if I do this?*

Nothing. They'd agreed on that, hadn't they? Nothing had happened and nothing was going to happen, if for no other reason than that Jack was busy trying to keep everyone alive.

His face heated up. His skin tingled with pins-and-needles. His feet seemed to be going numb.

God, I'm such a fuck-up.

What am I going to do with Grigory, Koichi, and Linda? Skyler thinks I should kill them. He didn't have to say it out loud. He's probably right. But … but …

A voice spoke in Jack's head then. It sounded just like his dad. "Thou shalt not kill. Is that so hard to understand?"

Jack cringed. Yes, I know, he argued silently. But … but … they're a problem. I've got too many problems already. It would be easier to just make them go away. Skyler would give me cover. Giles would approve. Alexei would hate me for it, but … but …

"NO," his dad's voice said.

Jack shuddered. Fear washed over him, cold and choking. Eyes wide open in the darkness, gloves splayed against the aluminum roof, he floated immobile until it passed.

*

Giles's laptop displayed ECNN—the Earth Central News Network. A fifty-mile tailback of RVs and pickups clogged a winding road somewhere in the Rockies. Volume was muted. The only sounds in the kitchen tent were plastic forks scraping on plates, and the occasional soft noise as one man or the other set his cup down.

Alexei watched Jack in between bites. Jack did not look up from his food. The bright light in the kitchen picked out the gray in his hair. He looked more than usually haggard.

At last Alexei spoke. "Sorry."

Jack looked up. "It's OK," he said, chewing. He swallowed and half-smiled. "We were getting too attached to the damn fish, anyway."

Two days previously, Grigory and Linda had made a second sabotage attempt. No malware required. They had been ordered to unclog the settling tanks of the sewage system—a revolting task that normally fell to Giles as part of his life-support duties. You had to stick your head inside a cabinet in the wall and stir the supercrap, as Giles called it, that had been around the back of the bioshield and gotten sterilized, but smelled no sweeter for it. It needed to be done often with 300 people on board, but Giles never complained. Jack had seen an opportunity to give him a break by making Grigory do it instead. Linda had volunteered to help. Alexei had volunteered to watch them.

Somehow, he wasn't quite sure how, he'd got chatting with them. It started with wry jokes about the smell arising from the tanks, and before long they were talking about Earth, about places and people they'd all known in the old pre-MOAD days. And while Alexei and Grigory were reminiscing about the ball-freezing winter weather back home, or maybe it was when Linda was talking about her shy, gifted son, one of them had reversed the flow of the sewage system, pulling water out of the settling tanks and sending it back upstream.

Contaminated a quarter of the hydroponics before the alarm was raised.

Which happened to include the tilapia tanks.

Which had killed every last one of those tough little fish whose great-great-great-grandparents had come all the way from Earth.

Which was why Jack and Alexei were eating MREs.

But that wasn't the worst of it. When the contamination was discovered, Brbb and his friends had beaten Grigory and Linda to a pulp. This was not a mere figure of speech. No square inch of flesh remained un-bruised, cut, or abraded by their fists and nails. Same thing they'd done to Kate before they killed her.

Alexei had forgiven them for Kate. At least he had tried to forgive them. There used to be fourteen *Krijistal* in this platoon, not just eight; the rest had died, mostly at Alexei's own hands, and if the survivors had forgiven him for that, could he do any less? They all had to work together.

But the sight of Grigory and especially Linda half-dead from the *Krijistal's* tender attentions had triggered a weapons-grade flashback, and—as Skyler put it afterwards—Alexei had gone Spetsnaz on their asses. It was lucky all he'd had to hand was a socket wrench, or there would be even fewer *Krijistal* on the ship now.

Everyone snaps at some point, but Alexei had thought he'd be the one who never snapped. Guilt dogged him. He chopped up his entrée with the side of his fork. Designed to be eaten in freefall, it was a solid slab that bore very little resemblace to beef bourgogné.

"God, this pudding is horrible," Jack said. He examined the wrapper. "Banana cream pie. I remember having this on the ISS. It tasted better then. I suppose it's just been too long since I ate anything sweet."

"You're gonna love the food in jail," said a voice from behind Jack. Although slurred and nasal, owing to the effects of a broken nose, it recognizably belonged to Linda.

They'd tied her up with spacesuit tethers and secured her, like a dog—Alexei's mind shrank from the comparison—to the legs of the kitchen cabinets, the only permanently fixed furniture in the hab. Those strong, lightweight poles went right down into the floor.

Ostensibly ignoring Linda, Jack said, "Well, we weren't really expecting to go home again, anyway." He pushed away his tray and wrapped his hands around his mug of tea.

"It's not too late, Jack," Grigory said. He was tied to the other side of the cabinets. His voice sounded even worse than Linda's. Halting, wheezy. "Take the *SoD* to the moon. Save the human race."

The sides of Jack's nose went white with the effort of ignoring Grigory. He said to Alexei, "It's the *Cloudeater* they want, you know. Same old story. People will lie, kill, and betray their friends for alien technology."

"It's a little more complicated than that," Alexei said.

Grigory had admitted the truth while they were chatting in SLS. "They were going to use the *SoD* as an orbital weapons platform. Point the railguns at CELL. Fire a warning shot or two. Make the Earth Party guys leave. Then land the *Cloudeater* and the *Victory* near CELL, walk in, and take over."

Pretty much what Alexei had first guessed, in fact. His GRU-trained instincts had been on target.

"The CELL guys are tech geniuses, but amateurs in politics. They would have quickly found out what happens when you accept gifts from the government."

Jack shook his head half-admiringly. "They really are cunts, aren't they?"

Alexei figured he meant the American and Russian governments, which had cooked up the Trojan horse scheme between them. He nodded in agreement, although part of him thought it was rather a good plan. That's why he'd let himself get distracted from what Grigory was doing with the settling tanks. When the *SoD* reached Earth, they'd lob their remaining plutonium rounds at the *Lightbringer*. Suppose it all went as planned—a long shot, but possible. Suppose they destroyed the alien planet-killer. Then what? Grigory had warned him that all four of the *SoD's* crew would face life in jail. Alexei didn't fancy that. And he couldn't stand the idea of being separated from Nene. What would happen to her? And the other rriksti? CELL offered a faint gleam of hope …

… as well as one deal-breaking drawback.

"They wanted the *SoD's* guns and the *Cloudeater's* technology, but they didn't want the rriksti. Or us."

Jack's mouth twisted. He sipped his tea. "It's good to have

real tea again. Now all I need is real milk."

"There won't be any more tea after the *Lightbringer* comes," Linda said, from behind the cabinets. "There won't be any more milk. But there may be people. If CELL makes it."

Alexei got up and went to fix himself a cup of coffee. He shared Jack's sentiment that real tea and coffee were the best things to come off the *Victory*. He could see the top of Linda's head through the gap beside the hot-water dispenser. Blood crusted her hairline. Sitting on the floor, facing away from him, she didn't know he was watching her. She stared emptily at the trellis of broad beans in front of her.

"I see people all around me," Jack said behind Alexei, so quietly that Alexei wasn't sure he'd been meant to hear. "They've just got more fingers and toes."

Alexei stirred a packet of liquid creamer into his Nescafe and sat down at the table again. It was weird to stretch his legs out under there, with no fish tanks getting in the way.

"How's Nene?" Jack said.

Alexei choked on his coffee.

Jack scowled. "I feel quite betrayed, Alexei. I can't believe you never said anything. It's almost as bad as that time you deleted my copy of *The Meaning of Life* to free up disk space for *Spaceballs*."

"Come on. *Spaceballs* is the best comedy about a spaceship in the history of comedies about spaceships."

"That's a very small category, and by the way, on this ship you're to refer to me as 'idiot,' not 'you captain.'"

"I didn't want you to look at me with that look you

look at people with."

"I'm not that stupid."

"I'm the stupid one. I should change my name to Asshole."

"How many assholes have we got on this ship, anyway?"

There was a short silence, broken only by the sound of spoon on mug as Jack pointlessly stirred his tea. Presently Jack said, "Maybe you feel as though you've let Kate down?"

"No," Alexei said immediately. The suggestion surprised him. It proved how far Jack was from understanding his relationship with Nene. He tried to explain. "This is completely different. Kate meant a lot to me. No one could compare to her. But that's my point, there is no comparison." He glanced at the cabinets. Grigory needed to hear this, too. "Drinking tea is not like chopping firewood."

"Huh?"

"Apples, apples and …"

"Oranges. Apples and oranges."

"Yes. Both things are good and beautiful, and you cannot compare one to the other." Alexei thumped his chest, getting a bit Russian. "She understands my soul."

"That's fantastic," Jack said. "I could not be happier for you. But how's the nooky?"

They put their cups in the wash-bucket and their trays in the recycling. They had yet to figure out what the *Cloudeater's* upcycler could do with MRE waste, but it would probably come in handy at some point.

As they left the kitchen, Koichi came into the tent, followed by Fewl and Difystra. "Hey, guys!"

Koichi had raised the alarm after Grigory and Linda reversed the flow of the sewage. Apparently he had known what they were planning, but had decided at the last minute that he couldn't go along with it.

If not for that, they might have lost a lot more of the hydroponics. So Koichi didn't get tied up, although Jack had told the *Krijistal* to keep a close eye on him.

"Got the therapeutic laser," Koichi said, holding up an aluminum case. "The squids are taking our ship apart. Um. Anyway. Should I get started now?"

"Might as well," Jack said neutrally.

They squeezed through the plants and around the back of the cabinets to where Linda was sitting. She raised her face and spat at Koichi. The Japanese astronaut's head jerked back. He pulled his arm across his cheek.

"Come on, Linda," Jack said. "Where are your manners? He's trying to help you."

"Fuck off and die," Linda said. "Traitor."

Koichi hunched his shoulders. He opened the aluminum case and took out a power source, a cable, and a wand with a rubber pad on the end. "MLS laser," he muttered. "Works on abrasions, edema, and so forth. Brings down inflammation. Pain relief, too."

"Nifty," Jack said. "They didn't give us one of those."

"We've got a lot of stuff that wasn't developed, or wasn't available, when you launched."

Alexei watched Koichi apply the laser wand to Linda's injuries. The technology might be state-of-the-art on Earth, but it could only do so much. Fewl and Difystra opened their mouths, no doubt reflecting, as Alexei was, that *they* could have fixed Linda and Grigory up in just a few minutes.

Could have ... but would not. Nene had refused, too.

Alexei couldn't blame her. Grigory and Linda had tried, *twice,* to murder every rriksti on board.

"When you finish, can we punish them again?" Difystra said.

Koichi had been given a headset so that he could communicate with the rriksti, although he he had yet to use it to talk to them. He cringed.

"Don't worry, he's just joking," Jack said. "Aren't you, Difystra?" The tall riksti shied from Jack's nudging elbow.

"Go do Grigory," Linda said. "They hurt him worse than me."

It was true. Around the other side of the L-shaped wall of cabinet, Grigory lay on the floor, eyes closed. His breath wheezed fitfully. Koichi pulled his limbs this way and that to apply the MLS laser to his injuries.

Jack squatted near Grigory's head. "You said CELL is an ark," he hissed. "You're completely deluded. Oh, I can see how it looks from Earth. It looks like the adverts on the news. Hot and cold running water and a playschool and a dog grooming salon and God knows what. But this is *space.* Back in spring, a ball bearing nearly killed everyone on this ship." Jack pinched his fingers together to illustrate its small size, and planed his hand through the air until it landed on Grigory's shoulder. "A fucking ball bearing. *This* is an ark, if you like. And everyone on board could have been killed by a ball bearing. Don't try to tell me the moon would be any different."

Grigory groaned, "Long shot … better than no chance. Survival of the species …"

"Is paramount. I fully agree." Jack stood up. "That is why we're going to catch the *Lightbringer* … and blow it into radioactive dust."

CHAPTER 34

It was too hot to work, so Skyler was doing astrophysics. 98° F in the shade.

In the shade of the *Victory,* that is, where rriksti were prying edible electronics out of the walls by the light of the emergency LEDs, and Skyler, flashlight strapped behind his ear, watched priceless scientific data flow in through the ship's external Ethernet connection.

Supervising the cannibalization of the small ship last week, he'd discovered a ton of scientific instruments. The space agencies had given the *Victory* every kind of 'eyes' they could think of, perhaps hoping they would give the crew advance warning of any nasty HERF-style surprises.

"What a bunch of tools," Skyler had said to Hriklif as they boarded the *Victory.* The ship had been a complete mess. The *Krijistal* had ripped open all the boxes looking for the Shit We Need that wasn't there. Powdered eggs and green smoothie mix swirled towards the vents from torn vacuum packs. Skyler had rubbed his eyes.

"What are you doing?" Hriklif said.

"Shedding a tear at man's inhumanity to man. OK, that's done." Skyler smirked. "Check out those instruments!"

Particle detectors, a centimeter-band RF receiver, high- and low-energy proton monitors, and a bunch of other goodies. Skyler had got Hriklif to write DO NOT EAT on them in Rristigul, and earlier today, because it was too hot to do any real work, they had scrounged a long pole and mounted the best of the instruments on it. The *Victory* was in the shade of Jack's giant aluminum umbrella. Couldn't see shit from back here, so they had to stick the instruments out on the end of a boom.

Pointing at their object of study.

The sun.

"No human being," Skyler said, "has ever had the opportunity to observe the sun from this close up."

The *Victory* was an oven. Although they'd cranked the little ship's reactor output down to 2%, its radiators were having trouble dumping enough heat overboard, as hot solar wind snuck around the umbrella, raising the temperature even in the shade.

"Neither has any rriksti," Hriklif said, his eyes reflective in the darkness.

The two had become close friends as they shared responsibility for monitoring the *SoD's* reactor, and now the *Victory's* as well. Largely on account of Hriklif, Skyler had quit the battle of the pronouns. *He* it was.

"We're probably all going to die anyway," Skyler predicted. "So we might as well get some science done." He sighed, watching the numbers pour in. He'd set up the main computer to show the most interesting readouts in sine-wave graph format. "In the old days we'd have killed for data like this. We had ACE and SOHO orbiting at the L1 Lagrange point, but neither of them got anything like this level of detail."

"They sold our mission as a scientific mission," Hriklif said. "That's why the Lightsiders signed up. It was supposed to unify the Darkside and the Lightside after the war. Think of the discoveries to be made! they said. Imagine the scientific gains! That's why *I* signed up."

Hriklif was a Lightsider, which went a long way to explain his oddball status among the rriksti on board.

"Of course, the Darksiders knew the truth all along," he added glumly. *"We are not warlike*—that's what they always say. And we keep falling for it."

"I can think of a lot of people like that on Earth," Skyler said. "I used to be an astrophysicist, you know. I should have stayed in academia."

"My girlfriend was a student," Hriklif said. Skyler understood that Hriklif was using both of the terms—*girlfriend* and *student*—loosely. *Student* was a lifelong occupation on Imf, and Hriklif actually used to be one himself, while *girlfriend* apparently meant a female you slept with on the weekend. "I used to sneak into her dorm in the middle of the week," Hriklif said, laughing with his hair, and giving the lie to his own definition. But Skyler knew that Hriklif had been crazy about this long-dead rriksti female, and still dwelt on his loss eighty years later, which was pretty freaking sad, but then again, who was Skyler to throw stones? *He* still dwelt on his bygone non-relationship with the *Lightbringer's* new Shiplord.

"We'd better winch the boom back in soon," he said. "The instruments are gonna melt if we leave them out there too long." He peered at the readouts. "Looks like the radiometer is already melting."

"What?"

"Look at that: that's weird."

The radiometer had picked up a spike in the energy distribution of incoming protons.

"It's like a narrow section of the incoming flux suddenly got very active." Skyler tracked the spike with his eyes as it travelled towards the left side of the screen. "2023 is a big year for solar flares …"

Which made this the worst possible year to be swinging around the sun.. Skyler had saved the *SoD* by disabling the malware, and now Jack was going to kill them all anyway by cooking the ship in neutron flux. At least they were breaking new scientific ground on their way to oblivion.

"Could this be a type of precursor flare we haven't seen before?" he pondered aloud.

The old, nearly-forgotten thrill of the quest for scientific knowledge came back. He could almost taste the sweetness of discovery. He pictured his name in lead author position on the paper to follow … the accolades, the career opportunities … and then he remembered that civilization was due to be blotted out in two months, so there'd be no prestigious scientific journals to publish papers in anymore. Well, crap.

"That's our comms maser," Hriklif said.

"Oh. Are you sure?"

"Yes, these are stimulated ions blowing back in the solar wind. If this instrument had better resolution, we could read the message."

"Bang goes my paper in *Astronomy*," Skyler sighed. "Well, we'd better winch the instruments in."

They donned their suits and went out. It was pitch-dark in the shade of the umbrella, as the *SoD* and its smaller companions were pointed straight at the sun, but the edge of the umbrella, ahead of the ships, caught the sunlight. It etched a dazzling circle on the void, so that they seemed to be flying straight into a solar eclipse. Beautiful, and frightening.

Skyler concentrated on operating the winches they'd

attached to the *Victory's* truss. The boom hinged back down like a flagpole flying a luminous crimson flower. The steel casings of the instruments glowed red-hot. Skyler whistled.

Hriklif said, "I cannot work out why he was using the comms maser."

"Who?"

"Keelraiser, of course."

Skyler knew that Hriklif had a complicated relationship with the rriksti pilot. It seemed to have started off as hero-worship, and soured as Keelraiser's feet of clay inevitably came to light. The demands of survival on Europa may have papered over their differences, but ever since they boarded the *SoD,* Hriklif had been allowing himself more and more comments critical of his supposed boss. (*Boss,* too, was a slippery term with the rriksti. They managed to be both feudal and Orwellian at the same time.)

"A snowball?" Skyler said, at the same time watching the red-hot instruments fade, and realizing how radically dumb a suggestion that was.

"Not very likely," Hriklif said diplomatically. "We are on the far side of the sun from the *Lightbringer,* anyway."

"Yeah, Jack was saying we won't have to worry about them intercepting our comms for a while."

"But not quite yet. Communications won't become impossible until we cross Mercury's orbit."

Hriklif grabbed Skyler's arm and towed him around the *Victory,* using his wrist rockets to vector them around the *SoD's* much broader truss tower. Untethered spacewalking made Skyler sick with fear to this day, but he had learned to deal with it. They landed underneath the *Cloudeater's* belly. The ramp was down, letting people in and out of the unpressurized cargo hold. Hriklif grabbed the edge of the cargo ramp and swung them both up and over it. *Whoops-a-daisy!* Just like going next door. Yeah.

"I don't think Keelraiser's on board at the moment," Skyler said, when his pulse steadied enough for him to speak.

"Exactly," Hriklif said. "He's not. This is our chance."

CHAPTER 35

Hannah floated in foot tethers too big for her feet, operating a lathe with a bed as deep as she was tall. She was in the *Lightbringer's* vacuum dock, the on-board shipyard and parking lot. Preparations for the invasion of Earth were well underway. All up and down the length of the kilometer-long cavern, suited rriksti labored over shuttles floating above Hannah's head. Every one of the shuttles was a blackened hulk, and many were missing their tails, as if they had been torn in half by immense hands.

Unfortunately, the vacuum dock, being well forward of the water tanks, had not blown up in the historic explosion eleven years ago. But Eskitul's gang had disabled all the shuttles. There used to be seventy shuttles. Now there were sixty-nine wrecks. Eskitul and her followers had escaped in the last shuttle to Europa, where it and they presumably remained.

So the Lightbringer now effectively had *no* shuttles. But Ripstiggr never wrote anything off, so they were cannibalizing parts from the damaged ones. Sparks flew and smoke drifted through the dock. A vacuum forge melted down scrap metal. Enormous printers spat out replacement parts. Had there been any air, the din would have been overwhelming.

The activity centered around a handful of shuttles designated for refurbishment. These would transport the infantry to Earth's surface after the first wave of bombardment.

Orbital bombardment used to be a mere science-fictional concept.

Now it was as real as the steel alloy rod in Hannah's lathe.

Cast of slagged metal, the rod measured about three meters long. She mechanically wheeled the cutting tool up and down its length, honing it to cylindrical perfection.

Of course, orbital bombardment never had really been a science-fictional concept. That's how most people thought of it, but aerospace professionals like Hannah knew it was all too easy.

Step one: Make a cylindrical projectile.

Step two: Line up your crosshairs.

Step three: Rods from God, baby.

She could have deliberately botched her work, so the projectile would tumble off-course in flight, but what would be the point? The guys working the other lathes would not botch *their* work, and final inspections would uncover any irregularities, which would definitely be blamed on Hannah. Besides, she clung to her professional work ethic. She would not make a mess of any task she was given … even if it was crafting a weapon of mass destruction.

Fortunately, she had a distraction from the job at hand.

"If people would disperse out of the cities, these things would have less impact," she visualized in biophotons printed on the black, greasy chucks of the lathe.

Iristigut emailed back about one minute later. He was taking longer to respond to her emails these days. She assumed he was being kept busy, too. She glanced up at the suited rriksti levering a turbine out of a damaged shuttle overhead, wondering which one of them he was … or maybe he was one of the repair crew working on the *Lightbringer's* HERF mast, since he knew a lot about weapons.

"The impact will depend on the accuracy of our targeting," he emailed. "The rods'll be mounted on guided missiles and fired from the *Lightbringer's* main railgun."

Ripstiggr had shown her the railgun after they finally got the rails fixed. A keel-mounted monster two kilometers long, it could theoretically accelerate projectiles so fast they melted. But that level of gee-whiz firepower wouldn't be needed to devastate Earth's cities. Just point and shoot.

"The calibration would only have to be out by a couple of decimals to divert the rods from heavily populated areas," Iristigut suggested.

The scope of their conversations had expanded over the months from Rristigul tutorials, which were frustrating for Hannah as her progress remained painfully slow, to brainstorming ways to sabotage the *Lightbringer's* assault on Earth. With the Shiplord chip, and Iristigut's step-by-step instructions, Hannah should be able to do *something*. But it was a lot harder than it looked to come up with a plan that would amount to more than a futile gesture.

She screwed up her nose. "They'd notice something was wrong the minute the first rod landed in a field somewhere," she transmitted. "No, it's got to be something bigger. Something they can't fix in a few minutes, or a few days, or a few years. Something like Eskitul did."

She gazed up at the shuttles. Rriksti industrial-strength light bathed the vacuum dock, still dim by human standards, but bright enough for each ship to cast a shadow on the 'floor' of the dock where the manufacturing equipment stood. The shuttles reminded Hannah of the styrofoam models of space shuttles she had hung from her bedroom ceiling as a child ... blackened, ravaged, as if her past had exploded, along with her future. The reality of the *Lightbringer* retrospectively tainted all her childhood dreams of spaceflight, and in some ways, that loss hurt the most. The magic was gone.

She turned off the lathe to clean up the fan-shaped field of scurf that had floated up from the cutting tool. She had a large magnet for this purpose. She waved it around to grab the shiny curls of metal out of the vacuum, stretching and twisting, and her muscles felt just fine, no aches anywhere. Even her crotch felt fine, when it should have been sore as hell, because there was no magic in the stars, but there *was* magic in Ripstiggr's hands … and what do you know, there he was, drifting up from behind her machine. He just couldn't leave her in peace. He floated up behind her and tried to wrap his arms around her. She pushed off from the lathe bed, writhed away, and her magnet came too near the work piece. It jerked in her hands and glommed onto the projectile with a clang that vibrated up her wrists.

"Damn."

She braced her feet on the lathe bed and jerked in vain at the magnet. Ripstiggr circled her in his arms, closed his hands over hers, planted his feet either side of hers, and pulled. The magnet popped free.

"Thanks," Hannah snapped. "Now go away. I'm busy."

"We need to talk."

"I am Shiplord, buddy. Scram."

"Is it something I did?"

"You figure it might be? You figure maybe you went a bit too far?"

Weekend had followed weekend and every weekend

Ripstiggr pushed her boundaries a bit further. She still went through the motions of hiding from him, but they both knew that was just the game they played. And why shouldn't she play? Why shouldn't she gorge herself on alien booze and alien cock? Her life was joyless enough the rest of the time. She had every right to grab the pleasures on offer. That's what she told herself. But if biology must have its due, flesh also had its limits, and Ripstiggr had definitely gone too far last weekend. She turned her back on him and went back to work. In the corner of her eye she saw him float away.

She had a new email from Iristigut waiting. "Hannah, I won't be able to email you for a couple of weeks. It's unavoidable. I'm very sorry. But please keep emailing me your questions, and I'll answer them when I'm able. I'll also try to come up with a solution to the problem we've been discussing."

Hannah responded immediately. "Two *weeks?!?*" The prospect of not hearing from Iristigut for that long pushed her to the edge of panic. He was her lifeline. "You can't just abandon me like that! Things are pretty bad with Ripstiggr right now, and I really need …" There was no *delete* key in the neural interface. You can't unthink a thought, if you're only human. "I really need your input," she finished lamely. *Send.*

Whine, whine went the lathe, perfecting the missile with NYC's name on it, or London's, or Shanghai's. A couple of minutes later, Iristigut's reply popped up. "What's going on with Ripstiggr? Please tell me."

They had never discussed her bizarre, fucked-up relationship with Ripstiggr. She figured if Iristigut was on board, which he had to be, he knew all about it, and anyway, it was beside the point, had nothing to do with saving Earth. But now the need for a friendly ear overwhelmed her modesty. "He just keeps pushing it. OK, I don't think I've got anything to be ashamed of. I'm Shiplord. I can have all the men I like. I've got a *harem*. Is there anything wrong with that? *No!* I deserve some fun to make up for having this chip in my head! But last weekend he really went too far. And now he's acting like *I* did something wrong."

She stewed anxiously while waiting for Iristigut's answer. "What did he do?"

Hannah sighed. She wished she'd never opened this can of worms. "Is group sex normal for rriksti? Is it, like, something you guys normally do?"

Minutes passed. No reply. That's it, Hannah thought. I've grossed him out. He'll never talk to me again.

A second later, an even worse thought came to her. What if Iristigut were actually one of the guys she'd screwed over the weekend?

It had been Ripstiggr's idea. Regardless of her claim to have a harem, she had not had one before this weekend. She'd never slept with any of the rriksti apart from Ripstiggr. But this time, he'd encouraged her—nay, *coerced* her, by threatening to cut off her access to *krak*—to do several of the others, separately and simultaneously. Hulk, Joker, and she didn't even know the names of the other … six? Seven? Eight guys? Just remembering it made her want to cry.

It wasn't that they'd hurt her. In fact they'd been very respectful, insofar as they could be respectful while having energetic sex with her (and one another; when she said group sex she'd meant it). No, what hurt was the memory of Ripstiggr watching. Mouth open. She'd actually caught him playing with himself. Not only did he not care that these other guys were doing her, he'd gotten off on it.

And now fear twisted the screw further. What if one of those other guys had been Iristigut? What if she'd fucked him without even knowing it?

"You have to tell me who you really are!" she emailed, desperately.

No reply came. Hannah bit her lip, stricken with regret. As if it wasn't bad enough to prospectively lose contact with Iristigut for two weeks, now she'd lost him forever.

CHAPTER 36

Minutes ticked away and still Iristigut didn't reply. Hannah's sense of loss shaded into anger as she glanced up and saw Ripstiggr harassing the rriksti at work on the shuttle directly overhead. It was all *his* fault. It had been *his* idea, and on account of him, she'd lost her only friend.

She switched off the lathe, kicked out of her foot tethers, and flew straight up through the vacuum dock. A shuttle loomed above her. She caught the wing and went hand over hand along its trailing edge to the fuselage. A jump took her into the forest of heat radiator fins. She kicked off again and used her wrist rockets to flip in the air. The aft hull plates had been removed. She dived down to the flayed spine of the shuttle, forward of the engine bell, where Ripstiggr was giving hell to the poor saps working on the reactor.

"It shouldn't be unfixable," Hannah said sweetly. She was so pissed off that she rashly revealed the depth of her knowledge about the disaster, gleaned in bits and pieces from Iristigut. "All they did was crank the reactors and disable the speed controls on the turbines. Result, the heat rejection systems melted, the turbines exploded, and in most cases, the back end of the ship blew off. This one's in better shape than most. The radiator fins are still there, and the reactor housing's undamaged, which probably means it's OK. You just need to test it out. Inspect the cooling systems, hook up a generator to provide a load …"

"Which is exactly what I told these *schleerps* to do, several hours ago," Ripstiggr said. "Have you finished your work?"

"Anyone can run a lathe. I'll do this. It's my specialty."

"I gave you *that* task," Ripstiggr said, pointing down.

"And I am Shiplord, and I'm giving myself this task." She jerked her helmet at the cringing rriksti workers. "Buzz off."

As soon as they were gone, Ripstiggr pinned her on the top of the reactor housing, where they couldn't be seen from the floor. "Damn these suits. They get in the way." He brushed his thumb over her right breast. Her nipple poked up against the material of her suit. "I want you right now."

"It's not the weekend." Hannah struggled. He had no business getting all handsy after what he'd let those other guys do.

"The weekend is a social construct," Ripstiggr said, in blithe contradiction of the biological facts as she knew them.

At that moment a long email from Iristigut plopped into her notifications. She read it hastily, superimposed on Ripstiggr's black-shrouded face and floating hair.

"This is not the kind of question I expected to be answering," Iristigut began. "I have been trying to think how to respond. Briefly, there is a rriksti concept which I can only translate as 'test to destruction.' As an engineer, you should be familiar with this concept in the context of materials testing. A substance is broken down to determine its strength. We do the same thing to people. It's sometimes called 'professional training,' sometimes 'intimacy,' and sometimes, with unusual honesty, 'punishment.' Context is all."

Hannah changed her mind about Iristigut being one of the guys she'd screwed over the weekend. Those dudes would be completely incapable of analysis like this, let alone such articulate and grammatical English sentences. She actually couldn't think of anyone on the *Lightbringer* whose English was as good as Iristigut's.

"You are Shiplord, but you were never tested. I think Ripstiggr is testing you now. He is trying to find out how much you can take—emotionally, physically—so that he'll know how far he can rely on you. I strongly advise that you refuse to cooperate."

Easier said than done. Ripstiggr was pawing at her. She could hardly keep the wobbling golden words in focus.

"I used to be part of that culture, too," Iristigut wrote. "I participated in the cycles of destruction. Then I changed my mind. I decided that extroversion is *not* next to saintliness, testing to destruction is *not* love, conquest is *not* healing, and war is *not* peace. In short, I saw what was in front of my eyes. It is all complete bullshit. You belong to the Judaic religion, don't you, Hannah? I found some Talmudic quotations that seem to apply …"

The Talmudic quotations followed, at length. Hannah stopped reading. "Screw you," she responded. "I didn't ask for a goddamn sermon! I just need a way to stay alive until I can figure out how to sabotage this ship!"

"Why are you staring at me like that?" Ripstiggr said.

"I wasn't staring at you," Hannah said. "I was interfacing with the chip."

… how to sabotage this ship …

She'd said it herself. That was the answer! They'd been brainstorming ways to sabotage the weapons systems, but that was small potatoes.

Go big or go home, Ginsburg.

Sabotage the *Lightbringer* itself.

My baby, she thought. I can't hurt my baby—but that was the Shiplord chip talking. She was not a rriksti and this ship was not her baby. It was the instrument of Earth's destruction.

"What's it saying?" Ripstiggr said, floating above her, caging her with his arms and legs.

She quickly instructed the chip to acquire telemetry from the reactor beneath them. "Wow." Her eyebrows rose in unfeigned surprise. "Good thing they didn't start this sucker up yet. The gauge field settings are screwed. Jacked *way* up. Let me have a proper look."

She slid free and floated down to the reactor control panels. The chip printed transliterated Rristigul on her optic nerve, augmenting the physical displays. She matched the words with the cheat sheet Iristigut had put together for her. "OK, gotta recalibrate the gauge field. Don't want to make it too strong, or it'll produce too much fleurovium-298 ..."

Ripstiggr floated behind her. She knew for a fact that he knew less about the proton-lithium-6 fusion reaction than she did at this point, although he would never admit it. None of the *Krijistal* were nuclear scientists. Not one of them was even a propulsion specialist. And none of them had an Iristigut to teach them about the finer points of muon-catalyzed fusion. They had gotten this far by reading the user manuals and pushing the right buttons. It was a miracle they hadn't blown themselves up yet ...

... *a miracle* ...

That's it.

I'll give them a miracle.

I'll give them the biggest boom they've ever seen.

It unfolded in her head like the solution to a knotty engineering problem, as obvious as 2+2.

Blow up the *Lightbringer*.

Save Earth.

She saw herself escaping from the big boom ... maybe in one of these very shuttles. Soaring away to safety. Leaving all her problems behind.

"Funny," she mused aloud. "This one really is different from the others." She waved at the other shuttles hanging in their mangled ranks. *"Those* ones blew up. This one didn't." And here, she thought, was the key to her miracle. She began to regret her irate email to Iristigut. "Sorry I yelled at you," she emailed. "Does calibrating the gauge field to a higher setting increase the *strength* of the strong force, or just cause it to operate across a larger region in the core of the reactor?"

Whoever disabled this particular shuttle, they had to have been going for a really spectacular explosion. Not satisfied with merely melting the tail off one shuttle, they'd tried to trigger a fission reaction which would have blown the entire vacuum dock out the side of the ship. They'd failed, but Hannah had worked with fission reactors for years. It was time to put her long-mothballed expertise to work.

All she needed was a *little* more help from Iristigut.

If he could help her to figure this out, she might even take him with her when she escaped.

His silence gnawed at her as she tweaked the gauge field settings. At the moment, with Ripstiggr breathing down her neck, she was just trying to get it right.

"Sorry," Ripstiggr said.

"What?" Hannah said inattentively.

"Sorry I went too far."

She turned and stared at him. He had apologized. She couldn't recall him ever apologizing for anything before. "What brought this on?" she said warily.

"Just thinking."

"Oh my God, it's a miracle," Hannah said lightly.

But later, back in the jewel-hued twilight of the Shiplord's cabin, they knelt on the bed, hugging. The height differential was so great that Hannah's face rested against Ripstiggr's sternum. She could hear his heart beating, faster than a human's. They clutched each other tightly, without moving, without speaking, until Ripstiggr rubbed his face against her hair and said, "Tell me exactly what I did wrong, because I don't know. I'm not human. I don't know."

"Oh, hell," Hannah said. "I didn't want to do it with all those guys, Ripstiggr! Why did you make me do it? I feel like a slut."

"But you enjoyed it," he said.

"Yes, because I was hammered." She beat her fists against his chest. "Drink and drugs make people do crazy things. You *know* your extroversion acts like a drug on me."

"I'm not doing it now."

No, he wasn't. And the sad thing was that she liked the feel and smell of him, anyway. Stone cold sober, she liked the suede-soft skin, the salty odor, the ribby breadth of his torso, the way he trapped her in his arms. It made her feel small, sheltered, safe. It made her want to stay on the *Lightbringer* forever.

"Do you want me to punish the others?" he said.

"Oh hell no. It's not *their* fault. Anyway, Eskitul used to play with the crew, right? We've got to keep them happy. It's all about morale." She heard herself saying these things, as if the rriksti really were *her* crew. But she had decided to kill them all. She nuzzled her face frantically against Ripstiggr's chest, knocking him over backwards. She landed on top of him, struggling with her own weakness.

"At least we don't have any damn introverts on the crew anymore," he said, cuddling her. "They're the ones you have to watch."

"Introverts?"

"Like the guy who blew up all those shuttles."

"I thought Eskitul did that?"

"Eskitul was more led than leader by that time. She may have started it but she didn't finish it. *That* was Iristigut."

Icy shock stabbed Hannah in the stomach.

"In English his name would be Keelraiser."

CHAPTER 37

So I'm getting the picture you're a demolitions expert.

Skyler strained to read the dark green words on the dark brown screen. Numb, he had to remind himself to breathe.

I'm guessing you're one of the guys who came aboard with Eskitul. In fact, now I remember you were there on that first night. I respect your privacy, so I'm not going to ask what you look like, or what name you're using now. Hell, maybe you've found somewhere to stow away in the lower decks.

That's cool, Iristigut. That's cool.

All I'm interested in is your expertise.

Does the gauge field exhibit hysteresis?

Skyler skimmed over the dense, technical paragraphs that followed. Using the key that Hriklif said was the back button, he returned to the previous email. This one was from Keelraiser to Hannah: a multi-page screed, mostly about the Jewish faith.

"Hurry up," Hriklif said, floating in the door of the *Cloudeater's* computer room, so that the autorip couldn't close. "He might come back any minute."

"There are thousands of emails here," Skyler said, hitting the back key again. The text danced like dim ghosts on the low-contrast screen. Words jumped out at him. Bombardment ... calibration ...gauge field ... harem ... *what???* He stopped to read that one. *I can have as many men as I like.* That simply made no sense. It must be code for something, he decided.

Back, back, back. Humorous complaints about food. Scathing behind-the-scenes commentary on the Hannah Ginsburg Show, every episode of which Skyler had watched as a form of self-torture. All of this interspersed with dry-as-dust lists of Rristigul vocabulary and technical essays. Giles would love to see this stuff. But what struck Skyler was ...

"She sounds just the same as ever." He pinched the inner corners of his eyes, blotting moisture. Mixed emotions whipsawed him. "She hasn't changed a bit." And she didn't seem to be pining for rescue—least of all by Skyler. His name didn't come up once. *I can have as many men as I like* ... No, that *couldn't* mean what it said, because not in a million years could he imagine Hannah writing that sentence. "She doesn't sound depressed or anything."

"Well, they're not exactly going to be mistreating her," Hriklif said. "She's the Shiplord."

"Why did they make her Shiplord to begin with? Why not pick one of themselves? Why didn't this douchebag Ripstiggr implant the chip in his *own* head?"

"I'm not absolutely sure," Hriklif said. "It's just a rumor. But apparently the chip has side effects. For one thing, Eskitul drank like a fish." Hriklif opened his mouth wide in that rriksti expression indicating amusement tinged with sorrow: *what a crazy old universe we live in* ... "And also, I heard the chip kills your libido."

"Seriously?" Was Skyler an asshole to think this sounded like good news?

"Yeah. I'm pretty sure it's true. Eskitul was a decorated mother. She had some kind of stupid Darkside medal for childbearing. I think she had like a hundred kids, which suggests a pretty active sex life. But she never hooked up with anyone while we were on Europa, and it wasn't for lack of opportunity. Keelraiser was wild about her."

Skyler decided not to get sidetracked by *a hundred kids,* which suggested yet more unglimpsed facets of rriksti physiology. "Do you think the chip would have the same side effects for a human?"

"I have no idea. Might, might not. Your biology is different." Hriklif looked over his shoulder. "Come *on.* We've got to get out of here."

"Wait, just give me five seconds. I've got to email her."

"No!" Hriklif shoved him away from the screen and hastily shut down the comms software, returning the computer to its state it had been in when they sneaked in here. "Are you nuts? He'd see it in the comms log."

Skyler saw that Hriklif was only willing to disobey his boss so far and no further. And anyway, maybe he was right. Skyler no longer trusted his own judgement. Given a second to think, he sank into a morass of hypotheticals. He followed the engineer out of the computer room.

The door sealed behind them. They flew down the hot, dark, silent corridor.

"I feel better now, anyway," Hriklif said.

"Why?"

"Oh, you know. I thought …"

"You thought he might be in contact with the *Krijistal.*" Skyler, unlike Hriklif, had no emotional investment in Keelraiser's integrity, and had suspected that immediately. The difference was *he* didn't feel better now. He felt worse.

"It shouldn't even have crossed my mind," Hriklif said. "But everything's so crazy. How do you know who you can really trust?"

They flew into the passenger cabin, cover story at the ready: they'd been using the *Cloudeater's* instruments to continue their scientific observations of the sun. However, no one even noticed them. The hospital was overflowing. Everyone extroverted was working flat out.

The newest batch of patients exhibited different symptoms from the former lethargic victims of malnutrition. They fought healing, or confusedly tried to get out of the cabin, walking into the walls in the expectation, Skyler imagined, that these would autorip and magically deposit them back on Imf, in a familiar world where the sun did not spit out flurries of lethal neutrons.

Nene, sleeves rolled up to her elbows, floated up to Hriklif. "There you are. Sorry, Skyler, I am stealing him." Hriklif was mildly gifted. He'd done extroversion on Skyler as a favor before. "People are suffering. Science will have to wait."

"That's OK," Skyler sighed. "The sun'll be there."

*

Four hundred septillion watts, blazing away on the other side of that crappy little umbrella.

Skyler sat near the top of Staircase 6, barely sitting, more like floating, because gravity was weak up here, elbows balanced limply on his knees. He had decided to weather perihelion right here, where the wind from the fans on the axis tunnel could at least cool the sweat encasing his body. Others had had the same idea. Rriksti lined the upper reaches of all six staircases, like birds on curving telephone wires.

When the rriksti try to escape the heat, you *know* it's hot.

There was nothing special about perihelion. It was the moment when the *SoD* would approach closest to the sun.

It was hot now and it would continue to be hot as they pulled away once again. Yet everyone on board had come to see it as some kind of a milestone: like, if we make it through this, we'll be OK ... when in fact, passing perihelion would just bring them closer to the the life-or-death decision at the end of their journey.

Closer to the *Lightbringer*.

Skyler knew perfectly well that in Jack's mind, there was no decision to be made. If they could catch up with the *Lightbringer*, they'd nuke it.

He'd considered telling Jack about Keelraiser's secret email exchanges with Hannah. He'd come very close, but indecision stopped him. He knew Jack well enough to know the information would not change his mind. Jack would say that eight billion lives mattered more than one, and ninety-nine people out of a hundred would agree with him.

Hell, even Skyler agreed with him.

Wasn't there any way they could save Earth *and* Hannah? Such as???

Skyler couldn't think of any way to affect an outcome that depended, anyway, on the *SoD* getting through perihelion without melting. He couldn't even muster the energy to move.

So damn hot.

Pings and creaks sounded through the wuthering roar of the fans. These were terrible noises. They meant the steel hull was expanding.

Not everyone had fled the floor of the hab. Determined gardeners worked their shifts, and shadows moved on the off-white tarps of the kitchen tent. Some of them had bio-antennas.

Melting here.

I can have as many men as I like …

Skyler buried his face in his hands.

*

"Neutron flux," Linda said. "We did warn you." She glared up at the squids in front of her. It was so freaking hot, she could not even manage to feel much anger or hatred. They could take it as read. "Neutron activation transmutes elements into other elements. What that means for the human body, apart from the radiation effects, which are bad enough, is that sodium turns into magnesium."

Koichi sat beside her, pulling his own hair and talking in Japanese. He bumped his head on her shoulder like a child. He had clearly forgotten everything.

"Sodium is essential to nerve cell function, OK? So his nerves are taking a holiday. He's suffering from fatigue, confusion …"

"Lethargy, muscular flaccidity, memory loss," said one of the squids, through the intercom speaker on the other side of the kitchen cabinets. The voice seemed to come from behind her but she knew it belonged to the squid that was waving its black tentacles at her right now. "We're familiar with these neurological issues. Many of us are affected, too."

"Well, excuse me for breathing," Linda said.

"Neutrons are like little bullets," said the squid with red tentacles. "Sometimes they hit you. Sometimes they hit something else before they hit you. It is pure luck."

"Hey, you're squids of science," Linda mocked, remembering the children's book series about Alastair, 'boy of science,' that she used to read to Rufus. The memory of her son came so vividly into her mind that she realized she was probably having neurological issues, too. Reality was breaking up. All she had to ground her was the weight of the tethers around her ankles.

"We are going to heal him," Red Tentacles said. "We just wanted you to know what we're doing."

"Yeah, whatever," Linda said tiredly.

They held Koichi down on the floor with their horrible flappy hands. Black Tentacles didn't join in the torture, or whatever it was. "Have you ever been to this moon base?" it said to Linda.

Linda struggled to think what 'moon base' it could be talking about. She was having difficulty recalling their mission. *Kill the squids,* yeah, but after that? And what were they supposed to do if they failed? To fail to plan is to plan to fail. But the *Victory* crew had had no plan B, because humanity no longer had a plan B. All their eggs were in one basket ... or were they? At last the pieces of memory fitted together. "Oh, OK. Camp Eternal Light. No, I've never been there, but my husband and son are there now. That was the deal."

"What is the population of Camp Eternal Light?" said the squid. "How many ships and shuttles have they got? What about their defenses?"

Linda shrugged. It was too hot to think. "Grigory. Where's Grigory? He knows that stuff. Ask him."

"He's dead," said Jack. Standing with folded arms, he watched the squids who were treating, or torturing, Koichi. "Don't you remember?"

Now she remembered. It crushed her that she could have

forgotten. Grigory had died a few days ago, or was it a few weeks ago? Heart failure, or internal bleeding, or sepsis from all the germs in this hab getting into open abrasions, who knows? Basically, he died of getting beaten up by a bunch of fucking aliens.

Some of which were pawing Koichi right now.

Koichi moaned, and rolled over. Linda started towards him. Her tethers tripped her. She fell back against the cabinets, banging her head.

Jack squatted in front of her. His body odor, although pungent, made a welcome change from the salty reek of the aliens. "He's going to be fine, Linda. Look—*look*. He's smiling."

Koichi's eerie smile put the exclamation point on this nightmare.

"I don't care what you do to him," Linda said, belatedly remembering that she was supposed to hate Koichi. "He's a traitor to humanity. Just like you."

Jack sighed. "Oh, Linda. Can't you just drop it?"

Jack had changed frighteningly. Gaunt, with silver glints in his blond hair, he seemed to have aged a decade in less than four years. New lines bracketed his mouth and a newish scar creased one cheek. She didn't remember this cold, detached attitude, either. Maybe it was just that he was still pissed at her, which, OK, would be understandable. But the really *really* fucking scary thing was the way he opened his mouth wide from time to time, while staring with raised eyebrows, *just like the squids,* and she wasn't even sure he knew he was doing it. This above all convinced her that Mission Control had been 100% right. The original crew of the *SoD,* as well as the squids, had to die.

So no, Jack, sorry. I'm not going to *just drop it.*

"Go to hell," she slurred.

Jack glanced at the squids gathered around Koichi. "They're finishing up with him. You'll be next."

"No! No fucking way."

"Grigory died. I'm not going to let you die. You've got a husband and son. They need you. Right?"

She hated him for using Stephen and Rufus against her like that. "My husband and son are on the moon. We're not going to the moon. You're going to go head-to-head with the *Lightbringer* and get us all killed."

"Give me patience," Jack muttered. Koichi sat up. Jack said, "Feeling better?"

"Uwah," Koichi said. "*Naotta. Honto ni naotta.*" He looked up at the squids who'd been pawing him. "You guys ... how do you *do* that?"

The dopey smile on his face disturbed Linda. But he was obviously back to himself.

She remembered to scowl as he came to squat in front of her. She even tried to spit at him, but her mouth was too parched.

"I feel like a million bucks. You should let them do you, Linda."

"Yes, you should," Jack said to her, "because I need you to pilot the *Victory.*"

"What?" Linda yelped.

"Um, pilot it?" Koichi said. "It's welded to your truss."

"As soon as we pass perihelion I want to go to full thrust. That means all three engines thrusting together." Jack floated a hand up from his knee; they all watched it rise as if it were a bird. "We're going very, very, *very* fast. We have to burn some of this momentum off. If we trim our speed just the right amount, and hit just the right vector, we'll catch the *Lightbringer* as they slide into Earth orbit."

"Has anyone ever told you you're mad?" Linda said.

Jack grinned, and for a second he was the old Jack she remembered from NASA astronaut training and the *Atlantis* mission. "You don't have to be mad to work here, but it helps."

"Green cheese," she said suddenly.

Jack looked blank for a second and then roared. "God! I completely forgot about that."

"'The moon is made of green cheese,'" said Black Tentacles. "Is this correct?"

"Blue cheese actually," Jack said. "While we were on the ISS, I took a picture of the moon but I Photoshopped a nice ripe Stilton onto it. It was very subtle. I was hoping it would make it onto NASA's website before anyone noticed."

"That answers your question about the moon base," Linda said to the squid. "It's made of Stilton cheese." Her laughter caught in her throat. It's made of dreams, she thought. It's made of hope. And Stephen and Rufus are there.

"So will you do it?" Jack said. "If not, I can fly the *SoD* by myself and Alexei can fly the *Victory*. It's not a very complicated maneuver."

Linda scowled. Koichi's dark eyes entreated her to say yes. To betray the mission, just like he'd done.

"OK, I suppose that's a no," Jack said. "Oh well. It would have been nice to feel like we were all in this together." He pulled a face, mocking himself.

"I could do it," Koichi said. "Would that help? I am qualified as a pilot, too."

Jack slapped his forehead. "Of course you are!" With only three of them on the crew, they had all had to qualify in everything. "Yes, that would be brilliant, Koichi. As I said, it's not a very tricky maneuver. I'll align the thrust vectors myself ahead of time. You'll just have to thrust on my mark."

Koichi nodded. "I will do my best," he said in his serious Japanese way.

"Fucking hell," Linda said. "Your family's at CELL, too, Koichi! Your mother and your brother and his family, right? Are you just going to write them off like they don't matter?"

Koichi gazed steadily at her. "If I don't do my best, I cannot look them in the face again," he said.

A wave of dizziness washed over Linda. She lay down on her side and wrapped her arms around herself. In her mind she was hugging Rufus. But her arms went right through him, and she wept.

"Do her now," Jack's voice said, in the distance.

Some time later, in a faraway place, caressed by cool wind, her glitching mind took her to the Colorado mountains where she'd grown up. There was Grigory sitting on a tree stump. Large as life, smoking a stinky Russian cigarette. She rushed towards him. He held up a hand: *stop*. "I am dead, Linda."

"I forgot," she said, eyes prickling.

"Have you forgotten everything? Have you forgotten Plan B? Yes, of course you have. You poor kid. Too many neutrons to the brain. But look, they are inducing accelerated neuroplasticity to help you heal." She tasted garlic. The mountain scene, and Grigory, started to grow misty. "Your mind will come back, and then you'll know what to do ..."

He was right. When she woke up, she remembered everything.

She could save Rufus.

Maybe she could hold him in her arms again, for real.

If she could get the timing *just right*.

And, of course, if the *SoD* didn't get blown to shit by the *Lightbringer*.

CHAPTER 38

Richard Burke cleaned out his office at Johnson Space Center. Two Texas militiamen watched him, cradling assault rifles above their bellies. Burke's wife, Candy, fed documents through the shredder. The last thing Burke put into his cardboard box was the *SoD* poster that had hung on his wall since 2016. The idealistic dove logo now looked as stale and quaint as the United Nations logo that had inspired it. The United Nations had become the Earth Party's rubber-stamp department, and the State of Texas had become the Free People's Republic of Texas, population 50 million people and approximately 500 million guns. For a while, an extra-territoriality arrangement had left JSC in American hands. Now, with the *Lightbringer* only 10 days away from Earth, Texas was evicting them.

Burke told himself it was just as well. He'd grown weary of living in one country and working in another, enduring invasive security checks twice a day, while Candy coped with people spray-painting YANKEE RAUS on their rented house.

Carrying boxes, they walked down the stairs. Friendly Texan #1 and Friendly Texan #2 tromped after them. The building already smelled of neglect. A skeleton staff had manned it while New Hope was operational. Now the whole place was empty …

… except for Mission Control. A dedicated handful of men and women had camped out in FCR-1, the mission control center, monitoring the parabolic flight of the *SoD* and its companions around the sun.

Burke set his boxes down on one of the many unoccupied desks, taking the strain off his lower back. "Time to go, guys."

Most of the computers had vanished off the desks. All but one of the big screens at the front of the room were dark. The single live one showed a computer-generated prediction of the *SoD's* path towards Earth, in red. Another line also converged on Earth. That one was blue. It represented the *Lightbringer.* An angle of about 120° separated the two ships' vectors.

Burke looked away from the screen after one glance. He had never been comfortable with the *Victory* deception. It preyed on his conscience. He didn't know what was worse—that the mission had failed, or that he'd approved it in the first place.

"Guys. Time to go."

"Sir?" CAPCOM—actually, the twenty-something comms specialist who now sat at CAPCOM's desk—spoke diffidently. "They're burning."

Burke hurried over. The youngsters made room for him. He tapped keys, bringing up data on the infrared telescope image on the screen ... and whistled. "Holy cow." They were looking at the *SoD's* drive plume. Formerly, the ship had been nearly impossible to observe, as it was hurtling at them straight out of the sun. But now, a flame of hot H2 and O plasma lit up the screen. The *SoD* was thrusting with all its might to decelerate. Its observationally calculated speed ticked lower as they watched.

"They might make it," CAPCOM said, choking up.

By *make it,* she meant *make it back,* without overshooting Earth at 60,000 kph. But something else jumped out at Burke. He moved to the adjacent computer and clicked up their observational data on the *Lightbringer*. He compared velocities and rates of deceleration.

"They're going to get here at the same time as the *Lightbringer*. To within a few hours."

"No way, sir!"

"Yes way," Burke said. Emotion choked him. After the failures, indignities, and hardships of the last two years, this news was almost too much to bear. It offered ... *hope*.

"What's the hold-up?" growled one of the Texans. "Y'all gotta be out of here by noon."

Burke and his young staffers cringed in a Pavlovian reaction to authority, the only kind of authority that mattered these days: the kind with firepower.

But Candy Burke, uncomplaining veteran of America's dissolution, who had put up with being the other woman in Burke's marriage to NASA, and with the loss of her home, and the defection of two out of their three children to the Earth Party, turned on the militiamen.

"This is the *Spirit of Destiny*," she yelled, jabbing a finger at the screen. "It's coming home. And it just might save the world, so give us five goddamn minutes!"

Save the world? Burke wasn't so sure about that. He knew the *SoD* still had three out of its original complement of four nuclear railgun rounds. Whether that'd be enough to take out the *Lightbringer* was another question. And that was assuming the *Lightbringer* did not swat the human ship out of the sky like a mosquito.

What moved him to the point of tears was the sheer achievement of the *SoD*'s return. Breaking speed records, varying its velocity wildly, swinging around Mars, hooking around the sun, while still hanging onto enough reaction mass to slam on the brakes at the last moment—it was an astounding feat that few non-professionals could fully appreciate. Just as the Free Republic of Texas hammered the final nail into NASA's coffin, the *SoD* had achieved the greatest triumph in the history of human spaceflight.

It hardly mattered to Burke, at this moment, that it was also their last.

He grabbed CAPCOM's headset. "Get me the secure channel."

The remaining staffers had begun to pack up their sleeping bags and hotplates. They looked at Burke sadly. The *SoD* never so much as acknowledged Mission Control's transmissions anymore. To be sure, for much of the last two months the *SoD* had been on the far side of the sun, where comms were impossible anyway.

"Here you go, sir," CAPCOM murmured.

Burke cleared his throat. "*SoD*, Mission Control. We're packing up the shop here. All good things come to an end, and JSC is being decommissioned. We will be moving to a new, secure location, but I can't guarantee reliable comms in future."

Where they were going, he wouldn't even be able to see the sky.

"Just wanted to say I am goddamn proud of you. Whatever happens tomorrow, you've pushed back the boundaries of the possible. Nobody on Earth, ten years ago, would have said a human spaceship could make it to Europa and back. You are shining examples of the spirit of endeavor NASA has always tried to promote. You're lightning in a bottle, boys. If this is the epitaph of the human race, well, we went out on a high note."

Candy slid her hand into his and squeezed.

Some of the young staffers started to cry.

Burke knew he had to address Earth's betrayal of the *SoD*. He said, "We let you down." He forced himself to put it in plain English. "We tried to kill you and hijack your ship, because we were afraid. Just like the Bible says, we tried to kill the messenger because we didn't like the message. I take full responsibility for what we did, and I am deeply sorry."

That said, for all they knew, the *Victory's* failure might have been the disaster it looked like to the NXC. Burke might be talking to a crew of squids right now. There was just no knowing. But he had to hope that his boys were still alive, because that's all he had now: hope.

From the top of one of his cardboard boxes on the next desk, a framed photograph peeked out. Flaherty's bold Sharpie strokes encircled four faces. Kildare, Ivanov, Boisselot, Taft.

"Killer, if you're there, if you can hear me ...Alexei, Giles, Skyler ... all four of you are amazing human beings. I know that Kate would be proud of what you've achieved. I wish I could offer you the support you deserve, the support we promised you under false pretences. It's too late for that. But I just want you to know you are in our prayers."

He pulled the headset off as emotion threatened to overwhelm him. "Anyone got anything to add?"

The staffers shook their heads. They huddled together, weeping. Candy was hugging CAPCOM.

Burke put the headset on again for a moment. "Blow the fuckers away," he blurted, and reached out to cut the transmission.

"Wait," CAPCOM sniffled. "I want to send them something."

"OK …" Burke smiled. *"SoD,* looks like we have one final musical selection for you."

CAPCOM keyed up the track. Burke rolled his eyes. "Queen? Really? You weren't even born when Freddie Mercury passed away."

The cheesy song provided a much-needed injection of levity. The staffers packed away their emotions, wiped their eyes, and shut down their computers. They were not allowed to take any of the equipment with them. Millions of dollars in state-of-the-art hardware would be confiscated by the Texans. Not that it would do them much good, Burke suspected. The US government might not control much territory anymore, but it could still craft a mean computer virus.

Before they finished, more militiamen arrived. "That's it, you're out of time," the sheriff shouted. "Move it, move it."

The sheriff wore a ten-gallon hat, a dime-store star, and an Earth Party t-shirt, the one with the Shepard Fairey poster of Hannah Ginsburg's face. Red, white and blue, an idealized goddess gazing at you above the single word *RAUS*.

Raus! The enigmatic one-word slogan had come from Germany, the Earth Party's primary stronghold in Europe. *Raus!* Get out, get out, get out!

Raus, said Hannah to her old mentor as the Texans herded them out of the building. *Raus,* Rich. You're the enemy now. Get out, get out, get out. All your bases are belong to us.

The staffers dispersed to their cars and camper vans.

Burke's youngest child, Savannah, eighteen, drove the family RV around the building to pick her parents up. Burke and Candy loaded the boxes into the back.

"I'll drive first," Savannah said. "It's a long-ass way to Colorado." She narrowed her eyes at Burke. "Dad, why do you look so cheerful?"

"Last day on the job," Burke quipped wryly. "Why wouldn't I be cheerful?"

"You're nuts if you think they're gonna let you retire. We'll *all* have to work. Mom and me will probably have to dig potatoes."

The small NASA convoy drove out through the gates, and passed through the border checkpoint for the last time, bound for the Cheyenne Mountain Complex in Colorado.

Savannah continued to chatter as she drove. To the eighteen-year-old, this was an adventure. Candy squeezed her daughter's knee. "What if the world doesn't end after all, honey?"

After considering that for a moment, Savannah said, "What an anti-climax that would be."

Candy smiled at her husband. Burke saw something in her eyes even more wonderful than the *SoD's* drive plume, something he hadn't seen for even longer ... hope.

*

Back in the mission control center, a voice crackled from the speakers. CAPCOM had left the secure channel to the *SoD* open, and put it on speaker, as a passive-aggressive present for the Texans.

"Well, that was very kind of you, Rich," said Jack Kildare. "Unfortunately it's too little, too late. But thanks anyway, man. Really. Thanks."

One person remained in the room: the sheriff in the Hannah Ginsburg t-shirt. He was wandering around touching stuff, picturing this Star Trek-looking pad as his own future headquarters. He stopped and gazed up at the speakers.

"It was also nice to hear *We Are The Champions*. Haven't heard that one in a while. To show our appreciation, we've got a song for you."

There was some crackling, and then four male voices began to sing in unison.

"Always look on the bright side of life! If life seems jolly rotten, there's something you've forgotten …"

More voices joined the chorus. It was like a church choir bursting out of the speakers, and most of the voices, from soprano to bass, sounded like synthesized angels. The sheriff shuddered like he hadn't done since he was eight years old and feared God.

"So always look on the bright side of death! Just before you draw your terminal breath …"

"Fucking fruitcakes," the sheriff said. He was panicking. He didn't know what to unplug, so he drew his .9mm, aimed at the speakers, and shot them to crap.

CHAPTER 39

In a high-ceilinged 19th-century house in Boston, Trekker Taft sucked on his nebulizer, tossed it aside, and dropped a hailstorm of keystrokes on his Mac. His sister Piper looked over his left shoulder. Their father, Avigdor, looked over his right shoulder.

"Stop crowding me," Trek said. "I've almost got it!"

The lines of code on the screen made no sense to either of the onlookers. They were part of a program Trek had written himself, based on commercial malware he bought from some guy in Slovakia. Trek wasn't a hacker. He was a gamer. But he used to mod games, which gave him a certain amount of coding expertise, and he'd taught himself more in the years since Skyler, the eldest of the three Taft siblings, vanished into space.

With the country rocking and rolling down the slippery slope to anarchy, it was no longer OK to sit around feeling sorry for yourself because you were gonna die of cystic fibrosis.

The internet had gone to shit, anyway.

Right now Trek was using the fiber-optic cable that connected Beacon Hill with Harvard University, where seven generations of Tafts had taught or studied. Skyler had been the last.

"Are you in?" Avigdor said.

"Yes, I'm in," Trek wheezed. "The problem is all these other asswipes are in, too." He turned briefly from the computer to explain. "The Harvard-Smithsonian Micro-Observatory is a robotic telescope array. The actual telescope is in Cambridge. There was one in Arizona, too, but that's gone. Anyway, you can remotely program the telescope to look wherever you want in the sky. But it's supremely hackable, obviously." He allowed himself a chuckle, and coughed. His father passed him his nebulizer. He gulped the cool, mint-scented mist before going on. "Everyone on the planet wants to look at the *Lightbringer*. So I have to deauthorize them before I can point the telescope somewhere else." He went back to typing.

Piper Taft wandered to the window and pressed her thin, sallow cheek to the icy glass. At the bottom of their steep street, torches flickered. Like every other city in the country, Boston had attracted hordes of Earth Partiers as the *Lightbringer* drew closer. Boston Common had turned into a ghetto. Piper had walked with the Earth Party herself for a couple of years, because they sourced the best smack. She was clean at the moment, but sobriety came with a side dish of smouldering fear. The torches looked like the spume from a fiery tide creeping up the hill to engulf her and her fractured family. The Taft money had almost all gone, but the stigma of wealth remained. Piper felt like there was a target painted on their front door. She bit her nails.

Trek whooped. "Got it! This telescope is mine, baby, all mine!"

He copy-pasted the coordinates put out by Harvard, whose astrophysicists had calculated the courses of both the *Lightbringer* and the *Spirit of Destiny*. No one was interested in the latter. The profs just did it for the sake of completeness and fairness, Taft thought, because this was still Harvard and there was still such a thing as high academic standards, even if the apocalypse was coming in four days.

All three Tafts clustered around the screen.

The telescope at the Cambridge Observatory resolved an image in the night sky. High up, near the location of Venus. Just a blur.

"Is that them?" Avigdor said.

"Lotta light pollution," Trek said. "But yeah, looks like that's them."

Piper kissed her fingers and touched the blur on the screen. "Skyler, you dummy, what are you *doing?*"

Trek reached for his pipe. He'd packed it with high-quality Vermont weed. You could still get that. He clicked his lighter above the bowl, inhaled, and blew out a cloud of aromatic smoke. "This one's for you, big brother."

Avigdor Taft grunted, perhaps about to issue his usual spiel about not smoking weed when you only had 15% of normal lung function. Then he changed his mind. "Gimme a hit."

"Dad, you old dope fiend," Trek said agreeably, passing the e-cig over.

Avigdor exhaled a long stream of smoke as he dialed on the cordless phone, consulting a printed-out email. "Hello? Yes, it's me. We can see them ..." He read off the coordinates.

*

"Thanks, Avigdor," John Kildare said. "Thanks very much." He hung up, having carefully copied down the *Spirit of Destiny's* coordinates.

In the UK, dawn was breaking. John had been awake for a hour already. Helen was still asleep. She had a marvellous ability to remain serene in the teeth of the approaching apocalypse. He almost hated to disturb the sweet, lined face resting on the pillow. "Rise and shine, love. Avigdor says we ought to be able to see them."

John had become close to Avigdor Taft, despite never having met him in person. They'd struck up an email relationship on the basis of their unique tragedy. Both of them had sons aboard the *Spirit of Destiny*. Superficially, not much else linked the dissolute American portrait artist and the British retired science teacher, but John believed he'd been able to help Avigdor in some small way by speaking to him of God's love for man: not a sparrow falls to the ground without your Father knowing it …

Now Avigdor had returned the favor. John and Helen put on their coats over their pyjamas and went out into the garden. John got his telescope out of the garage.

The dawn chorus of birds was tuning up. The half-light softened the village street of near-identical brick houses. Less identical were the gardens. A year ago, in her unfussy way, Helen had started replacing her artistic wilderness of flowers with vegetables. John set up the telescope between the cabbages and the potato patch. The smell of dew-wet grass rose up as he settled the tripod into the ground.

"Is that it?" Helen said, pointing up at a luminous star.

"No, love, that's Mercury," John said. "It just so happens that both Mercury and Venus are near maximum elongation at the moment. Yesterday when I went down to the shopping centre, there were more than a few numpties standing around with binoculars. It emerged that they thought Venus was the *Lightbringer*."

"Did you get the candles?"

"They'd run out."

"I should have thought of candles before," Helen said. "And extra batteries. And pepper spray. And a baseball bat. Some American I am." She hadn't lived in the States since they were married.

"If the aliens try to steal our cabbages, I'll hit them with this," John said. The telescope was quite heavy. Fiddling with the focus, he sighed in frustration, and then— *"There* it is."

The viewfinder cupped a bright, elongated blur, still invisible to the naked eye.

"Coming in at two o'clock high."

John stepped back to let Helen see. His heart thudded with longing and helplessness. Out of habit, he framed a silent prayer. Jesus Jesus Jesus. Recently, he had no words for their plight. He could only call on the name of the Lord in inarticulate desperation. Jesus Jesus.

Helen said in a choked voice, "Are you sure that's it? It really is the *Spirit of Destiny?*"

"Yes."

She stepped back from the telescope, shoulders shaking. Unflappable Helen was crying. "Oh, Jack," she whispered. "Oh, my little boy."

"He's coming home," John said as he patted her hand. "He promised he would come home and he's bloody well doing it!"

The actual sight of the *Spirit of Destiny's* drive plume hit them like a crowbar, knocking loose a four-year accumulation of hope and fear.

Despite the early hour, not everyone in Nuneaton was asleep. John wasn't the only one who found it near-impossible to stay in bed with the end of everything just four days away. A Prius cruised along the street. John ambled down to the curb. The Prius halted and an acquaintance from church put his head out the window. "You're out early, John. Morning, Helen."

"And yourself, Mike. Everything OK?"

"All quiet on the western front. Just having a check around."

The Kildares made understanding noises. Earth Partiers had been trickling out from London, making nuisances of themselves. They dossed in gardens, and sometimes broke into houses that they took to be empty. Hence Helen's wish list of pepper spray and a baseball bat. The small Catholic community of Nuneaton had formed a village patrol, as had the Anglicans and the born-again crowd at the Temple of the Living Word. The borough council had gone altogether to pieces.

"That your telescope, John?"

"Yes. Want a look?"

A few moments later, Mike (a general practitioner and father of four) stepped back from the telescope, visibly shaken. He turned to the Kildares and stretched out his hands in an impulsive gesture. "Do you know, the future of humanity probably depends on your son?"

"Terrifying, isn't it?" John said dryly.

*

Four and a half thousand miles away, in the foothills of Montana's Beartooth Mountains, it was still dark. As soon as Isabel Ziegler walked out of camp, she walked out of the 21st century. Trudging through the snow-trimmed pines, she could've been a Native American girl a thousand years ago. What, she wondered, would remain here a thousand years in the future, after the aliens landed?

She hadn't brought a flashlight, because she wanted her eyes to adjust to the dark as quickly as possible. She held up her hands to keep branches from poking her in the eye, knowing that she wouldn't see them coming. The scent of fir needles and pine resin prickled her nose. The trail was overgrown. The adults had let that happen on purpose, so it would be harder for outsiders to guess that they were here.

Isabel's parents, Bethany and David, had moved the family out here after California seceded. They'd joined a community of ten families headed by an old friend of Dad's. Yurts, an outdoor firepit, polytunnels where they grew stuff. No internet, no TV, no electric light. The adults had been lawyers, executives, doctors, stage mothers; now they chopped wood, hauled water, hunted deer, and quarrelled bitterly over the precise positioning of solar panels. Isabel's brother Nathan and the other little kids looked after the chickens and goats. Isabel, at sixteen, occupied an in-between place. There was no one else within a couple of years of her age. They'd assigned her to record-keeping, because of her meticulous nature. *Total* drag. Yet she enjoyed the outdoor life, despite the bitter cold and snowfalls they had weathered during their first months here. The only thing she really missed about Pacific Heights was swimming.

Her coach had thought she might make it to the Olympics in 2024.

But there would be no Olympics in 2024, because the aliens were coming in four days.

The trail Isabel padded along—her eyes now adjusted to

the darkness, her hiking boots crunching dead leaves crisp with frost—led to the lake, where she had swum during the winter, even when she had to crack the ice with her arms like a miniature icebreaker.

She came out of the trees on the bluff above the lake, and the stars exploded over her head.

This was one thing she liked about Montana. The *stars*. She had literally never known there were so many of them.

But tonight she was looking for one star in particular.

Out here, far away from any light pollution, it could already be seen with the naked eye.

Soon, it would be the brightest thing in the sky.

Last night and the night before, they'd all traipsed out of camp to gaze at it. The adults had joked dismally about the War of the Worlds. The ironic thing, Isabel thought, was that they'd hidden up here to escape the collapse of civilization. They were terrified of what they saw the Earth Partiers doing to the cities, and hoped the squids would restore the world to rights. But actually they were terrified of the squids, too. Isabel wasn't fooled. She'd heard her parents talking about things they heard on the ham radio network connecting similar farflung prepper communities. The squids are going to nuke the whole planet back to the Stone Age. They've got chemical weapons. *Genetic* weapons. Nanobots. Plague.

If the Zieglers had more money they would have run away to the moon, like the Silicon Valley elite had. But they didn't have *that* much money, so the best they could do was to run away to Montana, with thousands of dollars' worth of survival equipment in their brand new

4WD.

Last night, the adults' smiley-happy façade had cracked a bit. Isabel's mother had said, "Maybe they'll make an exception for us."

"Nukes don't make exceptions for anyone," Gloomy Greg, the former plastic surgeon, had said. The subject was dropped there—don't scare the kids!—but it touched on the reason the Zieglers had been welcomed into the community in the first place, when other refugees from LA got turned away, no exceptions.

They were special. Because Hannah Ginsburg was Isabel's aunt.

Isabel hugged her knee-length parka around her, and stared at the stars on the horizon. The mountain peaks on the far side of the lake gave her two points of a triangle.

The third point was a silver pinprick. It looked more like a faint planet than a star.

Definitely brighter than it had been last night.

"Hey, Aunt Hannah," Isabel said. "Are you coming to see us? It's been a while."

She snickered humorlessly. She'd admired and looked up to her aunt when she was little, but Hannah had rarely made the time to visit. Never came to any of Isabel's swim meets. And then there was the time she'd dropped Nathan in the pool because she was drunk. Isabel knew that her parents would forgive Hannah for everything in a split second if she used her influence with the squids to save them. *She* was made of prouder stuff.

"We don't need you," she informed the *Lightbringer*. "We're doing just fine on our own."

Except everything was already ruined. No Olympics. No

pool. No school, no friends, no future.

Isabel excelled at pretending everything was OK, but as she gazed at the *Lightbringer,* her defenses crumbled, and tears came to her eyes, making the alien ship twinkle.

"It's all your fault, Aunt Hannah," she muttered, echoing her mother's words four years ago. "You may be a great scientist, but you're a shitty human being, *and* you're an alcoholic."

CHAPTER 40

Hannah sipped *krak* on the rocks, glued to the view from the bridge. As the *Lightbringer* raced closer to Earth, the faint blue dot in the black sky gradually got brighter. She struggled to wrap her mind around the reality that after four years of hardship and misery, she was almost home.

The sight was all the more poignant because she knew now she would never get there.

She'd counted on getting Iristigut's help to steal one of the refurbished shuttles. But he had dropped out of touch for two weeks, and when he reestablished contact, he'd told her no way Jose. You needed a special type of implant to fly a shuttle.

Well, wasn't he a shuttle pilot? Didn't he have the right kind of implant?

Yes and yes, but he wouldn't or couldn't do it, and it was too late by then to think of another escape route. There *was* no other escape route.

So she'd just have to go down with the ship.

As a Shiplord should.

She raised her glass of *krak* to Earth. Tears blurred her vision.

The rriksti assumed she was toasting the success of their mission. They whistled and stomped their feet. They were in a festive mood, euphoric as the moment of victory approached. How she wished she could share their excitement.

"Shiplord! Shiplord! This is all thanks to you," they said, clustering around to touch her feet, which was the rriksti equivalent of hand-kissing. Every crew member had something nice to say about her 'achievement' in bringing them all this way. Even Gurlp: "Best Shiplord I ever serve with."

"I didn't do anything." Hannah rolled her eyes.

"Exactly," Gurlp said, rolling her eyes right back.

But Hannah was going to do something. *Soon.* Iristigut emailed her again, reminding her that time was running out.

"I know," she visualized and sent. "I know! I'm going to do it today!"

The Shiplord chip interrupted her. It had gotten smarter, figured out her notifications filter. Now, when it wanted her to see something, it put her name in the subject line. The messages were still in transliterated Rristigul, but she'd learned enough of the language from Iristigut that she could sometimes pick up the gist. It helped when there were pictures attached, like this one. "What's this?" She looked around for Ripstiggr. "Radar's acquired a potential enemy / ally?"

(Rristigul had one word that covered both meanings, which could be frequency-nuanced to mean either thing, but in alphabetic transliteration it was just the one word, *lividdr.*)

"Oh, that," Ripstiggr said. "See? Up there."

He pointed at the zenith of the transparent ceiling. Hannah shook her head. "All I see is stars."

"Maybe you need to take a closer look." Ripstiggr picked her up and set her on his shoulders.

"Put me down!" Hannah yelped.

"I will not put you down." His seven-fingered hands wrapped securely around her calves. His bio-antennas swayed in front of her face like velvety silver snakes.

She was still holding her drink. "Watch out below," she said, tipping the glass.

The rriksti stomped their feet as Ripstiggr tilted his head back and caught the stream of *krak* in his mouth. "Whew!" He shook himself. Hannah swayed. "Can you see it now?"

"Chip, give me some freaking help," Hannah said. "This *lividdr*. Where is it?"

The chip painted a red polygon around a very faint star.

"What is it?"

"It's that little drone ship Earth launched last year. Remember? It chased us around Mars," Ripstiggr said. "It went the other way around the sun, but now it's caught up. What do you want to do about it?"

Hannah shook her head. "It's unmanned, right?"

That was what the traffic intercepts said, according to Ripstiggr. Of course, he could be lying. Or the intercepts could be lying. But Hannah could not imagine that Earth would have launched *another* manned spacecraft, after the loss of the *SoD* and seven-eighths of the *SoD's* crew. That would be political suicide.

"Blow it away," she said. The decision came from a well of stored-up bitterness. Earth's politicians had sent Hannah and her crewmates to their deaths. They deserved to pay for that … and they also deserved to know that some lousy little drone ship was no match for the *Lightbringer*.

"Just what I was thinking," Ripstippr said. He carried her to the drive chancel. She stretched up and touched the sloping ceiling. Swarms of icons and menus flocked to her fingertips. Soon she'd figure out what they all meant … no, she wouldn't, because *soon* she was going to die.

"You have to authorize the weapons systems, Shiplord,"

Ripstiggr said.

Hannah detected tension, not in his voice, but in the bunched shoulder muscles under her thighs. He wasn't *quite* sure she would actually betray her species when it came down to it.

"Authorize all weapons systems," she said to the chip. She had to keep Ripstiggr from suspecting her disloyalty. The drone ship was a small price to pay.

Ripstiggr set her down, but wrapped one arm around her to keep her close. He worked what had to be the targeting board, using gestures and bio-radio signals that the chip translated to her brain as chirps and beeps. "It's right at the limit of the railgun's effective range. 50% probability of a hit. We'll wait until we get a bit closer."

"I thought the railgun was specced out to eleven million klicks," said Hannah, who had been doing a lot of base 14 to base 10 conversions recently.

"That would be with the original ammo. Lumps of slag just don't fly that well." Ripstiggr's hair stirred pensively. He stroked her upper arm through her suit as they watched the drone ship—just a clump of pixels on the radar plot—float in the *Lightbringer's* crosshairs.

"I need something to eat," Hannah said. Not that she was callous about the drone ship's fate, but … y'know. If she was going to destroy the *Lightbringer,* she had to keep her strength up. "Hey, Figgrit!" she called. "Any chance of lunch in the next day or so?"

The cook was downstairs in the kitchen, beyond the reach of the chip's weak broadcasting ability, but she knew the crew would pass her request along, because she was Shiplord.

"It'll be on the table soon," the response came back.

Soon. Do it *soon.* Every passing minute shaved another increment off her remaining hours of life.

Seeking to shore up her resolve, she stared at the targeting reticule. "Are our projectiles going to fly OK in atmosphere? I mean, we've got to have rock-solid targeting precision, or we won't hit the ICBM launch sites."

Ripstiggr's mouth shut in a tense line. "Might use the HERF mast for that."

Hannah nodded, thinking about what HERF attacks could do to Earth's cities, let alone the launch sites. There wasn't much to choose between a targeted HERF and a nuclear airburst. Iristigut had jettisoned all the *Lightbringer's* nukes, and blown up its long-range HERF mast, but the crew had jury-rigged a short-range HERF mast by cannibalizing the ship's scientific instruments.

"The trouble with HERFs," Ripstiggr went on, "and the muon cannons, is their power requirements. We can't use them while thrusting. So that'll have to come after main engine cut-off. But we're going to pass 160 kilometers above Earth's surface as we enter orbit." He squeezed her shoulders. "We can drop our missiles right down their throats."

Hannah nodded, faced with the terrifying reality that Ripstiggr was winging it.

Billions of lives hinged, not on some fiendishly detailed plan of conquest, but on the instincts of a non-com elevated by chance and disaster to interstellar warlord.

Oh, sure, there *was* a fiendishly detailed plan of conquest. Or rather, there had been. It had died with Eskitul.

And they still hadn't been able to contact Imf, and there was no instruction manual for conquering an alien species.

So Ripstiggr was just playing it by ear.

"It's going to be OK," Hannah said.

I'm going to kill you.

"You'll make the right decisions when the time comes."

You won't have to make any decisions, because you'll be dead.

"Of course it'll be OK," Ripstiggr said. "I'm a seventh-level lay cleric. Ystyggr will guide me in the path of victory."

The rriksti twittered their approval of this cliché, and Ripstiggr hugged Hannah tightly, as if apologizing for the bullshit he had to spout in his official role.

If she stayed here any longer, her heart would fail her.

What are you *saying,* Hannah-banana?

Wasn't it enough for her body to betray her? Was her heart now betraying her as well?

Yes. It was. She wavered on the cusp of relinquishing her loyalty to Earth, because fuck it, you know what? If you're Shiplord, you might as well do it properly. Call it Stockholm syndrome, call Hannah a traitor to her species, but she was compos mentis and perfectly capable of making her own decisions based on the facts, and the facts, the FACTS, Rich—in her mind she was talking to her old mentor, Richard Burke—are, I could live like this. I actually like this big silver-haired schmuck. He fucks like a god and he gives me all the booze I want. I am Shiplord of the most powerful interstellar spaceship ever built. That ain't nothing.

But. *But but but.* I *know,* Rich. If I live, everyone else dies.

She freed herself from Ripstiggr's embrace. "I'm going to make sure Figgrit's not cooking my lentils too long. I don't like them mushy."

She pattered downstairs. Heavier, lighter, heavier again. Don't want to die. Don't want to kill him. She passed Gurlp on the stairs. Don't want to kill her. Or any of them. Oh god*damn* it.

In the kitchen, sheer bad luck waylaid her. Some dumbass had spilled a whole serving dish of steamed suizh, and they were all crawling around picking it up. Given the marginal food situation, not a single precious grain could be wasted. Hannah couldn't reach the airlock without stepping on the stuff, which would have drawn howls. She decided with relief that escape was impossible at the moment. She'd wait until after lunch.

She checked on her lentils and potatoes, and chopped greens for her salad, and the domestic tasks further depleted her will to die.

Tonight. *Tonight* I will DO IT, she told herself, heading back upstairs, nibbling on an ear of young corn (her latest gardening success).

She found the rriksti whistling and stomping their feet.

"Got it," Ripstiggr said, opening his mouth wide. He picked her up by the waist and swung her around. "Blew that cocksucker away!"

High overhead, the red polygon enclosed a spreading shell of pixels.

"Well done, Shiplord!" the rriksti cheered her.

"I didn't do anything," Hannah demurred, although their congratulations reminded her that sooner or later, everything the ship accomplished got attributed to the Shiplord, for better or for worse.

After lunch, examining the infrared and optical record of

the ship kill, she reflected that the debris shell didn't look quite right. If that was the pesky drone ship that had been chasing them since Mars, she'd have expected there to be *more* debris ...

She put it down to NASA cutting design corners and trying to do everything on the cheap.

CHAPTER 41

"Well, they got the umbrella," Jack said.

The *SoD* had cut their aluminum sunshade loose a week ago. It had promptly outdistanced the ship, hurtling towards Earth in a slightly higher orbit. Jack thought of it as a trial balloon. Would the *Lightbringer* fall for it?

They had.

The optical telescope captured the flash.

"The *Krijistal* just can't resist shooting at things," Keelraiser said scornfully.

"And now we know their range," Jack said.

He and Keelraiser sat side by side in the center and right seats, respectively, of the *SoD's* bridge. The *SoD* was burning at full thrust, and had been for the last 48 hours. The low-pitched roar of the drive turbine had become a background noise like the fans. Jack wasn't using the *Cloudeater* or *Victory's* thrust this time. Their triple burn at perihelion had led to a near-disaster when the radiant exhaust from the smaller ships, flooding past the *SoD's* reactor, overheated it, forcing the smaller ships to shut down their drives ahead of schedule, though fortunately not before they'd burnt off enough speed. There was also the live load issue to worry about. It would be massively embarrassing to fracture the truss at this point, so Jack was keeping the *Cloudeater's* thrust in his back pocket as a last-ditch option, and he had another use for the *Victory* in mind.

Thrust gravity held the man and the rriksti in their seats. Their hands were joined across the gap. Dampness formed a seal between their palms. Jack felt almost intoxicated with anticipation.

"Our range is better than theirs," he mused aloud. "We can start shooting any time."

Alexei was loading the railguns as they spoke. Two plutonium rounds in the broadside facing the *Lightbringer*. They also had kinetic rounds, but there was no point firing those. If they couldn't take the alien monster out with the nukes, they couldn't take it out at all.

Keelraiser said, "My life changed when I met you."

In contrast to Jack's excitement, Keelraiser seemed unusually relaxed. Jack was treated to the rare sight of rriksti eyelids, descending in slow blinks over the big sludge-brown orbs. The parted lips suggested a lazy smile.

"Mine, too," Jack said. He rearranged his fingers around Keelraiser's, so that his fingers interlaced with the rriksti's first four fingers, joining their hands in a crushing grip. The skin-to-skin seal was what he enjoyed about this. It both comforted and tantalized him, and why shouldn't he just go with it? What did it matter at this point? Even if they survived the coming battle, which Jack in his heart believed unlikely, the shipboard life they had eked out for two years was about to come to an end. He pictured himself and Keelraiser naked, every square inch of their skin somehow pressed together like a living Moebius strip, and squeezed tighter, although the extreme unlikelihood of this actually happening saved him from having to think about the explicit implications of the scenario. He preferred to think of it as pure somehow.

He freed his hand from Keelraiser's and moved over to the left seat. He picked up the headphones. "What are you doing out there, admiring the view?"

"C'est ça," Giles said. "We can see Earth, you know.

What did Neil Armstrong say? 'I'm coming back in … and it's the saddest moment of my life.'"

"That was one of the Gemini astronauts."

"Same thing."

A few moments later, the airlock opened, and a mile of Mylar-backed insulation lolled out of it like a silver tongue, followed by Giles and Brbb. The gunpowdery smell of space wafted into the bridge. "Try it now," Giles said.

Jack moved back to the center seat and activated the *SoD's* radar. For the first time in a year and a half, the radar plot was not a blizzard of snow. He whooped, and aimed the dish at the region of the sky where the *Lightbringer* should be.

Giles and Brbb had dismantled the DIY paraboloid jammer, as there was not much point jamming the *Lightbringer's* radar when they'd soon be close enough for it to target them optically. Anyway, Jack planned to get off his rounds before they entered the range that the *Lightbringer* had obligingly demonstrated for them a few moments ago. For that, he needed the radar.

"There it is," he breathed. "Large and ugly as life."

The image on the radar plot was only a few pixels across, but it silenced everyone on the bridge. To Jack, it meant more than their first sight of Earth had. He hunched over the screen, and Giles, balancing his feet on the mounting of Jack's seat, squeezed his shoulders.

"They're burning like hell," Jack said, clearing his throat.

"Are we going to blow them away now?" Giles said.

"I'm going to start firing as soon as Alexei gets the rounds loaded. Maybe in twenty minutes."

"OK. I will go start dinner."

Giles gave Jack's shoulders another squeeze and dropped back to the aft wall, where he changed out of his rriksti spacesuit. *I'll go start dinner* ... Jack replayed the remark to himself with amused appreciation. Giles's blasé manner was hard-won, he knew. But it was appropriate. Many hours would pass before their rounds actually hit the *Lightbringer*. In the meantime, they had to keep eating and sleeping. Jack just wished he could be equally laid-back about it.

Giles and Brbb dropped into the keeltube and vanished.

Alexei announced on the radio that he was coming back in. A few minutes later he scrambled out of the keel tube. Jack reached down to give him a hand, boosting him into the left seat.

"Loaded," Alexei said, palming sweat off his scalp. He'd started shaving his head again, using the late Grigory Nikolov's razors.

"I'd better go back to the *Cloudeater*." Keelraiser swung his legs over the side of his seat, dropped lightly down to the aft wall, and left.

Jack moved into the right seat. The shabby padding held Keelraiser's body heat. He wedged his feet through the tethers.

Locked and loaded.

He punched up the ranging function and squirted a burst from the comms laser at the *Lightbringer*. While he waited for the ranging data to come back, he powered up the rails. The lights dimmed. The familiar, long-unheard hum scaled up to an agitated whine.

"Are you sure you want to use up two plutonium

rounds straight away?" Alexei said.

"Yeah. There's no point just crippling it. We know it can survive *that*. Anyway, that still leaves us with one, just in case."

The computer spat out the ranging data. Jack fed it into the targeting equation he'd already worked out.

Lightbringer's 9,010,637 kilometers away.

But the old whale's decelerating at a steady rate. Constant deceleration is like gravity: one half deceleration x time squared. That *squared* gives you distance graphs that look like logarithmic curves. So, when we aim at where the *Lightbringer's* going to be when our rounds get there … that gives us a path length of just 4,540,006 km.

"Here we go," Jack said. He sighed. He mashed his thumb on the firing button.

Zzzzoik!

Zzzzoik!

The plutonium rounds sprang away, one after another, streaking towards the *Lightbringer*. No way the *Lightbringer* could see them—they were just little slugs, coated with an easily volatilized substance that applied even more speed once they were off the rails. When they impacted the *Lightbringer,* they'd be travelling at a hundred and ten thousand kilometers an hour, too fast to evade or intercept.

The whine dipped and died.

"Bombs away," Alexei said. He pushed his joined hands over his head, stretching.

"And now we wait for forty-one hours," Jack said. He sighed again. "Wanna play cards?"

CHAPTER 42

"We're running out of time! You have to do it SOON!"

"OK, Iristigut," Hannah said, and visualized, and sent, through a mist of tears. "Stop bugging me! I'm doing it, I'm doing it!"

Two days had passed. They'd been busy days. The excuses practically manufactured themselves. But now she was all out of excuses. The *Lightbringer* would reach Earth in 31 hours. The *Krijistal's* preparations were done as they'd ever be, and Hannah had got extremely drunk. That was the only way she could suppress her desperate yearning to survive. She focused with inebriated single-mindedness on picking her way across the bridge without stepping on anyone.

The rriksti had been working so hard that many of them had fallen asleep as soon as their shifts were done. They literally fell on the floor of the bridge and dropped off where they fell. To see so many of them asleep at once was unusual, but the floor-sleeping thing was not. Coming from a world without a day and night cycle, they'd never evolved regular sleeping patterns—it was one reason why life among the rriksti could feel like an endless Super Bowl with no commercial breaks. A rriksti in Imf's pre-industrial era would simply have taken a siesta whenever and wherever it felt sleepy. Nowadays, they structured their siestas around their work, but the haphazard drowsing-off thing continued to be their preferred pattern. And of course, they did not require darkness. The perpetual gloom was both their day and their night.

The Shiplord was unique in actually having a cabin, which of course was more for privacy than for sleeping in. Hannah had left Ripstiggr curled on the fur-covered bed. She wanted to go back and snuggle up beside him. Instead, she went downstairs, pulled up her helmet, and went out into the darkness. Faint green arrows blinked, pointing aft.

"Where are you?"

"I'm on my way, OK? You don't have to keep bugging me!"

It had started to feel downright creepy, the way Iristigut kept pressuring her to kill the *Lightbringer* and everyone on board, presumably including himself. But Hannah had a theory about that.

"Where are *you?*" she asked him. Predictably, he gave her the same answer as usual:

"Not very far from you."

Hannah smiled grimly to herself. She flew on, following the green arrows, until she reached a knobbly steel wall. It looked like part of the hull. She ordered the chip to unlock the door, and flew in. Lights blazed on automatically. She squinted. The lights were no brighter than you would find in a public area on Earth, but after so long in the twilight, she was dazzled. "Hello, Iristigut," she sent.

While waiting for him to reply, she searched for him. The lights bathed a corridor lined with plate glass windows, like a shopping mall without signage. She flew down the corridor. Each window was the wall of a cell about 1.5 meters square—cramped quarters for a human, wretched for a rriksti.

But every cell was empty.

"Where are you?" Iristigut emailed.

"In the brig. Aren't you here?"

She'd only found out about the existence of the brig recently, when her command of Rristigul improved to the point that she could read the ship schematics.

Ripstiggr had never told her the *Lightbringer* even had a brig.

And she had concluded that must be because Iristigut was there.

That's what you *would* do with the person who blew a kilometer-long hole in your ship and disabled all the landing shuttles, not to mention ditching the nukes and slagging the HERF mast. You'd put them in a maximum-security cell. Wouldn't you?

Except, obviously, not.

The reason Ripstiggr had never mentioned the brig was simply because they weren't using it.

"I thought you must be here," she sent. "I thought that was why you wanted to die."

She kicked the nearest cell window and rebounded into the one behind her. "Ow. Ow."

"I did spend time in the brig once," Iristigut emailed. "But I'm not there now."

"I can see that!"

He was not there. She could not force him to steal a shuttle for her. She was out of time. There would be no escape for Hannah Ginsburg. Not in this lifetime.

She fled the deserted, silent cell block and flew on through the dark corridors, passing by the hole in the hull.

"How did you get out of there?" she emailed. "How are you still alive?"

Iristigut's answer came quickly. "Someone I care about helped me to escape. Is there anyone you care about, Hannah?"

What a cruel question! Her eyes filled with tears again, which was really annoying because they couldn't fall in zero-gee. "Yes," she said. "My sister Bethany and her family. I guess most of all my niece, Isabel. God, I love that kid so much."

She had answered her own question, not his question. The question was: Why do I have to die? And the answer was: For them.

Her mind cleared. Her reluctance didn't go away, but she simmered down from her overwrought emotional state. She opened the throttles of her wrist rockets and flew faster, past icefalls bursting from the sides of cargo holds, and other holds that had been sealed off so the water could be turned into steam and pumped out. At last she reached the reactor room.

She braked, grasping the bulkhead at the entrance.

The high-ceilinged cavern held an armored containment ring the size of seven RVs parked head to tail. In the center stood a sphere the size of a two-storey house. This was the reaction chamber. It had heavy armor as well, but you couldn't see it because the sphere was semi-translucent. So what did Hannah see from the doorway?

A star.

The fusion reactor was running flat out, roaring away inside its smart-material casket. Its light cast the shadow of the containment ring on the wall all around. Submerged in that shadow, four rriksti monitored the muon injection beam and gauge field generator.

Hannah drifted to the top of the door and clung onto the handholds that covered the ceiling like nobbles on black dinosaur skin. The vibration from the ship's enormous turbines gnawed into her palms.

She eased across the ceiling. None of the reactor techs noticed her. Reactor techs? They were just screen-watchers and button-pushers. As such, they never took their eyes off their consoles, frightened that Ripstiggr would flay them if anything went wrong.

Well, something was about to go wrong.

Sorry, guys, Hannah thought as she positioned herself directly above the gauge field generator.

*

In the engineering module of the *SoD,* Skyler and Hriklif were playing Monopoly.

Skyler had not even tried to stop Jack from launching the nukes that would pulverize the *Lightbringer.* He'd just hidden away back here and wallowed in self-hatred, too miserable even to play his guitar.

Then Hriklif had turned up with a handmade Monopoly set.

Although not a word about Hannah was said, Hriklif clearly didn't intend to let Skyler suffer through his vigil alone.

It was nice to have a friend, even if he made you play board games.

The Monopoly set was well-designed. Hriklif had printed magnetic pieces that stuck to the sheet metal board. The properties were named Sirius, Vega, Betelgeuse, and so forth.

"Conquering the galaxy is lucrative," Skyler observed.

"That's why the Darksiders decided to do it," Hriklif said, and landed on one of Skyler's utilities.

"That'll be five million dollars in wormhole transit fees, please," Skyler said, rubbing his hands.

Above their heads in the storage module, irritated human voices broke through the background noise of the turbines.

"Linda," Skyler said, cocking his head towards the keel tube.

Unconvinced that Linda had repented, Jack had kept her confined in the *Victory* since perihelion, guarded round the clock by the *Krijistal*. Now, however, he apparently wanted the *Victory* for something else.

"You know, Keelraiser's been asking me some weird questions," Hriklif said.

"What else is new?"

"He's not an atomic engineer, obviously. And he never showed any signs of caring about gauge field calibration or muon generation before." Hriklif opened his mouth wide. "But now he wants to know *all* about it. Like, even stuff *I'm* not sure about."

"Is there anything you don't know about fusion reactors?"

"Sure. I've never blown one up before."

"Jeez," Skyler said.

A tired Japanese face poked through the keel tube.

"Hey guys," Koichi said. *"Uwaah.* She's in a bad mood."

Koichi had had the unenviable job of telling Linda she would have to vacate the *Victory*.

"Is she ever not in a bad mood?" Skyler said. "Wanna play Monopoly?"

He felt at ease with Koichi now. Everyone did. The Japanese astronaut had a way of making himself useful without asking for praise, like Giles. Skyler appreciated people like that, especially compared to the big egos around here—Jack, and to some extent Alexei. And Keelraiser. And Brbb.

"Where is Brbb, actually?"

"They're cutting through the welds attaching the *Victory* to the truss tower," Koichi said. He dropped into the engineering module, managing to flip in the air. He landed in a heap beside the Monopoly board, and smiled weakly at Skyler. He wore a thermal hoodie. It must have gotten cold in the *Victory*. "How is this going to end?" he said.

Skyler swallowed. Thanks a lot, dude. We were trying not to think about that. "Well, either we survive …"

"Or we die," Hriklif said, hair dancing.

But Hannah would die either way. Skyler glanced at the clock on the reactor controls display. Only twenty minutes until the plutonium rounds would impact the *Lightbringer*.

Suddenly he hated Jack. He'd hated him before, and tried to get over it, but it turned out the hatred was still hanging out in his heart, ready to be put on again, like an old coat, smelly but all too comfortable.

Hriklif's hair stirred uneasily. "Do you know how to play Monopoly?" he said to Koichi.

"This, um, isn't the version I know," Koichi said. *"Wormholes?"*

"It is a vision of the future when Imf and Earth unite to peacefully colonize the galaxy," Hriklif said.

"Or we could watch *Spaceballs*," Skyler said.

*

"Hannah! Are you DOING it? We're almost out of time!"

"Yes! Stop distracting me." Hannah stared intently down at the gauge field generator. "Chip," she whispered, "recalibrate the gauge field. Turn it up to maximum strength."

Graphs and figures poured into her vision, but in the real world, nothing happened ... until the rriksti monitoring the gauge field generator noticed something was wrong. Its hair stood on end. She heard it shrieking to its colleagues.

When the gauge field was properly calibrated, the fusion reaction inside the core generated a *little* bit of flerovium-298. This wasn't a good thing, just an unavoidable side effect. But it didn't impede the fusion reaction, because flerovium has a magic atomic number: both proton and neutron shells are filled, and thus it has a very low cross-section to muon radiation. So the Fl just got circulated out of the way, and decayed into alpha particles of helium. Brownian movement nudged them out of the way of the muon beam.

But now, the star in the core was burning hotter and hotter as the fusion rate climbed. Helium steals muons like xenon steals neutrons in a fission reactor. By cranking up the gauge field, Hannah had forced the muon beam to catalyze the fusion reaction more efficiently. All the helium—the 'smoke' from the reaction's 'fire'—was being swept out of the reaction chamber, where it couldn't steal any muons. Sounds good, right? Except the hotter the 'fire' got, the more 'smoke' it made ... and an increasing percentage of that smoke was now being compacted into highly radioactive flerovium-298.

Hannah's mouth squared. She was crying. So scared of dying. But now it was too late to take it back.

Hotter and hotter.

More and more flerovium.

Big, fat atoms bursting with protons and neutrons.

Fusing together into *superatoms* …

… which are inherently unstable, as everyone who ever took a graduate-level physics class knows.

Just a few more seconds now.

"Love you, Izzy," Hannah whispered. "Hope you think about me sometimes."

The rriksti swarmed around the gauge field generator, panicking.

If they had looked up—but they didn't—they would have seen a black spidery shape clinging to the ceiling, like one of themselves, but smaller, with an unadorned spherical helmet.

And if they could have seen the face inside the helmet, they would have seen a tear-stained but radiant smile.

For the first time, Hannah was proud of being Shiplord.

CHAPTER 43

Six minutes to go.

"I can't take this," Skyler said abruptly. "I'm gonna ... gonna ... I dunno."

He pushed off from the aft wall and jumped up. Grabbing the bulkhead, he struggled into the keel tube.

Hriklif bounded after him. "Skyler! Wait!"

Koichi was left alone in the engineering module with the half-finished Monopoly game.

He stared unseeingly at the magnetic pieces and the plastic fake money. He listened intently for any sounds from the storage module. The turbines made so much noise.

The fate of Earth hinged on his actions now, yet the fear of discovery froze him.

As soon as they lost the fight to capture the *SoD,* Grigory had initiated Plan B. Grigory and Linda had fucked with the sewage just so that Koichi could blow the whistle on them and win the *SoD* crew's trust. Why him? Why not Linda? Or Grigory himself? Because Koichi had the best poker face, supposedly. So Linda had suffered an atrocious beating, and Grigory had died.

And Koichi had won the other men's trust.

What no one had anticipated was that he'd win the trust of the squids, too.

He could not forget the way they'd healed him when his brain was riddled with neutrons. They had magic in their fingers. That helped to explain why the *SoD's* original crew had self-alienated. For a while back there, Koichi had come close to self-alienating, as well.

But Linda had kept him focused on their mission. She'd

reminded him that these squids were the exact same as the ones poised to rain down death on Earth.

If the *SoD* could destroy the *Lightbringer,* that would be great ... but Earth would not be safe as long as a single squid remained in our solar system.

The squids on the *SoD* also had to die.

Now, Linda had said when he went to fetch her from the *Victory.* We have to do it *now.*

And while the *Krijistal* were poking around for any electronics they might not have eaten yet, she'd slipped him the thing she had extracted from its secret compartment in the *Victory's* hull.

Koichi jerked down the zipper of his hoodie.

"It's so hot in here," he said, in case anyone suddenly appeared in the keel tube—but no one did.

He lifted his t-shirt, feeling a mixture of relief and terror.

The thing that had lurked underneath it, flat against his stomach, came out.

*

In the kitchen, Alexei, Nene, and Giles sat around the table.

"Two minutes to go," Giles said, breaking the silence.

"I don't know why I am not happy," Nene said. She tossed her head back and rolled her double-jointed shoulders the 'wrong' way, letting her arms hang down behind her. She looked like a broken puppet sitting in a too-small chair. Alexei knew this posture indicated a blend of exasperation and despair. He picked up one of her seven-fingered hands and squeezed it. He himself should have been wild with excitement at the prospect of slaying the *Lightbringer*. He should have been up there on the bridge with Jack, anxiously watching the radar. But Nene's sadness tainted their impending triumph. He couldn't leave her to go through this alone.

Because she had every right to feel upset. Love them or hate them, the *Krijistal* on the *Lightbringer* were her people.

Giles said, "It's not necessary to be happy, Nene. This is war. It shouldn't make us happy."

Alexei said, "For a gay heavy-metal fan with fourteen fingers, you say some very profound things."

The flaps of the tent rustled. Skyler trudged into the kitchen. Opening the refrigerator, he said with his back to them, "This fucking sucks."

"One minute to go," Giles said.

Skyler let out a howl like a forsaken dog. He slammed the refrigerator and leaned his forehead against it.

Forgiveness isn't a once-off thing. You have to do it over and over. It never ends.

Alexei jumped up and pulled Skyler into a hug.

*

One minute to go, but on the bridge, Jack was already freaking out.

"This isn't right. It can't be right."

The metallic taste of fear numbed his mouth. He was concentrating so hard on the radar returns, he barely noticed that Alexei wasn't on the bridge, as he would have expected him to be. This was the grand finale of their two-year chase, the pay-off for all their sacrifices ... and it was going wrong.

Wrong. Wrong.

Lightbringer's not supposed to be *there,* it's supposed to be *here,* where my projectiles are going to be in 46 seconds.

"They've stopped decelerating."

I based my targeting solution on a steady rate of deceleration. It was a reasonable assumption. If they *don't* keep the brakes slammed on, they're going to overshoot Earth.

But some *Krijistal* just took his seven-toed foot off the brake. They're cruising at a steady speed again.

"Their drive plume has vanished," Keelraiser observed.

"That, too. What the hell happened?"

Both of them fell silent, watching the final seconds tick down.

5 … 4 … 3 … 2 … 1 …

Three and a half million klicks away, the *SoD's* plutonium rounds streaked through the place where the *Lightbringer* ought to have been, passing harmlessly astern of the place where it actually was.

Jack flung himself back in his seat. "Fuck," he shouted. "Fuck, fuck, fuck, FUCK!"

All color and sensation seemed to drain out of the world. All meaning drained out of his life, exposing the underlying pattern of failure.

He heaved himself forward and thumbed the intercom. "All hands, be aware …" he said heavily. "We missed."

Alexei came on the intercom, outraged, disbelieving—*what happened?*

"That's what I'm trying to figure out," Jack said. "Might've been a targeting error, or I might've miscalculated the closing speed of the projectiles, or maybe the whole universe is actually a simulation run by cruel deities for their own amusement." He switched off the intercom. He didn't even feel up to discussing it with his closest friend right now. Especially as he knew the reason they'd missed was none of the above. The *Lightbringer* had stopped decelerating. In effect, it had executed the only evasive maneuver it could have, with suspiciously good timing. What he didn't know was why. There was no way they could have seen those rounds coming.

Keelraiser said, "I told Hannah to shut down the *Lightbringer's* reactor."

Jack pushed himself up in his seat and turned to stare at the rriksti.

Keelraiser perched in the center seat, legs drawn up, hands knitted around his shins. His pupils were pinpricks in the bright lighting.

The inside of Jack's head turned into a blizzard of snow like the radar plot when they had the jamming routine running. His fists bunched.

"There are a lot of rriksti on that ship," Keelraiser said rapidly. "We haven't heard from Imf. The planet may have been utterly destroyed. Our colonies, too. The rriksti species may be extinct, except for us."

"I'm starting to think that if the rriksti species went extinct, it'd be rather a good thing," Jack said. His glacially calm tone resulted from a superhuman effort not to punch the shit out of Keelraiser.

"It's OK," Keelraiser said. "It's OK! The *Lightbringer* will enter an elongated orbit around Earth. They'll swing out halfway to Mars, like a comet, and then swing back. We'll make sure they can't restart the reactor. By the time they come back, we can be ready to intercept and board them. Same result, minimal loss of life. It's better this way, don't you see, Jack, it's better—"

"Screw that. I'm trying again."

He had one more plutonium round. And now the *Lightbringer,* unpowered, was a complete sitting duck, unable to do anything except plunge forward inertially.

However, by the time his next salvo would reach the *Lightbringer,* the alien ship would be so close to Earth that a nuclear explosion would fry every electronic gizmo on the planet, including things like, oh, the computers that control electricity grids and power plants. So that was out.

He decided to save the last plutonium round for when the *Lightbringer* came back around, assuming Keelraiser was right that it would get captured into a comet-like orbit. He'd have to do the calculations. Keelraiser had presumably already done them, to make sure his deception would work. Jack reached for the intercom. "Alexei?"

"Yeah?"

"Reload."

Kinetic rounds this time, he was about to add, when Keelraiser yanked him out of his seat. They fell gently back to the aft wall in a tangle of limbs. Jack was taken completely by surprise. Before he could fight free, Keelraiser pinned his arms behind him. One long-fingered hand encircled both of Jack's wrists. The other hand went around Jack's neck. Disregarding the pressure on his throat, Jack tried to headbutt Keelraiser in the face. He sank back, gagging.

"Please don't," Keelraiser said. "Please. *Please.*"

Jack struggled mindlessly until he had to give it a rest. His breath came in ragged pants. Keelraiser used the arm around his back to hold him tighter. Both were wearing shorts and nothing else. Their upper bodies pressed together. The sticky residue on Keelraiser's skin formed the skin-to-skin seal that Jack had fantasized about more often than he cared to remember. It was salt in the wound of Keelraiser's betrayal to experience it this way.

At the same time, it dawned on Jack that Keelraiser hadn't actually tried to hurt him. Jack had resisted the urge to punch Keelraiser's lights out, and perhaps Keelraiser was making the same effort, in his own way. Well, it was progress. Maybe someday they could have a civil dialogue about why Keelraiser kept lying to Jack and pulling the carpet out from under him.

Keelraiser released Jack's wrists. He wrapped his other arm around Jack's back, and delicately laid his cheek on Jack's. "I've wanted this for so long," he said. "Now I've fucked it up. Story of my life."

Jack slid his arms around Keelraiser's back, settling them underneath the broad ribcage, where it seemed they were meant to go. He nodded in sad amazement—yup, you get what you want and then you fuck it up: story of my life, too.

"You're just a complete bloody … *alien,* aren't you?" he said, looking up / down into the black tangle of bio-antennas.

"It must be possible for two intelligent species to exist in the same star system," Keelraiser said.

"We can't even exist in the same room without attacking each other."

"I keep getting it wrong," Keelraiser said. "What about this?" He lifted his head. Their faces were inches apart. "Is this correct?" He pressed his mouth onto Jack's in an open-mouthed kiss. Soft lips with sharp teeth behind them, metallic seaside breath, enticing wetness—the sensations startled Jack violently. He pushed Keelraiser away.

"Just hang on. Just wait a minute."

"Was that wrong?"

Jack licked his lips. Salty, piquant, moreish. "Yeah. Very wrong," he said.

"You never say what you really mean," Keelraiser said. "But I think I know what you mean. You don't actually trust me, let alone like me. And I admit that I have not always behaved correctly. I've broken the rules. I've abused the reciprocity cycle. I've lied to you and deceived you, over and over. I'm a piece of shit, Jack. Is this correct?"

The self-accusation took the wind right out of Jack's sails. "Well, now that you mention it," he said, trying for a humorous note.

Behind Jack, someone cleared his throat. Jack knew without turning around that it was Alexei. A hot blush spread up his neck to his face. He groaned inwardly and mustered his nerve to face it out. He arched his body backwards until he could see Alexei's head and shoulders poking out of the keel tube. *Why* didn't I close the damn door? "Come all the way in or go all the way out," he said. "It still gives me the willies to see anyone halfway through one of those things."

"If it's not a good time, I can come back," Alexei said, with a broad wink.

"No, come in, we're not busy." Jack flipped right way up to Alexei. He collected his scattered thoughts, willing the humiliating blush to go away. "Well. We missed."

"Do we know why?"

"The *Lightbringer* seems to have shut down its reactor.

According to Keelraiser, it's unlikely they can get it restarted."

"You're fucking joking."

"Unfortunately not. So we'll be firing further salvos, on the hour." Jack didn't look around. He didn't care what Keelraiser thought. Anyway, Keelraiser was sure to be aware that the *SoD's* kinetic rounds would do no more damage to the *Lightbringer* than mosquitoes stinging an elephant, unless Jack could put one straight into the hole in the ship's side, or score some other chance-in-a-million lucky hit. "I expect them to return fire as soon as they realize we're shooting at them, if not before. We're about to enter the effective range of their railgun. So I'm going to use the *Victory* as mobile armor."

Alexei nodded in understanding. *"That's* why you wanted Linda off the ship."

"Yeah." Jack sighed. He had hoped for the best but planned for the worst, and as usual, the latter turned out to have been the right move. "Where is she now?"

"In the main hab. Giles is giving her coffee."

"Coffee! God, that sounds terribly civilized."

"Well, it is their coffee."

"I just don't know what to do with her. We can't tie her up again."

"No. Like a dog. No."

"I suppose we'll have to have someone follow her around all the time. Get the civilians to take shifts."

"With the taser," Alexei suggested.

"Christ no. Imagine if she got it off them. No, we'll just have to trust in the squid intimidation factor." Jack looked around at Keelraiser, hoping to draw him into the conversation. "Or maybe keep her on the *Cloudeater?* Squid intimidation factor times a thousand."

"No," Keelraiser said. "You are aware that Brbb's lot wanted to kill her. You've already broken the rules by keeping her alive. I'm in no position to criticize you for that, but don't compound the error." He moved between Jack and Alexei to the keel tube and left without a word.

Everyone does that, Jack thought hopefully—but as soon as Keelraiser was gone. Alexei leered and gave Jack a punch on the arm. "Well?"

"Well what?"

"Well, what's going on?"

"Nothing."

"You were kissing him. That's not nothing." Alexei pretended to duck. "I can't help having eyes."

Despite all his grueling experiences in space, Jack was still English. This came close to taking the crown as the most embarrassing moment of his life. "I'm not gay," he said weakly.

"No one says you are."

"You just did say it."

"No, I did not."

"You did."

"He's an alien. It's completely different."

Jack remembered Alexei using this very phrase—*it's completely different*—to describe his relationship with Nene. "You're right," he said. "It's completely different. We're human and they're aliens. They don't think the same way we do."

"It's possible to understand how they think. You just have to get them to open up."

Jack was bursting to tell Alexei about Keelraiser's betrayal. But if he said anything negative about Keelraiser now, Alexei would take it as criticism of Nene and the rriksti in general.

"I have to organize the *Victory*," he said, shutting the conversation down, shutting Alexei out. He regretted it immediately. But fuck it. This was a distraction. He needed to stay focused on the mission. "We'll need volunteers to move it …"

Alexei's gray eyes darkened. "Right."

"See if you can round up some of the *Krijistal*. I've got to stay here and see what the *Lightbringer* does. They're freefalling towards Earth, no brakes … this is not going to end well."

CHAPTER 44

It hadn't worked.

Hannah had clung to the ceiling of the reactor room, waiting to die, for what felt like a lifetime. But nothing had happened. No big boom. The reactor's rate of fusion had leveled off. The rriksti button-pushers had frantically tried to recalibrate the gauge field. They couldn't, because the Shiplord's commands superseded their permissions.

Oh well, she had thought at last. Might as well help them out.

"Chip," she'd said in a flat, dead voice, "switch the gauge field off."

Then something had happened.

The star in the reaction chamber had gone out.

*

Now, fleeing back towards the bridge, she emailed Iristigut.

"You lied to me! You complete asshole, you LIED TO ME! You said the superatoms of flerovium-298 would be unstable and go fissile! THEY DIDN'T! When I switched the gauge field off, they just decayed into alpha particles."

She wasn't an atomic physicist. If she were, she might have seen this coming. But even with her patchy, second-hand knowledge, it was pretty clear with hindsight what had gone wrong. The goddamn lousy gauge field exhibited hysteresis, meaning that it took a while to go away after you switched it off. So the superatoms hadn't gone boom. Held in the decaying embrace of the gauge field, they'd just fallen apart like dandelion clocks.

What time is it, Hannah-banana?

Time to panic.

If flerovium was supercompacted 'smoke' from the reactor's fire, when it came apart, it reverted to ordinary 'smoke'—clouds and clouds of helium particles. All that helium stole muons, 'putting out' the muon beam.

No muons, no fusion.

So the fire in the reactor's core had gone out

And that left the *Lightbringer* without thrust, without any power source apart from what was in the batteries, and sure, rriksti batteries held a heck of a lot of juice, but not nearly enough to drive the ship's gargantuan MPD thrusters. So the *Lightbringer* was dead in space, hurtling towards Earth *way too fast.*

She flung her fear and rage at Iristigut. "You TRICKED ME! You deliberately misled me about the behavior of superatoms!" And on and on, long after she gave up any hope of getting an answer out of him. At last, the funny side of it struck her. She was yelling at Iristigut for *not* helping her to commit a suicide bombing. She drifted to a halt and laughed weakly at herself.

Checking the map, she was on Sleeper Deck 2, in one of the broad transverse corridors dotted with groups of furniture. She pulled herself down onto a sofa, feeling like Alice in Wonderland—the sofa was too big for her little human body. No vibrations came up from the deck. Without power, the turbines were just hunks of metal.

What was Ripstiggr going to do to her? Oh God. He'd know it had been her. Only the Shiplord could have overridden the reactor's operating restrictions. He'd probably kill her.

Well, they were all dead, anyway. The *Lightbringer* would

scream straight past Earth, go into orbit around the sun, and come back in 2070 or so.

So she'd saved humanity, even if it wasn't going to be as dramatic as she'd planned.

I did it, Izzy.

See you in fifty years.

She was just mustering her courage to turn on her suit radio when she noticed a green light at the end of the corridor.

It raced towards her, illuminating the tanks on both sides with a sickly, spectral glow.

As the tanks lit up, their occupants twitched, flexed their limbs, and opened their eyes.

Hannah bounced off her sofa. She floated in mid-air, heart pounding.

Fixated on the tanks in front of her, she did not at first notice the figures crowding towards her from the end of the corridor where the glow had started.

Too late, she whipped around in the air and confronted a horde of soldiers.

They still seemed to be half-asleep. They zig-zagged and bumped into each other in the air. Yet their long-ago training had saved their lives. Each of them, before leaving its tank, had donned the suit stored in an inner compartment of the tank. Cryosleep gel dripped off their black-sheathed limbs, forming a gelatinous rainfall in the vacuum.

Hannah retreated.

"Um, hi, guys," she tried. "I'm your Shiplord. What are you doing up?"

The corridor filled up as more and more soldiers burst

out of their tanks. They flooded in from the narrower dormitory corridors that crossed this one. They had no intention, clearly, of sitting down on the sofas for a drink of juice and a nice gentle re-entry into the world of the living. They had awoken in an emergency situation—the ship in vacuum, the drive dead—and now the first thing they encountered was a bubble-headed alien.

"Stay away from me," Hannah warned, putting out her hands to ward them off. "I'm your Shiplord!"

They had been asleep since the *Lightbringer* blasted out of Imf orbit eighty years ago. Why on earth should she think they understood English?

She frantically sorted through her Rristigul vocabulary. She could describe the process of proton-lithium 6 fusion, but she was short on everyday words. *"Muzl!"* Stop! "I said *muzl!*"

That worked about as well as a red flag to a herd of bulls. They closed in on her, grasping her limbs in steel-hard fingers—their suits seemed to be armored, more rigid than her own—prodding and pulling and scratching at her suit to see if it came off, or if it was her skin. They rapped on her fishbowl helmet, knocking her head sideways. One of them seized the helmet from behind, fingers closing over her field of vision like bars, and tried to twist it off.

In a blind panic, Hannah screamed, "Ripstiggr! *Ripstiggr!* Help! Stop them! They're trying to kill me!"

No response came for long enough that she wondered if this was Ripstiggr's doing, if he'd intentionally woken the soldiers so they would tear her limb from limb. Then his voice slashed across the drowsy muttering of the soldiers. As he bellowed at them in Rristigul, they let go of her arms and legs. She curled into a ball in the air. A nauseating flash of pain stabbed her right elbow.

The beams of chest-lamps cut through the green-tinted gloom. Ripstiggr and a couple of the other *Krijistal* forced a path through the soldiers.

Still yelling at them, Ripstiggr caught Hannah in his arms. She heard the word *Eskitul*. Of course, that was not actually the name of her predecessor. It was the Rristigul word for Shiplord.

The soldiers fell back. One by one, they mumbled a response to whatever Ripstiggr had said. Hannah got the impression of formulaic, grudging assent.

"What are they doing awake?" She trembled, shocked to the core by her narrow escape.

"Tanks were programmed to wake them when we completed our final deceleration into Earth orbit," Ripstiggr replied. "The system was synched with main engine cut-off."

"Oh."

"Yup."

As her fear of the soldiers ebbed, her fear of Ripstiggr returned. She licked her lips. "I did it."

"I know." His voice had never sounded colder. "Come on."

The other *Krijistal* stayed behind to sort out the soldiers. Ripstiggr dragged Hannah back towards the bridge. Their progress was slow. Every corridor teemed with dazed soldiers looking for their weapons, looking for answers, looking for enemies. Ripstiggr yelled at them continuously. At last they reached the kitchen airlock. Soldiers had begun to invade the shattered space outside the airlock, floating over the glacier and investigating the three-storey hole it had torn in the support decks. Hannah did not envy whoever got to fill them in on the *Lightbringer's* adventures in the last twelve years.

A dozen of them crowded into the airlock with Hannah and Ripstiggr. Hannah shied from the black-clad giants. Nervously, she said to Ripstiggr, "Thanks for rescuing me."

Ripstiggr did a rriksti shrug, jerking his head sideways and rolling his shoulders.

She wanted to ask: *Why* did you rescue me? Why not just leave me to die?

But the question answered itself. He'd rescued her because she was Shiplord. He might kill her himself, but he couldn't leave her to get torn to pieces. Not because he cared about her. Just because she was Shiplord.

They stumbled into gravity. Hannah yelped as her weight came down on her right ankle—it was twisted or sprained. Dozens of *Krijistal* crowded the kitchen. The soldiers doffed their suits and headed straight for the water dispensers. It was chaos. Ripstiggr yelled orders. On the way upstairs, he said tersely to Hannah, "Air is the big problem. They've only got a day or so in those suits. I've told the guys to cycle them through here to top up. They'll also have to eat and drink, obviously. We're going to run out of food, but we'll run out of oxygen first. We'll operate the electrolysis equipment around the clock. Who knows if it'll be able to keep up?"

The *Lightbringer's* electrolysis unit was actually the *SoD's* electrolysis unit, stolen from it in Europa orbit.

"Sorry," Hannah said, hobbling after him, nearly in tears. She couldn't stand the thought of her crew suffering like that. Her crew? Yes, they were her crew. She was Shiplord. And she'd condemned them all to a miserable, lingering death, very different from the miracle she had planned on. "I screwed up."

Ripstiggr shrugged again.

On the bridge, the wall sections on either side of the drive chancel had been polarized to transparency. Earth floated ahead of the ship, a blue marble adorned with swirls of white. Hannah stared at it through a mist of tears.

Joker reported to Ripstiggr, his bio-antennas inscribing loops of despondency in the air. "They tried to restart the reactor. It's not happening. Got the muon injection going, but the gauge field is fucked."

I probably smoked the CPU by turning it up that high for that long, Hannah thought. Without the gauge field, the muons would just decay before they could catalyze fusion. No power. No thrust. No *power*.

"How are you feeling?" Joker asked her.

He'd asked. Ripstiggr had not.

"Lots of bruises. Something's wonky in my right ankle. And I think I've got radiation sickness again. I feel really nauseous."

Ripstiggr acted as though he hadn't heard her. "Organize a work crew to inspect the chemical thrusters," he told Joker. "They should be in order, but make sure."

The *Lightbringer* had small maneuvering thrusters that ran on rocket fuel. The *Krijistal* had used them occasionally to boost the *Lightbringer's* orbit during its ten years circling Europa.

Hannah felt a flare of hope, and then reality set in.

"Those thrusters can't slow us down enough to achieve orbital capture. We're going to sail straight past Earth."

"No, we aren't," Ripstiggr said. He did not look at her. He stared intently at Earth. She saw that he was not going to give up as long as breath remained in his body. "We're going in hot."

CHAPTER 45

Jack frowned at the radar plot.

He looked back at the computer.

He said, "They're going to aerobrake."

Despite himself, he felt a shiver of respect for the *Krijistal* commander.

"Blin," Alexei swore. "That takes guts."

"Yup. No power, no brakes … so they're going to brake in Earth's atmosphere."

"Mad," Keelraiser said crisply. "The *Lightbringer* was not built for aerobraking. It won't work."

"It was built *tough,"* Jack said. "The hull is what? Three meters thick?"

They all gazed at the main optical screen. It showed the feed from the *SoD's* forward-facing camera. Earth, picture-perfect, the size of a watermelon. The *SoD* was just 200,000 klicks out now—half the distance from Earth to the moon. They could not see the *Lightbringer* on the screen but it was there. Not having slowed down at all in the last thirty hours, it had reached Earth first. In fact it was about to dive into the atmosphere, entering at an oblique angle over the Pacific.

Jack almost wished Mission Control hadn't gone off the air. He'd have liked to hear Star City and Houston's best guesses about the *Lightbringer's* course. As it was, all he had to go on was their own observations.

"One dip into the atmosphere won't slow them down enough."

"They'll have to swing out to the moon," Alexei said.

"That's what I said."

"No, you didn't."

"Well, I was thinking it."

"Once around the moon," Alexei said. "Back to Earth. Then they will have to skip off the top of the atmosphere several times to slow down and regularize their orbit."

Jack shook his head, not disagreeing, just because it was such bad news. "That'll give them plenty of time to fire on Earth at their leisure."

He deliberately didn't look at Keelraiser. Keelraiser had been wrong. He'd underestimated the *Krijistal* by the same factor that he himself fell short of their standards.

"So …" Jack rubbed his fingers together nervously. "We'll have to chase them to the moon."

Silence.

"Anyone disagree?" Jack shouted, turning from the screens.

Alexei sat in the left seat; Giles was perched for some reason in the center seat; Keelraiser, Nene, Brbb, Koichi, and a bunch of odds and sods stood on the aft wall, looking up—even Linda was there … They merely looked back at him. Their silence said they weren't taking responsibility for this. He was the commander.

A timer on Jack's console cheeped. "Oh, fuck it." Time to launch another salvo. In silence, he laser-targeted the *Lightbringer*, powered up the railgun, and fired another four kinetic slugs.

"Can you fill us in on the operational utility of these attacks?" said Linda, sweetly, as the whine of electrification died down.

"I'm just amusing myself, aren't I?" Jack snapped.

*

Hannah, said the chip, followed by a schematic of the *Lightbringer's* aft port quadrant, exterior view. The picture was worth the thousand Rristigul words that followed it. The hull sported a brand-new crater measuring 2 *zlimik,* or three-and-a-half meters, across.

"Someone's shooting at us!" Hannah yelped.

"I know," Ripstiggr said curtly. He stood in the drive chancel, working the consoles. Hannah stood close beside him, not by choice, but because the whole bridge was packed solid with people sitting and lying on the floor. They couldn't split water fast enough to resupply the suits of 16,000 soldiers, so as a last-ditch measure, they were packing them into the pressurized bridge and support decks to hang out and wait for oxygen supplies. The air had already started to taste stale and smell foul. It was like living in a crowded subway carriage as big as a cathedral. It broke Hannah's heart how quiet they were.

"Who's shooting at us?" she demanded. She didn't know how to make the chip give her that information.

"Humans, doubtless," Ripstiggr said. A mild shockwave ran up through the soles of Hannah's feet. The *Lightbringer* had returned fire. Unfortunately, the railgun ran off huge fuel cells that had been fully charged before the reactor went down, in anticipation of hammering Earth's cities.

Sickened, Hannah wondered who was about to get hammered now.

*

"Skyler," Jack said into the intercom. "There's been a slight change of plan. We're going to the moon." He paused, expecting pushback. Nothing. "I estimate that the

Lightbringer's going to catch up to the moon in its orbit and swing around it in a retrograde direction to slow down. So we're going to do the same thing. We're behind them now, but we ought to catch up, as they'll drop more speed than we will on the way around Earth. Just letting you know ..." He trailed off. Waited. "Skyler?"

"Got it," Skyler said. "Anything else?"

Jack pulled a face. "We'll be throttling back to two-thirds of max thrust after we bounce off Earth's atmosphere. You don't need to do anything until that time."

"Got it. Out."

"Someone's got his knickers in a twist," Jack muttered after he shut the intercom off.

"What do you expect?" Alexei said. He took another star sighting. They were going to reprise the 'skidding' tactic they'd used for their Mars flyby, with bonus enemy rounds flying at them. They couldn't do anything about that but they could ensure rock-solid positioning. The *SoD* had to bounce off the top of Earth's atmosphere at exactly the right angle to reach the Moon. They'd meet the stratosphere in another eight hours or so.

Jack felt Alexei moving away from him like an iceberg moving away from the shore. He had to do something to bring him back. He said, "Keelraiser's been in touch with Hannah. He told her to shut down the *Lightbringer's* reactor."

Alexei sat back. "You're not serious."

"As a heart attack."

"So *that's* why we missed."

"Yup. Keelraiser made sure we would miss."

Alexei reddened and seemed to struggle for words. He said at last, "Well ... it won't make any difference in the end, will it? We're going to nail them with the last plutonium round."

"Right, on the far side of the moon, where it won't matter if we EMP everything within a thousand-mile radius."

On the camera feed, the shapes of the Americas emerged from Earth's swirling veils of cloud. Jack breathed deeply, fending off homesickness. "We're doing this for Earth," he said, tacitly begging Alexei to understand. "For the people down there. For our families."

"My parents moved to Siberia. By choice. They're crazy, but they will be safe there."

"You don't bloody know that, and anyway, there are eight billion other—"

"I know, but we cannot just forget about Hannah! I never stop thinking about her. And for Skyler it's worse."

Jack squeezed his eyes closed. He wanted to say he thought about her all the time, too, but it would be a lie. He deliberately did not think about her at all, because if he did, he might not be able to do this. "She's not on our side anymore."

Without warning, the *SoD* leapt sideways.

Jack and Alexei, jolted out of their seats, scrambled back to the consoles, yelling obscenities.

A Rristigul shriek issued from the intercom, and cut off.

Keelraiser's voice crackled from the *Cloudeater*. "That was Brbb."

"The *Victory*," Jack shouted, already guessing what had happened.

In anticipation of attacks from the *Lightbringer,* they'd

converted the *Victory* into mobile armor. They had broken the welds holding the smaller ship to the *SoD's* truss, and used the *Victory's* RCS bundles to edge it backwards, past the bioshield, until it lay alongside the aft portion of the *SoD's* truss tower. This positioned it between the *Lightbringer* and the *SoD's* external tanks, which held their dwindling supply of reaction mass... and the *SoD's* most crucial, vulnerable component of all—the reactor.

Once the *Victory* was in position, no one needed to stay on board. In fact, they couldn't, because the whole ship was now behind the *SoD's* bioshield, bathed in gamma rays from the *SoD's* reactor. Just getting it back there had risked the lives of the *Krijistal* who'd volunteered to operate the RCS thrusters.

"It's hit," Keelraiser continued, imperturbably. "That jolt was the *Victory* colliding with the *SoD's* truss. Check your cameras."

Jack didn't need telling. "It must have stopped the slug, or we'd all be dead." The tactic had worked as planned, but it had been a desperate hack in the first place. "Shit ..." The aft-facing cameras that looked behind the bioshield revealed a terrifying sight. The impact had forced the *Victory* flush against the *SoD's* truss, so it nuzzled the larger ship, grinding dangerously on the *SoD's* external tanks.

Jack could actually see the *Lightbringer's* slug sticking out of the *Victory's* forward module. It looked like a telephone pole. By the mercy of God, it had not hit the *Victory's* reactor.

Black-suited rriksti flew past the cameras, heading for the *Victory*.

"Oi!" Jack yelled. "You can't go back there!"

Keelraiser said, "You can't see it from your angle, but atmosphere is venting from the hole in the *Victory*."

"Doesn't matter. There's no one in there—"

"It's not air, per se. It is smoke."

"Oh Christ," Jack said. "Impact must've started an electrical fire. If it reaches the oxygen and nitrogen tanks …"

Just like the *SoD*, the *Victory* carried big tanks of compressed oxygen and nitrogen in its bioshield. If those exploded, the *Victory's* aft modules would blow apart. Debris could damage the *SoD* beyond repair.

"Oh yes, Kildare, use a flying bomb as armor," Jack groaned. "Sheer genius."

"Better than if the slug would have hit *us*," Alexei pointed out. But that was no comfort, as the men watched the *Krijistal* swarm around the stricken *Victory*. All eight of them were out there. Two headed straight for the airlock. The others flew up and down the truss as if looking for something. They carried a piece of equipment. Jack couldn't make out exactly what it was, but it looked familiar—

"That's our laser saw," Alexei said.

Brbb came on the radio. His voice was a thin thread frayed by interference. "We will use the saw to punch a hole in the *Victory*. Escaping air will push it away. Just looking for the right place to put the hole."

Jack knuckled his forehead. Yes. Gotta do it before it explodes. "Center of gravity. But you'll have to offset it to compensate for the air escaping from the other hole."

He could see the air venting from around the *Lightbringer's* missile now. Linear jets of gray. Smoke.

"Difystra and Fewl are inside," Brbb said. "They cannot put out the fire. They are coming out. Now we drill."

The laser saw sparked up. It seemed to Jack that they were taking their time. He thought about the fire raging through the Victory's modules, and also about the gamma rays soaking into the *Krijistal's* bodies. Rriksti suits—good but not *that* good. The rriksti themselves—tough but not invulnerable.

"Get a move on," he begged. "You needn't drill straight through. Drill a circle and keep going over it—"

"Until the air pressure punches the middle out," Brbb said. "Jack, we have been in space for longer than you've been alive."

The drilling process went on and on. The *Victory* smoked. More people crowded onto the bridge to stare helplessly at the screen.

Suddenly the *Krijistal* flew up from the *Victory's* truss. They were through!

The *Victory* began to edge away from the *SoD*, torquing as smoke now gouted from two holes.

"It's going!" Jack yelled. "Come back in! *Now!*"

Brbb didn't reply. Instead, all the *Krijistal* leapt across the gap and clung to the *Victory's* truss. They scattered towards the back of the small ship, deploying their own body mass to correct its torque. The *Victory* scraped the *SoD's* external tanks. They pushed off with their feet.

"No!" Jack bellowed into the radio.

Alexei jogged his elbow, showed him his laptop. He'd done a quick and dirty calculation of how much radiation the *Krijistal* had absorbed in the sixteen minutes—only sixteen minutes?—they'd been out there. "They're dead," he said flatly.

Keelraiser said over the radio, "Their nervous systems are shutting down. Already they are having trouble moving."

Jack croaked, "Brbb, Difystra, Fewl…" He went through them all, these rriksti he'd once considered thugs and the bane of his life. "You don't have to do this…"

Brbb whispered, "Godspeed."

The *Victory* drifted away. At first its motion appeared stately. Then it got very fast.

It shrank to a dot before it exploded.

Jack burned with humiliation and grief. "Chuck Norris, eat your heart out," he muttered.

There were a dozen rriksti on the bridge by this time. They were crying: tiny pale flecks of skin floated from their faces and upper bodies. They were literally shedding tears.

Linda had come to watch, too. "Well, there goes our ship," she said. "Guess we really are stuck with you now." *She* was dry-eyed.

*

Jack waited until everyone else was off the bridge. There was no need for the entire crew to know about Keelraiser's treachery. When he was alone he radioed the *Cloudeater* again. "Do you think you could possibly ask Hannah to stop shooting at us now?" he snarled.

Keelraiser said, distantly, "She's not answering my emails anymore. I don't think she is even reading them."

CHAPTER 46

The *Lightbringer* tore into Earth's atmosphere like a meteor.

NASA trained astronauts to expect intense g-forces on reentry, but that was only if you had working engines. The *Lightbringer* did not. It was freefalling towards the planet. Hannah stood with a much-needed glass of *krak* in her hand, gazing 'up' at the Pacific.

Using the maneuvering thrusters, Ripstiggr had rolled the ship to present its undamaged side to the atmosphere. This gave the crew and soldiers on the bridge a fine view. The blue-and-white expanse of the Pacific Ocean filled the ceiling. Earth no longer looked like a globe, but a wall.

Notifications wobbled over Hannah's left eye. *Hannah Hannah Hannah.* Iristigut was emailing her again. She hadn't read any of his messages since the reactor shut down. Apologies? Weaselly explanations? Not interested. Delete delete delete. And now the bruise-colored text was spoiling her view of Hawaii and the West Coast.

"Turn off notifications," she muttered.

The text vanished.

Ahhhh.

Better.

But now the atmosphere was starting to drag on the hull. The *Lightbringer* juddered like a speedboat on a rough sea. People laughed, clutched each other for balance, sat down.

Hannah stayed on her feet, although she could feel herself getting heavier. Their deceleration would generate *some* gee-force. She drained her glass and watched the blue wall came closer. Hello, California.

Ripstiggr stood in the drive chancel, monitoring their descent. Hannah walked over to him, stepping over soldiers who sat on the floor. With every step she seemed to grow heavier and heavier. She'd been living in half a gee so long that it felt like having breezeblocks tied to her arms and legs. Yet she refused to sit down. She was Shiplord.

Turbulence tossed the floor up at her. She dropped her glass, staggered, caught herself on the edge of a console that came up to her breastbone. Dizziness speckled her vision.

Ripstiggr nodded coolly at her. "See that?"

He wasn't watching the view.

The targeting screen displayed a rendering of Earth with all its artificial satellites.

*

Richard Burke stood on the side of a mountain in Colorado. You weren't supposed to go out, but he was far from the only person who'd defied the rules today. They waited in silent groups around the bunker exit.

Perfect weather.

Sunny, brisk.

A juniper-scented breeze blew over scrub accented with snow.

Burke's daughter Savannah grabbed her father's elbow, pointing.

On the western horizon, a new star flashed over the Rockies. As bright as Venus, if Venus shone during the day.

People cried out. Sobbed. Cowered. They were all waiting for the big boom that would end everything.

Burke felt disgusted that this was how the remaining employees of the federal government greeted the apocalypse, and proud of Savannah, who stood erect by his side, shading her eyes with her hand.

"You can see it moving," she said.

"It's actually moving very fast," Burke said.

"It looks like a star."

"Yep. The hull is ablating off. It is literally burning." The sight brought back memories of the worst thing that had happened during Burke's early career at NASA: the day the *Columbia* broke up over Texas. It had looked like this. Like a day-star. Very bright and very quiet.

*

In his war room deep under the mountain, Flaherty gave the command to fire.

Nuclear submarine crews in the Pacific and the Caribbean executed the procedures they'd been drilling for months.

They fed up-to-the second satellite data on the *Lightbringer's* trajectory into their targeting software.

And pressed the big red button.

Trident II missiles with heatseeking nose cones, their nuclear warheads replaced with conventional explosives, surged up from the surface of the ocean, curving towards the *Lightbringer* on ballistic intercept paths.

A few seconds later, Russian submarines in the North Atlantic launched Sarmat missiles. Their first stages tumbled back towards Scandinavia. Contrails etched the sky, terrifying the faithful who awaited the aliens in Copenhagen, Stockholm, and Oslo.

The *Lightbringer* flashed onwards, gaining altitude again as its velocity pulled it out of orbit.

Point and shoot.

They're just satellites, after all. No need to feel guilty about them. Hunks of metal and electronics don't have feelings.

Key word, electronics.

All 3,000 or so of Earth's satellites were exquisitely vulnerable to HERFs.

Hannah aimed the short-range HERF mast with gestures, and fired its pulses with grunted commands, while fighting the gees that tried to crumple her into the floor. The HERF beam was a cone. It only had an effective range of a thousand klicks or so, but that soaked broad tracts of orbital space.

Ripstiggr could have done this himself, anyone could have, but he'd offered her the honor, because she was Shiplord. She was smart enough to know that he was giving her a second chance to prove her loyalty to the *Lightbringer*. And like it or not, she had to take it. At least this way she had a chance of minimizing the damage.

The crowd sitting on the bridge applauded her kills with high whistles. In their eyes, she was finally acting like their Shiplord.

What it felt like, though, was playing a 1980s video game. Space Invaders or something. Shooting at blips on a screen. Not real.

The *Lightbringer* swung back towards space, while Hannah grunted her commands, and more satellites died.

*

As the *Lightbringer* pulled away from Earth, Flaherty got a phone call from his best friend. That's how the other man described their relationship, anyway. He had a sense of humor.

Right now, however, he was in no laughing mood. "How is it possible that *all* of your ICBMs missed the fucking thing?"

"All yours missed, too, Vladimir," Flaherty pointed out. "It was going very fast and very high and the damn things just plain missed. The tech ain't perfect."

"We will not miss next time," said the dry voice from Arkhangelsk. "If they—"

Sudden silence.

Flaherty pulled the phone away from his ear, checked it was working.

"Line's dead," he yelled.

"Uh, sir, yes, sir. We are getting reports of satellite failure. Pretty much everything in low Earth orbit …"

"What about the ISS?"

*

"That was a blast," Hannah said, smiling brightly at Ripstiggr.

Then she collapsed, coughing. Flecks of blood speckled the consoles. What a time to get radiation-sick again.

Ripstiggr picked her up. Cradling her in his arms like a baby, he walked through the crowd.

"Do you understand now, Shiplord?" he murmured. "No one has to die."

*

Actually, however, people had already started to die.

The ISS and its overgrown sibling, CELL's Sky Station, caught in Hannah's indiscriminate HERF blasts, wallowed in low Earth orbit without power—without comms—without light, or heat, or computer controls.

In defiance of orders, a few hardy astronauts had stayed up there to watch the *Lightbringer's* arrival.

All of them would soon be dead, the first collateral damage in the war between Imf and Earth.

CHAPTER 47

"It took the Apollo astronauts three days to reach the moon," Linda said. "We're going a heck of a lot faster than they were. Jack says two days."

Koichi just nodded. The loss of the *Victory* had plunged him into depression.

Linda smacked his knee. They were sitting in the gloom of the main hab, under a tree that smelled like cheesy socks. Nobody monitored Linda's movements now that the squid enforcers were gone. Good fucking riddance to *them*. Now Koichi and Linda had to get rid of the rest of the squids … and then they could escape. This unplanned swing out to the moon was a heaven-sent opportunity. Every minute brought her closer to Rufus and Stephen.

"We can't hold off much longer. It's ready to go. Right?"

"Yeah. I just have to give it the final command."

A squid stalked past them, staring with its inscrutable bug-eyes. Linda knew the monsters were deaf. All the same, she lowered her voice to a whisper. "Now," she said. "Do it *now*."

*

Skyler was sleeping on the aft wall of the engineering module. It was too hot back here to use a sleeping-bag. But thrust gravity didn't have enough oomph to hold him down. His startle reflex disturbed his sleep. Again and again, he dreamt that he woke up in the darkness, fans off, turbines down, in the hideous silence of a dead ship.

Then he really did wake up in the darkness.

The glowing reactor and turbine controls soothed his fears. Hriklif had just turned out the light to let him sleep.

The *SoD* had not been HERFed, or blown to shit. *Yet.*

But he couldn't go back to sleep. He shook Hriklif, who was napping, too, splay-limbed amidst the floating game pieces and crumbs and the *mirip* twigs that rriksti liked to gnaw on. "Hey, hey Hriklif."

"Huh?"

Skyler had woken up with a resolution in his mind, fragile but fully formed. He could no longer afford to hang around in a paralysis of indecision. The loss of the *Victory* had proved just how quickly the end could come. There was no time to lose.

By hook or by crook he talked Hriklif into coming with him. "We shouldn't leave the reactor controls unattended," Hriklif objected.

"No, and we won't."

They flew up into the storage module. Rriksti were at work, extracting heavy metals from scrap in the alchemical-looking setup they had cobbled together at the machine shop bench.

"Guys, could a couple of you cover for us? Just hang out in the engineering module. Don't touch anything. If any alerts go off, ping me."

Skyler and Hriklif donned their spacesuits and squeezed into the airlock.

"We're going to get in such trouble," Hriklif moaned.

"Ditchlight," Skyler said, using the English translation of the engineer's name, "here's some perspective for you. We are all at risk of *dying*. Screw the rules."

*

The two rriksti Skyler had asked to cover for them settled into the engineering module. They eyed the Monopoly pieces floating around. They tried biting them, but spat them out. Only aluminum. Not nutritious.

Further aft, in the turbine room, the drive turbine and the housekeeping turbine thundered in their steel cabinets.

Skyler and Hriklif rarely went back there. Neither of them had noticed the rectangular hole, about the size of a hardback book, that had recently appeared in the back of the housekeeping turbine cabinet. It was easy to miss. A screen the same dull green as the cabinet covered it.

The screen was a solar cell. It soaked up the bright light in the turbine room to charge a capacitor on the drone that had made the hole, which was now squatting inside the cabinet.

Equipped to maneuver in zero-gee with gentle puffs of air, the drone had a miniature laser drill.

Over the last three days, since Koichi Masuoka released it in the engineering module, it had drilled a little ring of pits around the pipe supplying hot steam to the housekeeping turbine.

This task completed, it had gone into standby mode.

Now, Koichi, sitting in the main hab under Linda's eagle-eyed gaze, punched another command into his wristwatch.

The watch transmitted the command wirelessly to the drone.

The drone began to perform the last task programmed into it by the NXC.

It fired more laser pulses at one of the pits on the pipe.

Hitting the same spot over and over.

Weakening the metal.

Again, and again.

*

Skyler led the way through the *Cloudeater's* passenger cabin. For once there weren't many people in hospital. Enough heavy metals had been cannibalized from the *Victory's* electronics to give the malnutrition cases a new lease on life. Cleanmay, the rriksti doctor, greeted them amiably.

They flew into the darkness of the crew area.

Hriklif gripped Skyler's arm, dragging his feet along the sides of the corridor to brake.

Skyler edged forward until he could peek into the cockpit. Keelraiser slumped in his seat. He seemed to be absorbed in his screens.

Skyler gave Hriklif a thumbs-up. They backtracked to the computer room and shut themselves in.

Hriklif threw his head back and rolled his shoulders—*this is crazy!*—but he set up the comms program they had caught Keelraiser using before. Soon Skyler was staring at a blank screen.

He now realized that he hadn't planned out what to say.

"Hey, Hannah. This is Skyler," he whispered. Hriklif had to do the typing. Keelraiser had rigged some kind of conversion program to turn rriksti squiggles into English. "I just wanted to get in touch …" Stupid, stupid. "I love you," he whispered.

Hriklif opened his mouth; his hair danced.

"Just type it! I love you. I should have told you years ago. I was such a loser back then. I hope I've changed since then, for the better, hopefully. But my feelings haven't changed. I love you, I love you."

As he spoke, he ceased to see the slim, snarky beauty

who hosted the Hannah Ginsburg Show. He saw *his* Hannah, a touch overweight, unaware of how damn sexy she was. He remembered her grin, her acerbic streak, and her awesome professional competence.

He blurted, "I don't know what Keelraiser's been telling you. Just between you and me, he's a complete douche. But this is me, Skyler. Remember? The guy with the peace symbol and the bad hair. When I climbed into the *Shenzhou*, back in Europa orbit, I never thought it would be the last time I saw you ..." His emotions untwisted like a long-coiled spring. "I'm on the *Cloudeater* right now. That's the shuttle the good guys took down to the surface of Europa. It's kinda like a space 747. Um, it smells like rotting seaweed and it's hot as hell—"

"It is *not* hot," Hriklif said. "It's nice."

"OK, my buddy Hriklif is saying it doesn't feel hot to him. Aliens gotta alien, right? Anyway, I hope you're more comfortable where you are. I wish I was there. I wish you were here. I'd do anything to see you again ..."

"Why not just propose to her?" Hriklif said, laughing with his hair.

The reference to human marital customs surprised Skyler. "Do you guys do marriage?"

"Nope. We used to, maybe a couple of centuries ago? But I don't think the Temple allows it now."

"Huh. Well, a lot of people on Earth don't do marriage anymore, either."

"So do you want to say anything else?"

Skyler hesitated, second-guessing himself. A love-email would not save Hannah... *or* him. They were locked into a deadly dance determined by orbital mechanics and the ranges of the two ships' guns.

"Just this. I have total faith in you, Hannah. I know you'll do the right thing. Send it," he said, before he could change his mind.

"Done," Hriklif said.

"What did you just do?" Keelraiser said, in the doorway.

Hriklif and Skyler cringed.

"Ah, you've emailed Hannah. Let me see what you've put." Keelraiser floated past them. "'I love you, I love you.'" He opened his mouth at Skyler, just as Hriklif had done. The rriksti invariably seemed to react to the subject of love with derisive amusement. "What on earth were you trying to accomplish?"

"I just wanted to tell her how I feel," Skyler said. His lips felt stiff. He was afraid of Keelraiser.

"How very self-indulgent of you," Keelraiser said. "Well, she won't read it."

At that moment, the comms screen changed from dark brown to medium brown. A single, dim word appeared.

Skyler???

"She read it!" Skyler crowed. "Hriklif, can you reply? Tell her—"

A second reply popped up.

That's not very fucking funny, Iristigut. Skyler Taft is DEAD, and you will be, too, when I get my hands on you.

Skyler recoiled from the screen. "She thinks it's you pretending to be me."

"She thinks the *SoD* never left Europa," Keelraiser said.

"You lied to her as well as to us? You really are a

douche."

"Oh, shut up," Keelraiser said. He pushed Hriklif away from the comms console. Urgently, he started typing.

"What are you telling her?" Skyler yelped.

"At least she's checking her email now," Keelraiser muttered. Skyler had never seen anyone type so fast, apart from a few ex-hacker dudes he had known at the NXC.

Hriklif floated towards the door.

"I'm not finished with you, Hriklif," Keelraiser said without looking around.

"Too bad. I'm finished with you," Hriklif yelped. "You think rules were made to be broken, but if anyone *else* breaks the rules, watch out! What happened to our revolution? The guy just wants to tell his girlfriend he loves her, and you cut him to pieces. It's almost like you're a *Krijistal* officer or something! Fuck you, asshole." Hriklif darted away down the corridor.

Skyler, horrified and confused, stayed put. As much as he wanted to follow Hriklif and ask him what he was talking about—a *revolution?*—he wanted more urgently to see what Keelraiser was typing. Was he lying to Hannah about Skyler? Telling her that Skyler was dead, after all?

He edged around the computer room, behind Keelraiser's back. If only rriksti screens weren't so damn hard to read! He glimpsed a few words: *and, the, you, if, dirigibles*—

Keelraiser still had not looked around. He seemed to be unaware Skyler was still there. But unbeknownst to Skyler, as soon as he could see the screen, it also caught his reflection.

Keelraiser took one hand off the keyboard and backhanded him across the room.

CHAPTER 48

Tap tap with the laser on that little pit in the steam supply pipe. Tap tap, over and over ... until it gave way.

The pipe cracked under the pressure of the superheated steam within.

The steam jet slammed the drone against the side of the cabinet, crushing it.

Seconds later, the cabinet itself exploded.

The steam filled the turbine room and boiled into the engineering module. It came straight from the reactor, at a temperature of 500° Celsius. It killed the two rriksti there instantly.

On swept the wave of superheated death. Seven rriksti perished in the storage module, as scalding clouds of steam filled their lungs and boiled them alive.

Three seconds after the pipe blew, the housekeeping turbine's safety interlocks shut it down. However, there was still plenty of water in the steam drum. The secondary heat exchanger continued to relentlessly vaporize it. More steam boiled through Engineering and the storage module, and gushed into SLS.

The only person there was Giles.

He was unclogging the settling tanks. He had taken to wearing his rriksti spacesuit for this task. Yes, it looked eccentric. But it blocked out the smell. It also brought him closer in spirit to Brbb and the other *Krijistal* who had died on the *Victory*. And it served as a barrier between himself and the other humans, so that no one would say, "Turn that frown upside down," or "Cheer up, the world's not ending until next Tuesday," or, worst of all, "Want to talk about it?" No, Giles did not want to talk about it. He didn't want to tell anyone how the *Krijistal's* sacrifice had desolated him. What they had shared ... what was it? Merely sex, you might say, from the human point of view. Weekend jollies, from the rriksti point of view. But it was more than that. They had accepted him. Among them, he had the right number of fingers and toes, and his paunchy little body was no more laughable than any other human's.

He wept a little, steaming up his goggles.

When the module filled with steam, he mistook it for grief clouding his vision.

Jack screamed over the radio, "Explosion in the turbine room! Close the pressure doors, *close the fucking doors!*"

*

Jack groaned, stuck on the bridge, watching clouds of steam billow through the main hab. Within seconds, it obscured the cameras, blinding him. "Alexei! Skyler! Giles! Check in!"

Close the fucking doors, he'd said. But when the *SoD* was on its way to Europa, the first HERF attack from the rriksti had triggered the sensors that automatically closed all the pressure doors. Xiang Peixun, their original life support specialist, had died that day—literally cut in half by a closing door. After that they'd disabled autoclose on all the pressure doors. And disabled they remained, from that day to this.

Someone would have to go into that hell and close the doors manually.

"Copy," Giles said, hoarsely. "I go to close the door of the turbine room."

"Where are you?"

"SLS. It's filled with steam. Now I go aft. We find out

how good these rriksti suits really are."

He's in his suit?!? Why?

Jack didn't have long to wonder about it. The first wisps of steam licked into the bridge. It smelled like hot oil.

Jesus, I'd better put *my* suit on.

He would not close the door of the bridge as long as the other guys were still out there.

He grabbed his suit off the aft wall, shucked his shorts, slipped his arms through the straps and performed the writhing trick he had learned to reach the donning button. The silky smart material flowed up over his body. He gulped a last mouthful of tea from his squeeze bottle before the suit covered his face.

Linda flopped onto the bridge, followed by Koichi.

"Spare suits over there," Jack said, relaying his headset's transmitter through the intercom. "Get into them."

Instead, Linda started to crank the pressure door closed, and Koichi leapt on Jack with desperate ferocity. A karate-style punch that would have felled Jack in gravity instead sent him spinning across the bridge, gasping and coughing into his air supply mouthpiece. He bounced off the far wall, reflexively putting his dukes up. But Koichi was not a rriksti. He had learned his unarmed combat skills in the Japan Self-Defense Force. He knocked Jack's fists aside, grabbed the back of the right seat to stabilize himself, and pistoned a kick into Jack's solar plexus. Winded, Jack helplessly gasped for air. Linda struggled with the crank, while Koichi searched the lockers, probably looking for something to kill Jack with.

Jesus! I *trusted* him! Jack thought in disbelief.

More steam billowed through the crack in the door, and Alexei came with it, a shadow in the white clouds now filling the bridge. Unaware of what was going on, he grabbed spare suits from the aft wall and tossed one each at Linda and Koichi, then hastily donned his own.

Jack hauled breath into his lungs. "Watch out Alexei, these fuckers attacked me—"

"We just don't want to die," Koichi said.

"If you don't want to die, put the damn suits on!" Alexei yelled. The steam was now so dense that they could scarcely see each other. The LEDs on the consoles lit up the fog. Koichi and Linda, choking, donned the suits.

Jack knew how scary it was your first time. He waited until the smart material flowed over their faces, and then he went for Koichi. He wrapped his legs around his old friend and punched him in the face, *Krijistal* style. He had never done this to a fellow human. It horrified him a bit when he felt Koichi's nose break.

"Alexei!" Linda shrieked. "Make him stop! We've still got a chance to survive! We go into orbit around the moon, OK? The *Lightbringer* flies off into outer space. They *cannot* aerobrake, it's impossible. But we have a working drive. So we go into lunar orbit, then CELL sends up a landing shuttle—"

"Yeah ..." Alexei said slowly, and Jack froze. He forgot about Koichi even while the Japanese man bucked under him, choking on his own blood. He realized he was about to lose Alexei. The Russian had made a number of offhand comments about Camp Eternal Light, implying it actually might not be a bad plan to take refuge there ... He wanted to live, of course he did. With Nene.

"*Nyet.*" Decisively, Alexei shook his head. "If it's just us? Yeah, maybe. But it is not just us. It's three hundred other people, including my girlfriend. Probably you have killed them all, but anyway, I have no time for this stupid conversation. If any of them are still alive …"

He headed for the keel tube, then paused.

"Jack, you can handle these *svolochi*, yeah?"

"Yeah."

As Alexei left the bridge, Jack's paralysis melted. He kicked Koichi away and dived for the lockers. He kept his guns in several different hiding-places now. He snatched his blaster out of the first-aid locker and levelled it two-handed at the ghosts in the fog. "Did you do this?"

The possibility had not occurred to him before Alexei stated it as a matter of fact. Now it seemed both self-evident, and unthinkable.

"Are you going to kill us if we say yes?" Linda said. "Or are you going to kill us anyway?"

Jack's gloved fingers twitched on the trigger. He pictured the mess they would make. Just like Kate, when the *Krijistal* shot her, right here on this very bridge.

He had changed a lot, but he could not face the thought that he'd changed into a *Krijistal*.

"Just get out!" he roared. "Get the fuck off my bridge, and count yourselves lucky I'm not asking for the suits back."

He closed the pressure door behind them and lunged through the steam for the intercom. Thank God it was still working. "Skyler, Skyler, come in."

Skyler would've been in the engineering module. Right in the path of the steam explosion.

Terror gripped Jack. He'd never consciously realized how much he valued the young ex-spook.

*

Giles dropped through the clouds of steam into the engineering module. He couldn't see a thing. When he landed on the aft wall, a body rolled limply under his foot, dropping him onto a second body.

"Everyone is dead back here, Jack."

"Skyler?"

"I have not found him yet."

Giles eased down the keel tube into the turbine room. Fresh steam surged up around him. His rriksti suit had no heads-up display, but he estimated that he was moving through lethal hundred-degree temperatures. What's worse, he knew the steam had to be radioactive. Fear drove him back. Laboriously dragging the bodies, he retreated to the storage module.

"I am closing the door now." Seven-toed feet braced on the wall, he rotated the crank with his seven-fingered hands. They were strong and deft.

"Let me know when you're done," Jack said. "I'm going to vent the atmosphere in Engineering."

Alexei came on the radio. "I'm in the main hab. It is filled with steam, but the air is still breathable. People are alive."

"Thank God," Jack said. "Thank God."

The door of the engineering module squelched closed. The steam in the storage module thinned. A dozen lifeless bodies bumped over the aft wall. Rage suffused Giles. To make it all this way, and then die like this … "There is no God!" he shouted. "I knew it all along, but now I believe it."

*

As soon as Giles got the door closed, Jack vented the atmosphere from the engineering module and turbine room. Every module had spill valves, in case of fire. He took a few seconds to update Keelraiser. "The only thing is we haven't found Skyler," he finished, the words heavy with dread.

"Oh," Keelraiser said. "He's with me."

"Really? Brilliant!" Jack punched the steamy air in joy. "Send him over, I suppose ... hang on." Logistics cascaded through his mind, falling into logical, inevitable sequences. "Actually, no. Tell him to stay there for the moment. I'm sending everyone else over to you."

*

So they evacuated the *SoD*, again.

Two by two, rotating the limited number of spacesuits available, the civilians filed out of the airlock. With Engineering sealed off, the atmosphere in the storage module was painfully hot, but survivable ... for rriksti. Alexei made the mistake of doffing his suit to the neck. The air scalded his face, stung his eyes. Holding his breath, he donned the suit again as fast as he could.

The civilians laughed at him. "On the Lightside it is hotter than this!"

Alexei shook his head. Koichi and Linda had had no idea what they were dealing with, did they?

But the heat wasn't the only danger. The steam had also carried a perilous dose of radioactivity throughout the ship. They had to limit the civilians' exposure to *that*. The rrikstis' famous indifference to ionizing radiation was mostly based on their ability to heal the damage it caused. And with the eight *Krijistal* gone, there just weren't enough strong extroverts on board to heal everyone who might fall prey to radiation sickness.

Nene whispered, "And even that isn't the worst of it."

"Are you reading my mind again?" He slipped his arm around her waist. Despite everything, he couldn't sink into despair while she was alive and unhurt.

"It's the plants and the fish."

"Yes."

"Everything's dead or dying."

"Yes."

"Everything."

"I know." For once, Alexei couldn't think of anything to say to cheer her up.

She gazed grimly at the bodies stacked in a corner of the storage module. "We will take those," she said. "Just as they are. Flash-freeze them in the vacuum. Who needs a dehydrator?"

CHAPTER 49

The moon was not worth getting out of bed for, Jack decided, with due apologies to the Apollo astronauts. When you had been to Jupiter and Mars, this titchy gray ball of rock underwhelmed.

'Titchy,' of course, was the scientific term for 'actually quite big.' At 50,000 kilometers out, the disk brushed against the edges of the main screen. He could see all the famous seas and mountains. But he spent next to no time gazing at the view. He had other things to do.

As soon as everyone had evacuated to the *Cloudeater,* he vented the atmosphere in the main hab. Not all of it, of course. Just enough to dump the heat. Watching the pressure indicators unblinkingly, he closed the spill valves when the air pressure reached 5 psi. That was the equivalent of Himalayan air pressure, but it wasn't actually so hard on the body, as the oxygen / nitrogen mix stayed at 50/50. Thankfully, the algae had survived the steam explosion.

He equalized the bridge air pressure with the main hab, and opened the pressure door for the first time in twelve hours. He drifted out into still-warm gloom and silence.

This was not the living, humming silence he'd grown to love. It was dead quiet. A pungent smell of rot crisped his nostrils.

He worked his way along the outside of the axis tunnel, ripping the repurposed upholstery filters off the growlights.

Little by little, the full-spectrum UV light exposed the devastation on the floor of the hab. The jungle had turned brown, and putrid yellow, and moldy white.

Jack left the job half-done and went down to floor level. He wandered in a trance of disgust through sagging stalks of suizh and wilting yfrit. Mushy leaves squelched under his bare feet. The smell nauseated him. If the Imfi vegetation had smelled like overripe cheese and artificial bubblegum when it was alive, dead it smelled like a compost heap.

However, not everything was dead. Recycling bugs carpeted the floor, gnawing at the decaying leaves. He knew they were edible, and thought about gathering some up for the hungry rriksti in the *Cloudeater,* but they scurried between his fingers.

"Jack?"

"Just a minute," Jack grunted. He'd found a sack and some spare aerogel panels in the deserted village, and set up a trap for the bugs. Clapping his hands and stomping, he was trying to funnel them between the panels and into the sack.

"What are you doing?"

"What does it look like?"

"I think they usually catch them with sticky stuff," Keelraiser said.

"'Sticky stuff'? Easy to tell you're not a gardener." As he spoke, Jack lost his balance. He knocked over one of the aerogel panels, and all the bugs scurried away. "Now look what you've made me do."

"I'll tell some of the civilians to come over and have a bug-catching competition," Keelraiser said. "Can I use your radio?"

"Time for me to get back to the bridge, anyway." Jack wiped sweat off his face. "I assume Linda and Koichi haven't come with you?"

"They are on the *Cloudeater*. Strangely enough, they refuse to talk to us. They won't drink our water, either."

"They will when they get thirsty enough. I wouldn't expect any breakthroughs in the conversation department, though. I've never seen brainwashing like it. Koichi ... I trusted him! But he was faking it all along." Jack brooded as they climbed Staircase 2. "I blame sci-fi films. *Independence Day,* and so forth."

"Your favorite film of all time?"

"Yes, but I know it's a *film*. Some people can't tell the difference ... but just in general, we've been conditioned to see aliens as inhuman and implacably hostile. I suppose that says something about us."

"We were conditioned to see aliens as hapless pushovers," Keelraiser said, opening his mouth. "What does that say about us?"

They flew up the keel tube to the bridge. Thrust gravity turned the flight into a scrabble. The *SoD* was still thrusting at 66% of max. The housekeeping turbine was down, but the drive turbine was undamaged, so the MPD engine had power, although the life-support systems were running off the fuel cells.

The moon had grown larger. Its edges were now off the screen. "We ought to be able to see the *Lightbringer* on the optical telescope soon," Jack said, hunkering over the radar console. "I just want to get a little closer. One round left and I'm going to make sure it counts."

Keelraiser made his call to the *Cloudeater* for bug-catchers. Then he sprawled in the left seat, head hanging back. "Do you know why I attacked you on the day we left Europa?"

The never-mentioned topic brought Jack upright in his seat. He narrowed his eyes. "So it wasn't just your way of showing affection?"

"I was afraid."

"Afraid?"

"This low-tech nightmare of a ship. Oh, I no longer see it that way ... The *Spirit of Destiny* is a tough little beauty. She's stronger than any of us."

"She is," Jack agreed, filled with love for his ship, no matter how damaged.

"But it looked very different to me two years ago. Tin cans attached to a *fission reactor* ... and I was about to put my people aboard this thing? I was about to put them in *your* tiny little five-fingered hands? I panicked, Jack. I thought: There can only be one commander on this ship. Is it to be a *human*? No! Unthinkable! It should be me."

Keelraiser spread his hands and then clenched them into fists, as Jack stared, slack-jawed at what he was hearing.

"I was going to kill you."

"Shit. I mean ... glad you changed your mind. I suppose you remembered the rules at the last minute?"

"No. I just couldn't kill *you.*"

Jack sat back in his seat. "Well, I'd no idea what a close call that was. Thanks for telling me. I suppose."

"You're always saying I am dishonest. I'm trying to change."

Jack shook his head. "Mate, you are what you are. You've just got to accept it." The cliché embarrassed him as soon as it came out of his mouth. "By the way, what happened to those swords?"

"Oh, my service swords? We ate them some time ago."

"Shame. They were cool."

"They were nutritious."

Jack nodded. Nothing mattered more to Keelraiser than keeping his people alive. He understood that and respected it, although he couldn't go along with it as far as Keelraiser wanted him to. "Well, we've managed pretty well," he said after a moment, half to himself.

"You've managed pretty well."

"These tiny little five-fingered hands aren't so useless after all, eh?" Jack grinned, and flipped Keelraiser a rriksti salute.

Keelraiser reached across and grasped his hand. "I love these tiny little five-fingered hands."

Jack felt exasperated and sad. He freed his hand and pointed at the radar plot. "There's the *Lightbringer*. I am going to nuke it. Got it? Nothing you say or do will change my mind."

To his surprise and relief, Keelraiser didn't argue. "And then what?"

"What do you mean, then what?"

"After we nuke the *Lightbringer,* then what?"

People expected him to keep coming up with new ideas, but he was out. What he had was all he had. "Have you never heard of dying in the line of duty?" he snapped in irritation.

"In Darkside strategic thinking, that's an honor reserved for the other side."

"Good one."

"We don't believe in an afterlife."

"I'm not sure I do, either."

"But you wear this." Keelraiser climbed across the seats and jerked on Jack's rosary.

Jack took the crucifix from the long fingers. "I know it's sappy," he said, "but …" Self-pity welled up. "I believe in love." He reached up, wrapped his hand around the back of Keelraiser's head, and pulled him down. His dry, chapped lips caught on Keelraiser's lips. They stayed like that for a moment.

"There is no word for love in our language," Keelraiser said. He tried to pull Jack closer, as if they could melt into one another's bodies.

"As I've said before, your culture sucks." Jack sniffled. Before he could get really mushy, he pushed Keelraiser away and worked his rosary off over his head. "Take this."

"What? Why?"

"It's coated with tungsten. Very nutritious."

"It's a religious symbol."

"So were your swords, weren't they? You ate those."

They discussed matters a little further. Then Keelraiser went back to the *Cloudeater*.

A few hours later Jack increased thrust to maximum. Blasting with all its might, the *SoD* entered lunar orbit, only a few thousand kilometers behind the *Lightbringer*.

*

Ripstiggr said silkily, "Shiplord, I need you to reauthorize the weapons systems."

Each authorization expired after a set time, and had to be renewed. The *Lightbringer's* designers had been really, *really* keen on keeping the ship's awesome power out of dirty ditch-born hands.

Hannah tossed a bleak glance at Ripstiggr. "No." Curled

in her armchair on the bridge, she drew up her knees like a wall between herself and the crowd. She made the chip bring up Skyler's email again. Iristigut's. *Skyler's.*

That email had knocked her head apart like a pinata. The next time the Shiplord chip pestered her with an enemy/ally warning, she'd understood what she was looking at. That blip on the radar was an alien shuttle! *The alien shuttle that Eskitul had stolen twelve years ago!* Talk about a blast from the past ... It had followed them all the way here.

And Skyler Taft was on board.

Skyler Taft!

Now *there* was someone she hadn't thought about in ages.

It had been weird and a bit creepy to read his declaration of love. He seemed to be writing to someone else. The details convinced her it really was Skyler, but she had to bear in mind that he might have been writing under compulsion. Iristigut was one hell of a manipulator, after all. The likeliest scenario, she concluded, was that Skyler was a captive on the *Cloudeater,* just like she was a captive on the *Lightbringer.*

And yet ...

I have total faith in you, Hannah. I know you'll do the right thing.

Those words had lodged in her heart like bullets.

She had tried to do the right thing.

Failed.

Skyler's email had found her at a low point, when her only ambition was to not get killed by Ripstiggr.

But couldn't she do better than that?

If at first you don't succeed ... try, try again, Hannah-banana.

So she had a sort of a plan, a really shitty plan but the best she could think of. But if she were to have a chance of implementing, she had to make Ripstiggr believe she'd repented of her disloyalty.

But she still didn't want to blow the *Cloudeater* away.

But since Ripstiggr didn't know *she* knew that it was the *Cloudeater*, much less who was on board, she had to provide another rationale for not authorizing the weapons systems.

She shifted in her chair and moved her gaze to the moon. They were barely 5,000 kilometers up, freefalling towards the rocky disk for a retrograde flyby. With a thought, she spun and zoomed the image on the variable-polarization ceiling. It was an actual optical image, as if seen through glass, but at her command the ship's computer took over and rotated it around two axes. (She was getting better at this.) At the south pole, a tiny pool of infrared glowed. "Do you want to hit Camp Eternal Light?"

"Well ..." Ripstiggr said cagily.

It had impressed Hannah greatly to discover that humanity now had a moon base. "Tch, tch," she said. "Leave them alone. A few pioneers in dugouts, huddling around their solar panels. What threat could they possibly be to the unstoppable interstellar victory machine that is Imf?"

Whistles of approval.

Some striking differences existed between the newly awakened soldiers and Hannah's old friends who'd been awake all the way. One of them was that the soldiers, even if they had the ship's new auto-translate program running on their implants, did not get sarcasm. She and Ripstiggr had

had some good laughs at their expense.

Emboldened, she added, "And as for that pesky little ship that's following us? That would be one of CELL's shuttles. Jeez, you should see their technology. Chemical rockets. No kidding. We'd be lowering ourselves to fire on it, and also the optics would be terrible."

"Oh, *that* ship?" Ripstiggr said. He gave an impression of speaking through gritted teeth, even though he wasn't using his mouth to talk at all. Hannah felt a twinge of worry. Then Ripstiggr opened his mouth wide. "I'm not worried about that ship. It's our backup."

CHAPTER 50

Down we go.

Lower and lower, deeper into the gravity field, bending closer and closer to the surface.

The bright side of the moon blurs past, 500 kilometers below ... 400 ... 300.

I could do this in my sleep.

It *is* exciting, though. The thrill never entirely goes away.

Remember Alexei saying we could drop a bomb down Olympus Mons?

I could *spit* into these craters.

Alexei's not here now. Got him to stay on the *Cloudeater*.

And this was a new experience for Jack. He was flying the *SoD* all by himself. It gave him a giddy sense of power and control.

Lower, lower ...

The fly in his soup was that he couldn't actually see the *Lightbringer* anymore.

But he'd known this was going to happen. The orbital mechanics decreed it. As both ships dived towards the moon on close flyby trajectories, the *Lightbringer* had vanished around the curve of the rocky sphere. Catch-22! Jack could have fired from a distance of thousands of kilometers, sacrificing accuracy. But he was absolutely determined not to screw this up again. *One* nuke left. That meant getting closer, but *that* meant diving lower, and *that* meant he lost sight of the target. They say you can't hide behind a moon; well, you can when you're low enough to see the tracks of the lunar rover in Schiaparelli Crater.

(Yup. *Wish* I'd had time to take pictures.)

Schiaparelli lay far behind now, as the *SoD* raced towards the moon's terminator in an equatorial orbit.

A solution to the Catch-22 existed, of course.

Dive even lower.

Cut the corner.

Catch up.

And that's what Jack planned to do. The altimeter read 298 kilometers. He spoke into the radio. No hands—he was wearing his suit, as you should during risky maneuvers. Not his rriksti suit, but his smelly old Z-2. "What is the fucking delay?" he shouted, pent-up tension spilling out.

*

"Forget about it," Alexei said, sprawling on a crash couch in the *Cloudeater's* crew cabin. The cabin's transparent ceiling doubled as the floor of the cockpit. Above him, Keelraiser and Hriklif sat in the pilot's and co-pilot's seats. Waiting. Keelraiser wore Jack's rosary around his neck. When Alexei saw that, he'd gotten a bad, bad feeling.

"I miss the *Krijistal*," Jack's voice crackled over the radio. "They did as they were bloody told."

"Maybe you should have punched me in the face a few times, but I don't care. I am not doing it."

"What about the civilians? What about Nene? Are you going to let her die because you were *scared?*"

Jack's voice jabbed at him, lacerating, on and on. Alexei understood perfectly well that his friend was trying to get him mad on purpose. He breathed in and out, feeling his old scars twinge, refusing to rise to the bait.

And yet what Jack was saying made sense. In fact it was

what Alexei had been thinking for days, if not weeks.

"We can't take the rriksti back to Earth. Apart from anything else they'll die of starvation before we get there. We've got to cut the *Cloudeater* loose and it's got to be done NOW! I'd have done it at 30 K if they had enough fuel. They don't, so a thousand would have been ideal, but a hundred klicks is the absolute minimum, so get out there and break the fucking welds, Alexei!"

"It's too late," Alexei said.

"DO IT NOW."

"No, I mean it's too late for this. We've come too far together. I can't abandon you."

"I'll. Be. Fine. I've got plenty of MREs."

Alexei stared at the concave forward wall of the crew seating area. It displayed an optical feed of the moon, blurring past like the floor of the main hab when you looked down from the axis tunnel. He did not want to leave the *SoD*. Could they survive down there? It would depend on Keelraiser's piloting skills. If Keelraiser could land the *Cloudeater* close enough to Camp Eternal Light, they'd have a chance.

He made his decision. Rolled out of his couch.

Nene, in the couch next to his, caught his hand.

Thrust gravity pulled them both down to the aft wall.

Alexei caught her in his arms. He kissed her to hide the fact that his heart was breaking. She knew anyway, of course. "I have to stay with them," she whispered.

"I know. I have to stay with the *SoD*."

"I know."

"I love you."

"You are my life." This was her way of saying *I love you.*

"Perhaps we'll meet again when this is over."

Alexei nodded and kissed her again, taking his time because it would be the last time. The other rriksti in the crew seating area looked away. They considered public displays of affection unseemly. Did Alexei give a fuck? He did not. He had found the one woman in the universe for him, and now he was letting her go because he was a motherfucking Russian cosmonaut and he had to do his job.

He vaulted up the ladder and plummetted down the corridor into the passenger cabin. It felt like falling out of the future into an overcrowded third-class train carriage. Fine white dust floated in the air. People couldn't help crying, although they knew how bad it was for the air circulation system. Alexei knew how they felt. He worked his way back to the engineering decks at the rear of the shuttle. "I need the ultrasound pulse cutter. Quick."

Skyler elbowed between the rriksti thronging the corridor. "I'm coming with you."

*

Alexei aimed the ultrasound pulse cutter at each weld in turn. The tool had an ultrasonic transducer on the end of an extendable arm. Like many rriksti gizmos it was based on principles familiar to humanity, which could only be applied if you *also* had megawatts of power packed into a battery the size of a smartphone.

Welds are sintered powder.

Pulse ultrasound through them and they go back to being powder again.

They worked by the light of the moon, as if standing on their heads, while the Mare Fecunditatis swept beneath them. Suddenly darkness engulfed them. The *SoD* had crossed the terminator.

Alexei cursed and switched on his chest-lamp.

Skyler, aiming his own chest-lamp at the aft starboard weld, began to sing: "Breathe, breathe in the air. Don't be afraid to care …"

The lyrics floated to Alexei's lips. "Leave, but don't leave me …" Nene. Leave, but don't leave me.

"Pink Floyd depresses the shit out of me," Jack said, from the *SoD's* bridge. "Can't we have something a bit more cheerful?"

So they sang Monty Python songs until the final weld crumbled into powder and the *Cloudeater* floated free, cellar-depth below the *SoD's* truss.

"You're clear to thrust, *Cloudeater,*" Alexei said. "Godsp—"

An angle iron swung at him. Skyler was wielding it like an extra-long baseball bat. Alexei tried to dodge, too late. The angle iron caught him lengthwise under the ribs, knocking the air out of his lungs. He bounced out on his tether.

Skyler scrambled to the other end of the tether, released it from the truss, and threw the tether reel into the *Cloudeater's* cargo hold. He threw the angle iron after it.

Rriksti hands caught both things.

"Got him," their sweet voices said. "Got him."

As the ramp began to hinge up, the rriksti hauled in the tether, with Alexei on the end of it. "Fuck you, Taft," he shouted.

"No no no no no," Skyler said in his headset. "You saved my life. I'm just returning the favor. Anyway, they need you. Think those douches at CELL are going to welcome three hundred rriksti with open arms, without a human to vouch for them? If so, you're really naïve. And with all due respect to Giles, it better be a human with the normal amount of fingers. So that's your job, and I'm going to do my job."

The rriksti hauled Alexei over the cargo ramp. It closed, cutting off Skyler's voice.

The *Cloudeater's* drive turbines spun up with a noise like thunder.

The little shuttle broke away from the *SoD* and rolled into a steep climb, scrambling for altitude.

*

"Godspeed," Skyler whispered.

Then he went back in.

"There I was thinking I'd have peace and quiet at last," Jack said in his headset.

Skyler choked on the putrid smell of rotten vegetation that filled the ship. "Whew. Does it ever stink in here." The housekeeping turbine was still down. Fuel cells powered the emergency LEDs. He scrambled back to the engineering module.

"What are you doing?" Jack said.

"My job." Skyler checked the displays, settled in on the aft wall. Twiddled a Monopoly piece. Flipped it up in the air and caught it. The hexagonal display shone like the sun, solid yellow. Above it, Hannah's family smiled down from that curled old photograph.

"You keep surprising me," Jack said. "I mean that in a good way."

"Let's just get it over with," Skyler said.

He had made a decision. An irrevocable decision. The

Cloudeater was already thousands of kilometers away. He'd chosen the *SoD*. He'd chosen Jack. He'd chosen to be a party and a witness to Hannah's murder.

He could not have lived with himself any other way.

"You shouldn't have to do this by yourself," he told Jack. *"You* didn't sign up to murder people for the greater good. I did. I didn't know what the NXC was going in, but ignorance is no excuse. I could've quit at any time. After the first murder. Or the third one."

Oliver Meeks.

Lance.

Qiu Meili. (No, he hadn't meant to murder her, but it sure felt like he had.)

And now ... Hannah.

He'd stepped onto a bitter path, chasing the carrot of importance. Maybe this would put an end to it one way or another.

"If anyone makes a stink about the nuke, we'll say I held a gun to your head," he said.

"Don't count your chickens before they hatch," Jack said. "I can't even see the *Lightbringer* yet."

*

So he went lower.

Bending even harder. Yawing the ship to keep the nose pointed down.

The moon's horizon no longer looked smooth. Mountains crenellated it.

Quick glance at the altimeter.

Ooer.

But now that the *SoD* didn't have the *Cloudeater* clinging to its back, Jack didn't have to worry about overstressing the truss. And with less mass to shove, the MPD drive's thrust went further. So the ship was handling beautifully, and Jack felt confident enough to go lower still.

There it is!

Finally, the *Lightbringer* glimmered over the horizon. Radar said it was only 500 klicks ahead. Jack imagined catching up and overtaking the alien ship, giving it the middle finger in the rearview mirror. He snorted at the silly mental image. He bent the *SoD* even closer to the surface, narrowing the gap, and at the same time he reached up and powered on the rails.

"You should come up here," he said to Skyler. "There's nothing for you to do back there really, and it's an amazing view."

In the thirty seconds it took for Skyler to come forward, the *SoD* had closed the gap to 200 kilometers, but the Lightbringer had seen them coming and reacted the only way it could. With no main drive, this meant using its maneuvering thrusters to angle closer to the surface. Same thing Jack was doing.

"Look, the whale's trying to dive."

Skyler plopped into the left seat. White-knuckled, he stared at the main screen. "Oh. My. God."

"It's something, isn't it?"

They were scudding over the dark side of the moon at a height of *fifteen* kilometers. 'Dark side' turned out to be a misnomer. Earth hovered at the top of the screen, and its reflected light shone on the barren moonscape, turning it turquoise. Navy blue shadows puddled at the feet of jagged hills.

But Jack only had eyes for the *Lightbringer*. It kept going lower. The chase had become a game of chicken. Who would lose his nerve first?

Jack had the smaller and more maneuverable ship. He dived down to nine kilometers, confident that he could pull up at any time.

He ranged the railgun with the laser. A targeting reticule settled onto the radar plot, trapping the *Lightbringer* dead center of his sights.

Tracer rounds away.

They impacted on the *Lightbringer's* hull like fireworks.

"Firing ... *now.*"

Zzzzoik!

The last plutonium round sped away. Time seemed to stretch like a rubber band. Both Jack and Skyler shouted like sports fans, caught up in the moment—*come on, come on ...*

*

"Incoming," Hannah said. "This is a little bit worrying! If that's your backup, why are they shooting at us?"

Skyler! Why are you shooting at me?

But of course, it wasn't Skyler at the controls. It had to be Iristigut. *He* didn't trust her to do the right thing. Not anymore.

She clenched her fists, struggling with panic. She would *not* authorize the weapons systems. She would prove to them that Skyler wasn't wrong to have faith in her.

"Don't worry! It's their way of showing affection," Ripstiggr said, working the flight controls with grim concentration.

Hannah, said the chip, following her around like Isabel used to follow Bethany: Mommy, Mommy, Mommy. *Impact* something something Rristigul something, and a picture of yet another crater. This one could more fairly be described as a dent.

Relief flooded through Hannah. What do you know? Ripstiggr had been right. That had just been a symbolic shot. Or something.

"I guess that's the Imfi equivalent of a love tap," she said. "Now would you please pull us out of this nosedive?"

"It's not a nosedive. It's a maneuver," Ripstiggr said, unconvincingly.

Ripstiggr was not a professional pilot, of course. He was a professional reader of technical manuals. He was just winging it with enough flair and style to convince everyone that he knew what he was doing … except Hannah.

She twitched with eagerness to take over. But she couldn't do that. Not yet.

Somehow or other, he did pull the *Lightbringer* up a bit.

*

"I did *not* miss," Jack whispered.

Yet ahead of them, the *Lightbringer* hurtled on around the moon, completely undamaged.

"You saw, didn't you, Skyler? The round impacted the hull fair and square! I did *not* miss."

"It must have been a dud," Skyler said.

This obvious truth knocked the stuffing out of Jack. A dud. Of course. Given Jack's luck, it was a miracle it hadn't blown up on the rails.

The *SoD* glided on. After a few moments of mentally abusing the designers of the dud round, and all the factories that made all its components, Jack decided to stay low.

He didn't have any more ideas, but keeping up with the *Lightbringer* seemed preferable to getting left behind.

"What now?" Skyler asked. A few hours ago, Keelraiser, sitting in the same place, had asked the same question.

But the failure of the nuke's fuse, or detonator, or whatever component had glitched out, changed everything. Jack gave a different answer. "Back to Earth, I suppose."

"OK."

"It's still unclear whether the *Lightbringer* will be able to successfully inject into orbit. We can. Our tanks'll be bone dry by that time, but ..."

"Been there, done that," Skyler nodded.

"After that, I suppose we'll just have to wait and see if the *Lightbringer* obliterates human civilization. If it does, end of story. If it *doesn't* ... well, someone'll probably send a Soyuz up for us so they can put us in jail."

Skyler sighed noisily into his suit's transmitter. "Well, we tried."

"Yeah. We tried."

"I'm sorry."

"I'm sorry, too."

"But ..."

"When life seems jolly rotten, there's something you've forgotten," Jack sang.

"And that's to laugh and smile and dance and sing!" Skyler joined in.

"When you're feeling in the dumps ..."

"Jack, are those mountains supposed to be there?"

"Of course they are, they've been there for billions of years. Don't be silly chumps ..."

"Just purse your lips and whistle."

"That's the thing!" they bawled together.

"How, um, high, exactly, are they?" Skyler interrupted as the peaks came closer.

"And always look on the bright side of life … Do you know, I'm not sure. That wasn't in astronaut training. Come on! Always look on the bright side of life!"

Those mountains actually look as if they might be a bit higher than our current altitude, which is, let me see, *eight* kilometers.

Hmm.

Better pull up a bit.

Jack clutched the reaction wheels. For good measure, he fired the RCS thrusters, too. "Always look on the bright side of life," he hummed.

Skyler fumbled with his harness, strapping himself in.

That might be a good idea, actually.

Clutch with one hand, jam the straps into the buckles with the other.

Come on come on come on—

Jack waited impatiently, but without any real fear, for the gyroscopes to bring the *SoD's* nose around, correcting their flight path away from the moon for a rapid gain of altitude. It was going to be close. But he'd flown around Jupiter. Around Mars. Around the *sun*. He could do this in his sleep, remember?

Oh *fuck,* look at that horrible peak. Right in the way.

"Skyler, um, if you're at all religious you might want to start praying."

"I don't know any prayers."

Blasting hard, the *SoD* climbed towards the mountain peak.

Jack reached for his rosary, before remembering he'd given it to Keelraiser. A scalding surge of fear left his mind a blank. "Jesus," he screamed. "Jesus Jesus Jesus—"

Sometimes the difference between life and death is a crap detonator.

And sometimes it's three meters.

The bridge and main hab skimmed over the peak. The aft modules and the bioshield squeezed over, just missing it.

All this happened between one heartbeat and the next.

The reactor smashed into the peak.

At the *SoD's* current speed—north of 30,000 kph—the lunar rock acted like one of Keelraiser's tungsten-edged swords.

The truss sheared.

The reactor bounced down the back side of the mountain.

The rest of the *SoD* flew on for some way, spinning wildly, until the moon's weak gravity pulled it down. It crashed into a crater, bioshield first. Dust undisturbed since the birth of the solar system geysered into the sky.

Down at the bottom of the dust eruption, the *SoD's* bioshield split.

The rotating hab cracked off from the truss.

The pieces skidded across the crater floor, kicking up more dust, and came to rest separately, just short of a deep rille.

The ship that flew to Europa had found its resting place on the dark side of the moon.

CHAPTER 51

Three days later, the *Lightbringer*—undamaged, which is to say, no more damaged than it had been already—returned to Earth. It bounced off the top of the atmosphere like a stone skipping over water.

Hannah's teeth jarred together. She covered it with an ostentatious yawn. "How many more skips?"

"As many as we can manage," Ripstiggr said.

Hannah nodded. She'd just have to play it by ear.

The jolting stopped as the *Lightbringer* soared back into space.

"One hour until our next skip," Hannah said, converting the figures the chip supplied. That gave her time to grab a last drink.

She wriggled out of her hammock. The *Lightbringer* had no crash couches, since it was never intended to land anywhere, but it had emergency hammocks. Made of a smart material similar to the clingfilm that the rriksti used for everything, they'd fallen from the ceiling of the bridge like oxygen masks in an airline safety video. They were pretty comfy.

She dropped to the floor and padded across the bridge. Above her head, hundreds of hammocks blocked the view of Earth. She went into her bedroom—and screeched in outrage.

Half a dozen soldiers clustered around the safe in the corner, helping themselves to her booze.

"You goddamn *schleerps!* Get out of here!"

They fled the Shiplord's wrath, hanging their heads.

Her jug of *krak* was completely empty.

"Ripstiggr. These assholes have bogarted our booze. Tell someone to get more from the still."

"There's none left," Ripstiggr said.

"Please say you're kidding me."

"It is customary to pass out alcohol rations before going into action. It is customary on Earth, as well. I looked it up."

Hannah tilted the jug upside-down over her mouth. A single drop trickled out, piquing her thirst unbearably. "How'd those guys get into my safe?"

"I gave them the combination."

"You bastard."

"Did you see their insignias?"

"No," Hannah was forced to admit. She'd only had eyes for the empty jug.

"They're pilots. They will be flying the shuttles."

"Ah." Hannah had to admit that if *she* was going to climb into one of those Frankenstein repair jobs, she would want a drink, too.

But she wanted one *anyway,* it would have been her last drink ever, and when she got back to the drive chancel she ducked under Ripstiggr's hammock and punched him in the butt. "Don't you ever, *ever* give away my booze without asking me again."

"Gimme another love tap, baby," Ripstiggr said, stretching like a cat.

"Is the still running? Will it be done soon?"

"No, and no. We could ask the G9 leaders to bring supplies when they come up to sue for peace."

Hannah rode out the next skip thinking about what she'd most like to drink right now. For some reason she really craved Madeira. Or a dry white wine. Oh, or champagne.

Was there champagne in heaven?

Their skips got shorter as the *Lightbringer* lost speed.

Half an hour between skip two and skip three.

Twenty minutes after skip three, they braced for skip four.

Ripstiggr, lying on his side in his hammock, gestured at the consoles, and Hannah gathered herself, waiting for her moment.

Bump bump bump, her hammock soaked up shockwaves.

She once again reviewed the last email she'd ever received from Iristigut.

Ripstiggr wasn't a real pilot.

Iristigut was.

And he'd told her a few things about flying the *Lightbringer*, things she might need to know if they were really going to try this aerobraking shit.

Such as: *You must keep the ship's nose UP.*

OK.

Hannah took a deep breath—and snatched the flight controls from Ripstiggr.

She was Shiplord.

And her interface with the chip had improved a *lot* recently. For so long it had seemed like she was making no progress at all … but that's how exponential learning curves work. They look flat for the longest time and then they shoot up. So after all this time, her efforts to learn Rristigul were finally paying off, while the chip's own machine learning capabilities had allowed it to build up an understanding of how her brain worked. They had achieved the first-ever interstellar technological handshake.

Didn't feel like a handshake, though.

Felt like a hug.

My baby.

No. *Not* my baby.

With a thought and a gesture, Hannah pushed the *Lightbringer's* nose *down*.

The ship lost its balance. It pitched into the troposphere, diving towards the Pacific, out of control.

*

When she and Bethany were kids—this was before their parents died—they used to vacation at Shaver Lake, in the Sierra National Forest. The family car was a jeep. The girls delighted in going for off-road rides on the dirt roads around the lake. Securely buckled in, they'd shriek joyously, "Faster! Daddy, go faster!"

Little had they known that jeep would kill their parents when Hannah was ten.

Anyway.

Bump bump bump.

Faster, Daddy, faster!

Turns out bumpy rides aren't so much fun when you're 42, and instead of rocketing over a dirt road, you're freefalling through Earth's atmosphere, and your five-kilometer billion-ton jeep is melting.

The chip flooded her with panicky status updates.

Ripstiggr wrestled with the maneuvering thrusters but any idiot could see that that was not going to be enough to flatten out the *Lightbringer's* dive. In contrast to their previous flyby, when they zoomed in at a nice low angle, they were going in steep and hot.

Flung around in her hammock, Hannah thought: Look,

Skyler. Look. I did the right thing.

But when you fall from high orbit, you fall for a *long* time. Long before the *Lightbringer* reached the troposphere, her triumph had started to pall, as she listened to the soldiers and crew joke calmly about their impending death. *How big of a splash will we make?* They were professional. Composed. Everything astronauts should be. And she'd just killed them all.

Ripstiggr abandoned his futile struggle with the maneuvering thrusters. He climbed out of his hammock and leapt into Hannah's, landing on his hands and knees, straddling her. "You did this."

Hannah wiped her eyes and nose, leaving snail trails on the arms of her suit. She hadn't even known she was crying. "They think *you* did it," she said, turning her head to indicate the soldiers and crew. "They think you screwed up."

Ripstiggr grabbed her by the hair. She screamed. Balancing with his feet on the ends of her hammock, he lifted her by her hair. "This alien," he shouted. "This *thing* has sabotaged our mission." Hannah was still screaming, clutching at his wrists. "Death is too good for her. But there isn't time to punish her as she deserves, unfortunately."

He gripped her head in one hand, her shoulder in the other, and tensed to twist.

"No," Gurlp shouted, jumping out of her hammock. "She is best Shiplord we ever have!"

"Take your dirty ditch-born hands off her," Joker yelled.

"You killed one Shiplord already," Hulk rumbled. "You

go too far, Ripstiggr."

"That's right! Leave her alone!" Gurlp shouted.

Ripstiggr's grip slackened.

Hannah twisted free. She took a half-step, turning to face Ripstiggr in the swaying hammock. His mouth hung open. Never before had his people stood up to him like this. The rriksti were feudal, intensely hierarchical ... but when all was said and done, Ripstiggr was just a platoon sergeant. They hadn't forgotten that, even if he wished they would.

Hannah punched him in the crotch.

Then she lost her balance and fell out of the hammock, into the arms of her crew.

"He screwed up," she said, dashing her hair out of her face. "But I can fix this."

Could she?

Soldiers vaulted down from their hammocks and formed a living shield around Hannah. She hung onto them for support as the bumpy descent continued.

"We'll deploy the dirigibles," she said.

"What dirigibles?"

Hannah grinned. "You don't think they made a ship this big, this powerful, this expensive, and *didn't* give it an emergency unpowered descent option?"

She was cheating, kinda, because Iristigut had told her about the dirigibles, but it still felt great when they stared at her in awe.

"We can't use the dirigibles yet, though," she acknowledged. "They'd just burn up."

The hull was ablating in a cone of fire.

Ice broke off from stanchions and shattered decks, and showered out of the hole in the side of the ship.

External heat rejection systems were melting.

From the ground, the *Lightbringer* must look like the Chicxulub impactor.

"I need to calculate our trajectory. Can you get Ripstiggr out of the drive chancel? Don't hurt him. I just don't want him near me."

In a press of jostling bodies, she forced her way back to the drive chancel and got a boost into her hammock. The soldiers stayed with her, surrounding her hamock like a Praetorian guard. She concentrated on the screens and tried not to think about how badly she wanted a drink. She understood now that alcohol hindered her interface with the chip. It insulated her from the *Lightbringer*. That's probably why she craved it so much—

Oh, Hannah-banana, quit making excuses for yourseld.

The *Lightbringer* approached the coast of California, 120 kilometers up, doing Mach 35.

CHAPTER 52

"Shiplord, we should launch the shuttles," Joker said.

"What?" Hannah shook zoomed-in optical images out of her eyes. She'd found Pacific Heights, where Bethany and her family used to live. She'd been trying to find their house, but the neighborhood was unrecognizable. Many homes had been bulldozed. Smoke rose from outdoor fires. Swimming pools had turned green, or were empty. She remembered Isabel cleaving through the water in the Zieglers' backyard pool, and clenched her fists in a spontaneous prayer. Please God, let her be safe.

"Oh ... the shuttles."

The four refurbished shuttles waited in the vacuum dock, fueled up. Each shuttle carried a full complement of crew and infantry, 200 apiece. Plus bombs.

Hannah faced a split-second choice. If she refused to launch the shuttles, the crew would doubt her claim to be on their side. If she said yes ... the shuttles would be free to drop their payloads on Earth's ICBM launch sites.

It wasn't *that* hard a choice.

Hannah never had been a fan of weapons of mass destruction.

"Go ahead," she said, authorizing the shuttles with a thought.

Back in the vacuum dock, robot arms flung the shuttles at the wall, which autoripped. The little craft tumbled out into the *Lightbringer's* fiery slipstream, and powered up to full thrust.

Two of them climbed, turning 90°, into polar orbits. They would hook over the North Pole and stoop down on launch sites in Asia and Russia.

The other two screamed ahead of the *Lightbringer,* heading for Europe.

"We take care of North America targets ourselves," Gurlp said. "Shiplord, authorize weapons systems!"

Hannah looked into Gurlp's bright eyes, and died a bit inside. Gurlp had been the first crew member to speak up in her support. She owed her her life. How could she say no?

But this was the same as authorizing the shuttles. Right? They would only be hitting strategic targets. And wherever Hannah's family was, they sure weren't hanging out at a military airfield.

"Weapons systems authorized," she said in a low voice.

The railgun powered up. Gurlp pushed past her, bio-antennas stabbing at the targeting console.

A projectile screamed along the rails. It arrowed down through the atmosphere and slammed into Vandenberg Air Force Base, which now belonged to the Republic of California. The launch pad and associated facilities were instantly pulverized. A mushroom cloud rose over the wreckage, towering up to the stratosphere ... but the *Lightbringer* had already passed on to the east.

*

Underground in the Cheyenne complex, Tom Flaherty gave orders to scramble every fighter still under the command of the United States government. His comms section had fallen back on a patched-together network of third-party base stations and military radio. Nevertheless, the orders quickly reached Air Force bases in Alaska, Kansas, and Oklahoma. F-22s and F-35s took off in pursuit of the *Lightbringer*.

The floor bucked under Flaherty's feet.

Kuldeep, beside him, staggered and grabbed a desk for balance.

Insulation tiles fell from the ceiling. Dust filled the room.

The lights went out.

The phone in Flaherty's hand hissed static.

*

A missile sank New Hope off the Louisiana coast.

Cape Canaveral went up in flames. All that rocket fuel made an explosion so big it broke windows in Miami.

Wallops Island, the NASA facility off the Virginia coast, took a direct hit.

The *Lightbringer* charged on over the Atlantic.

Atmospheric drag had reduced its speed to Mach 10.

And now it was only 60 kilometers up, bouncing and roaring through the mesosphere.

Hannah, said the chip. Enemies/allies acquired.

"Oh, look," Hannah said. "We've got company."

She drove her hands into her hair, despairing. There was just no good way out of this. Each of those fighter jets had a pilot, and each of the pilots had a family …

… and gung-ho Gurlp was already targeting them.

Hannah focused on the *Lightbringer,* so she wouldn't have to watch the jets go down. She pulsed the maneuvering thrusters, just to confirm they were still working. Fuel was low, so she killed the thrusters again.

The Atlantic swept past below.

The *Lightbringer* punched down through the ozone layer.

The American fighter jets rose on a vector that would intercept the alien ship's descent.

Gurlp nailed the leaders with HERF pulses.

They fell to the ocean like stones.

The others, quick learners, hung back out of HERF range.

And down we go into the troposphere—the bottom layer of the atmosphere, the stuff we breathe.

Clouds covered the eastern Atlantic, so Hannah couldn't see exactly how much ocean they still had to cross. She tried to bite her nails, tasted filthy smart material, doffed the suit to her elbows and chewed on a thumbnail that wasn't much cleaner.

Back in the unpressurized regions of the ship, the soldiers who could not fit into the bridge were hanging on for dear life. Hannah figured out how to check in with them, and did it. "How's it going, guys?"

"Bumpy," they said.

Now there was air outside, albeit thin. It battered into the hole in the side of the ship, filling the interior corridors. At the same time, the Venturi effect tried to press the airflow out. *Bumpy* was an understatement. The soldiers had lashed themselves to stanchions, crowded into the least-exposed decks.

The *Lightbringer* tore through the cloud ceiling, cutting through thick cumulus. Hannah gasped in horror as she saw nothing but ocean to the east and west.

"Deploy dirigibles," she said. She had to stretch this glide out any way she could.

Hidden exterior compartments—at least, they used to be hidden before the outer layer of the hull melted off—snapped open. Thirty-five enormous sand-colored dirigibles burst out, inflating as their tethers jerked taut.

Inside them: very hot hydrogen gas.

The *Lightbringer* juddered. Hannah clung to the sides of her hammock, waiting to see how much lift and drag the dirigibles could deliver.

Answer: not much.

Still falling.

"Knew those wouldn't help," said a familiar voice. She glanced up and saw Ripstiggr looking down at her. He'd climbed into the web of support cables that held the hammocks. Crouched up there like a spider, he stared down at the group in the drive chancel.

"It was a good idea in theory," Hannah snapped.

"I know what they'll be good for," Ripstiggr said. "Release them."

"No!"

Back on Sleeper Deck 4, a soldier raised her head. Her suit flowed back from golden bio-antennas and an ecstatic face. Her companions grabbed at her in horror. "I can breathe!" she said. "Try it!"

Then she keeled over, because the *Lightbringer* was at the same altitude as the top of Mount Everest.

But all the time they were dropping into thicker, warmer air. More soldiers doffed their suits. It broke Hannah's heart to witness their delight as they inhaled Earth's air for the first time, knowing these might be the last breaths they ever drew.

"Those flyboys are catching up," Ripstiggr said. "HERF mast's out of power. Let me—"

He leapt down from his perch. They wrestled. Ripstiggr kicked Gurlp in the face, pinned Hannah's arms, and gestured at the dirigible controls.

Ten of the dirigibles flew away behind the *Lightbringer*—and exploded into fireballs, the hydrogen ignited by explosive bolts.

One F-22 flew straight into a burning dirigible.

The other jets veered clear.

Meanwhile, imprisoned in Ripstiggr's arms, in the warm cage where she used to feel so safe, Hannah fired the maneuvering thrusters, rolling the *Lightbringer* 50° off the horizontal.

All the hammocks swung and bumped each other.

The wall of the drive chancel became a steeply pitched ceiling.

Everyone who was out of their hammocks—Ripstiggr, Gurlp, Joker, Hannah, and a dozen soldiers—wound up in a heap on the opposite wall.

"You probably have this idea of a crash landing where you just glide in like a paper airplane," Hannah gasped. She was trapped in the pile of bodies, but Ripstiggr had shielded her with his body, protecting her from getting crushed. "That's not how it works. It doesn't matter how you come in, right side up or upside-down or backwards, as long as you keep your nose up. And because this ship is shaped like a freaking sperm whale, you know, with the magnetic field generator and all that business, rolling is the only way to do it. We'll probably land in the Atlantic, anyway. So it won't make any difference. But I tried."

Gurlp's voice said, "Is that land?"

"Land?" Hannah struggled upright, for their current value of 'upright.' Stepping on people, she fought for a view of the transparent wall.

Ahead of the *Lightbringer,* a purple smear lurked beneath the clouds.

"Land! It *is!* Oh, come on, come on, come on," Hannah begged. "Come on, baby! You can do it!"

The *Lightbringer* fell onwards and down towards the distant shore, while Ripstiggr released the rest of the dirigibles one by one, scaring off the few jets that still pursued.

A breadcrumb trail of fireballs traced the alien ship's course over the coast of Gabon.

Its sonic boom rolled like thunder, terrifying people and animals across a curve of Africa as wide as the path of a solar eclipse.

Everyone on the bridge shouted deliriously as the ground came closer. Cacophony reigned on the radio frequencies. The air was silent, except for the creaking of hammocks, and one hoarse human voice. Hannah was promising God that if she lived through this, she would give up drinking.

The *Lightbringer* tore through treetops, touched down, rebounded, ploughed into dense undergrowth, and skidded along for several miles while incinerating and flattening the jungle at the same time.

It came to rest on its side, smoking, in a sparsely inhabited region of the Democratic Republic of the Congo.

The bridge airlocks gave way.

Sweet, humid, rich air flooded in.

CHAPTER 53

As the *Cloudeater* glided around the moon yet again, Alexei and Nene butchered a dead rriksti in the cargo hold. She had died in the steam explosion on board the *SoD*. Alexei hadn't known her very well. That did not make the grisly task any easier, nor did the knowledge that many of the survivors would refuse to eat her flesh, even if he sliced it thinner than gourmet sausage. Rriksti funerals included ceremonial consumption of mummified flesh, but they drew the line at eating their friends as a source of calories. They would, literally, starve first.

The *Cloudeater* had orbited the moon nineteen times now. Every orbit changed their plane by a few degrees. They had started off in the *SoD's* equatorial orbit. To land at the south pole, they needed to get into a polar orbit. With limited reaction mass, Keelraiser had had only one option: Go round, and round, and round, burning for a few minutes each time, tipping their orbit south like the hand of a clock.

Every orbit took six hours.

Six hours times nineteen is almost five days.

But who's counting, when you're living in a flying gulag? Every hour dragged like a year. Alexei actually felt guilty relief at escaping to the cargo hold, breathing suit air instead of the stench in the passenger cabin. The ramp was open a crack. Sun shone in. Earlier he had glimpsed Earth in that crack. They'd learned from the internet a couple of days ago that the *Lightbringer* had crash-landed in the Congo.

What a mess. What a goddamn mess.

At the other end of the hold, suited rriksti were working at the smaller 3D fabber, the one that printed metal parts. He couldn't see what they were doing. Didn't have the energy to care. He drew the carbon nanofilament saw to and fro, while Nene placed the slices of frozen flesh in a bag.

When they were done, they tossed the bones and gristle overboard and went back inside.

Nene doffed her suit to the tops of her shoulders. A cloud of fine white snow floated out. She was shaking.

Alexei pulled his goggles off and shook tears out of them. He wiped his eyes, smearing wetness over his cheeks.

Nene threw her arms around him. They held each other for dear life, floating amid hundreds of other people, cocooned in noisome heat and silence.

And in the blackness inside his head, Alexei once again saw the wreckage of the *SoD* lying in that crater on the far side of the moon.

Keelraiser spoke in his headset. His voice struck a brisk contrast to the lethargy in the cabin. "Alexei, Nene, if you wouldn't mind coming to the cockpit."

Alexei wiped his face with his hands. "Be right there."

They flew forward. Nene distributed the frozen meat haphazardly as they went. Those hungry enough to eat it would nuke it in the *Cloudeater's* poky galley.

In the cockpit, Keelraiser gestured at the forward wall. "We'll be landing shortly. Please fasten your seatbelts." His hair danced like the limbs of a broken puppet.

Floating behind the pilot's seat, Alexei took in the rugged lunar panorama. Bright gray mountain peaks reared out of lakes of shadow. Disorientingly, the landscape was receding before his eyes as if seen in a rearview mirror. The *Cloudeater* was flying backwards. Keelraiser had flipped the ship during their last plane change, so they could use the drive as a brake.

"We're very low," he observed.

"Yes," Keelraiser said. "These are the mountains of the south pole. Camp Eternal Light is located on the rim of Shackleton Crater. We'll be landing on a small plateau between Shackleton and Shoemaker." He added, "I've established radio contact with them. They will send vehicles to meet us."

"I didn't know you were talking to them," Nene said.

Keelraiser shrugged.

None of them had much heart for conversation. When Hriklif, seated beside Keelraiser, spoke up, Alexei wondered for a second who was talking. It seemed like a year since he'd heard the atomic engineer's voice. "I think Alexei should have the co-pilot's seat. They might need to hear his voice on the radio."

Keelraiser shrugged again.

"See you on the ground, my life," Nene whispered. She kissed Alexei and went aft to settle the passengers.

Alexei strapped into the co-pilot's seat, while Hriklif went below to join the others in the crew cabin. Alexei glanced down through the transparent floor and saw Giles, watching the news on the wall screen. That's all Giles did now. Watch the news, and rant about the stupidity and chaos it portrayed.

"What's our descent plan?"

"Burn all the reaction mass we have left, and pray," Keelraiser said.

"That sounds like a plan."

The *Cloudeater's* drive turbine roared throatily. Thrust gravity pitched them forward in their straps. With so little reaction mass remaining, Keelraiser had braked as late as he dared. They were descending at a steep angle. Alexei gripped the armrests, which were at the wrong height and shaped the wrong way. He tensed every muscle, aware of the mountains behind the ship looming larger and closer.

This is how Jack died.

Oh Jesus, Jack.

Alexei remembered all the good things. Jack's unfailing cheerfulness. His willingness to make fun of himself. The way he never even thought about giving up.

Those stupid movie quotes.

The rope game.

Handmade crossbows.

A sunshade made out of plastic bags and seat frames.

It's a hard knock life.

You were my brother from another mother, Jack. I'll never forget you as long as I fucking live.

The *Cloudeater's* velocity dropped further. A barren hill drifted into view. They sank at walking pace towards the north side of the hill. "Velocity zero," Keelraiser said. "Firing auxiliaries."

Lunar gravity pulled the *Cloudeater* down, while the auxiliary thrusters pushed against it.

Alexei spotted a scattering of reflective geometrical shapes near the top of the hill. His heart clenched in his chest.

The long-unused landing gear bounced on lunar rock. Keelraiser's hands flew over the controls. They bounced again—and settled. Gravity pulled loose items in the cockpit to the floor.

The shuttle from Proxima b had landed safely on the moon.

"That," Alexei said, "was a nice bit of flying."

Keelraiser sat still, his head hanging forward. "Is there a heaven?" he said.

Alexei pointed at the geometric shapes atop the 'hill'—which, he now realized, was actually Shackleton Crater. It was smaller than he had expected. "I think that's it right over there."

White and orange dots trundled down the side of Shackleton Crater, kicking up dust.

Keelraiser muttered something that sounded like "this colony is a fucking joke."

The radio squelched. A strange voice crackled into Alexei's headset. "Identify yourselves, please."

Alexei raised his eyebrows at Keelraiser—I thought you'd established contact with them? Keelraiser gestured to him to speak.

Alexei cleared his throat. "This is Alexei Ivanov on the *Cloudeater*. We are the survivors of the *Spirit of Destiny*. Four humans and two hundred and sixty-seven rriksti. Hope you've got room for us."

The voice laughed. "We got the whole moon. C'mon out. Bring anyone that urgently needs first aid or other assistance."

"Roger that." Alexei stood. The lunar gravity seemed to strip away his tiredness. "Let's go."

"Wait." Keelraiser put a hand on his arm. He called out in Rristigul, and went ahead of Alexei down the ladder into the crew cabin.

Suited rriksti crowded the cabin. They were the same ones Alexei had seen at work in the cargo hold earlier. And they were holding …

Giles pushed between them. "Here, Alexei. They also made one for you."

"Crossbows?"

Keelraiser shrugged. "Easier to make from printed parts than guns."

Alexei handled the crossbow Giles had given him. Lightweight aluminum alloy. Those seat frames never stopped coming in handy. The crossbow was better-made than the ones he and Jack had put together from spare parts. He imagined Jack looking down from heaven and laughing his head off.

"Highly advanced alien technology," he murmured.

"We have an image to maintain," Keelraiser said. And then he took from his backpack a pair of sunglasses. He settled them on his nose over his suit. Much repaired, and retooled with wire to fit a rriksti face, they were Jack's old Ray-Bans.

Alexei smiled sadly. "Lead the way, then."

The small group of men and rriksti emerged from the *Cloudeater* into the airless lunar day. They stood with their crossbows lowered by their sides, waiting for the vehicles to arrive.

EPILOGUE

Jack's alarm clock was ringing.

He got the feeling the insistent buzzing noise had been going on for some time.

Better get up or he'd be late for class.

This astronaut training gig felt just like going back to school. Sit at a desk and learn about fluid science and robotics and what have you. Bored him to tears, to be honest. But at the end of it all, he'd get to go into space, so it was worth getting up for.

He opened his eyes.

Telemetry alerts pulsed in the darkness of his helmet.

Oxygen reserves: critical.

His body flexed in a startle reflex, and sagged back in weak gravity that reminded him of—

Europa—

It all flooded back.

He remembered where he'd been, and where he was now.

That he was alive seemed like the lesser miracle.

THE ADVENTURE CONTINUES IN BOOK 4 OF THE EARTH'S LAST GAMBIT QUARTET, *KILLSHOT*.

THE HUMANS

Spirit of Destiny
Acting Mission Commander Jack Kildare
Mission Specialist Alexei Ivanov
Mission Specialist Giles Boisselot
Mission Specialist Skyler Taft

Lightbringer
Eskitul Hannah Ginsburg ("Shiplord")

Victory
Mission Commander Grigory Nikolov
Mission Specialist Linda Moskowitz
Mission Specialist Koichi Masuoka

THE RRIKSTI

Cloudeater
Shuttle Pilot 1st Class Iristigut ("Keelraiser")
Medical Specialist & Lay Cleric Nene ("Breeze")
Atomic Engineer Hriklif ("Ditchlight")
Medical Expert Stawrrl ("Cleanmay")
Lance Corporal Brbb ("Pathbreaker")
Private Difystra ("Blackbone")

Lightbringer
Acting Commander Ripstiggr ("Godsgift")
Weapons Specialist Gurlp ("Rocky")
Life-Support Specialist Sokrine ("Joker")
Food Services Specialist Figgrit ("Tearflake")